The Pleasur

In spite of her terror, she managed to say, "Your Lordship, this is highly improper."

If she panicked, she could lose everything: her reputation, her freedom, and perhaps even her life.

"I shall show you improper," the stranger whispered, humor edging his voice. He removed the hand from her bum and slid it up her body in a quick exploratory caress. Then he shoved his fingers into her tightly braided hair, pulled her face down to his, and slammed his mouth awkwardly over hers . . .

The Accidental Courtesan

CHERYL ANN SMITH

THE BERKLEY PUBLISHING GROUP
Published by the Penguin Group
Penguin Group (USA) Inc.
375 Hudson Street, New York, New York 10014, USA

Penguin Group (Canada), 90 Eglinton Avenue East, Suite 700, Toronto, Ontario M4P 2Y3, Canada (a division of Pearson Penguin Canada Inc.)
Penguin Books Ltd., 80 Strand, London WC2R 0RL, England
Penguin Group Ireland, 25 St. Stephen's Green, Dublin 2, Ireland (a division of Penguin Books Ltd.)
Penguin Group (Australia), 250 Camberwell Road, Camberwell, Victoria 3124, Australia (a division of Pearson Australia Group Pty. Ltd.)
Penguin Books India Pvt. Ltd., 11 Community Centre, Panchsheel Park, New Delhi—110 017, India
Penguin Group (NZ), 67 Apollo Drive, Rosedale, Auckland 0632, New Zealand (a division of Pearson New Zealand Ltd.)
Penguin Books (South Africa) (Pty.) Ltd., 24 Sturdee Avenue, Rosebank, Johannesburg 2196, South Africa

Penguin Books Ltd., Registered Offices: 80 Strand, London WC2R 0RL, England

This is a work of fiction. Names, characters, places, and incidents either are the product of the author's imagination or are used fictitiously, and any resemblance to actual persons, living or dead, business establishments, events, or locales is entirely coincidental. The publisher does not have any control over and does not assume any responsibility for author or third-party websites or their content.

THE ACCIDENTAL COURTESAN

A Berkley Sensation Book / published by arrangement with the author

PRINTING HISTORY
Berkley Sensation mass-market edition / October 2011

Copyright © 2011 by Cheryl Ann Smith.
Excerpt from *The School for Brides* by Cheryl Ann Smith copyright © by Cheryl Ann Smith.
Cover art by Jim Griffin.
Cover design by George Long.
Cover hand lettering by Ron Zinn.
Interior text design by Laura K. Corless.

ISBN: 978-0-425-24397-8

BERKLEY SENSATION®
Berkley Sensation Books are published by The Berkley Publishing Group,
a division of Penguin Group (USA) Inc.,
375 Hudson Street, New York, New York 10014.
BERKLEY SENSATION® is a registered trademark of Penguin Group (USA) Inc.
The "B" design is a trademark of Penguin Group (USA) Inc.

PRINTED IN THE UNITED STATES OF AMERICA

10 9 8 7 6 5 4 3 2 1

To Duane, Paige, Regan, and Ethan, I love you guys.
And finally to Joan Smith and Joan Cole:
Thanks for your infectious enthusiasm!

Acknowledgments

First I'd like to thank everyone at Berkley Publishing for all the wonderful work they do. I'd especially like to thank my editor, Wendy McCurdy, for lifting my books to another level, and to Katherine Pelz, who is quick to answer a question or offer encouragement. I appreciate your patience and support! And to George Long, Jim Griffin, and the entire Berkley art department, you guys do fantastic work. My covers are stunning. Thank you so much!

As always, thank you, Kevan, for everything you do for me.

When I first started writing, I knew nothing about the publishing business. For teaching me so many things, I'd like to thank Romance Writers of America and the Greater Detroit RWA chapter. I'm always amazed by the camaraderie and giving nature of my fellow writers. There have been so many people throughout the years who've been quick to give helpful advice and the benefit of their wisdom or just made me laugh. For that, I appreciate you all so much and plan to pay it forward.

Chapter One

❧

Lady Noelle Seymour wobbled slightly on the trellis and bit her bottom lip to keep from crying out. Two stories up, the redbrick town house appeared much taller than when she'd decided to go through with this ill-conceived plan and had slipped across the lawn and into the shadows of the building like a sneak thief. Still, the intrigue of a grand adventure had trumped any final hesitation as she donned a pair of black, rolled-up trousers and matching shirt and set off for the Mayfair town house of the Earl of Seabrook.

She weaved her hands through the scratchy climbing vines and held the trellis in a viselike grip. If her sister Eva, Her Grace, knew what she was doing this evening, she would hand Noelle's head back to her on a platter.

Yet, she forced herself onward. Prickles of excitement were twisting through her. She was no longer a proper lady from a good family, but an adventuress without the encumbrance of society's rules. For this night, anyway, and she'd not let fear or common sense ruin her outrageous adventure.

Tomorrow she'd be tucked back in her corsets and stockings with no one the wiser. Prim, if not quite proper, Lady Noelle.

Tentatively, Noelle extended a toe toward the window ledge, her heart pounding loudly in her ears. Once her foot found a firm place, she removed one hand from the trellis and clutched the windowsill in a death grip. If she fell, it would be more than broken bones or possible death that faced her. If she were discovered breaking into the married Seabrook's house, in the middle of the night and dressed like a boy, the scandal would ruin her forever in the eyes of the Ton.

Mother would bury her so deep in the country, she'd shrivel up, dry and crackled, like a neglected daisy deprived of water and sunlight.

Noelle grimaced and brushed a leafy twig away from her chin with her gloved hand.

Death would be preferable to the shame of being sent off in exile. If she plummeted to the ground, she'd pray she landed headfirst and died instantly.

"Almost there," she muttered for courage, and slid her foot across the narrow stone ledge. Ever so slowly, she eased her body to the right, skimming her belly against brick; she was thankful the town house was blessedly quiet.

The earl was in Bath with his wife, according to gossip. This gave Noelle enough time to return the stolen necklace and save Bliss from prison or, worse yet, hanging.

Beautiful Bliss. The girl had the sense of a donkey.

Noelle smiled wryly. Clearly, at this moment, both were superior to her in intelligence. Neither courtesan nor donkey was about to commit a crime that might well land her into the cell adjoining Bliss's at the horrible Newgate Prison.

For an instant, Noelle considered which was worse: exile by her mother or getting caught by the Bow Street Runners and spending years in Newgate. Knowing Mother as she did, she'd almost prefer the latter.

Still, it was too late for regrets. The darkened window loomed before her. In a few minutes the item would be safely returned and she'd be on her way home.

Gingerly, she leaned on her right foot to test the strength of the ledge and reached for the window. She whispered a brief prayer, flattened her palms against the painted wood frame, and pushed the window up. Relief flooded through her as it opened easily with only a slight scraping sound.

She'd not have to fumble along the ledge to find a second or third unlocked window. Clearly, His Lordship didn't expect anyone to make such a perilous climb to steal his valuables.

With extreme caution, she poked her head into the room to make sure it was empty, then stepped gingerly inside. In the blackness, she heard nothing to cause her alarm. No snoring, no shifting of a body on a bed. The space was blessedly quiet, and she pulled in a deep soothing breath to loosen the tightness in her chest.

According to Bliss, either this room or the one next to it belonged to the earl. The girl wasn't certain which, as she'd been distracted during her brief visit by the amorous attentions of the earl. Though he kept a separate and smaller town house for his courtesans, he'd smuggled Bliss into his home some months ago, while his wife was enjoying the soothing waters of Bath.

With outstretched arms, Noelle walked around the room, searching for the bed and the blue coverlet that would assure her she was in the right room. If she was to return the necklace and lead the earl to believe it had only been misplaced and not stolen by his former courtesan, she had to put it in a place where he could easily "discover" it as soon as he returned.

A task that turned out to be easier said than accomplished.

The blasted room was too dark! Not even the moon offered its cooperation, as it remained well hidden behind the blanketing storm clouds. Lightning would certainly help, yet it also failed to make an appearance.

Luckily, she soon found the massive bed. The coverlet was dark blue, or black, or even a deep green. She lifted the fabric to her nose to squint at it close up, fairly certain now that it was green.

Blast! With no time to linger, Noelle dropped the coverlet and fumbled across the room. With outstretched hands, she felt around for a door, then eased it open. Once in the dark hallway, she followed the wall to the next room. The panel creaked softly as she pushed the door open. She froze.

When no alarm sounded, she rushed inside and softly clicked the door closed behind her. The space was even blacker than the first room. Perhaps she should have waited for a cloudless night with a full moon before venturing out.

"You can do this, Noelle," she whispered. "Find the bed, make sure this is the right room, and get out."

She stumbled around the room, arms swinging in wide sweeps. Eventually, she knocked into a small table and beside it found the bed. Sheer luck kept her from upending a lamp. She leaned to squint at the coverlet.

Was it blue? Frustration mounted. She'd have to drag it over to the window and pray for a slip of moonlight to know for certain. Remaking the bed afterward would also be difficult in the dark. The maids would be suspicious if they found the bed in disarray and would report the incident to the earl. If the Bow Street Runners got involved, she could be in serious trouble.

In a case like this, desperate measures were required. She'd worry about the bed once the necklace was returned.

Noelle rounded the bed to the area closest to the window. She had both fists gripped around the corner of the coverlet when an arm snaked out of the darkness and jerked her down on the bed.

"Oh!" she cried sharply, bouncing against a hard body before catching herself. "Release me!" she said in her deepest tone. A hand clamped over her bum, and she was dragged across a warm and naked chest; a naked and very male chest, by the feel of downy hair covering the firm, sinewy expanse.

The effort to sound mannish was rewarded with a low chuckle and a mumbled reply: "No man smells so sweet or has such delightful curves, love. Now give me a kiss."

A kiss? She couldn't see anything, though her captor's breath brushed the side of her face. It had to be the earl. This was his house. But what was he doing here? He was supposed to be in Bath!

Think! Think!

In spite of her terror, she managed to say, "Your Lordship, this is highly improper."

If she panicked, she could lose everything: her reputation, her freedom, and perhaps even her life.

"I shall show you improper," the stranger whispered, humor edging his voice. He removed the hand from her bum and slid it up her body in a quick exploratory caress. Then he shoved his fingers into her tightly braided hair, pulled her face down to his, and slammed his mouth awkwardly over hers!

Noelle stilled, her arms pinned against her sides. His firm mouth moved about for the correct position in the dark until he found it, fully claiming her with a searing kiss.

He teased her with his exotic scent and warmth, and her limbs turned to hot pudding. Shocked to find a rising tide of tingles in her body, she opened her mouth to demand a stop to the kiss. Instead of release, the bold stranger pushed his tongue between her teeth, and she tasted a hint of some unnamed spirit. The earl felt strong and untamed beneath her, unlike any of the tepid noblemen of her acquaintance. Beneath her open palms, his bare skin was warm and supple, and his thigh rested, hard and wrapped with thick muscle, between her legs.

A flood of desire poured through her body, and she went slack. She'd never been kissed like this before! This was no casual peck on the mouth, but the kind of kiss one shared with a lover.

Her virginal mind went blank as he rolled her onto her back and partially covered her with his upper body and a leg over her knees.

Why wasn't she fighting him? She should definitely be fighting him. But her body seemed unwilling to push him off. Suddenly, a horrified Noelle realized her arms were around his neck and she was hungrily returning his kiss!

"So sweet," he mumbled, breaking the kiss and trailing his mouth down to nuzzle the base of her throat. There was something about him, his voice, that didn't sound correct in her ears. Thankfully, it forced some reality into the situation. She felt a prickle of danger from this man and knew that if she didn't get out of the bed immediately, she'd lose much more than her freedom in the blackened room.

He slackened his hold briefly to shift their positions, and Noelle took the opportunity to give him a great shove. The earl fell back in the bed, far enough to allow her to roll out from under him and scramble to her feet. She bumped into a piece of furniture—a dressing table, she suspected—and had sense enough to pull the necklace out of her pocket. The color of the coverlet no longer mattered. This was clearly the earl's room.

She heard the earl climb from the bed, and she dropped the necklace on the table's smooth surface with a muted clink. She was disoriented by the kiss and the darkness. She wasn't sure which way the door was. All she knew was that she had to get out before he reclaimed her.

The sound of his bare feet moved away from her, and she heard him clatter around for a moment. Bright red coals sputtered to life as fire licked the sticks he'd dropped atop them. Quickly, the room became infused with muted light.

Noelle knew her chance for escape was upon her. She looked frantically for the door and launched herself toward the oak panel. A few steps and she'd be free!

"Halt," he commanded behind her, and she jolted to a stop. Slowly she spun about, fists upraised, and braced herself to fight for both her freedom and her innocence.

"You are not a maid," he said, narrowing his lids. There was no obvious explanation for her odd dress and boyish appearance. "I've stumbled upon a thief."

Fear chilled her limbs. She was about to be arrested. She was a criminal, a thief. No magistrate would believe that she'd come not to steal but to return the earl's stolen property.

There had to be a way out of this predicament.

The fire rose higher, and she got her first good look at the half-naked earl. Her breath caught.

He was wearing unbuttoned black trousers that sagged low on his narrow hips to a shockingly indecent degree. It was painfully clear he had nothing on beneath. Any sort of shift and the trousers could fall to his knees, leaving him without coverage altogether.

She flushed and pulled her eyes away from the thin trail of hair pointing downward beneath his waistband, to the most incredible chest she'd ever had the fortune to gaze upon. Well, truthfully, she'd never had the opportunity to see a male chest close up. Her experience was limited to one brief glimpse of a tenant's son in a distant field. Still, she was certain the earl's was magnificent in comparison to other men's.

There was very little about Bliss's hasty description to recommend him as His Lordship. But Bliss had been nearly hysterical when she'd described what she'd done, so Noelle had taken everything she said with a bit of skepticism.

Indeed, this man was as tall as Bliss had described, but he didn't have the pale skin of the gentry. His sculpted torso was a golden bronze, as if he'd spent all his time, shirtless, in the sun. His hair was light brown and streaked through by the sunlight that had darkened his flesh.

A pair of shadowed eyes peered at her from beneath a few strands of loose hair as he moved toward her, slowly and with a savage grace that wobbled her knees. She knew the earl was a well-respected member of the Ton—a status that didn't fit the untamed beauty of the man before her.

Just then she understood what it meant when her sister Eva explained the sensual feelings her husband, His Grace, evoked in her when he held her in his arms. Noelle had felt something for this man while sprawled beneath him on the bed and hadn't quite understood the feeling. It was a sensual pull toward a faceless stranger.

Sensual pull?

In that moment, a plan took root in her mind. If she

could find a way to distract the earl, she could escape. And there was only one way for a woman to distract a man fully and completely. That much she'd gleaned from her time around courtesans. So she waited until he was close enough to reach out and touch.

Noelle settled what she hoped was a seductive smile on her lips, then lifted her hand and placed it on his chest. He twitched beneath her fingers. She had to remind herself to keep breathing as she stared at his mouth.

"I am not a thief, My Lord Seabrook." Noelle fluttered her lashes and widened her eyes. "You mistake my intentions."

"Indeed?" He looked down at her clothing and tugged the black fabric at her waist. The effort brought her a half step closer. "You are certainly dressed as such, Milady."

The dark clothes *were* difficult to explain. She had to redirect his attention. Quickly.

Slowly, Noelle drew her hand down his chest, and the supple skin trembled beneath her touch. Curiosity and anonymity and fear of hanging led her to boldness. He was magnificent. She wondered if his skin tasted as exotic as it smelled. Scandalized by her thoughts, a virginal flush burned her cheeks and drifted all the way down to her toes.

"I've heard you are casting about for a new courtesan, and I've taken these desperate measures to be the first to offer my services." She touched the tip of her tongue to her bottom lip. "I find you very, very desirable."

The last was not a lie and slid easily off her tongue.

A slow grin passed over his face, yet he didn't speak. Instead, he turned his attention to the golden strands that had escaped her braid during her climb. He examined his find with a grin.

"I shall enjoy seeing it unbound."

The cool air of the room tingled across her skin. Noelle looked down to see he'd loosened her shirt. Her lacy chemise kept her covered and prevented his perusal of her breasts. Barely.

Noelle forced herself to remain calm as he shoved the

shirt farther up to cup her full and thinly veiled breasts. Her nipples budded beneath his palms. A wicked smile tugged his lips, and she ached to kiss him again.

In this moment, with this man, she wasn't the proper and soon-to-be spinster Lady Seymour, but a reckless adventuress who climbed a trellis and entered a window in the middle of the night to return a necklace and kiss a handsome stranger with abandon.

"How desirable do you find me?" he asked softly, his fingertips tugging at a nipple through the thin cloth. She suppressed a moan. Her legs threatened to collapse as a warning bell sounded in her head.

There *was* something strange about this man that had nothing to do with his scandalous behavior. Yet, she couldn't put her finger on exactly what roused her suspicions, no matter how hard she tried to focus.

She leaned against him to stop the fondling and peered into his red-rimmed blue eyes. It was then she realized he'd had more than a few drinks this evening; enough to explain why he sounded and appeared slightly off-kilter to her. Not drunk enough to wobble or topple over, but enough for her to use to her advantage and extricate herself from the situation.

Noelle grinned. She'd found her opening. "The first time I saw your face in Hyde Park, I knew I had to have you, My Lord." She pressed lightly on his chest with both hands, and he shuffled slowly backward toward the bed. He cupped her hips and they walked in a bumbling synchronization, locked together.

"When I discovered through gossip that your courtesan had flown your nest, I knew I had to get to you before the other women discovered her flight." Noelle spoke in a hopeful, breathless tone. He stared down at her breasts and groaned. "Tonight, I plan to give you a taste of my many talents. Then tomorrow we shall come to an arrangement."

Her seductive smile drew his eyes. He stared hungrily at her mouth and grinned. "I shall need to see everything."

"Of course, My Lord," she purred. This adventuress was relying solely on instinct and snippets of conversations she'd overheard from Bliss and the other courtesans on how to please men. Now was not the time to show her inexperience. Thankfully, the man was not a warty toad.

His knees hit the back of the bed and he stopped. He slid his hands from her hips to cup her buttocks. "Where would you like to start, Milady? We have all night." He leaned to press his lips against her neck, and whiskers tickled her skin.

Noelle sighed seductively. "Here?" She lowered her hand to cup the large erection beneath his trousers. Her face flamed at her boldness. She suspected he would be considered well endowed and required no padding to make it so.

Her virgin sensibilities were replaced by pure curiosity as she caressed the bulge. What did an erect male member look like up close? Did it hurt the first time a man put it inside a woman? Would she eventually become used to having such a large thing inside her?

The earl's second groan was deeper than his first. "Thus far, you have moved to the top of my list of potential mistresses."

The flush on her face was a clear indication of her innocence, but she hoped he was too deep in his cups to notice.

"I have learned my craft well, My Lord." Her shocking curiosity led her onward. With anonymity a perfect mask to hide behind, Noelle felt positively wicked, truly scandalous.

She would do anything to save herself from Newgate, even fondle the earl if it kept him from summoning the Bow Street Runners. His lids drooped, and for the first time he wavered on his bare feet. He pressed a kiss to the corner of her mouth, and it was all she could do not to turn her face to accept his kiss. It was proving hard enough to keep him upright.

Noelle splayed both hands on his chest, pushing gently so he fell limply back on the bed. She'd waste no time waiting for his drunken snores before she made her escape. The necklace was on the dressing table, and the dim light, mixed with his inebriation, would keep him from putting the Lady Seymour and the thief-courtesan together as one person.

"Good night, My Lord," she said softly with one last look at his handsome face as his lids began to droop over unfocused eyes. She shivered with regret.

And then she was gone.

Chapter Two

❦

Gavin Blackwell woke up the next morning with wool in his mouth and daggers piercing his brain. When he dragged open his eyes, bright rays of sunlight were streaming through the window and over his face, torturing him for his folly. He turned away with a parched groan and swore under his breath.

Tormented by his indulgences, he reached for the glass and its remaining splash of whiskey to wash some of the dreadful dryness off his tongue. Once he was able to speak, he cursed his poor judgment for dipping heavily into last evening's entertainment, and for not ordering the maids to close the drapes before he left.

The belated celebration of the opening of his shipyard had gone far past a few drinks with his cousin and his companions. He wasn't clear on much from the previous evening, but he did know one thing. He'd been carried home and up to bed while singing some nonsensical and very slurred Irish ditty. After that, the night was all a blur.

The clock chimed ten, and he pulled the sheet over his head with the intention of collecting a few more hours of sleep. He'd just begun to chase Morpheus back into oblivion when a light hint of lemon and cinnamon drifted up his nose to tease his battered senses.

He jerked upright on the bed. Pain shot through his head, and he cursed again.

A woman. He darted a glance around for signs of her but found nothing. Still, he wasn't completely deterred. A beautiful woman had been in his bed sometime during the night. He was sure of it. Well, mostly sure. He'd kissed her and tasted her lemon-scented skin and lush lips.

Hadn't he? Then where was she? Unless she'd climbed into the wardrobe or shimmied under the bed, she wasn't there.

He pressed both palms against his forehead and picked diligently through his muddled brain for a clear thought. The attempt proved futile. It might take a week to recover fully from his drunken stupor. Time he didn't have.

No, he assured himself, she hadn't been a dream. Her lingering scent on his pillow proved she was real, and not some delightful fantasy he'd conjured up for his amusement.

Gavin lifted the sheet and looked beneath. He was still wearing his trousers. He wasn't sure if he should be pleased he hadn't bedded the mysterious wench or bereft she'd escaped, unscathed, from his fumbling attempts to seduce her. With a face like hers, from what he could remember through the haze, it would be shameful not to recall every moment of their coupling.

What he did recall was the softness of her mouth and the scent of lemon and spice in her blonde—or was it brown—hair? He also seemed to recollect some sort of offer to become his mistress. But had the woman actually made such a bold offer, or was it a seductive dream?

Bloody hell! His head was ready to explode, and frustration weaved through the pain. If she'd been a whore given to him as a gift by Charles, she shouldn't be too difficult to hunt down.

He grinned. Next time he had her in his bed, he'd be fully sober and ready to enjoy the favors she'd offered. After all, it was high time to take a mistress. Brief couplings at brothels, with women of questionable cleanliness, had never appealed to him. He wanted a beauty to share the pleasurable intimacies of his bed. He wanted this mysterious beauty.

Knuckles rapped on the door and the panel swung open. Charles, Earl of Seabrook, strode into the room without invitation, dressed in lordly attire and ready to face the day. A wide grin split his handsome face. Clearly, one of them wasn't suffering the effects of too many drinks.

"I came to check your breathing, cousin, before I venture off to Bath." He grinned stupidly and claimed a chair by the window. Charles rarely slept past noon and was already impeccably dressed for his trip. A late night out hadn't changed his habits. "I wasn't sure a man could survive such high amounts of whiskey and live to see morning. I expected to find you cold and dead."

Gavin shot him a watery glare and slumped back on the pillows. "I seem to recall you kept my glass filled. Your tab at White's must be a level fortune."

Charles chuckled. "I can cover it. My father left me a bloody king's ransom." He stretched out his long, thin legs. Charles and Gavin revealed a hint of their shared paternal bloodline in their features and dark hair, but his English cousin was British-pale. By contrast, Gavin had spent most of his life in America, working on the docks and learning all there was to know about shipbuilding. His sturdier build and darker skin were the results.

"My father left me a worthless shipyard. I had to build my own fortune," Gavin grumbled. Though their fathers were brothers, Gavin's father had been one of the younger sons and reckless in every regard. He suspected the only reason his father hadn't gambled away the shipyard was that he'd won it in a card game, then promptly forgotten he owned the property. "Perhaps I should push you under a coach and claim your inheritance. Then I could spend my life indulging my pleasures rather than working my hands to callused imperfection."

It was only recently that Gavin had returned to this land of his birth, after the death of his Boston-bred mother. When his estranged father had died some years ago and left him the shipyard, he'd balked at returning to London. He had a life in Boston. But without his mother, there was little to keep him in America. Loneliness and curiosity drew him back to his birthplace, and here he would stay, for now, if this new shipping venture proved as successful as he planned.

"Don't forget Thomas and Cecil," Charles said, and swung out an arm. "They have claim over all this before you. Surely you wouldn't push them beneath the coach as well?"

Gavin shook his head. His two young cousins, Charles's sons, were being groomed by their mother to inherit once Charles finally dropped dead.

And, truthfully, Gavin was quite satisfied with his lot.

Charles chuckled. "I know you, Cousin. You'd hate the responsibility that comes with my title. I am wed until my death to a woman who despises me. I carry the weight of the financial burdens of keeping my coffers full, so that I may leave my children more than the lint in my pockets." He sighed. "You have the freedom I lack. Thus, I have to indulge in my pleasures when I can, to keep myself sane."

Gavin lifted the glass. "Then here's to your continued good health, Cousin, and to that of your sons." He swallowed the last few drops of liquid. "May you all live very, very long lives."

Charles chuckled. "If only your father had been born first. . . ." He let his wistful voice trail off.

Though his cousin complained about his responsibilities, Gavin knew Charles enjoyed all the privileges his title offered, Lady Hortense aside. From the stories Charles told, the woman was a veritable shrew, and Gavin had thus far taken pains to avoid meeting her. It was impossible for him to understand how Charles managed to get four children by her without snapping her scrawny neck.

Perhaps it was remembering the immense dowry old Lord Pottsworth had offered Charles to wed and bed his oldest daughter that allowed his cousin to perform his husbandly duties. The dowry rivaled the value of the crown jewels. Still, no fortune would have convinced Gavin to take Hortense, in spite of her rumored lovely face. Charles claimed her harsh voice was enough to freeze a man's bollocks blue.

Gavin shuddered and quickly changed the topic. "I would like to thank you for the woman you sent me, though I fear I did not get to indulge myself, thanks to you and your whiskey. I would, however, like to ask where you found her, so I can discover her whereabouts. I'd appreciate a second chance to taste her favors."

Charles frowned. "Woman? What woman?"

"The woman you sent to my room." Gavin watched Charles's confusion, and his stomach tightened. His cousin looked positively befuddled. "Didn't you send me a doxie last night?"

Charles shook his head and looked around the room. "A woman was here in this house?" he said, surprised. Then his surprise turned quickly to excitement. "Was it Bliss?" He gave Gavin a brief description of his vanished courtesan. His desire for the girl was clear on his face.

"It wasn't her," Gavin said. "The eyes and hair were not the same." His sneak thief–courtesan's eyes were a soft amber brown with flecks of what he thought might be green around the pupils, and her hair was lighter. That much he could remember from that moment they'd been nose to nose.

Concern drew him out of bed. Gavin stumbled to his coat and found his coin purse undisturbed. "Then who was she?"

Charles stood and walked around the room. "I haven't any idea. This is as much a mystery to me." Peering into every nook and corner and behind the drapes, he eventually stopped at the dressing table and lifted something off the surface.

"Hortense's necklace. I had the spider clasp repaired." Charles turned and dangled a very expensive piece from his fingertip. Sapphires and diamonds glistened in the sunlight. "Odd. I thought I'd lost it. Hell, I thought Bliss had stolen it a couple of days ago, during my last visit to her town house. That was right before she vanished without word. Are you certain it wasn't her?"

"Very certain. This woman did not have blue eyes."

The two men fell silent. Gavin was puzzled. Was the mysterious woman a thief? Or had she found and returned the necklace? The idea was absurd. How could she know the rightful owner unless she'd had a part in the theft? And if she was a real thief, why return it at all?

Perhaps Charles had accidentally dropped it and one of the maids found it and left it on the table. An improbable solution he quickly dismissed. A necklace such as this would be returned to the earl immediately, not left lying around for anyone to lift.

There were too many puzzling pieces of this story. Suspicion welled. What *had* she been doing in his room? Suddenly, Gavin wanted to find the mysterious woman and shake the truth from her.

"I did suspect Bliss had taken it. I'm pleased to see I was mistaken. Perhaps I should call the Runners to make an investigation," Charles said tightly, and closed his hand around the necklace. "If my dear wife had discovered I'd lost the piece, she'd have had me castrated. It is her favorite."

"I think you should wait," Gavin countered. He couldn't imagine his lovely little thief in shackles. He had other plans for her. "There was something about this woman that led me to believe she was not a common criminal. There's no proof she had anything to do with the necklace." More memories surfaced, and he grinned. "I do recall that she thought I was you and offered her services as Bliss's replacement. Perhaps it was as simple as a desperate woman looking to secure a wealthy patron."

Slowly, Charles relaxed. "Then I shall defer to your suggestion. No harm is done. Perhaps if you find the chit, you should send her to me." He walked to the door. "Clearly, the girl finds me worth risking her neck for. And, as you know, I am in need of a new courtesan. Bliss has been missing for two days. I fear she is not coming back. Pity."

With a wink, Charles left him. Gavin settled back and stared at the ceiling as his conversation with the self-proclaimed courtesan began to come back to him. Tension returned as he recalled her words. She mentioned spotting him in Hyde Park and hatching a plan of seduction. If that was true, then why didn't she immediately recognize he was the wrong man?

W hen Noelle returned to the courtesan school that morning, she discovered Bliss in a state of hysteria. The brunette's face was plum red from weeping, and tears streaked her cheeks, ruining her pretty features.

Bliss launched herself from the settee with a rustle of fabric. Noelle took a quick step back to keep from being knocked flat and held up her palms as a barrier. The girl clasped her raised fingers tightly and jerked Noelle's hands toward her.

"Did you return the necklace?" Bliss said, her eyes pleading and filled with unshed tears. She moved Noelle's clasped hands under her trembling chin. "Please tell me you returned the necklace!"

"I returned it." Noelle pulled free with some effort, sidestepped around the young woman, and pulled off her cloak. "You need not worry anymore."

Bliss went down to her knees in a pouf of pink, nearly vanishing beneath skirts and petticoats. Relief filled her pretty features. "Thank you, Miss Noelle. You have saved me."

Noelle frowned at how quickly Bliss had recovered from her hysteria. A smile spanned the courtesan's face.

Had the woman actually learned anything from her poor choice, or was she destined to get herself into more mischief in the future? Noelle had risked her neck for the girl, not knowing the earl was still in London, and she couldn't resist telling Bliss so. She had to make the gravity of the situation as clear as possible for Bliss's sake.

"You have no fear of Newgate this time, Bliss," Noelle said sharply. "However, if you ever steal again, I'll send for a Runner myself."

The courtesan shook her head so briskly that several

strands of hair escaped their bindings and fell around her shoulders.

"Oh, no, Miss Noelle. I never stole anything before in my life, and will never steal again." She pushed to her feet, stumbled a few steps, and dropped onto the settee. "But it was so pretty, and my maid, Freda, said His Lordship's wife did not deserve such a trinket. She said I should have it for myself."

This was the second time she'd heard the story, and Noelle wondered if the maid was up to mischief when she made such a comment. Though Noelle's acquaintance with Bliss was brief, she'd discovered quite quickly that the girl was not above being swayed by the whims of others. If this decision to steal the necklace was any indication, the maid had a tight hold on the courtesan.

Thankfully, Bliss was no longer under the influence of the maid or His Lordship. Bliss wanted to be free of her courtesan's life. Or so she said. She'd decided marriage was in her future; however, Noelle wasn't completely sure of her convictions. The girl talked about the earl in such loving terms, Noelle suspected it was only the potential consequences of stealing the necklace that kept her from returning to his bed.

"Though the necklace has been returned, the earl can still bring charges against you," Noelle said sternly. She had to make sure all ties to the earl were severed. Bliss was a chatterbox. If she made a confession to the earl in an unguarded moment of lovemaking, it could have serious consequences. "If he puts the two matters together and decides it was you who stole it in the first place, he could have you arrested. You must stay away from him forever."

Bliss's thick lashes fluttered as she looked downward. "Yes, Miss Noelle."

The earl's face flashed in her mind, and Noelle trembled. It was understandable why Bliss wouldn't want to give up such a virile man. In Noelle's opinion, he was a cut above all other men. Both women would be best served to keep as far from the seductive earl as possible.

"I smell strawberry tarts." Bliss instantly forgot her worries and moved happily from the room. In seconds, the shadow of Newgate had clearly been lifted from the courtesan's mind and again replaced by cotton fluff.

Noelle frowned as she walked over to lock the parlor door for privacy. The town house housed Bliss and Edolie, courtesans waiting for Noelle's sister Eva to return to London and start a new class. By the time school started, the house would be filled to the brim with runaway courtesans. Eva helped the women change into respectable young ladies and matched them with husbands.

While Eva was away, Noelle had promised to check on the women and make sure they were settled in for their stay. How could she know such a simple task would change so quickly into a crime caper?

Fatigue weighed heavy on her as she slumped into the nearest chair and closed her eyes. But the scandalous night had left her nerves frayed.

She'd actually kissed a stranger, a married stranger, and enjoyed his caresses. Immensely. Even now, her nipple budded against her chemise with the memory of his hands running over her body and tugging at that very same nipple.

Fire burned her face. She'd not only kissed him, she'd cupped his erection, caressed the most private part on a man. Never once had she experienced more than a chaste kiss on the cheek or hand from a suitor. Though her strokes had been delivered under the guise of a courtesan, she didn't feel any less troubled by her behavior.

She so desperately wished her sisters were in London! They would certainly know how to distract her from her lascivious thoughts and direct her attention elsewhere.

What they could not do was settle the aches the very married earl's attention had caused in her body. Or erase the shameful actions she'd committed to keep herself and Bliss from arrest.

Noelle dropped her face into her open palms and groaned. Thankfully, he was gone from her life. Forever, surely.

Chapter Three

Noelle decided that a shopping excursion was just what she needed to get her mind off the unavailable earl. There was no need to dwell on last evening when she would never see him again. Yet Noelle didn't feel entirely calm. Though Bliss had promised not to seek out the earl, some anxiety over the whole situation remained. Spending an enormous amount of money on new gowns would certainly turn her thoughts in a more frivolous direction.

Her cousin Brenna Harrington had recently returned to London and was in residence at her family's Berkeley Square manor. Noelle sent a note asking Brenna to meet her at Madame Fornier's dress shop for a day of shopping. She changed into a simple blue day dress and set off with plans to think of nothing but gowns and hats for the rest of the day.

Brenna was one of the three blackest sheep in the Harrington family, a family that had, through the years, an entire flock of black sheep to choose from. Having been born to—gads!—the daughter of a common Irish mother and a rapscallion Harrington father, the three were seen as untamed by the Ton. One could rob coaches, or run off with a married lover, or throw oneself off the Tower of

London over a broken romance, but one didn't dare marry an Irish commoner.

Uncle Walter had fallen instantly and madly in love with a dark-haired beauty, Kathleen, while visiting Dublin with friends, and wed her nearly on the spot. The tumultuous thirty-year marriage produced Simon, Gabriel, and Brenna, all of whom shared their mother's coloring and fiery temperament.

In spite of their inauspicious beginning, Noelle's aunt and uncle were still happily squabbling.

"There you are, Noelle."

Noelle watched Brenna alight from the carriage, a picture of loveliness in a pale green day dress that matched her eyes. The cousins kissed cheeks and shared a brief embrace. After the turmoil she'd been through, Noelle took comfort in the presence of her cousin.

Brenna looked her over. "I do love you in blue."

"I thank you, but it is you, my dearest Brenna, who makes heads turn." Noelle discreetly indicated a young man in a sensible brown coat and trousers staring at her beautiful cousin. "That poor man nearly tripped over Lady Pemberley's pooch while craning his neck to get a look at you."

Brenna sent him a flirtatious look and the poor fellow turned a bright shade of red, obviously shamed to be caught gaping like a spring trout. He spun on a heel and fled into the milling crowd.

Noelle giggled, hooked Brenna's arm with her hand, and led her into the shop. "You are awful, Cousin. It will take him weeks to recover."

With both of her sisters in the country and her mother hiding out from the scandalous marriage of her youngest daughter, Margaret, to an impoverished baron, Noelle had been left to her own devices. The prospect of having control over said devices had proved more desirable than the actuality of being left quite alone in her uncle's rambling house.

"I hoped you would be in town this Season, Brenna." Noelle sighed as they stepped into the cool interior of the shop. The scent of hot tea and the colors of bolts of exotic fabrics lifted her spirits and promised to be a delightful distraction. "Without my sisters, I am dreadfully bored."

Until last evening. She looked forward to suffering from boredom again, now that the nobleman was well out of her life.

"I thought Aunt Clara was chaperoning you this year." Brenna lifted a bolt of deep red cloth and held it against herself. The color complimented her skin nicely. "She can be quite entertaining."

Noelle gave a sheepish smile. "Aunt Clara had to rush off to Sussex to be with Pudding. Her dear daughter has suffered another one of her spells and needs her mother to talk her back from the brink of her impending death. So Aunt Clara put Aunt Bernie in charge instead."

The two cousins shared a knowing smile. Pudding, as Cousin Wilhelmina was affectionately known, was as plump as she was tall, and spent much of her time abed with a variety of ailments she conjured up in her head.

"I heard Pudding suffered a dreadful bout of consumption last month," Brenna said as she reached to lay a bolt of gold fabric across Noelle's upturned hands. "She should be dead and buried by now."

Noelle fingered the hideous gold cloth and held back a snicker. She did love the way Brenna spoke her thoughts without hesitation. "She had a miraculous recovery, dearest. The doctors have never seen the like."

The cousins giggled.

"Has Aunt Bernie been able to stay sober during the soirees?" Brenna asked with a wink. "The last time she attended a play with me, she almost toppled out of our box."

"I have yet to call upon her," Noelle admitted sheepishly. As Noelle usually attended functions with the express notion of having fun, she'd decided watching her aunt stumble about, making a fool of herself, was decidedly not fun. "I have been flouting convention and attending unchaperoned."

Brenna's green eyes widened in false surprise. "Careful,

Noelle. You might be added to the family list of black sheep if you continue to push the boundaries of society."

Noelle snorted. "I shall take my chances. With you and your brothers to distract the gossips, I have been able to parade about without drawing too many shocked whispers."

"Speaking of interesting gossip"—Brenna's eyes narrowed suspiciously—"I heard you have discovered a new relation. Evangeline, is it? There is some nonsense about her being a long-lost cousin I have never heard of. Explain, please."

The cousins locked gazes. Noelle had known it wouldn't be long before her family became privy to Eva's existence. Brenna couldn't have been the first to hear the gossip, so the matter was out. It wouldn't be long now before the ridiculous falsehood about Eva's actual connection to the family crumbled. She hadn't expected the news to travel so quickly.

She pulled Brenna behind a stack of cloth bolts and whispered, "You cannot tell anyone this secret. She is not our cousin but my half sister. She was recently married to the Duke of Stanfield."

"His Grace? He is so very handsome." Brenna made a wistful sound and stared off in the distance. "I'd heard the duke had wed. 'Tis a shame."

Noelle shook her arm. "He is my sister's husband."

Brenna blinked, and her eyes cleared. "Right. Sorry."

A quick glance about revealed several women lingering nearby. Too close for privacy. A tale such as this needed the better part of an afternoon to flesh out fully. "However, that is a story for another time and place. Right now I am in desperate need of a new frock."

Brenna accepted the brief explanation, knowing Noelle would eventually give her the entire story.

They spent the day shopping Bond Street, Noelle doling out pieces of information about her secret sister until the tale was largely told. By the close of the afternoon, Noelle's back was bent with fatigue and she was weighted down with packages. Brenna was similarly afflicted.

"I think I shall skip the party tonight and spend the evening soaking my feet," Noelle said with a soft groan. There was a second reason, one that didn't involve her throbbing feet, for avoiding public activities. The earl.

The chance was small he'd even remember her, yet there was no telling what the sot would recall. Likely he'd awoken feeling as if his head was cracked into pieces and thought her nothing but a curious dream. Still, she couldn't be certain. Even though he was not known to enjoy the frivolity of the social whirl since his marriage some five years past, it wasn't beyond comprehension that he wouldn't change his behavior and spread his presence throughout the Ton.

Tripping over him at some party was a risk. Better to let a few weeks pass before venturing out. It would give him time to forget he ever met her, and her, time to forget him.

As if she could.

The idea of living shut up in her uncle's town house for weeks was a grim prospect. Then, there was always Aunt Bernie for company.

"I have spent far too many nights of late playing the flirtatious minx for my own entertainment," Noelle explained. She did enjoy her amusements. After years of begging her mother to allow her to spend her summers in town, she took this respite from the country to socialize. Seclusion would be a dismal prospect. "Perhaps I should withdraw for a week or three."

Brenna watched her skeptically. "You, withdraw from society? The Season will fold in upon itself without the lovely Lady Seymour to amuse the young bucks. Wagers abound over who will finally break your reserve and wed you." She pondered Noelle's face. "There is something you're not telling me, Cousin. I've sensed your distraction all day."

Noelle considered confiding in Brenna. However, she

couldn't be absolutely certain her cousin could keep the secret from her brothers. The more people who knew of her midnight climb up the trellis, the better her chances of arrest.

Still, Brenna would not be assuaged by a shrug and some silly excuse. So Noelle decided to produce some weak half-truths.

"There is a man, an earl, whom I stumbled across last week at the Billbury tea. He was most disagreeable." She cast her gaze down to her feet. Noelle hated to lie to her favorite cousin, but the truth was worse. "I have tried to avoid him since."

"I see." Brenna frowned. "He is married?" At Noelle's nod, Brenna's mouth thinned. "Then you should attend the party with your head high and show the cad a Harrington will not be intimidated by his boorish presence. And if he makes an inappropriate advance, I shall summon Simon to beat him senseless."

Noelle smiled widely. "That will be entirely unnecessary." She couldn't bring herself to see such a handsome face damaged. He might be an unfaithful cad, but he was pleasant on the eyes. "I can handle the earl myself, thank you."

"Then you will attend the party?"

Reservations tightened Noelle's stomach. Until last evening, she'd never seen the earl. His wife lived most of the year in Bath, and he spent most of his time there. His presence at the town house last night had been a surprise.

Bliss had assured Noelle he planned to be away for many weeks. Clearly, her information had been flawed.

Noelle's vow to withdraw from society faded with the pleading in Brenna's eyes. Perhaps she could attend this one last party before her exile. If she kept watch for him and avoided a chance meeting, she could enjoy the party without qualms. This was her first summer without her mother shoving every available dandy under her nose as a potential mate. Noelle just couldn't let the earl ruin it for her. He'd taken enough from her already.

She sighed. "I will."

Brenna let out a squeal that drew the attention of several people strolling down the walk.

Noelle laughed at Brenna's open enthusiasm, said a brief good-bye to her cousin, and climbed into her carriage. As she slumped back in the seat, she hoped she'd have enough time for a short nap before the evening's festivities.

Gavin sat atop his gelding, his mind filled with the shadowy woman, berating himself for not having a clearer image of her face to work with. He remembered finding her enticing and delightfully sweet-tasting. Unfortunately, he couldn't recall enough to believe he could recognize her if he passed her on the street. Nor could he discover her identity with discreet inquiries in all the places they'd drunkenly weaved their way through last evening. She was truly a mystery.

If the woman had spoken truthfully about becoming his (er, Charles's) courtesan, she'd clearly changed her mind. There was no sight of her, nothing to clue him to her whereabouts.

So he picked his way gingerly down Bond Street after a fitting for a new coat, annoyed with the knowledge he might never see her again. He should be focused on his shipyard and the naval contract anyway. Still, the idea of a large payout in business didn't soothe the frustrating ache she'd left in his loins.

The street was jammed with shoppers and their conveyances of choice. Dust hung heavy in the air, and the smell of the masses and lathered horses assaulted his senses. He kept his hat low in hopes he'd not be accosted by anyone he knew and have to spend time in lengthy conversation.

The noise and the heat of the sun made him long for the days when, as a boy, he could swim nude in the chilly Atlantic whenever he pleased and lie on the grass looking at the clouds.

He casually tipped his hat at a young woman and elderly matron on the walk, both of them up to their knees in boxes. From beneath her bonnet, the chit leveled on him a less-than-innocent invitation with her eyes.

Gavin frowned and turned away. He wanted no part of the games virginal misses played to snag a husband. That trap had almost been sprung on him once, and he knew well the signs to avoid. He was content to remain a bachelor rather than shackle himself to an unfaithful miss who cared more about his fortune than the cut of his character.

There was a party this evening, and the ladies were out en masse, shopping for, well, whatever last-minute fripperies women shopped for. As he eased his horse around a slow-moving coach, a flash of color in an open carriage moving in the opposite direction caught his eye.

He turned his head and saw a figure in blue, a matching blue hat settled low on her head, with only the curve of a petite jaw exposed to his view from beneath the beribboned and lacy confection.

Gavin jerked upright, his senses fully engaged. Could it be her? There was something familiar about that tiny hint of her face that caused him to swing about in the saddle and stare after her as her driver skillfully avoided a man who had darted into the street.

Blast! He had to get a closer look. He went up half a block before finding an opening between equipages wide enough to pass between them. By the time he'd gotten turned around, all he could see when he stood in the stirrups was the top of her hat over a row of carriages. He eased the horse onward, weaving in and out as quickly as was manageable. In the distance, her carriage turned left and took a quiet side street at a rapid clip. A blue feather waved on her hat.

Teeth gnashing, he pressed on, only to discover, once he made the same turn, that her carriage was gone. He released a string of curses and slammed a gloved fist on his thigh.

If this was his scandalous beauty, she'd escaped him again. Gavin tapped his heels and turned the horse in the direction of Charles's town house, careful to stay clear of

Bond Street. He'd planned to spend a quiet evening at home, nursing the lingering headache that refused to abate.

There was little chance his mystery visitor would attend this evening's party. However, if she was not the courtesan she'd indicated she was, he would miss an opportunity to discover her true identity.

And have her in his bed by dawn tomorrow.

His cock twitched at the thought of the lingering feel of her hand fondling him. She was a bold little thing. She'd responded passionately to his kisses and teased him with her caress. Yet, she'd also had an air of innocence, a hesitation that he hadn't noticed at first. It took a clearer head to see she wasn't quite the daring seductress she tried to portray.

A wicked grin split his face. Whatever her motives, it didn't really matter. By the time he finished with her, he'd know everything she was hiding.

Noelle fidgeted while Martha carefully placed the last few pins in her upswept hair. Her eyes were red, and tension thinned her lips. An attempt to nap had failed. The seductive earl ruined her peace. Finally, she'd climbed from the bed with a curse and resigned herself to an evening stifling yawns.

The man was married! Well and completely married! There would be no covert glances across a crowded room, no secret assignation in the garden, no gushing proposal on bent knee. Any attraction she'd felt for him and his perfect male torso had to be buried forever.

"You must sit still, My Lady," Martha scolded, jerking Noelle from her unwelcome thoughts. "Unless you want your hair to tumble down during a dance."

The middle-aged woman had been with Noelle's family forever and wasn't the least intimidated by her title. She always said her piece, and scolded when required. And Noelle adored her.

"We wouldn't want that to upset a potential suitor," Noelle said absently, and plucked at the delicate lace on her cream-colored gown. The best thing that could happen to her this evening would be to meet a stunning unmarried gentleman with whom to laugh and flirt and forget the earl. Though Noelle had vowed never to wed, casual flirtation and stolen kisses in the darkness of the garden would be acceptable, if it meant pushing Lord Seabrook from her mind forever.

Martha snorted. "It is shocking enough to have you wandering about town without a chaperone. You need to be taken into hand before you find yourself in a disgraceful situation."

Noelle met her gaze in the mirror. "I just turned twenty-five. I think I am past the age when I need to worry about appearances. A spinster has certain allowances."

The last pin went in and scraped her scalp. Noelle winced. The maid was clearly put out with her. She braced herself for a continuation of the lecture.

"You are young and lovely, My Lady. Many men have asked to call, yet you refuse them all. There is no reason for you to remain unmarried and alone," Martha snapped. She patted the coiffure and stepped back to admire her work. "It is your stubbornness that keeps you a virgin still."

Noelle stared. "Say what you think, and please do not hold your tongue, Martha." Mischief welled to replace her annoyance with her outspoken maid. "How can you be certain I do not possess a string of lovers?"

Martha scowled. "You are as innocent as the day your mother birthed you. I'd know immediately if a man had taken your innocence." She shook her finger. "You cannot lie to me."

Noelle bit back a smile. Martha knew her very well. Still, she didn't know everything. Some things were better kept a secret; like breaking into houses and kissing strangers. "If it smooths your feathers, my cousin Brenna and her brothers will be at the party. Simon will chase off any men who dare launch a dastardly assault on my virginity."

The maid muttered something under her breath about the wild Harringtons not being fit chaperones. This time Noelle did smile. She stood and pulled the older woman into a tight embrace.

"Fear not, dear Martha. I shall return to you in the same condition in which I left. I have no plans this evening to lose my spinster's title by accepting any proposals, proper or not. I shall laugh and flirt and find my way home before my coach turns into a pumpkin."

Though Martha's plump arms hugged her tight, her lined face was etched in a scowl.

"If I thought it would keep you from spinsterhood, I'd pray for a bold man to drag you into the bushes and force a marriage." She cupped Noelle's chin and peered deep into her eyes. "You should have more than an empty future without a family to love."

"You saw the unhappiness of my parents' marriage and the misery it wrought." Noelle flounced over to retrieve her shawl and settled it about her shoulders. "Margaret and Eva have husbands, and soon I will be an aunt. I shall be content to love their children."

A couple of tongue clucks followed, but Martha remained silent as Noelle wandered into the hall and headed for the stairs.

An arranged marriage had made her father and mother miserable. Her sister Eva was the product of her father's liaison with his courtesan. Still, she loved her sister dearly and wouldn't change a single moment of history if it meant losing Eva.

Noelle had vowed long ago that she'd not marry a man she didn't love and who didn't love her. She intended to keep that vow. She had family who adored her, and that was enough.

Some women were not meant to be married and mothers. And if she could spend the evening avoiding the very married and intriguing earl, she'd consider the night a rousing success.

The coach dropped her at Tipton House half an hour later. The house was an immense four-story sandstone structure with an entrance framed by stately white columns. Noelle followed the flow of guests into the opulent home, pausing beneath an enormous chandelier to get her bearings. Clearly no coin had been spared in the decorations. White roses sat in gold vases on hip-high white tables that resembled Greek columns. Gold silk tapestries adorned the white plastered walls, continuing the white-and-gold theme.

This was Lady Tipton's first party of this size. Though Noelle didn't know the new bride intimately, they had spoken briefly several times and got on well. As Noelle moved gingerly through the house, she didn't see her hostess but did spot her handsome cousin Simon in a dark blue coat. She headed in his direction. If the dangerous earl was lurking, Simon was the perfect man to keep her safe.

Gavin clawed at his collar and felt a trickle of perspiration trailing down his spine. He was hot and out of sorts. Didn't the Ton ever open their windows? With the heat of so many bodies, how was one expected to breathe normally in the stifling space?

He reached to tug his high stock away from his neck and wished he could yank off his cravat and coat. However, some guests would find such behavior shocking, and he didn't need more whispers.

Though much of the Ton thought him an uncouth American, he was issued an invitation to every soiree because of his proper pedigree and wealth. Normally he avoided these large parties with all the marriageable ladies in attendance and hunting for husbands. Tonight he was on a mission, so he suffered for lust.

He'd been stalking the halls and rooms on the first and second floors for over an hour and had found no sign of his lovely visitor. The chance she'd be a guest was slim, yet he'd had to try. The time he'd wasted away from the ship-yard on this futile hunt raised his frustration. His body had been in a state of partial arousal since he'd pulled the courtesan-thief down onto his bed. It irked him that he couldn't seduce and forget her.

With his jaw clenched, and the cloying heat driving him toward the terrace doors, Gavin declared the night a waste of time. If he ducked out into the garden, he could be off without drawing his cousin Charles's attention.

Since Gavin's arrival in London, his cousin had worked hard to find him a bride. Charles had even had the gall to have his bookkeeper, Jones, give a matchmaker a sketch and his personal information, in hopes the woman could find him a bride. A former courtesan bride. Charles even came out tonight, a rare occurrence, in hopes of having Gavin engaged before the clock struck midnight.

No amount of protesting could keep Charles from his course.

If not for a fire at the hotel where he'd been staying, Gavin wouldn't have been forced to stay with Charles. Close quarters gave his cousin ample opportunity to press his case. Gavin needed to find a town house of his own. And soon.

The only positive of living with Charles was meeting the mystery woman. But she wasn't in the crush, and his cousin was busy lining up potential wives for introductions.

Fleeing the party was Gavin's best option, before his cousin arranged a wedding of inconvenience. Misery loved misery, and Charles desired all the men around him to be just as miserable as he was in his marriage.

Gavin nodded to an acquaintance and took the most direct route toward the doors. Several young women cast him covert glances that he chose to ignore. He had almost made it to freedom when someone finally threw open the doors and a light breeze filtered across his warm face.

But it wasn't the air that drew his attention and caused his body to turn stiff and focused. It was the light scent of lemon and cinnamon that brought him upright in his tracks.

Chapter Four

***

Instant awareness zipped through his body like a fox sensing a hare hiding under a nearby bush. His gaze moved from face to face as he searched for his seductive visitor in the swirl of party guests. She was here! He knew it as well as he knew his own name. Never once before had he smelled that combination of scents in the sea of lilac and lavender most women favored.

He might not clearly remember her face, but her scent was permanently etched in his mind. He'd not rest until he found her, even if he had to sniff dozens of necks. A slow grin spread over Gavin's face. What a stir that would cause among the esteemed guests. He suspected he'd spend the rest of the evening fending off dueling challenges from irate husbands and fathers.

Gavin moved slowly through the crowd, his head turning this way and that. Nothing could distract him from his mission.

He was following her fleeting scent, as difficult as looking for a hairpin in a field of hay. But the little courtesan-thief was near. She'd not get away this time.

It was nearly a half hour before he spotted a woman in

pale cream, her flaxen hair upswept to show the perfect
curve of her graceful neck. Her eyes shone as she turned
slightly and smiled at some witticism spoken by her companion. Gavin's eyes locked onto the side of her face.

There was something familiar in her fine features. With
his eyes he followed her neck downward to her trim back,
then to a perfect, graceful rump.

If this wasn't his elusive courtesan, she was a nearly
perfect replica from behind. The only way to know for certain was to cup her buttocks in his hands. He grinned. He
had to wonder about the severity of the pummeling he'd
receive from her companion if he tried.

The woman was in conversation with a tall man in blue
who smiled down at her with affection. The two seemed intimately acquainted as she brushed something off the man's
sleeve.

Gavin scowled. If the man was her lover, it was a complication he didn't need. If there was an arrangement between
the pair, it could be difficult untangling the relationship.
With her beauty, she wasn't the sort of woman a man would
give up easily.

There were bits of memories coming together, a piece at
a time. Gavin gnashed his teeth. Though he couldn't recall
everything about last night, he saw enough in the curve of
her tiny, delightful ears, and the way she tilted her head
slightly when listening to her companion, to gain confidence. He was certain his would-be courtesan tipped her
head in just that way. It would take a closer look to confirm
his suspicion.

Eyes narrowed, he began taking a straight path across
the space between them. Not wanting to alert her to his
presence, he kept the crowd between them until she was
steps away, then veered off to circle her and her companion.

The blur of moving bodies faded as he saw more of her:
her bright smile, her husky laugh, and a closer view of her
sparkling eyes. She was stunning—and clearly not a courtesan. She was a Lady from head to toe. He didn't need an
introduction to see how well she fit in at this party.

Still, it didn't mean she was nobility. Many courtesans could blend quite well into society, as some came from impoverished, albeit well-placed, families.

Desperation drew many to that life. Others saw it as a place of power in a man's world. Either way, this woman was no common doxie.

Gavin watched her place a gloved hand on her companion's arm a second time, and felt a rush of annoyance pass through him. He wanted to jerk her hand away and drag her from the room. He wanted her touch; he wanted to press his face into her hair to confirm her identity through her scent. To see the intimacy between the pair only succeeded in raising his frustration.

"You must excuse me, Simon," she said, leaning in. Her lilting voice carried through the din. It was filled with good humor. "I must find Brenna."

Simon? Gavin blinked as she walked away. Given names were seldom used in society. His curiosity rose tenfold as he shook off his musings, locked onto her swinging hips, and headed off in her wake. If she truly was his mysterious would-be courtesan, he intended to get close enough to find out.

Without her protector looming over her.

Noelle spotted Brenna, clad in dark green satin. Her cousin was deep in conversation with an animated elderly woman who tapped her cane frequently when speaking, as if to prove a point. She decided not to interrupt. She needed a moment alone to collect herself. To find a place out of the crush of bodies in which to breathe in some perfume-free air.

The evening was warm and the ballroom was stifling. A sheen of perspiration dampened the skin beneath her dress and caused the fabric to itch against her skin. Finding a cool spot to clear her head wouldn't be too difficult, if she headed for one of the three sets of double doors that led outside.

Of the three, the set farthest to the right appeared to

overlook the darkest part of the terrace. She could slip away for a moment of welcome respite.

Then a flash of gray caught her attention as someone stepped into her line of vision. Not twenty feet away, blocking the doorway and clad in a dark gray coat, striped waistcoat, and white breeches, was the earl.

She gasped, and her feet faltered. His gaze locked onto hers. There was something in his eyes that gave her a clear indication he wasn't just admiring an attractive woman. No, he seemed to recognize her!

Her stomach lurched, and the room wavered.

It was impossible he could recognize her! They'd spent perhaps ten minutes together with only a small fire to light the room. And he'd been thoroughly foxed.

It took every bit of the training she'd received since birth not to react to his appearance, in spite of the warmth flooding across her skin with the memory of his kisses. She lifted her nose and turned away as if they were strangers.

Several matrons walked past, and she ducked behind them like a coward. A set of doors opened to a hallway on her right. Noelle hoped it led to a hiding place.

The matrons stopped near the doors, and she slipped into the dim light of the hallway. A quick glance behind her confirmed that she'd lost him in the crowd. Relief flooded her mind as she stumbled into the nearest darkened room. With unsteady steps, she followed the trail of moonlight seeping through the drapes to a private corner of the room, behind a large potted plant.

Once hidden away, she closed her eyes and inhaled to steady her heart.

So close. She let her mind drift to the moment she'd caught his eye. Had he been looking at her only out of curiosity, or had he actually thought he knew her?

She hoped not.

He'd barely been able to stand last night. Likely the man thought her just a dream. Still, he was watching her as if he knew her, as if he wanted her. As if he wouldn't rest until he kissed her again.

Noelle groaned. It had been a mistake to attend this party. She should have allowed the full Season to pass before venturing out again. By then he'd have forgotten all about her.

Her shoulders slumped. Why couldn't *she* forget him? Why did her mind have to remember his perfect jaw, his blue eyes, and that muscled chest so warm beneath her exploring hands?

A whisper of heat brushed her ear. "I have decided to take you up on your offer, sweet."

Noelle shrieked and spun around, landing awkwardly against the intruder's chest. She lifted her gloved hands to ward him off. Her fingertips ended up splayed over firm and familiar muscle beneath his open coat and waistcoat. The earl stared down at her with the same intensity that he possessed in his bedroom. As if she were a meal to be feasted upon.

"Sir, please. Stand back!" Her outrage was genuine. He had no right to accost her in such an intimate fashion. If only she'd not been woolgathering and had heard his approach, the window would've been an avenue of escape.

He leaned back slightly and raked his gaze over her face. Her breath came out in little explosive bursts. He was too close, too all-consuming, to the point that she was certain she'd lose the capacity to breathe at all. She smelled his exotic, spicy scent, felt his warmth. Everything about him was burned, unwelcome, in her mind.

Her limbs stiffened, and she couldn't move.

It was he who spoke first. He leaned down as if to take her into his confidence, with his cheek pressed lightly against her temple. "I do apologize, love. I thought after the intimacies we shared, a few whispered words in your delightful ear would be most welcome." He lifted his head to stare at her mouth.

He did remember her! She wanted to cry. She'd be ruined if he decided to make their association public! All she could do now was deny, deny, deny, and hope she could convince him he'd made an egregious mistake.

"Intimacies?" She struggled to find a measure of calm. Difficult to do when her throat closed off and her heart pulsed so hard she was certain it would stop beating altogether.

"Yes, intimacies." He grinned wickedly.

"I do not know you, sir," she protested. She was certain he could hear her lies, the guilt in her voice. The press of his body and his wicked grin caused torturous feelings to overtake her body. She was aware of him with a painful ache that she knew wouldn't subside until his hands were on her again. "W-we have never met."

He cocked up a brow and flashed a row of perfect white teeth. "Indeed? I remember the night well. Shall I tell you, moment by moment, every detail I remember?"

Deep down she knew she should push him away, but she was pinned between his body and his arms, his hands flattened on the wall behind her. His hint of scent was brutally and sensuously male. It took sheer will not to press her face against his corded neck.

"I f-fear you have m-mistaken me for another, sir." She forced herself to remain stoic, regardless of his breach of propriety. Any reaction would confirm his assumptions. "I demand you step back, now, before I call for my cousin to eject you from the house."

He gave a low chuckle. Mirth lit up his beautiful eyes, and she bit back a groan. Laws should be passed to keep such a man from being allowed to move freely through the female populace. Looking down, he ran a hand along her arm and closed it over her wrist. She nearly toppled over.

"Mistaken? Perhaps I thought so once, before I stepped close and smelled your delicious skin." He lifted her hand to brush his lips over her knuckles. He smiled into her eyes while she gaped like a trout. "You have a distinctive scent, my dear courtesan. There is no mistake."

Before she could collect her thoughts and issue a sharp retort, he released her hand, pulled her against him, and closed his mouth over hers!

Noelle faltered against him as he stole her breath with

his searching lips. Besieged with confusing emotions, she gripped his coat to keep upright as his tongue plunged deeply into her willing mouth.

The image of his wife and children rose unbidden to quell her passionate response. She tore her mouth free.

"You are a married man, My Lord." Hard bands of sinew bunched in his arms as she tried to break his hold. He refused to give her any freedom. "I will not be your plaything."

He lifted his head and his eyes narrowed. "I think you are mistaken, mistress." He shrugged, confused. "I have no wife."

"We both know that is a lie," she snapped. At least he could have the decency to be honest. It wasn't as if marriage stopped men of wealth from taking lovers. "You not only have a lady wife but children as well. You would do well to turn your affections toward your family and leave me be."

At that moment a couple strolled past the open door to the shadowy hallway. Noelle took the opportunity to free herself with a shove. His hands dropped away. She lifted the hem of her gown and raced to the door, quickly peered out to assure herself she wouldn't be observed, and then hurried toward the ballroom at a rapid clip.

Just outside the ballroom doors, she pressed her hand to her heart and counted to ten. Once she was certain panic had been removed from her face, she walked inside with the air of a queen. She couldn't let the earl know how troubled she felt. She must continue to deny their acquaintance. If she fled now, it would further confirm his suspicion.

In the moment she'd pushed free of him, she was almost certain she'd seen a slight, lingering doubt in his eyes. Though he'd accosted her, he wasn't completely ready to call her out as the erstwhile would-be courtesan. And if he didn't actually know the truth, then all his behavior over the last few minutes confirmed he was a woman-accosting cad.

Forced gaiety kept her from hysteria for the next two hours as she stayed close to her cousins, never giving the earl a chance to approach her. It was nearing midnight when she walked through the dining hall with Brenna and spotted him leaning against a wall, talking to a group of men.

Her composure slipped, a condition that afflicted her every time she saw his face. She gripped Brenna's arm and pulled her into a private alcove before he spotted her.

Facing her puzzled cousin, she took Brenna's arms and whispered conspiratorially, "The Earl of Seabrook. What can you tell me about him?"

Brenna shot her an odd look, then peeked around the alcove wall. She scanned the room for a moment, then turned slowly back to Noelle. A crease appeared between her brows.

"The man you spoke of earlier? The one who has accosted you is the Earl of Seabrook?" Brenna took a second glance. "I don't see him."

Noelle poked her head out and saw the earl in conversation with an ancient gentleman in blue. Thankfully, her unwelcome would-be lover didn't seem aware of their scrutiny. It gave her a moment to glare daggers in his direction. "He is right over there," she hissed, and pointed.

"You are mistaken."

Noelle scowled. Did Brenna need spectacles? "In the gray coat. Leaning against the wall."

Her cousin smiled and shook her head. "That man is not the earl. He's the American import everyone has been twittering about. He's the earl's English-American cousin, Mister Blackwell, and he is said to be more American than English. He owns a shipyard and, from what I hear, is very wealthy."

A stone formed in Noelle's stomach. An American?

"There must be a mistake," she protested. Then the suspicions she'd had about him since their first meeting all made sense: the odd accent, his sun-kissed skin. All the questions that had formed in her head finally came together with a clear explanation. And he'd known of her confusion the first time she called him "Your Lordship." The cad had failed to correct her even once, knowing she'd mistaken him for the earl.

She planned to kill him at the first opportunity.

"He is the man who has taken liberties?" Brenna pressed a gloved knuckle to her mouth in a shaky attempt to hide her smile. It failed miserably. "He is very handsome. I wouldn't mind him taking liberties with me."

It was all Noelle could do not to remove her shoe and launch it at his head. The man was a cad, a rapscallion. He took advantage of her misunderstanding to press his attentions on her, knowing she thought him a titled lord. "He led me to believe he was the earl."

"Well, he is in line to inherit the title, after Seabrook and his two sons," Brenna said as she took another peek at the exasperating American. "If you don't want him, I'll let you introduce us." She turned to examine Noelle's face. "By the flush on your cheeks and seeing how upset you are, I would guess you are more acquainted than you've let on to me. How is that, by the by?"

"We have never been introduced," Noelle said sharply. Clearly, introductions were not required before he moved on to kissing and fondling strange women. "We've bumped into each other twice, and I find him completely without manners."

After a moment of silence, Brenna giggled and took Noelle's hands. "Deny it all you will, but I think, my dear cousin, you are smitten with the seductive American. He has finally broken through my reserved Noelle and melted some of the ice around your heart."

"I am not smitten. And my heart is not icy." The protest came too fast, and Brenna snickered. Noelle grimaced. If she couldn't convince Brenna of her distaste, how could she convince herself? "He is without a single positive attribute to redeem him. He is coarse, crude, and without merit. I have seen feral cats with more charm."

"I'm crushed, ladies." A deep, laughing voice startled both women as the American stepped around the wall and into view. "I am usually considered quite charming."

Noelle's face burned as Brenna coughed lightly into her

hand. From the light in his eyes, Noelle knew he found humor in her embarrassment. He'd been eavesdropping. It was another reason to keep him at arm's length and practice avoidance. His sins grew with each encounter.

Everyone knew Americans lived like savages. As his recent behavior proved, he was a perfect example of that theory. With a second chance to poke around his room, she'd likely find a deerskin breechcloth among his things. She knew from books that colonists wore animal hides as a matter of course, and the women indulged in snuff. They were a wild lot and best viewed from a distance.

Her flush deepened. The image of him nearly naked, thighs exposed, bare-chested, wearing only a scrap of cloth to hide his manhood, made her weak-kneed. It was Brenna's unladylike throat clearing that roused her from the beginning of a very hot daydream.

"I'm Gavin Blackwell," he said, and reached for Brenna's hand. He pressed a kiss on her gloved knuckles. The lovely brunette smiled prettily. "And you are?"

"Miss Brenna Harrington." She recovered quickly and reached out to pull Noelle to her side. Her tight grip kept Noelle from fleeing. "This is my cousin, Noelle Harrington, Lady Seymour."

Gavin released Brenna's hand and took Noelle's before she could jerk it out of reach. He lowered his mouth to her fingers, never unlocking his gaze from hers. Thankfully, her gloves kept him from contact with her skin.

Noelle fell into the vortex of his blue eyes. As he pressed his lips to her gloved knuckles, she felt a tingle spread up her arm. His warm gaze promised her much more than a casual press of his lips on her hand.

"My pleasure, Lady Seymour."

Beneath his attention, she felt bare, exposed. She knew he was recalling every second of their embraces, their kisses, with the same hunger she felt within herself. She wanted to slip into his arms and press her mouth to his, to feel his muscles beneath her hands, to see what other scandalous things he could teach her. And the light in his eyes told her that he was thinking of something else, too. Perhaps silently cursing Brenna's presence?

Noelle yanked her hand free, tripped over her gown's hem, and wobbled slightly. Only embarrassment kept her upright.

A flash of a smile lit his face. He nodded to Brenna, then turned back to Noelle. "If you will excuse me, ladies, my coach is waiting."

As quickly as he'd appeared, he was gone.

Noelle's knees quivered. She stumbled to the nearest bench and dropped gracelessly onto it. Brenna joined her on the smooth marble surface and took her hand.

"That man wants you desperately and won't stop until he has you," Brenna said simply, and squeezed Noelle's fingertips. "You are in serious trouble."

Noelle looked helplessly at her cousin as her body shook under the strain of the stunning encounter. "Yes, I am."

Chapter Five

Noelle peered between the curtains, her stomach a series of hard knots. She felt stalked, watched, as if her privacy was no longer her own. In the three days since the party, she hadn't left the house. In her rational mind, she knew the arrogant American (she refused to think of him any other way) had his shipyard to run and couldn't spend his time lurking outside her home. Still, she couldn't shake the feeling of impending doom.

Gavin Blackwell's intentions were clear. He wanted her, and he wouldn't be satisfied until he had her: every bit of skin, every strand of hair, every part of her covered by her undergarments, all of her. He was prepared to press his attentions, against her wishes, until she was completely under his control.

Maybe she should have one of the footmen jab around in the bushes with a stick to see if any cravat-wearing, cane-carrying critters might tumble out.

She put her hands over her face. "I have lost all measure of sanity. What is wrong with me?"

Madness plagued her. He'd not contacted her, had done nothing to warrant such suspicion, yet she could not turn her thoughts in any other direction. When she'd thought he was married, it made refusing him easier. Now there was nothing to stand between her and his pursuit. But there hadn't been any requests to call, no contact at all. Shouldn't she be pleased?

Had he accepted her rebuffs and turned his attentions elsewhere? There were several young women out this Season who were capable of attracting the handsome Mister Blackwell.

"If only my sisters were here to help," she muttered helplessly. Brenna was a perfectly acceptable confidante, but she didn't have the knowledge of men Noelle's married sisters had. Eva understood the powerful attraction to a robust man, and in fact had been a duke's mistress before they'd fallen in love and wed.

And Margaret was expecting her first child any day now. Clearly, she knew about men; or at least how to make children.

Gads! Where was her mind traveling?

There was little chance Noelle could love any man; she'd pushed that possibility firmly out of her mind years ago. Still, the dreaded Mister Blackwell had caused a deep restlessness in her that she couldn't untangle. It was the dreaded condition called attraction, and she hated to be thus afflicted.

Noelle crossed and uncrossed her arms several times before coming to a workable solution to her problem. There was a sensible way to get Mister Blackwell to leave her and her troubled mind alone. She had to confront him immediately and demand he never speak to her again.

The first signs that she was nearing her destination were the acrid fish scent of the Thames and the sight of gulls riding wind currents in the azure sky. She scrunched up her nose to deflect the smell and pressed a fingertip beneath it as the hired hackney slowed and the murky water came into view.

She'd decided to leave her carriage at home so as not to draw the attention of the curious to her destination. As a woman of advancing years, she was allowed to bend some rules, but visiting a single man without a chaperone, at his place of business, was not one of them. Particularly when the visit was, as she quickly discovered, in such an unsavory area of the wharf.

Blackwell Shipworks. The sign confirmed she was in the right place and brought deep apprehension. She should rap on the roof, demand that the driver take her home immediately, and forget this foolish endeavor. Unfortunately, her fist did not comply with her wishes and remained tightly clutched by the other fist in her lap.

The sight of the ships and the sounds of the bustling activity of workers left her oddly excited. Hammer against steel, flapping that she could discern came from sails catching the wind, and voices raised to be heard over the din of ships being built and readied to sail.

In all her years of spending the spring and summer months in London, she'd never visited a wharf or been on a ship. Mother found sea travel a frightening proposition, and their trips had been limited to overland travel. Fortunately, Noelle had no similar notion or limitations. She hoped one day to sail the world.

Anticipation welled when the hackney pulled off the street in front of the sign. She wriggled on the seat as a tall ship bobbed in its mooring. Perhaps she might press Mister Blackwell to give her a tour of one of his ships before she demanded he never speak to her again.

Noelle pondered delivering a proper set-down as the driver descended from his perch. By the end of her visit, Mister Blackwell would know how deeply she despised him and his behavior.

Several shirtless men watched as she alighted, and Noelle kept her eyes carefully averted. Any careless glance could be taken as an invitation to approach. Without a burly chaperone for protection, she'd be vulnerable to unwanted attention.

Beneath her oversized bonnet and simple, unadorned yellow gown, she knew she stood a good chance of passing the throng of workers unrecognized.

Noelle looked about for the office and spotted a tidy building with a smaller Blackwell Shipworks sign over the door. She had taken several rapid steps in that direction when a sharp whistle stopped her. She raised her head to locate the source of the sound.

A man was tangled high in the ropes of a sail, several dozen feet above the deck of a ship. He raised his hand, and it took her a moment to realize she'd found Mister Blackwell.

The devilish American was shirtless in the sunshine, and his skin held a golden flush. Muscles bunched while he strained and shifted with the sway of the ship. Several locks of hair blew in casual disarray about his face while the majority of his hair was fighting to remain in a ribbon tied at the base of his neck.

She touched her hand to her throat and did her best not to openly admire his fine form. The impropriety of his half-naked state was negated by the fact that she found him utterly attractive and could not turn away.

It was difficult to believe that this man was first cousin to an earl and not bred and whelped in an alley. Still, though he had no problem with flouting convention at every opportunity, there was nothing crude or lowborn about him. Even now, her heart fluttered dangerously at a second viewing of his magnificent chest, this time in bright daylight.

He wavered slightly when a gust of wind snapped the partially lowered sail near his head, and he ducked to keep from being hit in the face by the heavy canvas.

Noelle gasped. When she was certain he was about to plunge to his death, he easily righted himself and actually laughed as he began the process of climbing down to the deck.

Her skin tingled as he retrieved his shirt and walked toward her, taking his sweet time covering himself. The man was a preening peacock, showing off his attributes. It was obvious he enjoyed flaunting his sculpted body for her perusal. He was sweaty, gritty, and disheveled. And all she could think of was ripping off her gloves and exploring each curve and angle of his body with her bare hands. For hours, if she had her druthers, until she was certain no muscled plane had been left undiscovered.

Sweaty or not.

"No need to worry, love," he said, coming to a stop before her and squinting in the sunshine. His hair was damp on his forehead, and perspiration gave his skin a damp sheen. "I have been climbing in the rigging since I was a boy. My maternal grandfather owned a shipyard much like this one. Only grander. Until it was sold to settle bad investments." He looked down the row of ships, and pride was clear in his eyes. "I will outpace him someday in ships and coin." He turned back to wink at her shadowed face. "Count on it, Milady Thief."

Noelle lifted her nose. She should have known her disguise wouldn't keep him from recognizing her. Even at a distance. He'd been intimately close to her, several times. He probably realized who she was as soon as she alighted from the coach.

"You are awfully confident, Mister Blackwell."

"Success takes confidence," he countered, scratching the side of his head. Noelle locked onto the action. It aggrieved her greatly that his every movement fascinated her. She should find his dusty appearance repulsive. Instead, she wanted to know if he smelled as earthy as he looked.

"Some find working in trade beneath them," she said, hoping to remove the confident smile from his face. The hungry look in his eyes rattled her. She let her attention fall to his callused hands. "They leave labor to the laboring classes."

Mister Blackwell chuckled. "Spoken like a true aristocrat, dearest, from one used to living off the earnings of their ancestors and the hard work of others. Tell me, Lady Seymour, did you manage to get into that frock of yours unassisted, or did you need a slew of maids to help?"

Involuntarily, her hand went to the trail of buttons on

her dress. She gnashed her teeth when she realized he was mocking her. "You also have been living off the coin of others, sir. Your father was an earl's son. That makes you as connected to the indulged upper class as I."

He cocked a brow. "Perhaps. Once. Now I find I enjoy watching the fruits of my own efforts grow and flourish." He held out a hand to indicate the ships. They were beautiful against the blue sky and the Thames behind. "Did you know my father cut Mother off when she refused to return with me to England? If not for a small inheritance, we'd have been left with nothing. He paused and returned his attention to the ships. Pride seeped from his every pore. "Everything you see before you is mine. Every shilling that purchased these ships, I earned with back-bowing work."

Noelle felt a welling of admiration for the exasperating man. She hated the feeling. It was more acceptable to see him as a debaucher of innocent women, or a tradesman less than her equal. In truth, he was her superior in that he actually earned his way in life. She'd lived off her father and her uncle and all the generations of Harringtons before her. Truthfully, she wasn't certain which previous Harrington was responsible for the family wealth.

For the first time she saw herself as he must see her, a spoiled and indulged brat. Her throat burned.

Something on her face must have caught his attention, for he reached out to cup her chin with rough fingertips. "Worry not, love. You have many other admirable qualities."

She sniffed lightly. He lowered his arm and closed his hand around hers. Her gloved hand was nearly encompassed by his. Only her fingertips showed.

"Come," he said. "Let's get you out of this heat."

He pulled her toward the building, her feet moving quickly to keep up with his long strides. He opened the door and allowed her to pass inside the dim interior. The air was several degrees cooler than the heat outside. A row of open windows overlooking the Thames was the source of a cool breeze.

Noelle looked around and realized the large building wasn't just an office, but some sort of workshop, too. There were various woodworks in progress, parts she assumed belonged on ships to help them sail.

Several men clanked tools and sent brief speculative glances her way. Gavin led her toward an open door and into a cramped but tidy office. While he removed his soiled shirt, took a clean one off a peg, and pulled it over his head, Noelle walked over to a model of a ship that was similar, she thought, to the one on which Gavin had been climbing among the sails.

"It's a frigate, a warship." Gavin joined her and touched a fingertip to the delicately carved mast. "The navy has commissioned me to build a dozen of them." He smiled softly and ran the same fingertip over a tiny sail. "My grandfather should be turning in his grave with envy."

Noelle smiled. She couldn't help herself; his humor was infectious. "Is this one of the ships I saw moored outside?"

He shook his head, and several straight locks fell over his eyes. "I have yet to begin building. We start next week."

The ribbon at the back of his neck had proved ineffective against the wind and rigging climbing. His disheveled hair gave his face a boyish slant. Noelle's hand twitched to brush the hair out of his eyes. But to do so would inform him of her desire to touch him and also offer unneeded encouragement on his part. Mister Blackwell was already free enough with his hands.

She forced her eyes back to the model ship. "It's beautiful." A wistful sigh followed, and he chuckled.

"Would you like a tour of a schooner?"

Noelle nodded eagerly. "Yes, please."

Gavin watched her pale face turn animated. She colored with a light blush, obviously excited at the prospect of putting her pretty little feet on the deck of a ship. Most women saw ships as a means to get from one place to another and thought of little beyond that. Noelle seemed intrigued by the ship itself. He realized that besides his aching attraction for her, there was much about her to like.

"Then let us proceed." Gavin took her elbow and led her outside. The bright sun had moved temporarily behind a fluffy cloud. He wondered what she was thinking beneath the shadows produced by her bonnet. Everything about her puzzled him. One minute she looked like she wanted to lick cream off his chest, then the next, like she wished to put a bullet between his eyes and be done with him.

He much preferred the former.

Gavin chose the three-masted schooner less for its interesting lines than for the fact that it was currently unoccupied by workers. The ship belonged to a duke and had taken a beating during a stormy journey to Paris. Gavin had refitted the damaged pieces, and it would be sent off to Dover in the morning. It was the perfect place to get the lovely lady alone.

It had come as a surprise to see her alight from the rented hackney in her drab costume. Gavin knew she'd been avoiding him. To see her arrive at his shipyard unattended by a chaperone had almost cost him his footing, and quite possibly his neck.

Not that he was complaining, mind you. Her scent mingled with the salty sea air and teased his nose. He'd never thought sea salt and spice and fruit could arouse him until his cock twitched beneath his dirty breeches. The combination stirred up images of her in his bed, kissing him with that delicious mouth of hers. He was beyond tempted to taste her again, if only to assure himself she was not some heated daydream about to dissipate on the wind.

Noelle lifted her face to the breeze, and her bonnet fluttered. He caught a brief glimpse of her pert little nose and fine angled features as the bonnet blew backward against the tightly tied ribbons beneath her chin. Just as quickly, the wind died, and the bonnet returned to its previous position.

Gavin wanted to snatch it from her head to expose her face, and to crush the unflattering bonnet beneath his boot.

He was stopped from doing so by fear of retribution from the petite miss. If he angered her and she ran back to the waiting hackney, then he might never discover the reason for her visit.

And he was nearly expiring from curiosity.

"I own the land from the warehouse down there"—he paused and pointed to the low, squat building perched on the end of the row, then turned in the other direction—"to just beyond the ketch with the pink sail."

Noelle screwed up her mouth, and Gavin chuckled at her puzzlement. "The marquis who owns it wants to present the boat to his wife for her birthday. He spent a sizable chunk of his fortune getting the sail tinted her favorite color."

Her amber eyes softened. "He must love her very much."

Gavin shrugged. It wasn't his business why the marquis had requested a pink sail. The money was good, and he'd have outfitted it with black dots had the marchioness liked dots. "She just presented him with an heir. Had the babe been a girl, she might have gotten a tea service."

Clearly she didn't like his comment. "Are you always so unromantic, Mister Blackwell? In spite of the practice of chaining men and women together for financial or social gain, some people do find love and happiness in their marriages."

The lovely lady was a romantic. A surprise, for Lady Seymour seemed more of a practical sort. He knew very few couples who had genuine love and grand passion after their weddings, and none since his arrival in London. Most couples tolerated each other and found happiness outside their marriages with lovers.

He stepped around to face her. "If you are so intrigued by the institution, then why, Lady Seymour, are you unwed?" He perused her upturned face. There was a tinge of annoyance in her eyes. He bit back a smile. "Certainly at least once since you were dragged out of the schoolroom and had your first Season you've received an acceptable offer to wed?"

Her glower deepened. "Just because I believe the marquis loves his wife does not mean I believe all couples are happy. I have seen, firsthand, the destruction a miserable marriage can bring to a family. I have no desire to bind myself for eternity to a man I loathe." She drew in a deep breath as if to collect her thoughts. "I am quite content to live my life as—"

"A courtesan?"

Noelle stewed. How dare he remind her of her folly again and again? Clearly, the man was missing even a small measure of manners.

"You, sir, are insufferable." She lifted her nose as high as she could comfortably do so without falling over backward. "As I have told you before, you have mistaken me for someone else."

Skepticism filled his eyes, and his square jaw twitched. She'd grown to despise that smug look. It showed her that no matter what she said, how many arguments she launched, he'd always know she was lying.

If only the Thames were closer. She'd greatly enjoy pushing him into the vile water.

"Oh, there is no mistake, Milady."

Before she could protest again, he grabbed her arm and fairly dragged her toward the schooner. Noelle sputtered at the mistreatment but was unable to pull away. He rushed through a litany of ship terms while dragging her across the deck. Boom, gaff, topsail, stern; her mind whirled, and she soon found herself belowdecks. When he finally saw fit to stop, she took the chance to breathe and scowl at her molester.

"I hope you paid attention to your lesson on ships, Milady," he said, chuckling. "For I intend to test you on all the terms and what purpose they serve. If you fail, I shall have to kiss you."

She shot him a stern look. He was impossible! Choosing to ignore the comment, she examined the small space that she assumed to be some sort of cabin, and dug her nails into her palms. If he planned to ravish her on the narrow bunk tucked against one wall, he'd be in for a fight.

"Are you always such a charmer, or is there something about me that you find distasteful, Mister Blackwell?" She raised her closed fists to about waist level. He made no move toward her, nor did he appear worried. "I came to speak to you privately, and you accost me publicly." She took a small sidestep toward the door. "I think I made a grave mistake believing I could plead my case to you."

This time his brows shot up. "What case is that, exactly?"

Noelle focused on his chin and kept her eyes averted. In the enclosed room, he seemed large, bold. Her body was emitting small shivers, and she was having a difficult time remembering the words to explain why she'd come. She opened and closed her mouth several times with the struggle.

"Perhaps I can be of help." He took two steps to close the narrow gap between them and reached for the tie of her bonnet. Noelle's breath caught. "You have come to fulfill your offer to become my courtesan."

Chapter Six

Her teeth snapped shut with a *clack*. "Certainly not!"
Why did he have to repeat that sentiment? It was as
if confronting her with her shameful behavior was some
wicked way to break down her denials and get her to confess to her misdeeds. She was not, and would never be, a
courtesan! If he expected her to submit to the scandalous
pledge, he would be extremely disappointed!

While her mind filled with virginal indignation, her
body shimmered with heat. The idea of playing courtesan,
and freely giving herself to him for even one night, warred
within her mind. He was too close, too perfectly male.

His mouth curved up at the edges, his confidence overflowing. It was as if he knew her struggle. Knew how much
she wanted him. He'd give her everything she wanted, and
more. All she needed to do was ask.

Alarmed, she stepped back and hit the wall behind her
with her shoulder blades. In perfect synchronization, he
followed, his body forcing her to press against the wall in
an attempt to keep from touching him. He was so close she
could feel his heat and the rough homespun of his shirt
brushing her uplifted hands.

"I c-came to remind y-you once again of your m-mistake." She stammered like a child caught stealing a cookie by a stoic-faced nurse. "Y-you must stop saying s-such things. Until the Tipton party, we'd never met. Your confusion has left me rattled. I am not, and never have been, a courtesan. To call me such is an insult."

The words came without bite, and he chuckled softly under her weak protests. It seemed that with each heartbeat, he drew closer to her, until she was forced to place her hands flat on his chest to keep him from pressing against her.

"Mister Blackwell, please! You must stop this at once. I did not come here to be manhandled again. Surely you have some manners?"

"Manhandled?" He looked down to her hands resting on his body. "It appears it is you, My Lady, who has your hands on me. I am the one molested."

Exasperation welled in Noelle. He was finding joy in her discomfiture. The only thing she could do was use her limited strength to keep a modicum of space between their bodies.

His hands moved to capture her hips and shift the lower half of his body against her. The act put her in intimate contact with his thighs. Her core pulsed, and her eyes widened in shock. Only his grip was keeping her upright. Somewhere deep in the back of her throat her breath lodged, causing her head to spin. She could do nothing but watch helplessly, and breathlessly, as his smiling mouth descended toward hers.

This time she managed a strangled whimper as his perfect mouth brushed her lips. His tongue pressed the seam. Then, without a moment of hesitation, she opened up to his exploration and he plunged his tongue inside her ready and eager mouth.

The floor fell away beneath her feet, and she momentarily clung to his shirt to get her balance before sliding her hands up to lock her fingers behind his neck. Desire raced through her. Noelle boldly lifted to her toes for a better fit, aching to feel his body against her in its entirety.

There was nothing outside his heat, the way he felt, his hands, his mouth. This man, this American-Englishman, fired something inside her that she found impossible to fight. She kissed him with everything inside her, wanting everything he had to give.

And more.

Gavin dug his fingers into her hips and ground her against his hardness. Noelle felt wild, untamed. The smell of the sea and the musty room added to her excitement and sent her imagination soaring. The adventuress and the ship captain were lost at sea in a storm, the raging swell matching the ferocity of their blinding passion.

She smiled for the briefest moment before realizing he was turning her around and backing her toward the narrow bunk. With the rush of reality came crushing disappointment. She'd refused to become his courtesan, and yet she was moments away from becoming what she denied. Once he took her innocence, there was no taking it back. She would be ruined.

Noelle broke the kiss. "I cannot," she begged, and twisted to free herself. His hold was too strong. He leaned to nuzzle her neck with hot kisses. She moaned weakly, unable to fight his powerful draw.

"My beautiful lady courtesan," he breathed against her skin, and ran a hand up to caress her breast. Her nipple hardened beneath his touch. "I cannot resist you. Come to my bed."

"No!" she cried, bracing her hands on his shoulders to shove him back. She would not bed this stranger, no matter how greatly her body ached for him. She was Lady Seymour, not a common strumpet. It would serve her to remember her place.

"Unhand me!" The demand worked. He released her, and she stumbled back. Noelle jerked her skirts into place and smoothed her rumpled bodice. The desire still in his eyes did nothing to cool her body. How much she wanted him! "I think it best if we never see each other again, sir."

With the air of a noblewoman of high birth, she collected her skirts in both hands, lifted the hem of her dress, and walked out the open door.

Gavin watched his Lady courtesan flee him, the *clack* of her boots like rifle fire on the wooden ladder leading up to the deck. He wanted to go after her, bring her back, lock her in the cabin with him, and make love to her delightful body all afternoon long. If not for the deep sense of propriety that always lay beneath her seductive surface, he would at this moment be relieving her of her clothes.

Her boots clomped across the deck, speaking her ire through the heavy footfalls that passed over his head as she found her way off the ship. He moved to a small window and peered out, watching the stubborn sway of her hips. Keeping a careful watch to make sure she returned to the waiting hackney unmolested, he chuckled when she climbed inside without assistance and slammed the door closed behind her. Once the conveyance could no longer be seen, Gavin turned and leaned back against the wall.

He closed his eyes, remembering her slightly parted lips and the hunger in her eyes in the moment he lowered his head to kiss her. He'd felt her heartbeat against his chest and heard her breath catch. Though she denied their encounter in his bedroom and refused to acknowledge her attraction, she couldn't control her body's response to him, no matter how hard she tried. She wanted him with a vigor equal to his desire for her.

"I will have you in my bed, My Lady," he whispered, and chuckled at the image of her pink flush when she'd fled the cabin. Her desire was strong. She'd be back. "And you will eagerly welcome me when that moment arrives."

Lady Noelle Seymour was a fiery witch with amber eyes and a passion that took his breath away. Beneath her cool exterior and silky white skin beat the heart of a courtesan.

Patience would bring her around.

And he would not be satisfied until he taught her all the carnal delights he had to offer.

* * *

Noelle thought the courtesan school would offer a distraction from her riotous emotions, but when the driver pulled up to the town house, she found she could not alight from the hackney. Her boots felt nailed to the gritty floor.

Though there were only two courtesans in residence and class would not begin for two weeks, Bliss and Edolie made more racket than a flock of magpies. At times their endless chatter could be diverting, but Noelle had no desire for it now. Gavin's attempted seduction was too fresh, his taste still lingering on her lips.

So she urged the driver on to Mayfair, requesting to be let off a distance from her house and using the walk in the brisk air to clear her mind.

The dreaded American had launched a volley of cannonballs over her defenses and breached the line behind which she carefully kept ardent suitors at bay. It wasn't that she didn't enjoy the company of men; she just didn't care to be courted if marriage was the end result.

Sometime between the carefree moments of her childhood and her marriage to Noelle's father, Mother had grown drawn and bitter. Noelle's fear was to become the same, should an arranged marriage turn out badly. She much preferred to continue living off the good graces of her absent uncle and to slowly and happily slide into spinsterhood.

And once the bloom had diminished from the rose of her youth, she'd no longer have to suffer the amorous attentions of men, and she'd be content. Well, as content as she could be, never having children of her own. That was the one negative to her plan: giving up motherhood.

The first thing Noelle noticed when she finally pushed open the door to her uncle's town house was the overwhelming smell of roses. The second was the scent of lilies mingled with the roses, then other flowers she couldn't quickly name. Then came the strange sensation that she was passing through a garden of flowers in full bloom. The combination made her want to sneeze.

"What have you done to the house, Alfred?" she asked, easing her bonnet from her head. "Has the gardener brought the garden inside?"

The middle-aged butler smiled, showing a small gap between his two front teeth. He'd been with the family for ten years and well knew how to keep the family secrets.

"The garden *is* inside, Milady; however it is not Mister Brown who brought it in." He indicated the parlor. "You must see for yourself to believe it."

Noelle handed him her bonnet and began to walk hesitantly down the hallway. She'd never been one to enjoy surprises.

She stopped in the open parlor doorway and gasped. The sound brought Brenna to her feet. In vases on every surface of every table, and in one particularly large vase that had no surface on which to rest and was left in the center of the floor, were every kind of bloom, in every color one could imagine. It was a horticulturist's dream.

"Good lord." Noelle pressed her hands to her chest and glanced at her cousin. "Brenna, what have you done?"

"It wasn't I," Brenna said, pressing her knuckles to her smiling mouth. "I think my dearest Noelle has an admirer." She turned an encompassing glance about her at the vast array of blooms. "A very zealous admirer."

Noelle stepped slowly into the room. She loved to spend time reading in the garden but never thought to bring the whole inside. Add a buzzing bee and a skittering butterfly or two, and the picture would be complete. "I'm worried that if I don't leave a trail of bread crumbs for Alfred to follow, I may become lost in the maze of vases, never to be found again."

Brenna laughed lightly. "I shall send for a full king's regiment should the need arise to launch a rescue." She joined Noelle, and they stood shoulder to shoulder. "Perhaps you should look for a card."

"I suspect I know the sender." There were several men who'd made overtures toward her this Season, gently rebuffed of course, but none as bold as the dastardly Mister

Blackwell. She would be shocked to her toes were the man behind the grand, and somewhat embarrassingly excessive, gesture any other than the outrageous American.

The mystery remained: How had he pulled this off so quickly? She'd left him no more than two hours ago. The cost for the rushed purchase and delivery must've been staggering.

"Mister Blackwell?" Brenna asked. "Do you think he is the mysterious suitor?"

"He has expressed his, shall we say, enthusiasm for me several times." Noelle stepped to the closest bouquet and leaned forward to search for a card. There was nothing but flowers. So she moved on to the next. "Unless you have another suspect with such abject boldness, and the wealth to pull off such folly, I think we need not find the card to name the culprit."

Brenna picked the vase nearest her and helped with the search. She sighed dramatically. "I so envy you, Cousin." She plucked a pink rose from a vase and held it under her nose. "I have never been the recipient of such devotion."

Noelle scowled. She'd been trying to rid herself of the pesky American, and Brenna found the man admirable. If only Mister Blackwell had the same feeling for her cousin, Noelle would happily match the two.

"Then you are welcome to run off to Gretna Green with him if he'll have you." On her fifth vase, she finally spotted a square of white paper. She gingerly reached between the lilies to extract the note. "He is not the sort of man one seeks as an admirer."

"Indeed?" Brenna put the rose back and walked over to peer at the envelope. It had Noelle's name and address carefully penned in black. "Devastatingly virile? Wealthy? A face women swoon over?" Brenna cocked a brow and looked at Noelle like she'd clearly lost her mind. "You are absolutely correct, Cousin. He has absolutely none of the qualities one seeks in a mate."

The cousins frowned at each other.

"And sarcasm doesn't become you, Brenna." Noelle ripped the envelope open and removed the folded paper.

She snapped it open and scowled. "Wait until you stumble upon a man who annoys you and challenges you and feels free with his hands, and then tell me you will welcome the crush of his attentions."

I didn't know which flower was your favorite. G

Her hand and the note dropped to her side. Brenna reached to take the paper from her. Noelle wandered to the nearest high-backed chair and lowered herself into it. She hated that the note, in his carefully penned hand, had the ability to send her stomach tumbling. She hated that part of her that found his gesture, though more than a little garish, impressive. The cost for the flowers alone must have severely lightened his purse.

"G?" Brenna asked, drawing Noelle's gaze. She waved the note. "Perhaps you should explain just how intimate your association is. This is not from a man who once kissed your hand and found the taste of your knuckles delightful. This man feels he knows you well enough to rush past any and all formalities."

"In spite of your suspicions, we have no intimate association. I have insisted several times that he end his pursuit, and he obviously has no intention to do so. I cannot allow this to continue."

"Has he taken liberties?" Brenna pressed.

Maybe too vigorously, Noelle shook her head. One wrong word, and Simon would pound Mister Blackwell into the dirt. Though the idea had merit, she couldn't do it. "No. Unless one calls a few stolen kisses liberties."

"He has kissed you?" Brenna slumped onto the settee. Her eyes narrowed. "Tell me his kisses were sloppy and repulsive."

"Unfortunately, they were not. His kisses are perfect. He makes me shiver in places I should not, and did not know one could shiver in. Every time he puts his arms around me and pulls me close, I cannot think outside of wanting him to kiss me again."

"Oh, dear." Brenna placed the note on a side table. "This is a bother. Chasing him off is almost impossible now that he knows of your attraction."

"And I do try to resist," Noelle said helplessly. "I resisted all of a full second this last time before I kissed him back. Surely he can sense my distaste."

Brenna giggled and leaned forward to put her elbows on her knees. "Perhaps next time you can offer him an onion scone before he pulls you into his arms. Then his breath will be so foul you won't want to kiss him."

Onions would be a deterrent to kissable breath.

"Remind me to ask cook to purchase a large bag of onions," Noelle said, and closed her eyes. "I fear not even onions can stop my attraction for the beast. He has fully engaged my body. I do so ache for his touch."

Silence fell for a long stretch.

"Perhaps you should wed him and be done with it." Brenna toyed with her cream-colored skirt. "You could choose worse."

"I cannot." There was no force behind her words. Mister Blackwell had battered her defenses so fully that she had no will to fight. "I will not."

Noelle looked around the parlor, with its plain white walls, dark furniture, and bland cream upholstery and drapes. The simple taste of her uncle had been transformed by the beauty of the flowers. This house had been a place of laughter when her father was alive. Then a place of mourning, then the place she escaped to when her mother became overbearing.

Now Mister Blackwell had brought life back into this house, this room, and Noelle wasn't sure what to make of the change.

The only touch left of her father was a miniature painting on the mantel of him as a young man. Most of his personal belongings had been sent to her mother or stored when her uncle claimed the title. Noelle kept his pipe, a second miniature of him, and a few trinkets in her room. She supposed she should be grateful there were few reminders of her loss. Even now, years after his death, the pain was still fresh.

Not once had she considered that her mad flight through life was a way of running from the grief that always seemed to nip at her heels. She loved her sisters, had a strained relationship with her mother, and possessed a general affection for others around her. But she did nothing, nothing, to risk her heart.

As she thought about the man behind this audacious attempt to woo her into his bed, she worried that her one grand adventure was nothing compared to what he wanted her to risk. What she would risk for him if he pressed her.

With a groan, she dropped her head into her hands.

Chapter Seven

"What I can't figure out is why he is so intent to seduce you," Brenna said. "Other than your obvious physical merits, of course. This situation goes past a simple courtship. Certainly, having been raised American does not make him unable to control his baser needs. Well, as much as men in general can control their needs," Brenna scoffed. "There has to be something he wants other than kisses."

Noelle wrinkled her nose. "Isn't it obvious what he desires? It is what all men desire: a woman to warm his bed. And clearly his focus is on me."

"He's well aware you are a Lady, and therefore not a common trollop with whom he can frolic below stairs. No, he has a reason for his keen interest, and I think you know exactly what it is. Now why don't you tell me the truth? You can't keep secrets from me forever."

Noelle worked very hard not to squirm in the chair and give away her guilt. She was a terrible liar. The entire family knew she couldn't lie to save her hide. One stern look from Mother or Nanny, and she'd break down and confess all her misdeeds.

Pressure pulsed in her temples. Knowing Mister Blackwell lacked a wife and children had taken away the one large barrier between them. And obviously he had plans to slobber over her at every stolen opportunity. The cad!

Lud, if only he did slobber! But his kisses were divine!

Perhaps confiding in Brenna would help ease her worry. Between the two of them, they might find a solution to the matter of the haughty American and discover a way to chase him off.

"I offered to become his courtesan." The simple statement brought Brenna to her feet. Her cousin had the surprised look of a woman about to be run down by a speeding mail coach, knowing there was nothing to do but brace for the impact.

"You did what?"

Noelle lifted her hands and hid a smile. The shock on her cousin's face was delightful. Brenna wasn't easily ruffled.

Noelle felt better already. "Well, it wasn't the proper Lady Seymour who made the offer, but a nameless adventuress who allowed stolen kisses in an effort to keep from being arrested." She let out a wistful sigh. "That adventuress is certainly without control."

"An adventuress?" Brenna dragged the chair she was sitting in across the narrow space between them, the legs making a squawking noise against the polished parquet floor. Once the two cousins were face-to-face, she sat down and glared. "Tell me everything. Now."

For the next quarter of an hour, Noelle filled her in on every detail. From finding the sobbing Bliss on the courtesan school steps, to her little trip to the docks to beg her tormentor to leave her be. She skipped over the most heated exchanges between her and Mister Blackwell, dismissing his kisses as nothing more than brief pecks on the mouth. She couldn't admit to her cousin that she'd almost allowed him to make love to her on a narrow bunk on a rocking ship, without one squeak of protest. The matter was too shameful to share.

"Did you offer him any explanation for your appearance

in his bedroom?" Brenna said. "If you continue to deny you were the desperate courtesan seeking a wealthy lover, you need to do a much better job of fibbing to the man. Blushing and plucking at your sleeves will give away your involvement."

"I have denied any knowledge of the break-in, and I do not pluck my sleeves when I'm lying. Not anymore, anyway. In fact, I denied knowing him at all. I still do." Noelle rubbed her forehead. She tried to remember if anything she'd said or done would have given away her guilt. Truthfully, she couldn't think of a single thing. Still, he'd not believed her, and she knew why. "It was the lemon-cinnamon bath oil I purchased from the peddler that gave me away. He followed it like a hound right to me."

Brenna snorted. "Men. They are dogged in their determination. They believe once they are on the scent of their prey, a woman no longer has a choice but to succumb to their paltry charms." She tapped her foot. "If not for your absent mother who has given up on ever seeing you wed, and mine, who doesn't believe in forcing her daughters into unwanted marriages, we'd both be chained to pompous lords who believe women are to grace one's arm and not be heard."

Noelle thought for a moment, then realized Mister Blackwell was not the kind of man who'd want a woman with little substance between her ears. He appeared to enjoy their verbal sparring. It certainly hadn't dulled his ardor. She'd felt proof enough of his ardor against her thigh. More than once.

"The question remains, what am I to do about my situation?" Noelle knitted her fingers. "I can deny our acquaintance until my face turns puce, and he believes I am just being coy. I can explain the real reason for my nocturnal visit and throw myself on his mercy. He might accept the return of the necklace with grace, but what of the earl? Would he be kind? I have a title behind my name, but what of Bliss? The woman has no family to protect her. The earl cannot take kindly to the theft of such a costly item, even if it was returned. She could hang."

Brenna's eyes widened. Finally, her cousin seemed to grasp the seriousness of the situation. "Certainly he would not be so cruel?"

"Does either of us know the earl? No." Noelle flinched. He'd probably want a front-row seat at their double hanging. "I have never met the earl, nor had I met Mister Blackwell before that night. Have you?" Brenna shook her head. "Other than setting the ladies of society all atwitter, he could be a deranged murderer who's left a trail of dead women from here to the colonies."

"You cannot think that!" Brenna said, appalled. "He seems like a very nice man. If he was a murderer, someone surely would have figured out his evil deeds by now."

It didn't matter about Mister Blackwell's history or whether he spent his free time changing the soiled nappies of baby orphans. A crime had been committed, and Noelle was a sort of accomplice after the theft. She jutted out her chin and briskly shook her head.

"I must protect Bliss from her bad decision. For all her history as a courtesan, she is a simple girl." Noelle recalled the tears with which Bliss begged for her help. She'd done wrong but didn't know how to fix it. "She sees the world through childlike eyes, as if all people are good. It was the influence of her maid that caused her to take the piece. If anyone is to blame and deserves time in Newgate, it is that woman."

Brenna fell silent for a long moment to ponder the information as Noelle's mind flicked to Gavin.

A little tremor tickled her skin. The adventuress he knew would have pulled him down to his bunk and torn open his shirt to expose his magnificent chest. She would have taken him into her body and let him show her all the pleasures one found outside the cold marital bed.

It was the Lady Seymour in her who could not take a man to her bed, in spite of her deep desire to do so.

But not just any man could relieve the ache in her body. Mister Blackwell had shaken her to her foundation and shown her what desire was. And unchecked desire had led many women to ruin.

If she found herself unwed and with a child growing in her belly, the scandal would knock the entire Harrington family tree onto their collective rumps, and they would be shunned by society.

The elder members would weather the storm. Wealth and titles always opened doors. But what of her young and unwed female cousins who were not yet launched into society? Would her fall from grace drag them down, too?

Finally, Brenna sighed. "There is only one thing you can do, my dear." She made a dramatic pause. "You must become his courtesan."

Noelle's jaw dropped. "Have you lost your wits?"

Brenna smiled widely. "What choice do you have?" She indicated the flowers with her hand. "He is determined. Eventually, he will begin to ask questions and want to know the real reason why you climbed through his window."

Noelle groaned. "I suspect he believes I was looking for a lover, then panicked. At the moment, he has no connection between my appearance and the necklace." She stared blankly at the ceiling. A spiderweb fluttered in a corner of the room, moved by the breeze from an open window. "Can I sell my innocence to a stranger to keep Bliss safe? I know little about her. She might have a long history of thievery. She could come from an entire family of thieves."

"Do you believe that?" Brenna asked.

How easy it would be if she did. She could confess her deed and allow the magistrate to decide both their fates. "I do not. She was far too upset to make that plausible. Besides, why wouldn't she take the necklace and flee? Its value alone could allow a thieving family to retire into obscurity. No. It was an impulsive act. I will have to keep her secret."

While Brenna stared at the flowers, Noelle pondered a way out of this fix. Of course she could not become his courtesan, but perchance there was another solution. If she could figure out exactly what it was. A powerful attraction wasn't reason to throw off years of semiproper behavior to frolic between the sheets with a most improper man.

Even if it meant it could save a life?

"I think I shall take a few days to contemplate what to do about Mister Blackwell," Noelle said, her heart heavy. "I cannot rush into a rash decision. Becoming a courtesan is not a bargain one enters into lightly."

Gavin worked until nightfall, hoping to get the sloop ready by morning. He'd sent his workers home when daylight faded enough to make dangling from the rigging dangerous. But it wasn't just the danger of falling to the deck on his head that finally forced him to quit. It was thoughts of Noelle and the unfinished business between them. He knew if he died of a broken skull, he'd never know the pleasure of seducing Lady Seymour, and that would be the real tragedy.

He grinned and silenced a happy whistle as he walked the short distance to the stable to retrieve his horse. The evening was quiet but for the sounds of revelry from a tavern one street over and a few crickets in song. The area was what one could call seedy, and not the type of neighborhood for Noelle to visit unchaperoned and without an armed escort. But as it seemed to be her wont to stumble into mischief, she hadn't allowed something such as traveling to a dangerous part of London to deter her from seeking him out.

Noelle. His extremities tightened with the image of her smoky eyes and delightful mouth. She was certainly an unusual mixture of prickly quills and the softest silk. One had to traverse the barbs to get to the latter, but it was well worth the effort for a chance to taste her mouth.

So caught up was he in his musings about what she would look like sans clothing, he failed to hear running footfalls behind him until a footpad was upon him.

Gavin spun about just in time to take a cudgel to his left brow. Thankfully the blow was ill-aimed and glanced off his head. He dropped back and managed to keep his footing. He faced his attacker and quickly realized the blow had been meant not to kill but to weaken his defenses. The giant of a man could have killed him quite easily.

A second man rushed from the darkness, and then another. There was a time in his youth when the odds would have been against the men, but age had certainly slowed him down, and his fighting skills had grown rusty.

He had no time to clear his head and come up with a plan to outwit the footpads when he caught a fist to the chin. Fireflies danced in his eyes. The man landing the blow was huge in both height and proportions. He didn't wait before taking Gavin to his knees with a ham-sized fist to the side of his face.

Gavin briefly considered staying down and letting them have his purse. Unfortunately, his pride wouldn't allow such a thing.

Wobbling back to his feet, he felt one of the men catch his arms behind him, and the stranger with the cudgel circled around to bend and look into his face. The sour smell of an unwashed body drew Gavin upright, past the pain to his face. He met the man's eyes with defiance. Any sign of weakness would please the trio, and he had no intention of adding to their fun.

"Where's the necklace?" the cudgel wielder asked, his breath a foul mix of rotten teeth and ale.

"Necklace?" Through the tufts of linen currently occupying his muddled brain, he realized quite quickly these were no common footpads, trolling for any hapless victim who had the misfortune to cross their path. They clearly thought he possessed a treasure they wanted back. "I have no necklace."

Ham-Fist cuffed him again, and it was the hands on Gavin's arms that kept Gavin upright. Cudgel-Wielder chuckled. The two resembled each other enough to be kin.

"The necklace with the purdy blue stones." Cudgel-Wielder tipped his head and stared. At least Gavin assumed he was staring. It was difficult to see anything in the darkness and through one good eye. The other was already swollen shut. By morning, the eye would be of little use. "Ye have it, and we want it."

Gavin opened his mouth to protest, then snapped it shut. Could these dimwits be speaking about the necklace Charles had discovered the morning after Noelle's visit? The item was a sapphire and diamond confection. The question remaining was how they could know about that particular necklace. It had spent most of its existence in Bath, decorating the neck of the lovely and sharp-tongued Lady Hortense.

His cousin had brought the item to London to repair its unusual clasp, but Gavin was certain Charles had it tucked away for safekeeping. There was no possible chance the trio had seen it in any public setting.

"Perhaps you gents should give me further details." He peered up at Ham-Fist and relaxed his body in a sign he was cooperating. "I cannot recall the item of which you speak."

Ham-Fist and Cudgel-Wielder darted befuddled glances at each other, then began a full minute of angry whispers back and forth. They outmanned him with brawn but were unarmed with wits. They had obviously been hired for the former.

Finally, they turned back to him. "The leidy stole the necklace with the spider clasp. The leidy with the pretty hair," Ham-Fist said slowly, as if speaking thus would help Gavin to understand their request.

Noelle had lovely hair. Noelle stole Charles's necklace? His confusion grew. He had a lot to contemplate with this curious turn of events. However, first he needed to get free of the trio and their desire to beat him senseless.

With his relaxed stance, the man holding his arms had loosened his hold slightly. It was enough for Gavin to pitch forward, breaking the hold. He came up under Cudgel-Wielder's chin with his head, hitting him hard enough to loosen teeth.

The man let out a pained yelp as Gavin gripped his

arms, swung him about, and shoved him into Ham-Fist. The two men staggered back. Gavin dipped down when the third, thinner man made an attempt to reclaim him, and launched the man over his back to the ground. The stranger landed with a choked grunt.

Seeing his opportunity, Gavin ran for the stable while his attackers untangled themselves and tried to regain their feet.

Thankfully, the stable boy, Elot, was efficient as always and had his horse saddled and waiting. The boy lay curled up in a corner of the stall. The lad barely opened an eye when Gavin rushed inside. Gavin pulled the beast from the stall and swung onto his back, kicking the horse into motion before he was fully settled in the saddle.

"My thanks, young man."

The sound of running feet caused him to let out a whoop as he broke through the open stable doors. Cudgel-Wielder took the full force of Gavin's boot to the chest. He cried out and fell backward into a post.

Gavin didn't look back but bent over the bay's neck and plunged into the comforting cover of darkness. The trio of attackers was quickly left behind, with nothing but shouted curses to show him their displeasure.

Normally, winning a fight would give him immense satisfaction and bring a confident grin. Not this time. Something stank tonight, and it wasn't rotting fish bobbing lifeless on the Thames.

The game was over. It was time to get answers.

Chapter Eight

Noelle wandered the darkened halls and rooms of the Harrington town house until well past midnight, unable to find any relief from the heavy burden of her thoughts. The house felt stuffy, and her body responded to the lack of any noticeable circulation of air with a thin sheen of perspiration dampening the entirety of the skin beneath her corset.

She could not imagine lowering herself to become the unwilling courtesan of an American colonist, yet if she couldn't discover a way to convince him she was not his erstwhile lover, the consequences could be deadly.

Certainly, should she agree to the disturbing proposal, her body would keep him occupied and his mind off searching for the real reason for her nocturnal visit. The necklace. Maybe he hadn't put her together with the sudden appearance of the sapphire beauty in his room. She could be worrying for naught.

She pulled her bottom lip between her teeth. It wasn't her body that took issue with her becoming his courtesan. He made her feel hot and cold mingled together in a mishmash of sensations. How easily his touch caused her to lose any measure of sanity and sent her rushing eagerly down a path toward ruin. Like all young women of her class, she'd been raised with the deeply ingrained knowledge that a lady saves her virginity for her wedding night. She doesn't fall headlong into the arms of a handsome groom, she doesn't allow a wicked lord to take a close-up peek at her drawers, and she doesn't get caught in the bushes with her father's secretary. Innocence is the highest gift one gives to the man with whom she will spend her life.

Even if the marriage is unhappily arranged and she despises him with everything in her, a husband, and no other, is still entitled to that gift.

Regardless of the fact Noelle planned never to wed, she still had the virginity rule buried in her mind. She was fairly certain the layers of clothing women had been forced to wear throughout the ages had been specifically designed by some outraged father as an added barrier to male seduction. A man had to be determined to find his way clear down to the skin.

Even now, without boned corsets and hoops to tightly bind a body, a man still had to be resolute in his seduction.

Dragging a hand over a tabletop, she wandered through the dining room and back into the hallway. The staff had gone to bed, and the house was silent.

There had been a time in the not-too-distant past when she and her sister Margaret raced down these halls, their boots tapping on polished marble and wood as their mother called for the nanny to get them under control. Now, the house was hers alone, and she ached with loneliness.

Her shoulders slumped. No Margaret, no Eva, and now no Brenna. Brenna's parents had shuffled her out of London to visit an ailing cousin and she wouldn't be back for several days. Any decisions Noelle made about Mister Blackwell from this moment forward would be hers alone.

Noelle gathered her skirts and headed through the back of the house and out into the cool night air in the garden. Though she knew wandering alone in the garden at night wasn't her best idea, she couldn't stand the confinement of the house for another moment.

Mister Blackwell would certainly find her discomfiture amusing. He'd likely puff up his chest, knowing she couldn't get him out of her mind. Lord help her if he ever discovered how he made her body ache in inappropriate places.

She had wandered halfway down the short path when a feeling came over her that something was gravely amiss. She stopped dead and listened for sounds out of place.

With only the flickering light of a distant streetlamp to illuminate the moonless evening, she darted a glance up and down the path, her heart pulsing wildly in her chest.

There was nothing to give her pause other than the odd notion she was being watched. She started to dismiss the thought as foolishness, until she heard a footstep crunch on a stick near a patch of lilac bushes.

Panic sent cold dread through her bones.

Realizing her servants and the residents on either side of the town house were probably tucked in their beds, leaving her without rescue should a thief be prowling the night, she lifted her skirts and walked briskly back toward the house.

She had managed to get within feet of the kitchen door when she slammed sideways into an immovable object. A large, obviously male object. Arms came up to catch her as she bounced backward and lost her footing. She let out a shriek and flailed her slippered foot. A grunt followed contact with some part of her attacker's leg.

"Let me go," she cried, and opened her mouth to scream. The scream became a muffled squeal when the man clamped a gloved hand over her mouth. She raised her eyes to get a good look at what was probably the last face she'd ever see.

She slumped with relief.

"Hush," Gavin whispered. His eyes danced with amusement. "We wouldn't want to awaken the neighbors."

Noelle's eyes widened, outrage replacing fear. She jerked free and slapped him several times on his hands and arms before settling back to stew.

"How dare you lurk around my garden in the middle of

the night? You gave me a fright," she snapped before casting a glance toward the windows and quieting her voice. If she was discovered trysting with him, no matter how innocent the meeting, she'd be ruined. "I demand you leave at once, lest someone see you."

His soft chuckle boiled her blood. "You broke into my room first, Milady. I thought it fitting to return the favor."

Footsteps along the sidewalk beyond the iron fence sent Noelle into a second panic. It was the night watchman taking his nightly stroll about the neighborhood.

She slammed both hands on Gavin's chest, shoved him back into the shadows of a narrow hedge, and pressed one finger to her lips in warning. If he made any sound to expose their whereabouts, she swore to herself that he'd suffer greatly. Thankfully, he remained silent as a tomb, but for the sound of his light breaths near her forehead.

The watchman wandered off, unperturbed.

It took a few deep gulps of air to slow her own breathing enough to allow her to speak. When she did, he faced her full wrath. "I told you I did not break into your room," she hissed between clenched teeth. "When will you get that through your stubborn head?"

A hand slid up to caress her spine, and he tipped his head to brush his mouth against her temple. "Never."

Her face burned. If she didn't regain control of herself, and soon, she'd end up bearing the man a passel of bastard children, her life in shambles.

"Clearly you have mistaken me for someone else." She shook out her skirts and tried not to think about his mouth, his eyes, his finely sculpted muscles; anything that he might use to get into her drawers. "You were very well into your cups and barely standing upright."

The moment the words left her lips, she let out a gasp and clamped a hand over her mouth, horrified.

A grin tugged the corners of his mouth. "How could you know I'd been drinking if you weren't there, My Lady?" He crossed his arms and leaned back on his heels. "Let us forget the charade and get to the business of you making good on your offer."

Her fists clenched. "Oh! You are despicable!"

The man had no sense of honor or decorum. His shirt strained over defined, muscled arms. Clearly, wearing a coat wasn't part of the costume of a prowler. She noticed the garden's ancient oak tree was close enough to the house for a climb through her second-floor bedroom window.

She grimaced. "You were plotting to break in and seduce me in my very own bed. Had I not been walking about instead of sleeping, you'd have been free to wander into my room and pounce on me before I could awaken and defend myself."

Gavin shrugged. "That was not my most pressing reason for coming. However, we can discuss your seduction after I have my questions answered."

"You are a cad, a bounder," she whispered angrily.

"I am." He nodded. "Now that we've settled that matter, my little thief, we have some arrangements to make." He gave her a thorough once-over. "You broke into my cousin's town house, sneaked into my room, kissed me at least twice, and offered to be my courtesan. I must say, I knew you noble classes like to pretend to be proper while secretly playing lascivious games, but I was quite stunned by the scandalous offer. However, in spite of the unorthodox manner in which the offer was made, I accept."

Outrage burned through Noelle. "You are without honor, sir."

He cocked a brow. "I thought the way you vigorously pushed me against the hedge here meant you wanted to consummate our arrangement. After all, I'm stuck with you in this garden until the watchman finishes his rounds, am I not?"

"You know the watchman cannot find us together," she grumbled. If only she'd thought to bring a pistol when she'd decided to wander around tonight. One shot, and she'd be rid of him for good. "In spite of what may have happened in the past, I have no intention to bed you. Not now, not ever."

His grin slowly faded, and his eyes narrowed. "Then your presence in my room that night was for a darker purpose." He locked onto her gaze. "Stealing a very expensive sapphire and diamond necklace, perhaps?"

The words pounded through her head like rifle shots, and it took Noelle a few seconds for the full impact of his comment to take root. He wasn't there to seduce her; he was there to have her arrested! She was bound to spend the rest of her life suffering the horrors of Newgate.

Her legs buckled. Somewhere, from a distant place, she felt herself lifted, carried off the path, and lowered onto a bench. Once she was settled on the damp stone surface, she began to reclaim her senses, and with them, terror.

Gavin sat beside her and looked into her eyes. She gripped his forearm with clawlike nails. "Please," she whispered, numb to her toes, "do not send me to Newgate."

Surprise lit his features. "Newgate?"

She felt the sting of hot tears burn her eyes and spill down her cheeks. "The necklace was returned in perfect condition. The theft was a mistake. There isn't a reason to ruin lives." The words rushed from her unchecked. She lifted his hand and clamped it to her chest. "Please. I will do anything to keep from prison. Anything."

Desperate, Noelle opened his palm and placed it over her right breast. He jerked it away as if scalded and stood.

Noelle closed her hands over her face and sobbed. The image of living in that dank, rat-infested prison, with guards who abused women without fear of consequence, was too much to bear. She'd beg to be hanged before she'd suffer that fate.

What had begun as a lark, an adventure, a way to help Bliss, had become her darkest nightmare. The shame brought to her family with her arrest would be acute.

The bench moved slightly as Mister Blackwell reclaimed his place beside her. She hardly noticed him as her body shook uncontrollably with wretched despair. "It was a mistake, a stupid mistake," she sobbed over and over again.

Gavin drew her to his side and settled her in his arms.

She clung to him in her misery, wetting his shirtfront, uncaring if he was the key to her downfall. She was falling into a bottomless abyss, and he was the only stable handhold she could cling to.

Though he knew of her deception, he had not brought a magistrate. She understood that much in her befuddled brain. Perhaps she could still dissuade him from his plot if she could stop the flow of tears and figure out a course of seduction.

Unfortunately, the blubbering continued unabated, despite her best efforts to quell her sobs.

Shhh." Gavin pressed his mouth against her hair and inhaled her sweet fragrance. She felt so small and fragile as she shook uncontrollably and sobbed as if her heart was breaking. It brought out unexpected protective instincts, and he did his best to calm her. "Shhh. You must regain control of yourself lest the watchman hears you and comes to investigate."

There was no sign she heard him. Concerned, he turned her face so her sobs would be muffled by his chest.

Her reaction to the mention of the necklace had thrown him off balance. He had intended to get to the bottom of the matter, not send her into hysterics. It took a moment to realize, when she mentioned Newgate, that she thought she was about to be arrested. Arrested? What crimes had she possibly committed, outside of breaking into the town house, that could send her to Newgate?

He managed to make out something through her hysterical rambling about returning the necklace and how sorry she was for the trouble. She kept saying "we," and he sensed she wasn't the thief but perhaps knew the culprit. The missing courtesan, Bliss?

However, the theft of the necklace was the least troubling matter he had to ponder. He'd been attacked over the bauble, and that lifted the crime to another level. There were deeper and more nefarious forces at work than Noelle climbing in a window. Now he had the added worry that somehow his reluctant courtesan might have put herself in danger.

When her crying slowed, then stopped, he tipped her chin up to the lamplight and brushed lingering tears from her cheeks. Her beautiful eyes were so full of despair; he felt guilty, knowing he'd unwittingly been the cause. He cupped her cheek and bent to look into her flushed face.

"I would never send you to Newgate," he said softly. A beauty like Noelle would be a target for all sorts of debauchery in prison. She wouldn't live a week. "It's no place for a woman."

"Truly?" she asked with a hiccup.

He nodded. "Truly."

The tension in her face melted. She let out a soft cry and circled her arms around his neck. "Thank you. Thank you."

Her soft body ran the length of him, and all sorts of improper reactions filtered through him. And he felt like a cad. She was emotionally frail, and what he wanted very much to do was nuzzle his face in the curve of her neck and run his hands over her perfect figure.

Thankfully, she couldn't read his thoughts.

For the last several days he'd planned to bed her, but not like this. He didn't want her to feel obligated to him, or desperate enough to allow a seduction in order to save herself from prison. When she pulled back and unlocked her hands from his neck, he let her move away. She looked down at her lap as if shamed by her tears and unchecked emotion.

His arms felt bereft without her in them. He cleared his throat, leaned over, and braced his elbows on his thighs. His aching face deserved some justice, and Noelle was the key to lead him to the identity of the culprits. Somehow she'd gotten mixed up with some questionable characters. He found it difficult to believe she could have just stumbled upon them during her daily activities. If it took all night, he'd have his answers.

"Lady Seymour, I think we need to start this tale from the beginning."

Chapter Nine

Noelle slid back on the bench as far as she could go without falling off and clutched her hands tightly in her lap. She looked so morose that Gavin wondered if another bout of tears was looming behind her thick brown lashes.

Thankfully, the dam held. He wasn't entirely sure he could handle a second round of such raw emotion. His mother hadn't been much of a weeper, not even as she lay dying. The only tears she'd shed were for him, as she begged him to take his rightful inheritance and turn his life to one of purpose.

It was because of her, and the sacrifices she'd made, that he'd returned to England and entered Noelle's life. And he still wasn't entirely sure he should be thankful for it.

"I don't understand what you want from me." She stared down at her feet.

"I want to know the truth. I want to know how the necklace ties in to your little visit to my room."

Her eyes were wary. Gavin suspected Noelle didn't fully trust him not to have her arrested.

Could she be a thief? Could she be the sort of woman who'd give up respectability to become a courtesan? He didn't think so. Still, there was much about her he didn't know.

Her tightly crossed arms pressed her breasts up to a delicious swell, and those eyes of hers made him wonder if they would change color when she was in the throes of passion.

He cleared his throat. Lusting after her was getting him nowhere. Inhaling her lemon-cinnamon scent mingled with the flowers in the garden was getting him nowhere.

"Since you were in possession of the necklace in order to return it, you must have somehow had the opportunity to steal the piece. Perhaps you should start there."

Slowly, she nodded and swallowed before speaking. She seemed intently focused on some distant object over his right shoulder, and fingered the folds of her skirt. He took both actions as a clear sign she was about to hand him a steaming pile of horse shit.

Gavin crossed his arms and waited.

"I saw this beautiful necklace dangling from the earl's pocket and knew I had to have it," she said in a rush. Then she sucked in a deep breath and slowed her pace. "So I brushed up against him and plucked it from his coat."

The chit was a terrible liar. "Where?"

"Almack's," she said firmly, nodding as if satisfied with her tale. Her attention remained squarely off in the distance, as if looking into his eyes would give away her secrets. "He was distracted by the dancers. It was a fairly easy feat to lift it."

Gavin let out a very long and exasperated sigh through gritted teeth. "His Lordship despises Almack's. He much prefers to spend his free time in London at White's."

"But I swear it is the truth," she insisted, her eyes wide and fearful. "It was me. I stole the necklace. I'm a thief."

The woman was protecting someone. A lover? A friend?

There was only one way to get the truth out of her. She needed a good slap of reality to break through her loyalty to this unnamed confidant. He stood and slowly turned toward the closest streetlamp. Pale light infused his face through a narrow space in the hedge. He hoped it was enough. He did not need a mirror to know it had born the brunt of several well-placed fists to his countenance.

She gasped and scrambled to her feet. She took a step toward him and scanned the damage. "Good God! What happened to your face?"

Gavin touched the tip of his forefinger to his swollen lip and winced. Though there was little pain, his attackers had done their job well. If not for his skill at dealing with criminal types, he might currently be residing at the bottom of the Thames with a knife in his belly.

"A trio of footpads came upon me as I was leaving the shipyard." He watched her eyes widen with shock. Obviously, she hadn't set the men on him. Thank goodness. "They caught me unaware. My mind was occupied elsewhere."

"Did they break anything?" She pressed her fingers against his rib cage with a surgeon's precision. "Do you have any bleeding?"

He reached down and caught her hands. As much as he enjoyed her attentions—and he did, very much—she had explanations to make, and he wasn't about to be put off before he had the complete picture. "They were looking for the necklace, Noelle."

Her mouth parted. Pain flitted through her eyes. Slowly, she eased her hands free of his grip and returned to the bench. She lowered herself onto the surface and rubbed her bare arms with her palms. A shudder shook her.

"Would you like to tell me the name of the real culprit in this caper?" he asked firmly. In order to save himself, and perhaps her, too, he needed her to recognize the gravity of the situation and be completely truthful.

She shook her head. "I cannot."

Gavin sighed impatiently. Clearly she was as stubborn as she was beautiful. He wanted to grab her and shake her until her teeth rattled. He could have been murdered tonight, and still she kept her secrets.

He went to her anyway and reclaimed his seat beside her. The intimacy of the moment wasn't lost on him. He was in the shadows of a darkened garden with the unchaperoned woman who'd haunted him since their first evening together. It wouldn't take much to have her flat on her back and his mouth pressed between her nicely rounded breasts.

It was nearly impossible to remain focused.

He crossed one leg over the other to hide his growing arousal. He rested his arms on his thighs and spoke.

"I know you don't trust me, Noelle, and you have no reason to. We are strangers still, in spite of our previous, shall we say, close encounters." He tipped his head to look into her eyes. "But what happened tonight changed everything. Three men tried to remove my head from my neck. This is no longer just about a stolen and returned necklace. Someone wants it badly enough to possibly kill for it."

"But I promised to keep the secret, and I cannot violate her trust."

"Her?" Gavin straightened. Noelle blanched.

It all made sense now. Charles's suspicion had been confirmed. There was only one woman foolish enough to steal from Charles and think he wouldn't notice the loss. "It was Bliss."

Noelle pressed her clasped fists to her mouth. A moment passed before she answered, "She was pressured to take it by another's influence. As soon as she took it, she realized her error. Then she panicked. It truly wasn't her fault."

The plot grew. Noelle. Bliss. Someone unnamed. Now there were three. If he shook the tree of thieves, who knew how many more would tumble out? "How did you become involved?"

"A, uh, friend has a small school that helps courtesans escape that life and matches them with husbands." Noelle paused, and her shoulders slumped forward. "Bliss knew of the school and came to ask Eva for help. Unfortunately, Eva is in the country at present. So I offered to assist." Noelle jumped to her feet and lifted her arms, her eyes beseeching. "I thought I could return the necklace and no one would know. Then I stumbled upon you. Entirely by accident, I assure you. I made the disgraceful offer as a way to distract you. I never intended to become your courtesan."

Noelle watched his face, knowing he held two lives in his possession. If he wanted to see a double hanging, he had only to call for a magistrate, and she and Bliss would be arrested.

However, it wasn't anger she saw on his battered face. He was frustrated over the situation and how her innocent adventure had almost had fatal consequences. And she felt horrible that he'd suffered for her actions. She wanted to reach out and touch the bruise under his eye.

His handsome face would bear the marks of her bad judgment for days to come.

"I could not let her go to Newgate," she said helplessly. The one way to right this and save Bliss was to try and make him see her point. "She is an innocent in spite of her profession, and is easily swayed. If not for her maid, Bliss wouldn't have taken the necklace."

"Her maid?" Quickly, his frustration changed to curiosity. This was an interesting twist. "Who is this woman?"

Noelle shook her head. Bliss knew almost nothing about the woman. She'd come into the courtesan's life, then evaporated just as quickly after the necklace was lifted.

"Bliss said she arrived about three months ago, looking for work. She had letters of recommendation. Though Bliss found her somewhat terse that first week, she did her job well and was kept on. It was during the last month that the woman began to place ideas into Bliss's head. Telling her she was not getting everything she deserved from the earl for her services."

Noelle's embarrassment flared. It was scandalous to be speaking of the intimacies between a man and his mistress with this stranger. Yet, she had to get the complete story out.

"It was during, ah, a visit with the earl at her town house

that Bliss casually mentioned the necklace to the woman. She'd stepped out of her bedroom to call for refreshments and gushed to the maid about the beautiful piece. It was then that the woman urged her to take the item."

"So she slipped it out of his pocket?"

Noelle nodded. "Almost immediately, she knew she had to return it, but she could find no way to do so without getting caught. She was trapped. It was then she came to me."

She watched his swollen face and felt the crush of responsibility weigh on her. He'd become entangled in this mad adventure and was paying the price for her impulsive game. She played at bravado, but she wasn't an adventuress, not really. Climbing the trellis to enter the town house and accepting her illegitimate half sister into her life were as far as her adventurous spirit stretched.

She hated that now, even with his bloodied face, she didn't want this adventure to end. Secretly, she had liked the thrill that came from climbing through the earl's town house window and from Gavin's stolen kisses. She liked being the kind of woman a man would pursue with enthusiasm and for whom he would sneak through a garden gate to spend stolen moments in her arms.

Impulsively, she reached out to brush her thumb gently over the tiny cut at the corner of his mouth. His skin was warm under her fingertips. He winced under her touch but didn't pull away. Little butterflies danced in her belly.

"I am sorry," she whispered regretfully. His handsome features were all but ruined, temporarily, giving him a rakish bent. "No one was supposed to get hurt."

His eyes softened as his gaze roved over her face. A playful smile lifted the uninjured side of his mouth. "I'm quite sure kisses would make it feel better."

Noelle clicked her tongue and shook her head. "You are impossible." Then, feeling both a rush of guilt and a bit of mischief, she carefully pressed her mouth to the bruise beneath his eye. He tasted lightly of salt and dust. She felt him go still. Good! She'd shocked him.

"Better?" she said, pulling back. Perhaps she *was* an

adventuress beneath her proper upbringing after all. Her mother would fall into vapors if she knew what her oldest child was doing this evening.

The thought emboldened her to brush a few strands of hair out of his eyes. She was handling fire and knew she could be scorched. Yet, he remained still and let her do with him what she wished. Without his protest, she found she didn't want to stop her exploration.

Gavin's stare was intense. "Somewhat. But they had very hard knuckles." She bit back a smile at Gavin's thick tone.

"I can see that." She placed a hand on his knee and leaned to brush her lips across the pair of red knuckle marks on his chin. His breath caught.

This time she did smile. There were so many reasons for this being a terrible idea, but she couldn't think of a one. She liked to kiss him, wanted to kiss him.

Gavin stared at her mouth, his lips slightly parted. There was a shaky quality to his breathing. "Certainly, there are other places on my face needing attention. They pummeled me for a good several minutes."

Noelle let out a short, clipped laugh. He *was* impossible.

With her hand gripping his knee, she pushed to her feet and came around to face him. She bent toward him and put both hands on his legs. She felt his thigh muscles twitch.

"Here?" she said, and kissed beneath his other eye. "And what about here?" With care, she gingerly dragged her mouth over a mark along his cheekbone. The odor of spice filled her senses.

The man moved not an inch. He seemed frozen in place. Finally, she turned her attention to the small red split on the corner of his excellent mouth. Thankfully, it wasn't bleeding. It would be a shame to ruin such a mouth.

"Last one," she breathed softly, and made a brief, close-up assessment of the spot. His breath brushed her skin. Very slowly, Noelle pressed her mouth lightly on the injury.

This time, his hands swept up to catch her waist. She didn't pull away. She moved from the cut, across his mouth, pressing more kisses as she went. She felt him draw her down on the hard stone bench until she was half atop his chest and lap, her legs between his. Covered by the darkness, with the heat of him beneath her, Noelle traced her tongue along the seam of his mouth, begging him to kiss her in return.

Gavin groaned and obliged. Noelle turned her head for a better fit and plunged her tongue deep into his warmth. He caught her head and ravaged her mouth with equal vigor.

The kiss was long and passionate. Their breaths and tongues tangled in a sensuous dance. Forgotten were his battered face, the necklace, Bliss, and Newgate. Noelle was swept away by the sensation of his lips beneath hers.

When she finally lifted her head to stare into his smoldering eyes, a mischievous smile tugged at her lips.

"Feel better now?" she whispered.

He let out a clipped laugh and spun her onto her back. He caught her to him and said, "Ask me again in a few minutes."

Gavin reclaimed her mouth in a searing kiss.

The fit of her body in his arms left Gavin hungry to rip clothing from her in spite of the discomfort of the position and the scrape of his thinly clad knees against stone. He wanted to share with her his vast knowledge of the female form. But he feared frightening her, just as she was beginning to trust him.

So he matched her kisses with several of his own and hoped his erection wouldn't spear through his breeches like a finely chiseled sword. One look at his hardened cock, and Noelle would flee in virginal terror.

For in all her boldness he sensed an innocence that assured him she was a virgin still. It was a complication he certainly didn't need. It was one thing to bed widows and courtesans with a careless, casual flair. A Lady-innocent was entirely another matter.

He groaned as he lifted his head and peered into her soft face. For a woman possessing a cool, delicate beauty, she had a passionate streak. He couldn't help but envy the man who'd eventually wed and bed her. The lucky bastard would never tire of a wife like Noelle.

As he brushed one last kiss across her delightful mouth, he found the idea of another man enjoying her perfect body and delicate lips unsettling. And having her sprawled casually against him was beyond unsettling—and dangerous, too. He needed to remove her body from beneath him quickly, before he lived to regret his actions.

"I am cured," he said reluctantly. Cured of the pain in his face, if not the pain much lower in his manly extremities. He had a feeling she could cure that, too.

But he had no time for a wife, and his wife Noelle would be if they were caught. He'd almost fallen into that trap once and would not do so again. His business was his spouse, and she demanded all of his time and energy.

Noelle smiled sleepily, as if he'd just awakened her from slumber. Her hair was mussed and tangled, her simple gown was askew, and he had regrets that with all the kissing, he'd managed to keep his hands away from any of her softer parts. And in his eyes, no woman had ever looked more beautiful.

With deep frustration, he rolled off her and slid back on the bench. "I think we should discuss the necklace before I do something we both might regret."

Chapter Ten

Noelle startled up onto her bum at the rough sound of his voice, realizing she'd been sprawled out like a wanton on the mossy bench. She was floating in a dreamy fog of kisses, a fog that had scrambled her senses and left her feeling weightless. The reality of what she'd been doing with Gavin brought a prickle of shame, and her face burned.

She turned quickly away. What he must think of her! She denied meaning to the offer to become his courtesan, yet she proved time and time again that she could easily be swayed to become his trollop!

Lud! Thankfully, one of them had been rational and able to stop the madness, and it certainly hadn't been her!

Keeping her eyes averted, she settled on the furthest corner of the bench and began the process of smoothing every wrinkle, not matter how small, from her skirt. There was no reason for him to see the heat in her cheeks; he'd certainly find her being flustered amusing. Not even the dim light could hide the proof of her humiliation.

"I have told you everything I know," she said, her voice tight. "I find it difficult to believe Bliss would be part of your attack. If she'd wanted to keep the necklace, she could have disappeared over the border into some obscure corner of Scotland where no one would ever find her."

"From what I hear, Bliss wasn't chosen by Charles for her intelligence," Gavin said wryly. "Her skills are in other areas."

Noelle's flush deepened until she was certain her face was about to burst into flame. She could feel his warmth, smell his enticing scent. Those alone were enough to fray her nerves without discussing Bliss and her profession. She could only imagine what sorts of skills would make Bliss popular with gentlemen. She had literally no idea what sorts of things Bliss knew.

Noelle had the basic knowledge of what it took to make a baby and the virginal blood that was spilled a woman's first time. Man on top, the woman bracing herself for penetration. The whole act sounded messy and distasteful. It was impossible to imagine what some women found pleasurable in the act.

The kind of act Gavin was well on his way to showing her when he'd abruptly stopped.

Thank goodness! The humiliation of painfully losing one's innocence on a damp garden bench, with a man she hardly knew, would be appalling, to say the least. She might as well hang her damaged, virgin bloodstained drawers on the fence for all of London to see. Her ruination would be complete.

"I'm sorry I cannot be of more help." She stood. The unpleasant path of her thoughts was leaving her close to insanity. If she didn't get free of her handsome tormentor immediately, there was no guarantee she wouldn't be reduced to a serious case of blathering and thumb sucking. "Good evening, Mister Blackwell."

She walked stoically back to the house. She knew if she turned around and saw even the hint of hunger in his face, she likely would run back to him and launch herself atop his long, perfect body.

Why did he have such an incredible mouth? Put that mouth with his pitifully battered face and the warm, toe-curling scent drifting off his skin, and she was one step away from losing all control. A man who looked like Gavin should never be allowed to wander about London without a feed sack over his head.

When God gave him that face and mouth, they should've been countered with a big, deplorable hump on his back and a hairy, spiderlike wart on his nose. Anything less was terribly unfair.

The kitchen became a haven he couldn't penetrate as she hurried inside the warm room. She quickly locked the kitchen door behind her and wandered back through the house. There was no hurry to get to bed and suffer through restless attempts to sleep. The rest of her night would be very, very long.

Gavin watched her stiff spine and curvaceous rump as she stalked to the town house and slipped inside. He suspected she'd slam the panel shut, had she not worried about waking the staff and the neighbors.

He chuckled softly and stared at the huge oak tree. He wanted desperately to climb it and enter her window. They had business to finish. Their shared kisses, though a tasty nibble, were not nearly enough to satisfy the hunger she left inside his body. He'd like to kiss, to lick, his way across her curves, smell her lemony-cinnamon skin, bury himself so deeply inside her body he might never want to come up to breathe.

He knew she saw his reluctance to bed her tonight as rejection. There had been hurt mixed with humiliation. She should be relieved he'd left her innocence intact; a noble act for a man whom very few women would call noble.

A light flickered on in a window on the second floor, and a shadow passed behind a sheer curtain. He grinned and wondered if she had checked the sturdiness of the window lock.

The idea of her undressing for bed roused his cock for a second time tonight. The image of her creamy skin, rosy nipples, and the patch of curls between her legs, in the golden glow of candlelight, left him competing against yonder garden oak over who was more rigid.

Bloody hell! He'd never promised any woman more than brief encounters and shared pleasure. Truthfully, Noelle was the only woman he'd spent more than a fleeting amount of time thinking about at all. Perhaps it was the contradiction between the cool lady she portrayed to society and the passion she evoked with her mouth that kept him intrigued. Perhaps it could be her beauty. No. She was lovely, true, but he'd known several women who were her equal or superior in that regard.

It all came back to the night she'd crawled through a window and found her way into his room. She was disheveled and dressed as a lad. There were bits of plant debris in her hair as it tumbled over her shoulder in an unkempt braid. And never in his nearly thirty years had a woman so shocked and captivated him as his little thief-ruffian did at that moment.

No, it was the desire to see what she would do next that was keeping his mind locked onto her with a single-minded focus.

There was nothing predictable about Lady Noelle Seymour other than her unpredictability. Once she'd made the hasty decision to return the necklace, he suspected she'd discovered she'd liked the adventure. It had opened a door to a side of herself she'd never been allowed to explore freely.

And now, after his attack, she'd continue to be an integral part of his life until the mystery was solved. Somehow she and Bliss were deeply involved in a dangerous plot with the necklace at the center. He felt surprisingly and fiercely protective of Noelle, considering they'd only just met, and wouldn't allow her to be hurt. If the thugs found out about their connection or her title, he hated to imagine what lengths they'd go to, to get the bauble back. Fortunately, Charles had it, and Gavin knew nothing of its current whereabouts.

Gavin retrieved his coat and shrugged into it. With a last look at the one lit window of the town house, he walked down the path and quietly exited through the garden gate.

Since he expected not to sleep the rest of the evening, he'd spend it working on a plan to solve the mystery of the necklace. He knew a man who was considered an expert investigator. If anyone could find the identity of Bliss's maid, Mister Crawford could.

Once she was flushed out of hiding, working things out from there would be easier. From experience, he knew the trio of thugs didn't share enough intelligence to plan an elaborate plot to steal the necklace. Someone was working their strings.

He intended to find out who, before anyone else got hurt.

Noelle used her sleepless night to formulate a course of action. She'd slipped into a simple white nightdress and robe, stoked up a fire in the study to fight the chill, and lit a lamp. Settling behind the desk, she wrote notes on a sheet of parchment about everything that had transpired and any questions she had about the case.

Thinking about the necklace and the frightening attack on Gavin—Mister Blackwell—kept her focused on the seriousness of the situation and off the memories of his heated kisses.

Well, as far off the memories of the kisses as was possible.

By the time morning dawned, she'd discovered that every avenue of plotting led back to Mister Blackwell and the earl. So she called for her maid and dressed in a simple rose muslin day dress. After grabbing a fig pastry to eat during the ride to the earl's town house, she pulled on her old bonnet and left the house.

The hackney covered the distance between the two houses far too quickly as her body tensed with nervous energy.

She'd never called on a man without a chaperone and never visited the home of an unmarried gentleman. Alighting from the rented hack, she glanced up and down the street for anyone who might recognize her, then lifted the hem of her dress and hurried up the steps toward the large oak door.

"I have come to see Mister Blackwell," she informed the butler who answered her knock, and was ushered into the earl's large parlor. She very much hoped the earl was elsewhere today. Her unannounced visit was highly inappropriate enough, without the earl becoming aware of it. They had never been properly introduced.

She walked to the fireplace and ran a gloved hand over the intricate carvings on the mantel. Studying the scroll-work helped to momentarily distract her from intently listening for his approach.

Footsteps in the hall set her heart fluttering, and she carefully kept her head averted from the door. She'd planned to present a cool picture with the hope, for once and for all, that Mister Blackwell would keep his hands to himself.

"Now this is an interesting turn, My Lady." Blackwell's voice behind her was heavily weighted with humor. "Had I known I'd be entertaining you this morning, I would have instructed the maid to freshen my sheets."

Noelle spun about, her mouth agape. She readied herself to unleash a tirade in response to his outrageous comment, but the sight of him standing there in black boots, buff breeches, and a white shirt hanging open off one broad shoulder left her speechless.

It took a few seconds to manage one intelligible sentence. "Had I known you were dressing, I'd have instructed the butler not to hurry."

His chuckle prickled the hairs on the back of her neck. It annoyed her to see the casual ease with which he appeared before her half-dressed. Still, the highly inappropriate behavior he'd displayed toward her from their first meeting should have prepared her for any eventuality.

Truthfully, she should be thankful he was wearing breeches.

Gavin looked at the mantel clock and back to her. His gaze slid casually down her body, and he cocked a one-sided grin. "It is half past eight, love. A few minutes earlier, and we would be having this conversation bedside."

She felt her cheeks warm at the seductive change in his tone. Could she never get through one encounter with the man without wondering what the rest of him looked like without clothes?

Her hand twitched. She wanted to reach for the fireplace poker and clobber herself silly with the heavy item. Thinking of him naked was not acceptable. Unfortunately, she had no guarantees a head fracture would actually eject him from her lusty thoughts.

Perhaps braining him would be a better solution. It would certainly render him unable to batter her with sensual images. "Make no mistake, sir, we shall never do anything bedside, in bed, or over the arm of a chair. I am here on business, not to spend time exchanging sexual barbs with you while fending off your continuous advances."

One brow went up, and his lips curled at the corners. Her mouth dropped open a second time when she realized his intention. That was exactly what he'd been thinking was the reason for her surprise visit! A sexual romp!

The space between her shoulder blades tightened until it cramped. She closed her eyes and pulled in a long, deep breath for patience. His arrogance knew no bounds! The man had a talent for setting her back on her heels, and he knew his power. He needed to be taken down a peg.

And the poker was very close.

"If your visit is not to fulfill every fantasy I've been carrying around since our first meeting, then why have you come, My Lady?" His gaze settled on her mouth.

Noelle stewed under his impertinence. It was time to exact a bit of revenge for all the gaping and dithering and sputtering he caused her to suffer through. She felt a strong desire to knock him, figuratively, off his feet. So she lifted her eyes to his and touched her tongue to her bottom lip.

"After much consideration, sir, I have decided to become your courtesan."

Chapter Eleven

✦

Gavin felt as if he'd been punched in the stomach. Lady Noelle Seymour was offering to become his courtesan?

The desire to shout for joy and drag her down on the nearest settee was tempered by the mischievous gleam in her eyes. Whenever she had that glint, it didn't bode well for him. There was something suspicious beneath her offer, and he suspected it had nothing to do with her overwhelming desire to climb atop his manly frame and ride him all night. He had a feeling Lady Noelle never did anything without first carefully thinking through the consequences.

And yet, he couldn't resist reaching for her before a return of sanity turned her back into the frigid Lady Seymour, the frosty half of her personality he disliked immensely. He much preferred the mussed-up and well-kissed courtesan-thief who'd offered to share his bed.

"I accept." He pulled her gently against him, pushed back her bonnet, and leaned to press a kiss against the side of her neck. She smelled lemon tart-sweet, and her skin was just as soft as he'd remembered. "Shall we begin?"

It would take more than an hour or two for him to work

through all the delicious things he wanted to share with her. Regretfully, he believed getting one or two minutes to seduce her into submission was the limit of her allowance. Even now he sensed her hesitation start to build. He had to work quickly.

Thankfully, he had nothing more pressing to accomplish at the moment than getting her naked. His foreman could watch over the shipyard this morning.

"Shall I help you off with your gown, or call for a maid? I am very skilled with buttons and bows."

He felt her stiffen, and he knew his moment of seduction was at an end. A flicker of annoyance danced through her amber eyes. The day wasn't to continue abed.

A string of curses filled his head.

His reluctant courtesan pressed both gloved hands against his chest to place space between them. "Your courtesan I shall be, but in name only. I have devised a plan to catch the thief-master, and I need your help. I fear the lives of you and Bliss depend on your compliance."

Slowly his brewing erection withered. Icy Lady Seymour had that effect on his ardor. The woman might enjoy public flirting in the company of men, but do not expect her to drag a suitor off behind a bush for kissing and groping.

"Perhaps you should explain this plot, Milady, for I have a feeling I will not find my part in it favorable."

Slowly her hands slid downward to splay over his stomach. His eyes narrowed. She delighted in tormenting him to get him to comply with her wishes. One day he'd return the favor, only it would be his wishes, his desires, they would be following.

"Does not the idea of spending days and nights in my company satisfy your desire to maul me?" She looked down at her hands. Her fingers twitched on his stomach, and fire burned through his tormented cock.

Gavin grinned evilly. He felt his flagging erection flash back to life. "Even brilliant conversation cannot squelch desire, Milady."

Noelle was a temptress, a handful, and he wondered if he might be wrong about her innocence. Were she not born to privilege, she would make an excellent and sought-after courtesan. Staring into her eyes would make any eager protector offer her anything to get her into his bed.

Had she already shared a bed with other men?

He cleared his throat. "You cannot be my courtesan without sharing your body with me." He drew a knuckle over her jaw. "Lovers look at each other in a certain way. They connect intimately with their gazes, subtle touches, and give off a heat when they are together. How can you lead others to believe we share a bed when every time I touch you, your spine stiffens?"

"I can act any part," she assured him. Noelle slipped a hand around to caress the side of his buttock. She leaned to stare into his eyes. "Undoubtedly, even I can fake attraction for you, Mister Blackwell."

The insult was a direct hit to his masculinity. Had her sighs and moans all been faked? Was she truly capable of making him believe she wanted him, and yet felt nothing? Were any of her responses to his kisses real, or were they ploys to save her lovely hide from the hangman?

Reluctantly, he took a large step back and scanned her eyes for the truth. Normally, he'd enjoy her toying with him. However, now was not the time or place to enjoy her feigned favors. He was puzzled. Was it possible he'd read her wrong? That the cold Lady Seymour had played him with the kind of skill a player on a stage would envy?

Noelle fluttered her lashes once, twice, and then sighed dramatically, as if she was bereft to no longer have him in her arms. This was a game. Her eyes held the clues.

Gavin snorted. One day he'd have the disagreeable wench in his bed, and he'd keep her there until she responded to him with real passion.

And to hell with the consequences.

"I have been thinking about your recent visit and the attack that brought you to me." She tugged the bonnet strings and pulled the item free. She dropped it on a wing-backed chair. "All this started with a courtesan. I think if I become one, we shall have a better chance to roust out the den of thieves."

"Absolutely not." His voice boomed in the large room, echoing off white plaster walls and dark furniture. "The moment you are seen anywhere on my arm, as my courtesan, you are ruined and your family will be thrust into scandal. I'll not have it."

Once a woman was touched by scandal, it was nearly impossible to recover from it and have any sort of satisfactory life. Hypocritical, he knew, considering he wanted to bed her without marriage vows.

Her eyes narrowed. "I wasn't asking your permission, sir."

Fire blazed in the pit of his stomach. She had no idea of the ramifications of her ill-conceived plan. Or if she did, she didn't care. She was hooked on the silly notion of tying up the caper herself.

"If I have to lock you in a wardrobe, I will," he warned.

His threat lit up her eyes. "If you try, your face will fare far worse than the bruises that currently occupy the space."

Damn, he wanted to kiss her! The spitting cat!

Forcing himself to be calm, he expelled a breath. The wardrobe idea had serious merit. He wondered how long he could keep her locked up before a servant stumbled upon her and let her out. "Have you considered all you are risking, Noelle?"

"I am not an idiot," she snapped. "I would be in disguise, of course, and our outings would be limited to places where it is unlikely I will bump into anyone I know." She tapped her open palms on her thighs. "I shall start at the courtesan school. I'll learn all I can from Bliss and Edolie about courtesans so I'll be able to pass as one. Then you and I shall go to the courtesan ball at Vauxhall Gardens on Saturday and see if we can draw your attackers out of hiding. If we can manage to catch one, then we can use him to gain information on the others. I believe that if they approached you once, they will do so again. However, this time we will be ready."

Gavin felt the walls press in around him. "And if I refuse to help you with this potentially dangerous scheme?"

"Then I shall proceed without you."

Noelle watched his face and wondered if he'd make good his threat and lock her up. From what she knew of the man, she wasn't sure he wouldn't. She had no information about his years in America. He could be a criminal, a thief, a murderer.

She shot him a skeptical look. "I shall shriek to the rafters should you consider making good your threat." She sighed and continued, "When Bliss disappeared, the maid must have suspected that she planned to return the necklace. It took your attackers no more than a few days to connect you to the earl's home. They were probably sent here to spy with the hope of discovering the whereabouts of the necklace. How long will it take for them to find Bliss and connect her to me? Bliss is not the kind of woman who is easy to hide. Men fall at her feet when she strolls down the street. I have her safely hidden, but for how long?"

There was a long pause as he stared into her face, as if contemplating her argument. Or perhaps thinking of where he might find a length of rope. It was impossible to read his blank expression.

"I have a business to run and ships to build," he said finally. "I have wasted enough time looking for my mysterious courtesan and not attending to my work. The more time I spend traipsing around London after you, the less time I devote to fulfilling my lucrative contract."

"You have workers, and it won't be a twenty-four-hour investigation," she snapped. "Surely you can take some time to help me with this matter. Unless you'd prefer I take care of this nasty business myself."

If he refused her, how could she proceed? She needed Gavin to pose as her lover to make it work. He was the key to drawing out the men. The footpads would have no reason to attend the ball otherwise. Until they were caught, Bliss and Gavin would be in danger.

Noelle felt partially responsible for the situation and wouldn't rest until she helped extricate the two of them from this very deep pit she had helped dig. The very public courtesan ball was the perfect place to start.

First, she had to become a courtesan. Though Eva worked with them, Noelle spent little time in their company. This was Eva's rule, about which she had grown more insistent since her marriage to her duke. Society couldn't know about the secret life of their newest duchess.

It had been Eva's mother's sudden illness that sent the duke and duchess to the country and put Noelle and a former courtesan, Sophie, in charge of the school. Unlike Sophie, Noelle was woefully inadequate in the position.

As there were currently no classes until the end of the month, her responsibility was only to settle courtesans into the town house and see they were cared for.

Bliss changed that simple task.

If Eva found out what she was up to, her wrath would rival a hurricane.

Noelle grimaced. Hopefully, Eva's stay at Highland Abbey would be lengthy. By the time she returned, Noelle prayed this adventure would be at a conclusion and her sister none the wiser.

"Workers tend not to work when there is no supervision." Gavin scowled. "If I lose this navy contract, I can lose everything. Not only a fortune in earnings but my reputation as a shipbuilder. People will not trust a shipbuilder who fails to build ships."

"The last thing I want is for you to suffer for my misdeeds. You cannot know how deeply I regret getting you involved in this caper." She wondered if his financial situation could end up as dire as he imagined, or if he was using his company as a reason to dissuade her from following through with her plan. "If I promise not to venture out without you, and to go out only during times when we can be together without taking you away from your work, will you say yes?"

"Is there even a small chance I can convince you to give up this impulsive endeavor and let me handle the matter alone?" At her head shake, Gavin rubbed the side of his face. She'd arrived so early, he hadn't yet shaved. Dark bristles added to his rakish appeal. "I thought not. You are a most stubborn woman."

"So I've been told." She nearly smiled. He was wavering. It was a good sign.

"If I agree to this scheme, will you follow my directives without argument?" He leaned in and pointed a finger in her face. "I will not help you if you don't agree. I cannot worry that you will do something impulsive and foolish."

His bossy tone stiffened her shoulders. She truly hated to take orders from anyone. Still, if she had to agree to take his manly commands as law, so as not to have to face the criminals alone, she would. In theory, anyway. He certainly couldn't expect her never to argue or to trot about at his heels like a dog on a leash. Did he know nothing about her?

"I agree," she said, and watched mistrust edge his eyes. He didn't believe her promise one bit. However, there was nothing else he could do but take her at her word.

This time she let her smile escape. He'd agreed. That was all that mattered.

"I shall return home and ready my disguise. Then I shall go to the school and learn all I can about courtesans and their lovers. By this evening, I should know all there is to know about the profession." She snatched up her bonnet and, with a little wave, left the town house.

Gavin listened to the sound of the door closing behind his new courtesan; his courtesan in word but not in truth. How, exactly, did their agreement work in his favor? He'd already lost valuable work time thinking of the beautiful and fascinating courtesan-thief. Now he'd agreed to her scheme to catch the crooks. He'd spend even more time with her, and none of it abed. By the end of this adventure, he'd be broke, existing in a full state of burning arousal and living in squalor as his shipyard failed.

And heaven help him if the chit actually could learn everything there was to know about courtesans and seduction in one afternoon and then used those skills to tease him further. His life would be pure hell.

"Lady Seymour, you do try a man's patience," Gavin grumbled. He dropped in the nearest chair, stretched out his legs, and settled his chin in his upturned palm. Exactly how much information could she could glean from a group of courtesans in a few hours? The idea of Noelle speaking to a gaggle of soiled birds about how to satisfy a man in bed roused his slumbering erection. Again.

The courtesans knew about men; that much was true. Nevertheless, their teaching would be limited to explanations, and Noelle would be limited by having no actual experience. His cock twitched. He should call Noelle back and give her a real lesson in how to please a man, as a good courtesan should.

Bliss screwed up her beautiful face. "Of course a courtesan allows a lover certain liberties in public, in the right setting." The girl shot Noelle an odd look. "But never on the street. His wife might pass by and witness the act. A courtesan is always kept separate from his family."

Noelle plucked at the thread on her sampler and tried to appear bored. She didn't want to appear too eager for information. That could arouse suspicion as to the reason for her desire to know about courtesan behavior. The two women, Bliss and the russet-haired Edolie, knew her as Miss Noelle, a friend of Miss Eva's. They hadn't an inkling that she was a Lady. Eva preferred it that way, and Noelle agreed. In fact, Eva wore a spinster disguise when she was teaching classes. Very few people, outside of Sophie and Noelle, knew this secret side of her life.

Though Noelle wasn't disguised, she wore simple clothing and told the ladies she was a widow with charitable intentions and a desire to help abused courtesans. The women accepted her presence in that capacity.

They were fleeing a life of sexual servitude. All they wanted were husbands and families. Noelle was of little interest to the women. They had their own worries.

"Interesting." Noelle wished she could put pen to paper and write everything down. To her surprise, there were a dizzying number of rules a good courtesan had to follow. It tore apart her notion that all the women did all day was lie abed, awaiting their lover's pleasure. "And the clothing?"

"It depends on the man," Edolie said. She had possessed three lovers in her twenty-four years, and the third actually wanted to wed her. Unfortunately, the elderly baron had died during their last visit, in the midst of a particularly enthusiastic romp. The trauma had been enough to finally convince Edolie to give up her profession for a husband and children.

"I thought all courtesans dressed scandalously," Noelle interjected. It was interesting how little she knew about courtesans. Everyone knew about them in a general way, as most husbands, fathers, and brothers had one. To spend time with them up close was a lesson in the depths of her ignorance. "Bright colors, low necklines, overflowing corsets?"

Edolie nodded. "Sometimes yes, sometimes no. While a few men do prefer that their lover dresses modestly in public and scantily in private, other men find it pleasing to have her forgo a corset and wet the front of her dress so her nipples show."

The courtesan paused and frowned. "I heard of one particularly naughty earl who took his courtesan to a ball where she wore only a long cloak, stockings, and slippers. Of course, it is an unconfirmed rumor."

Heat crept up Noelle's neck. She tried to imagine any woman engaging in such appalling behavior. Yet she knew that in the world of trading sex for money and security, anything could happen. Debauchery and abuse were what sometimes led courtesans to this town house's door.

"It is rumored that a duke took his mistress to a party where clothing wasn't required," Bliss added. "The party guests spent the entire weekend naked." She leaned in. "And the men were whispered to have swapped their lovers."

Dozens of outrageous questions popped into Noelle's head, but she kept them to herself. She'd retain some sort of propriety. If her questions got back to Sophie and, through her, to Eva, her sister would not be pleased. She'd want to know why Noelle was suddenly interested in courtesans.

"Shocking," Noelle said simply, wondering if Gavin would ever take a mistress to a ball sans clothing, or wander around all day without a stitch on. Worse, she wondered what kind of proclivities he enjoyed in bed, and why she really wanted to know.

"There have been several of those parties," Edolie added with a brisk nod. "The last was at Huntworth Manor. The earl lost his wife two years ago and has turned his home into a house of sin." She screwed up her face. "I cannot believe anyone would want to see the earl in that state. He is quite robust in his midsection."

Noelle gaped at that news. She had visited Huntworth with her mother and sister, once, many years ago. The countess had been a lovely woman, albeit a bit shy. The earl had been loud and red-faced with a barrel chest and a dark red beard. She tried not to imagine the man strolling about his grounds with a doxie on each arm and not a stitch of clothing between them. Unfortunately, the image planted itself in her imagination and refused to dissipate. She'd never again look at the earl without that disgusting thought popping into her head.

There was an entire world of debauchery she'd not been privy to. Faces she'd seen at balls and parties. Who knew what sorts of vile acts were committed in the privacy of some of the homes she'd visited as an innocent child?

A world she wanted to visit under the guise of finding out who was stalking Gavin and, indirectly, her. Could she pull off the charade with Gavin, knowing she was about to expose herself to who knows what?

Though Bliss and Edolie had given her several valuable pieces of information, she knew nothing, absolutely nothing, about the secret life of a courtesan! She'd never so much as had a man's hand on her unbound breast or bare thigh.

The closest she'd come to any sort of seduction was with Gavin, and even he had been a gentleman. Well, sort of. Kisses certainly hadn't led to nudity, and they certainly hadn't led to her agreeing to gallivant around London, bare beneath a cape.

Aches began in her secret places. Would the heat in his eyes turn to fire if he knew a cape, stockings, and slippers were the entirety of her clothing? Would he reach for the tie at her neck, knowing that with the flick of his wrist, the cape would puddle at her feet and she'd be naked to his unfettered gaze?

"Goodness, look at the time." Noelle jumped to her feet, upending her sampler so it clattered to the floor. She scooped it up and clutched it to her breast. "I really must go. I have a prior engagement."

Stumbling over both her words and her feet, Noelle hurried for the door, snatching up her cape and bonnet as she went. She didn't want him. Sex was for procreation and not for sport. Only men seemed to find it such. Women saw it as practical and a duty. A duty she had no interest in pursuing.

Sadly, her body wasn't in agreement.

A light fog rolling across London helped soothe the heat in her face and body as she hurried to retrieve her gig from the small stable behind the town house and climbed onto the seat. Taking up the reins, she snapped them over the back of the horse, thankful she'd chosen to drive herself this morning rather than take a hackney. The fresh air helped to ease the burn in her cheeks.

Beneath the bonnet, she thinned her lips and wondered

how many men who had danced with her, laughed with her, all properly behaved, shamelessly enjoyed chasing naked doxies around. How many men who had pursued her in the years after her coming-out were the same men who swapped mistresses at the house party?

How many wives knew of their husband's despicable behavior and could say nothing?

Did Eva or Margaret know such things were happening under their noses whenever they attended a society function? There was no telling what information Eva knew and kept to herself. She'd wandered among courtesans, listened to their gossip, for years.

What had her shy sister Margaret learned from the courtesans during the weeks when she lived among them?

There was a brief time last year when Noelle had insisted Margaret don a courtesan disguise and enter the school in order to get information on the mysterious Eva. Having a third and illegitimate sister could have caused problems had the connection come out publicly. But both Harrington sisters had learned fairly soon that Eva wasn't at all what they'd expected, nor did she want anything from them. They'd quickly grown to love their father's secret daughter.

This courtesan rescuer with a big heart.

A thread of anger crept up her spine. She knew men of circumstance took mistresses, courtesans, but what of their families? Didn't they care that their behavior could shame their wives, their children?

Her father had loved Eva's courtesan mother, Charlotte, and she'd born him a daughter. Noelle and Margaret's mother had lived to make him miserable long before Charlotte had come along, so how could Noelle have resented his happiness?

The conversation with Bliss and Edolie confirmed what she already knew in her heart. Spinsterhood was a far better path for her. She'd never lie awake at night, knowing the man she'd vowed to cherish for her lifetime might be mistress swapping with other husbands. And she'd never risk her heart.

* * *

A few hours later, Noelle called for the maid, Elsie, to help her into her costume. The young maid was easier to dupe than Martha, who never did anything for Noelle without first battering her with questions about who, what, and where she was going, and why. Martha was a mother hen in a maid's serviceable clothing.

If she was to convince Gavin she could go through with her plot, she had to convince him she was taking no chances with her reputation. "No one will recognize you now, My Lady," Elsie said, and made one last adjustment to the wig. Noelle leaned in for a better look in the mirror.

Beneath a crown of dark brown hair and enough powder and rouge for three women, she hardly recognized herself. A beauty patch had been placed above the corner of her mouth, and Elsie had lined her eyes in black for a dramatic flair. The gown was gold satin and cut low, tight to the waist. The fabric flowed in watery waves to her feet.

Noelle had convinced Elsie she was attending a costume party where the best-costumed guest would win a prize, and she wanted to be well disguised.

In truth, there was only one man she needed to convince that her disguise would fool anyone who knew her. If Gavin didn't recognize her, she'd be satisfied.

"It is perfect," she said. It *was* perfect. She'd be horribly disappointed if he quickly caught on to her ruse. If he, a man she'd known only a few days, saw through her disguise, then how would she fare with men who'd known her for years?

The maid nodded. "Your own mother wouldn't know you."

Sliding on her gloves, Noelle spun one last time before the mirror. She quelled a tightening in her stomach and nodded while Elsie drifted off to tidy up the room.

"Let us hope Mister Blackwell doesn't," Noelle mumbled. If she fooled Gavin enough to make her point, then this evening would be a success. She could attend the courtesan ball without any worry she'd be exposed and ruined.

They could publicly trick the thieves into making a mistake and catch them before they could do more harm.

But first she had to fool Gavin.

She walked down the stairs and found her footman waiting. He smiled. "I followed the gentleman from White's. He went to a carnival with two friends, Milady. I have hired a coach to take you there."

"Thank you, Timothy."

Noelle nipped nervously on her bottom lip as she left the town house.

Chapter Twelve

Gavin wandered through the carnival with no particular destination in mind. He'd allowed two young acquaintances, Cyril, Lord Creighton, and Hugh, Lord Sinclair, to drag him from White's for a chance to meet young women at the carnival. They'd managed to keep him in tow for a short while before the duo vanished into the crowd, chasing after a pair of young women dressed in bright skirts.

Truthfully, he wasn't put out to be left behind. After the morning he'd spent with Noelle, he wasn't in the mood to socialize. His thoughts were bleak as he worried what sort of mischief she might come upon if she broke her vow and decided to venture out on her own.

For all her bravado, the woman was innocent about anything outside the protective walls of society. All parents gave their children a general warning about staying out of certain parts of London, especially at night, and away from certain types of people. If she decided to toss aside caution and wander about the seedier areas alone, there was no telling what might happen.

No, Noelle was intelligent. She wouldn't willingly risk her life or virtue. Whatever trouble she might stumble into would be entirely accidental. That was what worried him most.

He'd failed to come up with a way to extricate her from this mess and convince her he had the situation well in hand. He believed her patience was limited. Eventually, she'd take matters into her own gloved hands.

Gavin wandered for a few minutes more. He'd taken care tonight to make sure he hadn't been followed. Watching over his shoulder, closely examining every shadow, tensing up at every noise was growing tiresome. He almost wished he had been followed so he could release some of his pent-up frustration on the footpads with his fists.

Fatigue pressed on him, and he longed to spend the rest of the night buried in bed if he couldn't spend it pummeling his attackers or, better, buried in Noelle.

The situation was becoming dire. He needed some relief from the tightly wound state his body was in. He ached for and wanted Noelle desperately, but he knew she was beyond his reach, unless he wanted to risk a wedding.

Truthfully, they had no promises between them. He was free to pursue other conquests. Perhaps if he found a woman to ease his needs, he could settle for treating Noelle like a friend or business acquaintance.

Oddly, the thought of bedding anyone but her left him feeling woefully disappointed.

Laugher turned his attention to a fellow in red and yellow silks with his face painted white. He watched the performer juggle five wooden balls at once, then clapped politely when the man bowed for his audience. Gavin tossed a couple of coins in the direction of a tin cup and turned back toward the entrance to the park.

A flash of gold caught his eye. A stunning woman floated slowly across his line of vision. She was lovely, made up in the extravagant style of another century with a high wig and tightly cinched waist. The dress flowed in waves down her body, leaving no delicate curve untouched. In the sea of carnival goers, she was a beacon of shimmering color in the flickering torchlight.

He watched her as she wandered around the carnival, clearly looking for someone. The sway of her trim hips and the curve of her back enticed him, and he imagined the delight of trailing kisses along the length of her body. Not since Noelle and, before her, Anne had a woman caused his extremities to take more than a brief and casual interest.

Gavin noticed rather quickly that she wasn't chaperoned. By the cut of her dress, he suspected she was a courtesan, a very expensive courtesan. It was quite possible she was looking for her lover as she ventured about alone. In the heated state he'd been in since meeting Noelle, and knowing there was little chance he could take her to bed without those dreaded wedding vows, this woman would certainly be a delightful substitution.

Sidestepping around a group of young bucks, he waited until she passed into the narrow shadows between two tents before maneuvering to cut her off.

She snapped upright with a small cry as Gavin appeared in front of her. Her kohl-lined eyes widened for a second before she calmed down, obviously realizing he wasn't a footpad out to rob her.

In the encompassing darkness, he couldn't make out the color of her eyes, but it didn't matter. The intensity with which she looked at him from beneath a palette of heavy face paint and curls left him feeling she wasn't at all put out by his unexpected appearance. In fact, she looked intrigued.

"Looking for someone?" he asked softly. Her mouth curled up at the corners. She drew her gaze down his frame, and he could see she wasn't uninterested. Truthfully, she was clearly admiring what she saw beneath his blue coat and breeches.

"It depends." Her voice was low and husky. Beneath the fringe of loose brown curls that partially obscured her features, she looked at him sidelong, her lips slightly parted. "I'm not looking for just anyone."

The invitation was clear, and he stepped close. He caught her gloved hand and pressed it to his lips. The woman was seeking a lover. A wealthy lover. And though he found the maddening Noelle delightfully enticing, her innocence would always be a barrier between them.

Perhaps if they had met years into the future, when he was settled and ready to be shackled, then he'd consider Noelle as a candidate for marriage. For now, he'd keep his attachments financial and lusty.

"I think an arrangement can be made. I am not without means." He didn't care if he was rushing into an arrangement that might prove unsuitable if their personalities didn't fit. He usually took his time when selecting a lover. However, it had been months since he'd bedded a woman, and this one was sending all sorts of amorous thoughts and feelings through his body. At this point, he'd risk all, pay anything to have her.

A flash of white teeth followed his offer. She leaned against him with her full breasts, and the scent of lavender filled his senses. Though he preferred lemon and cinnamon, he found he could settle quite well for lavender if it meant bedding this glorious creature in gold.

"Then perhaps we can move to your carriage and finalize our arrangement." The husky-breathless sound of her voice, and the soft flesh rising to view in two perfect mounds from beneath her corset, hardened his cock painfully. He nodded, distracted. If he didn't get beneath her skirts in the next few minutes, he'd spill himself into his breeches.

He took her hand and slid his arm about her waist. She was a perfect fit. She leaned into him, tucking herself close as he hurried toward a row of waiting carriages. He spotted the crest of Lord Creighton and knew the chap wouldn't be put off if Gavin borrowed the coach for a tryst.

Quickly, he ushered his new mistress toward the coach at a rapid clip, a soft giggle following his haste. He jerked the door open and all but pushed her inside the nearly black interior. She spun and dropped onto the seat, her back against the squabs. She sighed softly as he knelt over her, pushed a knee between her thighs, and pressed his mouth against the curve of her neck. The sweet warmth of her skin burned through her dress. His body was fully and blindly aware of nothing else but her.

She let out a low mewling sound as he slid a hand up from her hip to her waist, to cup one of her delightful breasts.

Lud, she was driving him to insanity! He liked to savor a coupling, enjoy the smell and taste of a woman's soft flesh. Not this time. His first moments with his new courtesan would be brief and without preliminaries.

He lifted his head to capture her mouth. The taste of her sweet lips and her passionate response sealed the contract between them. He didn't need to see what was beneath her clothing to know by her kiss that he'd be fully satisfied with their arrangement.

Gavin slid down her body and pressed his mouth against the silky curve of her right breast. She moaned helplessly and shifted beneath him. The creamy swell rose against his mouth, and he drew his tongue over her skin like a starving man.

"Your name," he urged. "I must have your name."

"Noelle," she breathed. "It is Noelle."

Gavin froze, his mouth still pressed to her breast. Slowly, he lifted his head, stunned. He reached behind her to shove open the curtain. With equal care, she slid back the wig to expose a cascade of blonde hair and dropped the item to the floor, her eyes wary. Even without the curls to shadow her face, and beneath the thick paint that covered her features, he'd know those wide amber eyes anywhere.

"Noelle?" His voice sounded harsh and distant through his heavy breathing. She'd claimed to be able to carry off the charade, and he'd not believed her. He had clearly misjudged her abilities to fool anyone, much less him. And she'd done so brilliantly. He'd not recognized her. Not once.

"I chose lavender." She reached up to stroke his chest. The sweetness of the simple and tentative caress showed she was no longer the fiery courtesan beneath him. She was the innocent Noelle. "I knew you'd recognize the lemon."

Foolish, that was how he felt. After all their meetings,

after all the times he'd kissed her, held her against him, she'd duped him. Surprise quickly faded to anger.

"You certainly learned your lessons well, My Lady." He jerked up her skirts and ground his erection against her woman's core beneath her drawers. She gasped. Good. She needed to learn a lesson. Terrible things could happen when a woman foolishly enticed a man.

"Mister Blackwell . . ." Eyes wide, she stilled. Then he felt her hips shift, and she pressed against his erection. It was an instinctive reaction and not feigned. His stomach flipped. In spite of his previous suspicions that she was playing games with him by feigning desire, she did truly want him. He saw it in her eyes.

All his doubts fell away. This was no game.

"Goodness," she breathed. Sprawled beneath him, her hair flowing in hopeless tangles around her shoulders, she was wanton and so very beautiful.

He instantly released her and sat back against the squabs. If he didn't put some distance between them, he'd take her violently and passionately, here in the borrowed coach.

"No." Noelle rose to her knees. "I need you. I ache so desperately. Please help me, Gavin." She reached to cup his face and pressed kisses along his cheek and jaw. He grabbed for her hand, but she was determined. She crawled over him, pressing fervent kisses until she was straddling his hips. In spite of his mind telling him this was wrong, she wasn't a courtesan, he couldn't help feeling such over-whelming desire for her, and he ached painfully in both his mind and body.

"We cannot," he said roughly, his teeth clenched, as she slid her body up against his. She was so warm and willing. His reserve began to crack. "You are an innocent."

"I am a spinster," Noelle gasped as she settled firmly over his erection and cupped both the back of his head and the side of his face with her gloved hands.

Arching against him, she kissed him hard on the lips. With a growl, he opened his mouth, slanting his lips over hers. She thrust her tongue between his teeth, and he nearly exploded.

She pulled back and said against his mouth, "You will not ruin me. I will never wed."

Gavin felt his world tumble out of control. Thankfully, he knew several ways to satisfy their hunger without taking her innocence. And he desperately needed that experience now. If he didn't release his need immediately, he'd never again be able to walk upright.

"Move back." She slid back to his knees and watched as he freed his erection. She gasped again, her eyes filled with both hunger and uncertainty. Before she could fully assess the situation and flee screaming from the coach, he caught her around the hips and settled her covered core atop his cock.

She stared deeply into his eyes as he ground against her. After a moment, she must have understood his intention, and she pressed herself more firmly against him to match his motions.

A low gasp escaped her mouth, and Gavin pulled her face down to his. He kissed her soundly, her little moans and whimpers driving him onward. He lifted a hand between them and loosened her bodice. Two perfect breasts sprang free. Noelle let out a cry when he broke the kiss and captured a dusky peak between his teeth. Her eager body drove him as he moved to suckle her other breast, his hunger taking on a life of its own.

His courtesan-thief rocked like a wild thing as he ground against her, seeking a release, her own pleasure. Gavin had no time to concern himself with who might be listening outside the coach as he tugged the nipple deep into his mouth. Noelle dropped her head back and called out his name.

Shudders rippled through her, and his body clenched. Half a second later, he spilled his seed onto the clothing between them with a sharp groan. Noelle slumped with a gasp onto his chest.

Gavin closed his eyes and nuzzled his face into her hair.

The powerful near-coupling had left him spent. He ran a hand up her back, listening to her uneven breaths begin to slow.

Never had he shared such an intimate act with a woman that did not follow with his cock inside a silky sheath. He'd satisfied them both without removing a stitch of her clothing. Noelle was still innocent—technically, perhaps—though certainly no longer as innocent as before. He felt a flood of warm emotion for the maddening miss and knew he'd never look at her again without remembering her eager response to his touch.

"Are you satisfied, Milady Courtesan?" he said, noting the good humor in his voice. He'd assuaged the pain in his cock and could do nothing more than grin dumbly.

"Quite," she murmured in his ear. She slowly lifted her head, and her eyes were smoky-soft. "How skilled you are, sir." She kissed him gently on the mouth. "I shall certainly regret my scandalous behavior in the morning. But at this moment, I have not a single negative thought."

Noelle watched his lips curve up and knew he was quite happy with the shared intimacies. She finally understood why Bliss found it so difficult to leave her lover. All the things women claimed to suffer with their husbands in bed were certainly not present here. Perhaps it wasn't that the women were born frigid, but the ineptitude of their husbands and lovers that made them so.

With Mister Blackwell, Gavin, these stolen moments of passion had certainly been unexpected. Though she'd promised herself she'd not go beyond a few kisses when proving herself a competent courtesan, she'd lost her senses again with his first touch. He was extremely difficult to resist. She also knew he'd sacrificed to keep her virginity intact, and she would appreciate his efforts in the morning. Nevertheless, even now, she ached to feel that erect part of him buried deep inside her body.

The adventuress in her wanted more. She wanted to feel

their naked bodies locked together. She wanted to kiss his skin and lick his nipples and explore all the angles and planes of his beautiful male form. She wanted to forget her title and become his courtesan in every way.

Thankfully, he possessed the good sense she lacked.

"I could stay like this forever," she breathed, disappointed that the stolen moment would end too quickly.

"Alas, My Lady Courtesan, this coach does not belong to me. There is real danger we might get caught." Gavin sighed as he adjusted her bodice over her breasts and tied the laces. He lifted her gently off his lap and covered himself. Noelle felt dampness on her chemise, a reminder of his release.

With care, he covered her hair with the wig and shook out her skirts. Noelle felt awkward as he cared for her, yet he said nothing to ease her discomfort. No words of affection. No tender stares shared between lovers.

Was it he who felt regrets? She was the one who should be regretful, even angry. At the first opportunity, he'd chased after another woman, a courtesan, when her back was turned. It didn't matter that the two women were the same person. He didn't know that when he dragged her into this coach. It was no wonder she didn't trust men. They were faithless creatures.

Fortunately for him, she felt no betrayal. They had no formal connection on paper, no verbal agreements between them to keep him from seeking the company of other women. They'd enjoyed a pleasurable moment, nothing more.

At last, he finished straightening his own clothes and lifted his eyes to hers. He appeared thoughtful, almost pensive. A change from the man who'd spent the last few minutes making love to her with such reckless abandon.

"Gavin," she began. He put a finger to her lips, then pulled her close and kissed her. Noelle suspected the tender kiss was meant to assuage her unease. It helped very little. The relationship between them had changed. There was no hope of going back to the days of innocent stolen kisses. Oddly, she felt no desire to do so.

"Come, we must go." He took her hand and helped her

out of the coach. Tucking her hand under his arm, he led her down the row of coaches. "Did you bring your carriage?"

Eyes averted, Noelle shook her head. "I took a hackney." At his frown she added, "I was careful to watch for anything suspicious. I believe my identity is still safe."

He nodded and kept walking.

In the aftermath of their love play, their conversation had ground to a halt. Silence stretched between them while he retrieved his horse from where he'd left him tied behind a coach and helped her mount. He climbed up behind her and settled her against him in the protective circle of his arms.

When they reached her town house, he went around to the back, so as not to alert the servants of her arrival. As he led her quietly through the garden, she felt his tension undulate off him. She wanted to say something, to assure him he'd not done anything she hadn't willingly begged for, but couldn't find the words.

He drew her to a stop at the shadowed kitchen door and stepped in front of her. He lifted her chin. "I need to speak to Bliss."

She nodded.

He pressed a kiss on her knuckles and said, "I will send a coach for you. Until then." He gave a slight bow and walked away.

Chapter Thirteen

Noelle was positive she'd changed somehow after the encounter with Gavin in the coach. Yet, no matter how many times she stood in front of a mirror, with or without clothing, and looked herself over from top to bottom, she saw no visible evidence to support this conclusion.

No flushed cheeks, no kiss marks on her skin, no dewy eyes when thinking of her sort-of lover. She was the same as always on the outside.

Everything she'd experienced was locked secretly inside her. Not even Martha seemed to notice anything untoward when she poked and pinched and fussed over Noelle as she always did. So went the maid's theory: She could read every secret on Noelle's face; and this was a big secret.

"Stand still, Milady," Martha scolded. "It is difficult to dress you when you fidget."

Noelle scowled. "I think this dress is too tight." She grunted and pulled at the fabric of her waist. It wasn't really too tight. She needed an excuse for fidgeting.

"The dress is fine." Martha gently slapped her hand out of the way and shifted the dress into place. "There."

The serviceable green dress was perfect for a visit to the

courtesan school, but she missed wearing the borrowed breeches and shirt she'd worn the night she met Gavin. She envied men wearing such comfortable garments. She longed to go back to that night, when she'd been a nameless adventuress in borrowed breeches and had felt free.

It was quite different from last evening, when a moment of passion had been tainted by guilt and regret. His.

Though she knew Gavin had found as much fulfillment as she had in their wicked love play, his subsequent behavior was a bit of a puzzle. Whereas most men would have taken her fully and without consideration of the consequences, he had became somewhat aloof afterward.

Could it be the anonymity of darkness that he found appealing? All of their previous encounters, where kissing and fondling were involved, had been in dim or darkened spaces.

Was it possible he didn't find her attractive in daylight? Her confidence slipped a notch. Disheartened at the idea, Noelle slumped onto the settee as Martha reached for a brush.

"What shall we do with your hair?"

The courtesans were napping when Noelle arrived at the school. Sophie went upstairs to rouse Bliss, leaving Noelle alone with her disconcerting thoughts.

She'd behaved improperly last evening. What must Gavin think? Was he appalled by how easily she'd succumbed to his seduction?

"Miss Noelle?" Sophie's voice brought her around. The former courtesan had on a simple yellow frock, and her blonde hair was tied back with a matching ribbon. She was in charge of the school when Eva was away, and took her duties seriously. "I must protest again. Your sister will be put out, should I allow you to follow through with this troubling plan."

Noelle had expected some resistance when she'd told Sophie she intended to use the school to learn how to be a courtesan and to keep watch over Bliss. However, Sophie was a mother hen protective of the school and the ladies. She worried that Noelle would bring danger to their door.

"I am always careful when I visit and would never allow anyone to discover the whereabouts of this town house. I will come in disguise and lead the others to believe I am a courtesan on the verge of leaving my protector. There will be no link between myself and this school for the thieves to discover."

"And what of Bliss?" Sophie's face tightened. "Do you actually think she might be involved with a band of thieves?"

This was the question Noelle had wrestled with. "I do not believe so, yet what do we know about her?" Noelle shrugged. What did they know about any of the young women who came to the school? Eva trusted them all explicitly, unless they said or did anything to break that trust. And thus far, she'd never had to toss a young woman out. "If there is anything wrong with her story, appearing as a fellow courtesan is the best way for me to find out. Her guard will be down. And I will be gone before Eva returns in two weeks to begin lessons."

The lines in Sophie's hard-edged face deepened. "I don't like deception," she said. "Miss Eva will have my hide of she discovers I allowed this."

Noelle felt her will falter. She placed a hand on Sophie's arm. "Should I get caught, I shall take the full brunt of my sister's anger. She will hold you blameless."

After a few more muttered protests, Sophie reluctantly consented to go along with the deception, once Noelle agreed that Sophie could call off the ruse should there be any inkling of danger directed toward the school.

Noelle hurried from the town house and into the garden behind it before Sophie could change her mind. The only way for the ruse to be a success was with Sophie's cooperation.

Hopefully, the next time Noelle returned in her disguise, all of Sophie's concerns would be settled.

It had also been difficult to get Sophie to allow Gavin to come and speak to Bliss. Men faced strict rules when visiting the school. Though Sophie was very protective, she had come to see this visit as unwelcome but necessary in order to protect Bliss from future harm.

Once the culprits were rounded up, they'd all be safer.

Ten minutes passed before a coach, its shades drawn and its windows painted black, pulled to a stop behind the house.

Noelle held her breath. Dragonflies flitted in her stomach. The large driver, Thomas, was also protector of the courtesans. He climbed down and nodded at Noelle. He had replaced Harold, who'd been Eva's friend, confidant, and protector until he'd married their sister Margaret.

Her heart thumped as Thomas unlatched the coach and swung the door wide. Noelle leaned forward against the gate but could see only a shadowy outline of Gavin in the darkened interior. Her heart tumbled about and her chest tightened.

"You may remove your blindfold, sir," Thomas said.

Gavin impatiently pulled off his blindfold and pushed to his feet. He paused, hunched over, at the open door and blinked in the sunlight streaming across his face. Noelle realized she was twisting her fingers together and forced her hands to her sides. In daylight, her erstwhile lover was magnificent in black clothing.

He scowled as he climbed from the coach.

Her heart beat so hard beneath her ribs, she was certain he could hear the thumps.

Beneath his stare, she was thankful she'd carefully chosen the color of the dress. The green muslin was edged at the bodice in cream lace and brought out the almost invisible bits of green around the pupils in her amber eyes. She had had Martha upsweep her hair into a soft crown around her head with a few loose strands to frame her face. If she'd thought he'd find her lacking in daylight, there was no indication of that worry as he met her eyes.

From the heat in his stare, she knew he found her more than a little suitable. It was the same look he'd held her in when he'd pushed up her skirts and settled her on his erection, ground against her core, and brought her to release.

Gavin drew her hand to his lips. "My Lady."

Her heart caught. "Mister Blackwell."

He held her hand longer than necessary, and it took Thomas clearing his throat to break the spell. Gavin released her fingers and frowned over his shoulder. Thomas settled into a position by the coach and ignored the frown.

"Was all this subterfuge necessary?" Gavin asked. "One would think the queen was in residence."

Noelle smiled. "Some of our courtesans are fleeing abusive men; the kind of men who don't take kindly to their absence." She peered at the nondescript brick town house. There was nothing to indicate there were wayward courtesans in residence, and the high hedges along the fence offered a measure of privacy from the neighbors' prying eyes. However, if there was ever any breach of security, Eva would pack the lot of them up without haste and move to another house. She'd had to do that once in the past. An angry baron had somehow discovered the address and made trouble.

"They must know they are safe," she said. "Miss Eva will not risk a scorned lover hunting down one of her girls."

"Miss Eva?" His eyes narrowed. "Her name is familiar." Gavin took in the garden and the house with a sweeping glance as Noelle turned and led him through the garden gate. "I believe I was invited here some time ago, to a party. An invitation I declined. So this Miss Eva is the woman who matches courtesans with husbands?"

The comment took Noelle by surprise. "You are in Eva's book?" How did she not know this?

"Not by choice, I assure you." Gavin snorted. "My cousin's bookkeeper was matched last year and is blissfully happy. Or so I hear. Charles thought I needed to be shackled myself and arranged the matter without my consent. Sketch included. And since I am in no danger of inheriting the title, he deemed a former courtesan as good as any other woman to become my wife."

"You don't sound enthusiastic at the prospect." The grim line of his mouth was a clear indication of his displeasure.

"I have nothing against courtesans." He turned back to her. "I just have no desire to wed one. If I were inclined to shackle myself to a bride, which I am not, it would have to be to a woman of impeccable reputation." He watched her expression. "As a gentleman, I do have a bloodline to preserve."

Noelle tried to hide her dismay. Oddly, she'd attended the party he spoke of. It was the day Harold proposed to Margaret and Nicholas proposed to Eva. How close she'd come to crossing paths with Gavin then.

"I shall see that your picture and biography are removed at once. The men in her book must be actively seeking wives."

His mouth quirked, and his eyes dipped to her bodice, where the slightest curve of pale flesh was pressed up to view. "I'd appreciate your assistance in the matter, My Lady. I am most certainly not looking for a wife."

A hot blush slipped down her body. Wifely was not how she'd behaved last evening. She'd been bold and scandalous. Clearly, by the look in his eyes, he'd gotten over his reluctance to face the situation head-on. He was staring at her as if he meant to gobble her up, and it was only the close proximity to the house, and Thomas, that cooled his ardor. She took some feminine satisfaction in knowing he still found her attractive.

Had they been alone, Noelle was certain there would have been a repeat of last evening. She gulped. Her core pulsed, and she regretted the lack of privacy.

Why did he have to affect her so?

His chuckle spilled over her. "You needn't worry I will accost you behind the hedge, my dear Lady Noelle." He took her arm and tucked it under his. "Should you decide to repeat your delightful actions of last night, I assure you we shall not be rolling about in the dirt."

Her face burned. It wouldn't do to have him think she was so overcome by his manliness that she couldn't control herself. His arrogance was already at too high a level. She forced her chin up and her eyes to hold steady.

"I fear I may have acted inappropriately, sir. I was merely playing a part, and it went too far. It will not happen again."

One brow cocked up. "Truly?" His handsome face above a high white stock was filled with what she could only guess was . . . regret? "I was hoping to share with you many, many more of the delights I have learned during my travels." He shook his head. "I shall have to live with my disappointment."

Delights? He was far too confident of his skills and her response to him. "I am convinced there are many women in London who would be pleased to be the recipient of your teachings. Our dealings will be businesslike from this moment forward."

G avin watched as Noelle walked off, her back stiff and her demeanor stiffer. His teasing had gotten under her skin and prickled her to ill humor. He'd planned to treat her respectfully and as if he'd forgotten her passionate hour in his arms. It took but one look at her, and he knew he could never, ever again treat her with casual indifference.

A grin broke wide across his face. Even now, he longed for a private moment to see if he could draw out the passionate lady he'd discovered in the coach. He'd never known a woman so uninhibited, so untamed. She'd cast off her veil of propriety and sought—no, demanded—her pleasure as if it was her right. And he'd willingly given it to her, as if it was his right.

His smile wavered. So caught up with the game, he'd almost forgotten she wasn't a courtesan and never would be. This school belonged to a friend. Noelle's bloodline likely went back as far as the first man who'd stumbled onto these fair shores wearing nothing but a bearskin robe.

If only she'd been born on the other side of the blanket, he could seduce and cherish her as a lover. Then the heavy weight of societal rules wouldn't bear down on his sensual thoughts as if he had no right to think them.

The best thing that could happen was to flush out the conspiracy behind the necklace as quickly as possible and return to what he did best: building ships and avoiding emotional entanglements.

The first would prove easier than the second, he thought, as he followed the path toward the town house. There were already enough entanglements between them to last for years. And Noelle wasn't the kind of woman easily forgotten. She'd hooked him in the gut, and he'd need more than the butchering of a surgeon to get the steel barb out.

Chapter Fourteen

Bliss proved to be no help at all. Gavin cajoled, outwitted, and occasionally battered her with his forceful glare, yet she had no new information to offer. It was like she was only a casual observer in her own life. If he wanted to know her favorite frock or all about Charles and his proclivities in bed, he suspected that she could expound for hours on both matters. But ask her what she knew about the woman who had lived in her house for months, and she could hardly remember what the mysterious maid looked like.

"Other than dark hair, you have nothing?" He wanted to take her by the shoulders and give her a shake. "No moles, no scars, no limp? Anything that might help identify her?"

"She was a servant," Bliss whimpered. "She fixed my hair and dressed me. What else was I supposed to notice about her?"

Gavin looked at Noelle, and she felt the weight of his frustration. He turned back to Bliss and pressed her with several more questions.

Finally, when the girl was near tears, he motioned for Noelle to follow him into the hallway.

"I think Bliss *is* innocent," he grumbled. He raked his

hands through his hair and closed his eyes. "The chit would have difficulty deciding which pastry to eat with her tea. I cannot see her leading a ring of thieves."

Noelle agreed. "I told you as much. I've spent enough time with her to discover quickly that she is incapable of such complicated deceit. She simply became entangled in this affair and saw Eva as a way out. When I informed her Eva was away, she crumbled. When she dropped at my feet on the stoop, sobbing and clawing at my skirts, I couldn't refuse to help."

Gavin's mouth thinned. "I think your first hunch was correct. Her maid is the key. I have an investigator searching for her now." His shoulders slumped and he leaned against the wall. "It's easy to see what Charles found attractive in her. She is a fetching chit, if one has no desire for intelligent conversation. If only she'd been wise enough to see she was being manipulated and put a stop to the matter before it went too far."

"Many mistakes have been made from the start," Noelle said. "Bliss's theft and failure to return the necklace immediately to the earl, before he'd left her town house, started the downward tumble. Looking back, my ill-conceived plan to return the necklace might have been better accomplished if I had sent the necklace anonymously, by courier."

Gavin grunted. "The fact that Seabrook had possessed the audacity to slip Bliss into his own home, the same home he occasionally shared with his wife and children, made you confident that Bliss had information about the floor plan to make returning the necklace in person possible. Outside of the address, Bliss clearly hadn't gotten much else about the property right."

"True," Noelle replied. Mistakes aside, the earl now possessed the necklace, and though he'd likely suspect Bliss, there'd be no proof she had a hand in the theft. Gavin promised to keep the matter between them. For now. "Still, I could have planned better. I have always been impulsive."

He shot her a funny look, and she smiled. "I guess that comes as no surprise to you, Mister Blackwell."

Reaching out a finger, he touched her under the chin. "It is one of the things about you I find most compelling."

Noelle couldn't regret all aspects of the situation. If she hadn't stumbled into Gavin with the stolen necklace hidden in her pocket, she might never have met him. She'd gone halfway through the Season without once catching sight of him.

"What is our next step?" she asked.

Gavin scratched his fingertips over his chin. "I shall check back with Mister Crawford, the investigator, and see what he's learned about the missing maid."

"I know Mister Crawford. He is very competent."

"He is," Gavin agreed. "If we discover no new information before Saturday, we will attend the ball."

"And use yourself as bait." Noelle saw him stiffen. "The footpads know who you are. That's why I instructed Thomas to use care when bringing you here." She paused. "They likely follow you everywhere. The ball is in a public place. It will be safer for you, for both of us, if they confront you there."

"Charles has the necklace," Gavin protested. "They should be chasing him."

"Unfortunately, the footpads think you have it. They probably assume Bliss gave it back." Noelle shrugged. "You said they weren't bright. I suspect they've mixed up you and your cousin. You do look a bit alike, and you live in his town house. With His Lordship in Bath, you are their focus."

Gavin shook his head. "They did call me 'Your Lordship' while pounding my face." He touched his bruised lip and darted a glance at Bliss. "I should give Charles a beating for getting me involved in this. He never has thought with his head around women."

Noelle ignored the salacious insinuation. "Having me with you at the ball will help cover our trap. They will not suspect you are drawing them out if you are with your new lover. That is why I must learn my part."

From his expression, Noelle knew he hated the idea of putting her in harm's way. If she hadn't pushed him to allow her a part in the investigation, she would be home now, walking grooves in the parquet floors and resenting that he was digging up clues without her.

She wanted to run her fingertips along the jerking muscle, and some kisses, too; anything to soothe the tension on his face.

"Sophie has mentioned that three courtesans are expected to arrive today," she said, mentally shaking herself free of her musing. "I shall return home, get into costume, and join them at the meeting place. They will not suspect another courtesan joining their group. Perhaps there is some gossip I can glean from the women." She smirked. "We women do love to share news. By the night of the ball, I will be a perfect courtesan."

Gavin's tension finally faded, and a smile emerged as he stepped close. He leaned in and said, "If you learn anything of, shall we say, an intimate matter, I'd be happy to discuss any questions you may have. Perhaps I may start a school of my own. What can innocent young society wives learn from courtesans to keep their husbands home and in their own beds?"

Noelle choked mid-swallow. Gavin thumped her gently on the back, chuckling as he did so.

"You are a libertine, Mister Blackwell." Glowering, she peered at him through watery eyes. "Have you no morals, no sense of propriety?"

His mouth lowered dangerously close to hers. "If I did, I don't think you'd find me quite so appealing."

The man was maddening! "You assume much, sir. Perhaps I find little about you appealing. You cannot read my thoughts. A few moments of madness does not make me yearn for you with the intensity of a thousand suns."

"Who said anything about yearning?" He smirked and drew a hand down her arm. "I think you find me every bit as fascinating as I do you. One day, when we have time to explore your, ah, yearnings to their fullest, I will be a very happy man."

"I do not yearn for you," she snapped. The man was too

confident and enjoyed knowing his seductive power over her. He needed to brought down a peg. "I am not your courtesan. We have no arrangement. I am playing a part to gain information, nothing more." She turned and headed through the house with her boots *clack-clacking* as she went. She didn't look behind her but assumed he had to walk at a brisk clip to keep up.

Though he held his tongue, she felt his humor, and it rankled. She led him through the garden to the gate where the coach stood just outside. Thomas pushed off the side of the coach and waited patiently at the door. There was a rumor he'd been in the army with Harold. It certainly explained his ramrod-stiff way of standing. And his serious demeanor.

"The servants are the ones who seem to know every scandal before it happens. Perhaps disguising yourself as a maid would be a more fitting avenue to overhear gossip."

A smile tugged at her mouth. She drew a slow, measuring gaze down his body and then back up to his face. "Yes, but it will not bring me nearly as much pleasure."

The direct hit to his manhood flared his nostrils. Teasing a man to arousal wasn't a brilliant idea. However, when the man was her outlandish Mister Blackwell, and he had no compunction about teasing her back with his own seductive words, she felt it was her duty to torment him in return.

His blue eyes turned stormy. "You worry me, Milady. You are enjoying your part as a courtesan far too much for comfort. I fear trouble is brewing ahead if you're not careful."

Noelle screwed up her face. With Gavin at her side, how much trouble could she get into? "Are you warning me that I am not safe with you?" she asked innocently. She might not be safe with him, but she didn't fear the thugs. Gavin had taken on three and won. "Should I have the metalsmith fashion a chastity device that I might wear beneath my drawers?"

If it was possible for a frown to deepen to a dangerous level, his did. She almost stepped back beneath the intensity of his glare. She didn't know why she was teasing him, outside of the amusement it brought her. The wicked adventuress in her wanted Gavin to yank her into his arms and kiss her silly.

There were several places in the garden where the feat could be accomplished quite nicely.

Gavin shifted from foot to foot. She dared not look down at the front of his breeches for proof of his arousal.

"I'm warning you, My Lady Noelle. If you stoke the fire too high, you will get burned." He gave her a terse nod and left her with the slam of the garden gate. Thomas fitted him with the blindfold, and Gavin awkwardly climbed inside the coach.

She wondered if he actually kept the blindfold on during the ride, and suspected he did not. Still, the painted windows and curtains would keep him from finding his way back.

"Oh, dear," she whispered as the coach pulled away. His warning rang loudly in her ears. He was telling her she just might get what she was asking for if she wasn't careful. Gavin had made it clear that if she didn't want to remain innocent, she should continue her bold behavior.

A shiver raised the fine hairs on her arms. What *did* she want? Did she hope for an affair with a deliciously seductive man? Did she want this one opportunity to feel fully and completely desired before she became an old and dusty spinster?

She did. Lud, she did!

Noelle managed a weak smile for the pair of women, Blythe and Sally, sitting opposite her in the coach. The third woman never showed up at the bookstore, so she didn't have to explain the presence of four women to Thomas. Truthfully, she was grateful he didn't recognize her.

How could he? She was fluffed, laced up, and powdered to such a degree that she'd make the bold Marie Antoinette envious, were the ill-fated queen still alive. The cream-colored vintage gown was slightly yellowed with age and smelled a bit musty. After spending decades in her attic, buried in a trunk, it needed more than one hour to air out.

Time Noelle hadn't had. The bookstore owner, Mister Potts, had been a client of Eva's and was married to the first courtesan Eva had rescued. Satisfied with the outcome of his marriage, he'd offered to help Eva collect the courtesans at predetermined times each month for transport to the school. Unless there was an emergency and a woman was in danger; then he'd send a note around to Eva and the woman was sent immediately to the school.

Bliss had somehow convinced him of her emergency. That was how she'd arrived unannounced.

If the other women found Noelle's appearance odd, covert glances aside, they kept their opinions to themselves. They chatted amiably about gowns and shoes and left her to herself. A few minutes later, the trio was ushered into the town house and directed to the parlor. Sophie joined them for an introductory tea. As she explained the rules of conduct and poured tea, Noelle let her mind drift. She'd spent much time in the town house of late but never had seen it through a courtesan's eyes. If she was to live as a courtesan, she had to see things as they did. She examined the uninteresting room and smugly realized the walls needed a new coat of paint.

Not exactly a stunning revelation.

So she sipped her tea and watched the four courtesans, Bliss and Edolie included, trying to focus on Sophie's words. The four shot her curious glances, trying not to be impolite. Per Eva's instructions, all were dressed in subdued colors. She was the only "courtesan" with enough lace and bows on her gown to sink one of Gavin's ships.

She bit back a sigh. She'd fully forgotten rule number one. Subdued. As she looked around the parlor, she knew, regardless of the muted color of the gown, that she stood out like a peacock in a pen of chickens. Sophie had arrived late and flustered to start the first lesson, so Noelle hadn't had a chance to speak with her alone. Although Sophie expected her to make an appearance at some point during the day, Noelle was amused to discover that Sophie didn't immediately recognize her. Perhaps the woman was so stunned by Marie Antoinette's appearance in the parlor that she couldn't bring herself to openly stare into Noelle's face for fear of appearing rude.

"You will carry yourself as ladies. Clothing with fabric thin enough to see through is forbidden," Sophie said. Noelle's attention drifted in and out. The former courtesan knew her part well.

"You are here by choice," Sophie continued. "If at any point you decide you do not want to obey the rules, you are welcome to le—" A commotion in the hallway interrupted her speech. After a flurry of rapid footsteps, Sophie broke into a smile. She stood.

All pairs of eyes turned toward the door as Eva, the Duchess of Stanfield, glided through the door in a simple gown of gray muslin, a wig similar in color to Noelle's that hid the true copper-gold color of her hair, and a pair of spectacles perched on her perfect nose.

Noelle almost let out a gasp of alarm.

"Sophie." The two women embraced. In a year they'd become old friends. "Mother has recovered nicely, and I had to come back. The fresh country air was getting tiresome," Eva said with a smile. She swept her gaze briefly around the room and seemed satisfied all was in hand. The courtesans would know her only as Miss Eva, spinster and courtesan savior. No hint of the beautiful duchess showed through her drab disguise.

Although she'd missed Eva, why did she have to return now and ruin everything?

Noelle's stomach clenched, and she slid down in her seat.

Chapter Fifteen

Noelle watched as Eva moved from woman to woman, introducing herself as Miss Eva and welcoming them to her school. The young women seemed pleased to be part of the new class and twittered excitedly, knowing they were just weeks away from altering their lives forever.

Seated a bit off to the side, Noelle was last in the row; not close enough to launch herself out the narrow window, and farthest from the door, making an unnoticed escape impossible. She was trapped, fully and completely, beneath her high, stiff wig.

Unfortunately, no matter how desperately she wished it, and how many silent prayers she frantically rolled through her mind, the floral-patterned settee did not open up and swallow her whole.

She'd have to hope against hope that the disguise was enough to fool her painfully observant sister. Not likely!

What was Eva doing back so early? Noelle had received a letter from her sister just two days ago, advising her that she and Nicholas would not be back for almost two weeks. And unless time had sped forward while she was sleeping last evening, she still had twelve days! Twelve days to find out what she could about courtesans without her sister hovering over her like a hawk circling a hapless mouse.

All too soon, Eva stepped over to Noelle and extended her hand. She might as well have handed over a dead cod, for Noelle looked at the outstretched hand with the same enthusiasm.

"Welcome to my school. I am Miss Eva."

Staring down at Eva's sensible hemline would only delay the inevitable. She breathed deeply and lifted her face. It took all of two heartbeats for Eva's breath to catch, and two more to recover from her surprise when Noelle shot her a pleading stare.

"How very nice to meet you, Miss Eva. I am Grace Templeton," Noelle said smoothly, and took her hand. Her sister smiled tightly and pulled her to her feet. They bumped together as skirts and feet tangled.

"If you will excuse us, ladies, I would like to speak privately with Miss Templeton." Noelle watched as finally a dawning came over Sophie's surprised face, and she shot Sophie a silent plea for help that went unanswered. Eva all but dragged her from the room and didn't release her until she'd closed the parlor door tightly behind them.

Noelle winced.

"What are you doing here, Noelle, dressed like you just stepped out of Napoleon's court?" Eva's voice was tight. "Did I miss the note about today being costume day at my school?"

Noelle forced a sheepish smile and patted the powdered wig. "I am in disguise. A pretty good one, if I say so myself. Even Sophie didn't recognize me."

Noelle kept silent about Sophie being in on her plan.

Eva spoke through gritted teeth. "We are not here to discuss the height of your wig or the cut of that gown. I want to know why I came back from nursing my sick mother to find you seated among my courtesans."

How much information should she share? If Eva knew what Noelle had been up to these last few days, what she'd done in the coach with Gavin, she'd be outraged.

Still, Eva was her sister and they shared a bond. Though they hadn't known each other long, Eva could read her very well. Lies wouldn't come easy. The best way to settle the matter would be to tell Eva the truth and take her lumps.

Besides, she'd been dreadfully lonely lately. Confiding in Eva would certainly help ease the burden of her secrets. And Eva might be able to help with the case. She was privy to all sorts of gossip.

Noelle slumped onto a narrow padded bench near the door. "I got myself into a pickle, and now I am working to get myself out of it." She began the tale with Bliss and continued with the edited version until the entire tale was exposed—well, she left the coach part out. No sense ruffling Eva further. "After Mister Blackwell was attacked, we knew this was more than a simple theft. There are some dangerous characters hunting for the necklace."

"Why would they attack Mister Blackwell if the earl is the owner of the piece?" Eva pressed a palm to her forehead.

"I can only surmise that when Bliss disappeared with the necklace, they thought perhaps she'd gone to return it to his lordship." Noelle screwed up her brow. Another thought came to mind that helped explain the mix-up between Gavin and Seabrook. "I wonder if one of them was watching the house that evening and saw me climb the trellis. They might have seen me come and go and thought I was Bliss." She paused. The puzzle had grown much larger. "If it is true, then someone was lingering outside. I'm lucky to have gotten away unmolested."

"You were very lucky you weren't killed," Eva said tightly. "Are you certain no one followed you home?"

Noelle shook her head. "I was careful. I didn't want the earl putting Bliss and me together. I paid a hackney driver to wait for me two streets over, and kept watch out the coach window for anything suspicious. There was no one on my trail."

Eva put her hands to her mouth and joined her on the bench. Her eyes were both troubled and angry. "And now you have offered to become Mister Blackwell's courtesan as a way to flush out the criminals? Isn't there any other way?"

Noelle shook her head. "It is like acting a part in a play," she rushed to explain. She brushed past images of Gavin's mouth on her nipples. "I am not about to become his courtesan in truth."

She hoped if she kept her eyes averted, Eva wouldn't see guilt on her face. She'd never consider herself his courtesan. It wasn't proper. However, she'd acted like one in the coach. If Eva found out, she'd have Noelle locked in her cellar.

There was a long moment of silence while Eva pondered everything she'd learned. There was no indication of the direction of her thoughts.

"Who is this American, and can you trust him not to attempt to seduce you? I understand colonists live by an entirely different set of rules. Some actually live like barbarians in log huts. Or so I've been told."

Rules that didn't exclude kissing, and fondling, and sucking the nipples of virginal spinsters, Noelle thought, and those very same nipples began to tingle beneath her bodice.

"He isn't actually an American. He was born here and *is* first cousin to the earl," Noelle said weakly. It was impossible to think clearly when her body was recalling his seduction. "He's in your book. I've been instructed to remove him."

Eva's head snapped up. "Wait. Your Mister Blackwell is *the* Gavin Blackwell?"

At Noelle's nod, Eva expelled a harsh breath. "I have never met him, though he came well recommended. I hear he is quite handsome." Her amber eyes scanned Noelle's face. "Many women wish he'd find his way into their beds."

Noelle felt her cheeks sting with heat. She was speaking of necklaces and footpads one moment, and the next, Gavin forced himself into her mind and her body was betraying her in a burst of tingles.

"Noelle, what is it? Your face is flushed." Eva placed the back of her cool hand to Noelle's cheek. "You don't have a fever." Eva pulled her hand back and cupped Noelle's face. She stared hard into her eyes. "It's Blackwell, isn't it? Oh, dear. What have you done, Noelle?"

Noelle was trapped. No amount of stumbling around, searching for the right words, would help her now. Eva was on a mission for truth and wouldn't be satisfied until every sordid detail was brought out and examined.

"I may have kissed him," Noelle admitted.

"And?"

What to tell? "And we had a brief encounter in a borrowed coach. But nothing horrible happened. Not really." She rushed ahead. "We were both fully clothed."

Well, mostly clothed. One part of Gavin had been exposed. A large, fully erect, and pleasing part he'd used to pleasure her quite nicely. But Eva didn't need to know those details. Some things were better kept private.

Eva stood and began pacing. "I am going to send Nicholas to beat him senseless. How dare he take advantage of a vulnerable young woman for his own pleasure? You are a Lady, for heaven's sake. He should learn to keep his hands, and all other parts of him, to himself."

Noelle clasped her hands to her mouth to keep from smiling. Eva was brutally direct. "The coach was my fault." Eva abruptly stopped pacing. "He wanted to stop. I sort of seduced him."

"You did what?" Eva's lips thinned.

"I climbed into his lap," Noelle admitted as her humor vanished. She'd disappointed Eva. Her shame was complete. "He is so very handsome and his kisses are delightful." Her lower lip quivered. "I am a year or two away from spinsterhood. Just once I wanted to know what it felt like to be touched, desired."

Eva stood tense for a moment, then reclaimed her seat and reached for Noelle's hand. "Many men desire you, Noelle, as you know. If you opened yourself up to suitors, they would form a line to wed you."

Noelle shook her head. "I have no wish to marry. You

know my greatest fear is becoming old and bitter like my mother, suffering through an unhappy marriage."

Both their mothers had suffered because of their father. He'd been a good man, but Noelle's mother had never loved him. Eva's mother, Charlotte, had slipped into a deep melancholia after his death and still endured bouts of it.

"I do know," Eva said. "But your mother's situation should have no bearing on your happiness."

But it did. "To allow a man to have such control of my life is a fate I cannot bear. Love and hate are dangerous tools when put into the wrong hands."

Their eyes met. "You are playing a dangerous game, Sister, and I'm not speaking of the thieves." Eva squeezed Noelle's fingers. "This man has crossed a barrier and has offered you no promises. What if next time he decides to take what you offer and not hold back? And if you become with child, then what?"

Noelle had no answers to give.

G avin examined the card in his hand, puzzled at the name printed on the surface. He seldom had visitors at the town house, never a strange woman, and never one so highly placed in society.

At first he'd thought the woman had come for Charles, but the housekeeper, Mrs. Mayhew, assured him he was the intended host of the visitor. He supposed he'd never find out what she wanted if he loitered in the hallway.

With that thought in place, he wandered to the parlor, passing an unfamiliar maid perched on a chair outside the open door.

Hmm. A chaperone of sorts. The woman didn't plan to seduce him. Once inside, he discovered the Duchess of Stanfield, quietly pacing the floor with clear impatience. He'd heard she was a beauty, and all of the gossip proved to be true.

From sculpted cheekbones to a pert nose to a mouth that might inspire men to all sorts of wicked thoughts, she was lovely. The question was why a married duchess would lower herself to pay him an unexpected visit.

"I must say, Your Grace, this is a surprise." He flashed what he hoped was a charming smile as he stepped inside the room. She leveled a weighted glare upon him in return. "Have we met? I'm certain I would remember if we had."

Her Grace did not smooth out her scowl. In fact, she clearly wasn't charmed by him. She looked annoyed, put out, angry.

"We have not met, Mister Blackwell," she said in a low, even tone that belied the dark emotion in her eyes. Had she been armed with gun or sword, he'd currently be bleeding on the carefully polished floor. "Though I do know many things about you, sir, not all of them pleasant."

Her frank comment took him aback. He tried to recall a single reason he might have inspired her wrath and could think of nothing. He hadn't been in London long enough to make enemies, though some in society found a man in trade, even a man with blue blood, beneath them. And he certainly would have remembered Her Grace had he made an untoward and unwelcome attempt to seduce her. Drunk or otherwise.

"Then I will apologize for anything I have done to offend you, Your Grace," he offered, attempting to look contrite. He knew she was married to a very powerful duke. It would be a great advantage to find a way into her good graces. "I have to admit, however, that I have no idea of the nature of my crime."

From beneath her wide-brimmed blue hat, she seemed to be taking his measure, and she wasn't appreciating his manly form. Obviously, she'd come on some sort of mission, and he knew she'd get to it at her own pace.

So he crossed his arms and waited patiently.

After a moment, she spoke. "I have come here on a matter of great concern, Mister Blackwell." She took a few steps closer. "It has come to my attention that you have recently become acquainted with a young woman. Noelle, Lady Seymour."

She paused; he nodded. His stomach clenched. It wasn't

implausible that Noelle and Her Grace knew each other. How well, was the question.

"We've recently met." He picked his words carefully.

The duchess waved a dismissive hand. "Let us be honest here, sir. You are more than casually connected. If my information is correct, there was a certain meeting in a coach between the two of you that was entirely improper."

Gavin's mouth went dry. Oh, hell! How could the duchess know about his near-seduction of Noelle?

She continued unabated. "What I'd like to know is what your intentions are toward Noelle. For if they are even remotely dishonorable, I have the connections to see you ruined."

He found he had nothing to say. The frontal attack and threats had thrown his thoughts into chaos. He had behaved dishonorably toward Noelle, but a consensual encounter between adults should not cause him to lose everything he'd worked years for.

It took a moment before he could find a worthy response, and with it came anger. Her punishment did not fit any of his crimes. Even this irate duchess should see that. "Clearly you have become privy to private information." He glared back. She didn't flinch. "I want to know why you feel what Noelle and I do is any of your concern, Your Grace."

A slow, tight smile crossed her mouth as she stepped closer. With a sweep of her hand, she slid her hat back to fully expose her face. His stomach dropped to his booted toes as he peered into her amber eyes.

"I do believe my sister is my business, Mister Blackwell."

Chapter Sixteen

Gavin was struck speechless. Of the many things Her Grace could have said to him, this was the last he expected.

She and Noelle were sisters? This certainly explained why the duchess had her petticoats ruffled. Her Grace was behaving as a sister would when a man was sniffing around her sibling, intending to bed her without the benefit of a wedding.

His next thought slammed through his mind. He realized he had heard some gossip about the new duchess, and was just now putting her together with the woman standing before him. She was the notorious Evangeline. Noelle's Eva. The courtesans' Miss Eva. What were the chances they were not one and the same woman?

In his casual inquiry into Noelle's history, he'd never discovered she had more than one sister. Margaret, Lady Lerwick, was a baron's wife and seldom came to London. From what he knew, she was not as social as her sister. Finding out a duchess was in the mix left him very uneasy.

He had no hope of finding a graceful way out of his predicament. Noelle had evidently informed her sister of some, if not all, of the details of their acquaintance. The best he could do was to attempt to soothe the duchess's ire and hope she had no plans to see him taken out into the country and shot.

"You have surprised me, Your Grace." He rubbed a hand across the back of his neck. A dull pain tightened the area from the base of his skull to his forehead. "I did not know of your connection."

Thankfully, Noelle had no father or brothers to call him out. He tried to imagine the duchess meeting him with pistols at dawn or, worse yet, forcing a marriage. With his history as a guide, he'd much prefer the former.

She stepped back a pace. "Not many do. Noelle and I pass ourselves off as cousins, and I would appreciate your discretion."

Gavin nodded. The secret might be used, later, if she did decide to have him horsewhipped. "Your secret is safe."

"Thank you." She tugged her hat back into place and crossed her arms. "Now about my sister . . ."

Her Grace wasn't a tall woman, yet she was an imposing presence. Oddly, there was a hint of vulnerability in her also, as if she was still getting used to the power behind the title. He wondered how long she'd been wed and what her background was. He surmised she hadn't been bred to become a duchess by a social-climbing mother. Otherwise, the two sisters wouldn't fear discovery.

His curiosity flared. Two amber-eyed sisters unable to claim each other publicly. What was the reason he'd never heard of the connection? He knew he wouldn't be satisfied until he learned the answer, and why the duchess was a courtesan rescuer and matchmaker.

But now was not the time to probe. Having an enraged sister-duchess on his tail was not a situation he'd like to be mired in. Her husband had the power to make his life miserable.

"I have no excuse for my behavior, Your Grace. I'd like to say I was slobbering drunk when I took advantage of Noelle, but that is not the case. I was sober when I allowed myself to succumb to your sister's charms. She is lovely."

"Hmmm." The tension in her shoulders appeared to ease. "I can see why Noelle finds you attractive, Mister Blackwell. You are a handsome man. I am certain she isn't the first young woman to fall victim to your charms."

The last comment was bland, yet he felt a veiled insult anyway. Did she believe him a despoiler of virgins?

"If you think I set out to seduce her, I assure you such is not the case." The lie flowed smoothly from his lips. Regardless of the sisterly connection, the duchess didn't need to know how intensely he had wanted Noelle in his bed.

"From what I've learned, that is difficult to believe."

Gavin had been hunted by an irate husband or two in Boston, but never an irate sister. He held back a grin. "That first night, it was she who offered to become my mistress. True, it was a means to escape. Since then, I have no excuses. Your sister has a way about her that makes me forget my manners."

"She is strong-willed."

"An understatement, surely, Your Grace."

Her lips thinned, and she gave him a sidelong glance before she turned away. Gavin believed she was hiding a smile. If the lady had not been married, and he had never met the vibrant Noelle, he'd consider Evangeline worthy of his attentions.

However, it was paler blonde hair and a kissable pink mouth that he much preferred.

"There are many aspects of Noelle's life you do not know, sir. Both our childhoods were emotionally tenuous." She turned back to face him. Any humor was gone. "You may not see it, but she has vulnerability in her that I fear you may exploit. I cannot and will not allow you to seduce her and then cast her aside. If I discover you have ruined her, I will see you hog-tied and dragged before a priest before you realize I'm coming."

His chuckle was explosive. The woman was a tigress when it came to her family. His admiration rose.

Gavin dipped into a low bow. "Yes, Your Grace."

The duchess tucked her reticule under her elbow and

stepped close. The scent of lavender filled his senses. "I do not agree with your plan to parade her around the courtesan ball in an effort to draw out your thieves. But Noelle is stubborn." The duchess frowned. "If you let anything happen to her, the priest will be called for another reason: to pray over your coffin."

Gavin's laughter followed her out of the house.

When he was alone again, he pondered both the differences and the similarities of the sisters. Both were strong-willed, almost to a fault. He suspected the duchess's husband was forever busy keeping up with his wife. Any man married to her would need a firm hand. Still, spending nights with such a spitfire would be well worth dealing with her feisty nature. He believed any man sharing Noelle's bed would feel the same.

Gavin knew Her Grace's threats were not made lightly. If he ruined Noelle, he'd find himself burdened with a wife. There wouldn't be a hiding place far enough away for the duchess not to find him and fulfill her threat.

With Eva hovering with a deep-set frown creasing her face, Noelle finished dressing for the courtesan ball, knowing tonight could lead the investigation in a new direction. Hopefully, Gavin could catch at least one of the footpads and force him to give up information to tie the thugs to their leader.

Not that she expected the culprits to confess willingly. And truthfully, the night could end with no captures or fresh clues at all. Still, being with Gavin would be worth the time spent getting into disguise.

She wished they could get the Bow Street Runners involved. It would help ease her worries. But between her and Bliss, their crimes were many. Until she was sure Seabrook would not prosecute for the theft of the necklace, or for her break-in at his town house, she'd have to trust that Gavin would keep her safe.

"A little more rouge, please," Eva instructed the maid.

Martha's lips were pressed tightly together. She didn't know the full extent of the plot, but what she did know, she didn't like. She slathered Noelle's cheekbones with color, and Noelle wondered if too much scowling could eventually cause one's face to harden that way.

"Not too much," Noelle protested as Martha dipped her fingertip in the rouge pot a second time. The maid set down the pot and wiped her hands on her apron. Her mouth worked silently, and Noelle knew she had much she wanted to say. It was the presence of Eva that kept her from voicing her disapproval. Noelle was grateful for Martha's respect of her sister's title.

Martha stood back and sighed. "'Tis done." She met Noelle's eyes in the mirror, frowned, and left the room.

"She is displeased," Noelle said. "I'm positive I'll be lectured tomorrow."

Eva nodded. She picked up a pearl and ruby necklace and settled it around Noelle's neck. "Perhaps I should have left the two of you alone. A second sensible mind might have convinced you to give up this folly."

Noelle cocked up a brow. "Have you ever known me to change my mind once I've made a decision?"

She'd spent two days in disguise at the courtesan school, and the only thing she'd learned about courtesans was the enjoyment men received when women kissed their private parts. The shocking frankness in the way the women spoke to each other over tea was astonishing. Of course these conversations were kept entirely to the moments when Eva was not in the room.

She'd have to play the courtesan for Gavin off her natural attraction for him. Her lessons had been a failure.

"If I had any sense at all, I'd call Nicholas over and have him shake some sense into you," Eva said.

Noelle stood and ran her hands over the tightly cinched waist of her gown. Though fashion dictated gowns of a looser fit, she had discovered this treasure in the attic and knew she had to wear it. The style was outdated, but the red color and the cut were perfect for a courtesan. Or so she thought. A few nips here and there, and it fit her as if it had been sewn to her proportions.

Eva tugged Noelle's bodice up, and Noelle tugged it back down. The frothy black lace at the bodice managed both to entice and to keep Noelle's nipples hidden from view. More lace edged the cuffs and hem, and matching ribbon was at the waist. The satin dress shimmered in the lamplight. Eva knew wearing such a daring gown would draw attention. It was exactly what Noelle wanted.

"You should be home in bed with your husband, or whatever you old married couples do when not making the rest of us envious of your happiness," Noelle scolded. She stepped back before Eva could reach for the bodice again. She peered at the simple yet elegant coiffure Martha made out of her new wig.

"Occasionally, Nicholas and I do manage to tear ourselves from the bed," Eva retorted. She leaned back and stared. "You will have every man at the ball tonight hating Mister Blackwell."

Eva had all but ripped the Marie Antoinette–era monstrosity from Noelle's head and replaced it with a more stylish wig. Martha had done magic with the new item. Without the heavy wig to hide her sister's face, Eva suggested a filmy veil attached to each side of her new wig with clips. The cloth would both hide her lower face and add an air of mystery.

The overall effect was stunning.

"I don't think this is the kind of thing one could wear to a lawn party." Noelle swished this way and that in front of the mirror, her skirts flashing in the light. There was no possible chance she could be recognized tonight. She was a courtesan in every way. She hoped Gavin would be pleased.

"Your Mister Blackwell will be a fool if he lets you out of his sight, Sister." Eva moved behind her and adjusted the necklace. "Another man might snatch you away."

"I will be far too busy looking for signs of trouble to notice who is noticing me," Noelle said. "And I would not consider a man who attends a courtesan ball a good catch."

"It isn't the lords and rakes I worry about."

The note of concern in her sister's voice brought Noelle's attention from the mirror. Eva's eyes were fearful.

"He will take care of me, don't you worry," Noelle said. "He understands the danger in this charade and will not let anything happen." She pulled Eva into an embrace. "Though I do appreciate your concern, I will come through this adventure unscathed. You'll see."

"I do worry," Eva admitted, pulling back. "How can I not?"

Noelle smiled. "Have you met Mister Blackwell? Can you see him allowing anyone to abscond with me? If anything, you should concern yourself with when we are alone in the coach. That is where the real danger lies."

Eva narrowed her eyes. She obviously didn't find the reminder of Noelle's bad behavior at all amusing.

"Perhaps we should add a few more layers of drawers and sew up the openings," Eva snapped. "That would keep his hands from roaming freely where they ought not to be roaming."

A tinkle of laughter spilled from Noelle. When she'd first met Eva, her sister was starchy and fiercely private. Laughter had been difficult for her, under the weight of her mother's illness. Between Noelle and Nicholas, Eva had found happiness. Still, it was during moments like these when the stubborn and protective part of Eva made a return appearance.

"I think nothing less than drawers made of steel would keep him from finding a way to breach such a barrier," Noelle teased, and was rewarded with a glare. She snatched up her shawl from the bed and draped it over the daring bodice. "You worry far too much, Sister dear. Now get yourself home to your handsome husband and leave Mister Blackwell to me."

Gavin listened to a distant clock chime eleven. It was getting late, and there was no sign of Noelle. With her insistence they go through with this debacle, and the excitement in her eyes at the prospect, he'd expected her to be timely. Instead, he'd been left to cool his heels, and he gnashed his teeth tightly together.

Where was she? She should have arrived an hour ago. He knew women liked to fuss over their appearance, but this was extreme. She wasn't hunting for a husband. They were setting their caps for a thief. There was no reason to keep him waiting.

Could she have changed her mind and decided to stay home? Somehow, he doubted that was the case. She'd taken to her courtesan persona and lived it with enthusiasm. There was no possible reason she'd give up this chance to end her game without the culmination of this night's activities.

A coach drew his attention as an old hired hack rolled up the street and stopped in the line of gilded and polished coaches. The pair of chestnut horses looked as old as the rattletrap conveyance, their matching gray muzzles catching the light. Gavin wondered absently which of the pair would drop dead first while carrying a fare.

He watched the weary-looking driver climb gingerly down from his perch and snatch open the door.

A woman's dark head appeared, followed by a pair of creamy white shoulders and a shocking red dress. It took him a full ten heartbeats to realize it was Noelle as she exited the coach with the light grace of a butterfly.

Her shawl had slipped free of one shoulder, exposing an expanse of velvety flesh. Noelle's breasts were pushed high by the cut of her gown, and her corset barely covered her nipples with a thin line of lace.

His breath caught. She paid the driver and turned. She spotted him and walked in his direction, her hips undulating with the sway of the gown. The sight of her in her finery, with her assets almost completely exposed in a sinful display, caused him to stand paralyzed with anticipation as she approached.

When she got close enough to make out her features, he saw that beneath the black veil covering her from nose to chin, a smile marked her full lips. He didn't realize he was gaping like a fish until she reached out a finger and pushed his chin up.

His mouth closed with a *clack*.

"Am I to assume you find the costume to your liking?" She spun slowly, allowing him time enough to rake his eyes over each delicious inch of her. His eyes moved from her waist to her hips and across her perfect buttocks. He wanted desperately to see if the pair of rounded curves would fit the span of his hands.

He swept his gaze over her arms and shoulders when she completed the spin, and her sister's warning evaporated. The duchess could have him castrated and fed to sharks as long as he could spend the night slowly stripping her out of that dress and loving her body with his.

Gavin took her gloved hand and pressed it to his mouth, his eyes dancing. If she knew how recklessly he wanted her, she'd have every reason to be concerned. "Any more to my liking and I'd have to return home and change my breeches."

It was her turn to gape, followed by a sweet bark of rich feminine laughter. "You are scandalous, Mister Blackwell."

"And you are stunning, Lady Seymour."

His compliment was met with the touch of her tongue on her lower lip. He hardened. She tempted him and knew full well her effect on his body. He had to wonder if it had more to do with her costume and the part she played, or if it was because she wanted him as passionately as he wanted her.

He knew he should hope it was the former, but deep inside his body, he couldn't help wishing for the latter.

Gavin slowly shook his head as her mouth tipped into a saucy grin. "The gown isn't too daring for this company?" she asked with mock innocence. She ran her hands gently over her waist. The movement drew his eyes to her décolletage. "I understand that some lovers enjoy displaying the wares of their courtesans. However, I couldn't bring myself to forgo my undergarments and wet my gown. Though"—she lifted

her eyes and gave him a sidelong stare—"if you think it would
help the investigation, I might reconsider."

The little minx! She didn't care about propriety or a wet
gown. She'd clearly learned some aberrant tricks for enticing
a lover from the courtesans. She was playing the coquette
for him. He wasn't sure if he should find a private place for
her to show him her new tricks or turn her over his knee for
teasing him to a raging erection.

"Indeed, it is not too daring a gown for the company."
He tucked her hand under his arm, his tone turning grim
with pent-up frustration and dark humor. "But I think you
should refrain from sneezing, My Lady, lest you find your
breasts fully exposed."

Chapter Seventeen

If Noelle thought a Ton crush was spectacular in its garishness, the courtesan ball brought revelry to a new level. Displays of flesh, gowns in every bright color imaginable, beading, sequins, gauzes, and silks, with deeply cut necklines meant to shock. The rotunda was packed with bodies, and rogues of all ages and sizes thought nothing of publicly placing hands in places on their lovers where hands shouldn't be. It was quite possible—no, it was certain—she'd never again see the like.

Thank goodness.

Noelle had been to Vauxhall once or twice during the day and had enjoyed the labyrinth of arbors, the endless walkways, and the sheer beauty of the place. To see tawdry displays in what she'd once considered Eden was a blow to her senses.

She paused, bringing Gavin to a stop. "Is there something wrong, My Lady courtesan?" he asked. There was a knowing in his eyes as he looked at the company, then back to her. She shook her head. He seemed to understand her hesitation and gave her a moment to collect herself.

"The last time I visited these grounds, there was much

less exposed flesh," she jested. She waited until the last few strains of the orchestra faded before continuing. "The gardens look much different filled with courtesans. I fear I am not as worldly as I profess. This goes far beyond what I imagined."

Gavin squeezed her hand. "We can leave at any time you wish. Now, if you prefer."

"Absolutely not," she said. Her eyes twinkled with amusement. Sheer bodices and rouged nipples aside, she wasn't about to forgo the adventure of the evening. "I wouldn't miss the sights of this outrageous ball for anything in the world."

Her companion's handsome mouth twitched. "You surprise me, My Lady," he said. "I was certain one look at nipple displays and you'd beg me to return you home."

The graphic speech warmed her cheeks. "If I cannot look at dozens of pairs of nipples without blushing, what sort of courtesan would I be?"

Gavin tipped up his head and laughed wholeheartedly. His blue eyes danced when he peered down at her. "I think you've spent too much time with the courtesans. You are starting to speak like one."

"Then perhaps I will make an acceptable courtesan after all," she teased. A bit of fondness edged his eyes when he examined her face. Clearly, he liked her and enjoyed her company. She enjoyed his as well. What wasn't there to like when accompanied by a fine-looking man?

He chuckled. "Remember this is a game, My Lady. If you run off tonight with a dandy and his fat purse, I will be sorely disappointed. I need your help catching the thieves."

Noelle leaned to press her breasts against his arm. "I only have eyes for you, my darling," she purred. For a moment their gazes locked. The intense sensuality in his face left her breathless. Her skin tingled in hopeful anticipation of his touch. He didn't disappoint. Gavin turned her until they were face-to-face and slid his hands slowly up her bare arms to her cap sleeves.

Her lips parted as he lifted the bottom of the veil. She wanted his kiss and cared not who might be watching.

After all, a kiss was the least scandalous of all the possible courtesan ball experiences. And if the thieves were watching, they'd expect two lovers to act . . . loverly. Gavin dipped his head, and she watched every movement, anticipating what was to come.

Unfortunately, a pair of drunken lovers chose that moment to stumble past. The man's elbow caught Gavin on the arm and jostled him sideways. Gavin righted himself, but there would be no kiss. The veil fluttered back into place.

The attractive young man shot a rueful look over his shoulder. "My apologies, sir." He winked and rushed off after the giggling woman, who was moving at a fair clip toward an arbor. There was no question of the reason the man was so eager. There were dark places in the garden perfect for trysts.

Gavin frowned as the pair disappeared into the night.

Envy. That was what Noelle felt deep in her quivering heart. The woman was about to be kissed, and who knew what else, by her lover. Noelle was standing on a path, an arm's length away from the most handsome man in all of London, regretting a lost moment.

Clearly, Gavin felt it, too, down to his slumped shoulders. He jerked his coat into place and tucked her hand back under his arm. "Shall we continue onward?" He led her farther into to the rotunda. With each step, her stomach added another knot until the space was full.

"Have you seen any sign of the men who attacked you?" Noelle asked and casually glanced around. She saw no one who matched Gavin's descriptions. She saw nothing but well-dressed men and their colorful courtesans.

"Not yet," Gavin said, "but it is still early."

With her veil in place, Noelle didn't fear recognition by several men whom she knew casually, each with a garishly dressed woman on his arm. One was a duke. A very married duke. No, it was the tension of not knowing if they'd entice criminals to act that overshadowed any worry about discovery by someone she knew.

To her surprise, Edolie was correct. There were indeed

women dressed as befitting a society gathering. However, those were few. Her entire body tensed with distaste when a man dressed in a red velvet jacket tweaked his companion's left nipple through the thin fabric of her clearly dampened bodice.

"Easy, love. You are a much sought-after courtesan. Every man in attendance longs to share your bed," Gavin murmured in her ear, his warm breath teasing her flesh. "I am the luckiest man in all England to have you on my arm."

Noelle leveled her breathing and smiled. She wanted to appear as a woman well versed in seduction. Unfortunately, she could only shake her head slowly as a middle-aged gentleman in green followed a redheaded woman in deep russet into the shadows. They had barely broken free of the flickering lamplight before their groping began in earnest.

"No, it is I who am lucky," she said absently. She shifted her eyes away from the spectacle, mortified by the display of lascivious behavior.

Gavin cocked a brow at the couple. He seemed quite comfortable in the setting, as if he commonly frequented courtesan balls. Still, in spite of the goings-on around him, he had eyes only for her. "I can see by your face, love, this was a mistake. We will go."

"No," she said sharply. "Please let us stay." Noelle straightened her shoulders and her chin. "I am well beyond the age when a bit of exposed flesh and questionable acts should permanently damage my sensibilities. It isn't as if I have never seen a couple take advantage of a quiet garden."

Or coach.

A light cough made her tip her head up, and she found Gavin struggling with his mirth. "How many times have you seen that in those darkened gardens?"

The man in green had his lover's breast freed and was making strangled sucking noises on her flesh. This time it didn't shock her. Another emotion bubbled up in her throat as the man lifted his head and the pair finally moved deeper into the shadows.

She pressed her fingertips to her lips and shook her head. "Never."

No matter what happened tomorrow morning, for this night she was his courtesan. She would laugh and flirt and perhaps even allow a few kisses and a caress or two—in the interest of flushing out the thieves, of course. It wasn't as if she planned to enjoy his attentions. Not in the least.

"If at any point this evening you become weary of nipples and bottoms and lengths of leg, say the word, and I shall spirit you away from this den of debauchery. We can worry about catching our culprits at another time."

The comment gave her confidence. "No worries, sir. I shall uphold my part in this scandalous production." She slid a fingertip down the center of his chest. "Can you?"

His grin broke loose, and he reached up to cup the side of her face. "It will not be difficult to play the part of a besotted lover, sweet. You are beautiful."

Noelle felt the heat in the rotunda notch up a full dozen degrees as his appreciative gaze ran down her body in a slow caress. Gavin's fine-looking male form was bedecked in a deep blue coat and striped vest over a snowy white shirt, with matching cravat. His cheeks were freshly shaven, and she caught a hint of an earthy-spicy scent on his skin.

She fluttered her lashes and turned her fingertip into a flat hand on his chest. His heartbeat was slow and steady. "I think it is you, Mister Blackwell, who is beautiful."

Clearly, several women loitering nearby also found him so. Their heated stares promised Gavin anything he wanted.

Noelle tensed. She shot them damning glares, and the trio turned away. From the courtesans' gossip, she knew a rich protector was to be closely guarded at all times, lest another brightly plumed bird swoop in and snatch him away.

It didn't concern her that she was only playing a part. She didn't want a scandalously dressed strumpet putting any part of her anatomy anywhere near Gavin. For this evening he was hers, and hers alone. She'd unsheathe her claws if she had to.

Ignoring the other courtesans, Gavin pressed a kiss to the side of her neck. "I've never been called beautiful." She felt him inhale deeply against her skin. She'd worn the lemon and cinnamon scent just for him.

"Then the women of your acquaintance have been remiss, Mister Blackwell. Gavin." His mouth moved down her neck to her collarbone and on to her bare shoulder. All sorts of delicious sensations followed his heated mouth. "You most assuredly have a male beauty to be envied."

He chuckled against her skin, then nipped her shoulder gently. She gasped, and was certain she heard the trio of women twitter. In her disguise, she was seductive and free to behave as she wished.

Noelle struggled to remember the real purpose of their attendance. A difficult task when Gavin was teasing her breathless. "You must look for your footpads. You cannot do so with your lips pressed against my neck."

Gavin murmured against her skin, "Unless they are in disguise, I've seen nothing to indicate their presence."

The clearing of a throat reluctantly brought Gavin's head up from her collarbone. He peered, annoyed, at the intruder. He slipped an arm around her as a gentleman wearing black, and a wide leer, stopped before them.

Noelle flinched, planning to back away from the familiar face, but the veil and Gavin's arm kept her still. She'd momentarily forgotten her disguise.

"Blackwell." He reached out a hand to Gavin, but his eyes were fully on her. Noelle peered at the broken blood vessels on his bulbous nose and grimaced. A sour taste filled her mouth.

The Earl of Cranbrook. The man was a known lecher, and Noelle had always taken pains to avoid him. She had suffered through an unexpected encounter with the cad at a party three years previous, when his hand had found a resting place on her bottom. She'd quickly refused his fumbling advances with a loud slap to his cheek.

"Your Lordship." Gavin frowned and tightened his hold on Noelle. She took comfort in his nearness. In a setting such as this, there was no telling what a man such as the earl might do. If she let any distance open up between her and Gavin, she might find herself dragged into the bushes by the earl and debauched.

"I see you have plucked the finest bird from the flock." His voice slurred, and Noelle glared into his red eyes. If she'd felt sorry for his long-suffering wife before tonight, she felt renewed sympathy for the sweet-tempered woman now. To be married to such a man had to be hell.

The earl needed a sound beating, or two, or ten. According to gossip, he'd all but run through the fortune his father left him and was on the verge of seeing his family left penniless. Noelle vowed to do whatever she could for his wife and daughter, if there ever came a day they were thrown into the street.

The earl licked his thin lips. "Perhaps when you tire of her, you can send her to me." He reached for her, but Gavin blocked him, catching Cranbrook's wrist in his grip. The earl winced. Gavin scowled and released him.

"You are touchy, Blackwell." He rubbed his wrist. "A whore is a whore. Enough coin can get any one of these women in bed."

Noelle lightly dug her fingernails into Gavin's hand as a warning, then faced the earl. She needed to defuse the tension before the two men came to blows.

"I fear, My Lord, you couldn't you afford me"—she paused and opened her eyes wide with feigned innocence—"and I fear Gavin has ruined all other men for me. I would find your awkward fumblings in my bed very unsatisfactory."

The middle-aged man turned ruby red and blustered, casting a few drops of spittle into the air. "Why, you impudent whore!" He appeared to strain for further insults but produced only strangled gasps.

Gavin shook with rich laughter as the man spun on his heels and launched himself into the crowd. "Well done, love."

Noelle didn't know what warmed her more, being complimented for her tart tongue or being called "love" several times this evening. Either way, she felt pleased to be the recipient of his affectionate regard.

"He desperately needed a set-down." She inhaled deeply. Her first test had been a success. "To call him a pig only serves to insult swine."

"Then we shall forget about the earl and concentrate on making you a successful courtesan-spy. Then, when you've captured the thieves and the Home Office calls to press you into service for king and country, you will be able to use your success with disguises to flush out traitors and foreign spies."

Noelle smirked. "I shall single-handedly take down the dangerous band of thieves and become revered all over London. My mother will be proud." Her mother would be horrified. That thought alone was enough to bring a smile.

Gavin nodded, and his hand squeezed her waist. "But first we must bring this caper to a successful conclusion."

Covertly, Noelle glanced around. She peered into the shadows and looked at many faces for any sign of danger. She saw no one who matched Gavin's descriptions.

"I fear our presence here has been a waste." She sighed. "It has been nearly an hour, and we have we flushed out nothing more than one drunken lord."

"We may not gain anything tonight but an assault to the senses," Gavin said. "But you have become a very successful courtesan. All the true courtesans are filled with envy."

She scanned his face. "Why, Mister Blackwell, I believe you mean that."

He tipped his head to press his lips against her temple. He said against her skin, "I do. All of your lessons have paid off. If this night doesn't end as we hoped, it will not be your fault. No one would ever suspect you are a Lady."

Normally, Noelle would take offense at being called unladylike. Instead, she reached up to pat her wig. "Thank you."

He lifted her hand to his lips. "You, My Lady, are an incredible adventure."

Touched, Noelle moved into his arms and slid her hands

around his waist. He was warm and inviting. "And you are a charming rogue. From the moment we met, you have made sure you are the one thing in my life I will never, ever forget."

A crooked grin was his response.

In this setting, it was easy to remember their stolen moments in the coach and forget they were not truly lovers.

Oh, how she wanted them to be! It would be easy to make it so. But she couldn't. Couldn't! She was Lady Noelle Seymour. As such, she had to live by certain rules.

It was becoming difficult to concentrate on anything but Gavin. Her thoughts were never far from him, and worry crept into her mind. She started to feel as if she was setting herself up for a broken heart. It was time to take a few steps back. She needed to look at their situation with a clear mind.

She reclaimed her hand. "Since we have failed miserably as investigators, perhaps we should go."

He frowned. "Is something the matter, love?"

"Must something be wrong?" She tried to keep her tone casual. "Can I not just be tired of nipples?"

Noelle's face flamed when he chuckled. How could she have said such a scandalous thing? Gavin's presence in her life was certainly having a negative influence. It reconfirmed her need to put some distance between them. He was far too handsome, and she was far too interested in his sensual draw.

She opened her mouth to speak again but was interrupted by an approaching couple.

Gavin didn't bat an eye as an older man escorted a woman past them. The courtesan winked at Gavin as she tottered by, and he returned her wink with a nod.

Noelle sighed, frustrated and a bit jealous. "If you'd care to run off that randy old goat and spend the rest of the evening in her bed, I can undoubtedly find my way home without your help."

He dismissed the pair and turned back to her. "Is that so?"

"I wouldn't want you to miss an opportunity to find a new lover. A real lover. I know men such as yourself suffer from needs they have difficulty controlling. I hear that if you don't slake them frequently and with due diligence, certain parts of your body can turn a vicious shade of blue."

It took a full minute for him to settle from his laughter. "My dearest Lady, you are a delight." He caught up her hand and drew it to his mouth. He held her with his gaze and turned the hand over to nibble on the bare flesh exposed at the top of her glove. "You're jealous."

"I am not," she insisted. "I don't care enough for you to be jealous. We are only casually acquainted. I simply find it rude for a man to escort a lady to a social function, only to find his interest focused elsewhere."

"Trust me, love." He lowered her arm and leaned to whisper in her ear. "My interest is fully engaged right here."

It was impossible to remain angry with him when he ogled her with a mixture of raw sensuality and teasing humor. He was a cad, an arrogant cad. But when he held her in his blue eyes, there was little she could remember to be angry about.

"I despise you," she said breathlessly as he bent and pressed his lips to the corner of her mouth. She smoldered beneath her gown. "You are far too arrogant and confident for your own good."

He straightened and collected her hands. "And you are far too beautiful. Come, let us partake in one dance before we call this night at an end."

The waltz was still considered shocking among the older members of society, yet it had been widely accepted for years. However, not many mamas allowed their newly minted debutante daughters to partake in the seductive dance.

Gavin led her through the crush to join the other dancers and pulled her into his arms. Noelle tried to keep from getting too intimate. Gavin refused keep a respectable distance between them. His hand on the curve of her back kept them close together. "Clearly you have decided my annoyance with you isn't enough to keep you from attempts to seduce me," she said tartly.

"My dearest Noelle," he countered, and pulled her closer. "The thugs could be standing at the edge of this dance floor, and I'd still want nothing more than to charm my way into your drawers."

"You are despicable," she wheezed, surprised by his frankness. It took lots of will to keep from smiling. Even the most annoying aspects of his personality left her wanting to laugh. "Do you ever think of anything but launching a coup against my drawers?"

He shrugged. "I'm afraid not."

This time she did laugh. Somehow, even his lack of manners was charming. He was bold and arrogant and far too free with his hands. And he was unapologetic about it all.

"I believe it is time to change the topic before you break into an explanation of how to launch a successful attack on my undergarments." She narrowed her lids.

He faltered ever so slightly, then easily regained his footing. Her saucy comment was only a temporary distraction. He was an expert at seductive banter.

"Perhaps later, when we have privacy, you'll let me draw you an assault map." He stared at her mouth. "That way you will know every attack point on your body before it comes, and can eagerly anticipate my next move."

Noelle rolled her eyes heavenward and shook her head. "You are entirely too confident that I would enjoy your seduction."

"You will."

"There has to be at least one woman who left your bed dissatisfied."

"Never."

The conversation was shockingly intimate. "You are saying that only in the hope that by the time I realize you are a braggart without skill to back up your claims, it will be too late. I will have already sacrificed my innocence to your lackluster ability."

Intensity took any humor from his face. "My Lady courtesan, I will make you this wager. If I ever fail to satisfy your every desire, in bed or out, I will give you my entire fortune, down to the last ship and shilling, to compensate you for your disappointment."

From someplace outside herself, Noelle felt herself treading on his toe. He didn't flinch. She was locked onto his eyes and her whole body exploded with heat. "You are that confident," she whispered as the music died.

"I am."

She felt his hand flex on her back, then dip to just above her buttock. She leaned into him until her breasts flattened against his chest. "Then I accept your wager."

The music swelled, and she hardly noticed they were dancing again. She'd just agreed that if she ever lost her common sense and became his lover, she'd accept a wager that would financially ruin him. By the look of shock on his face, he hadn't expected her to accept the bait.

For the first time, she'd won against his sharp wit. He was speechless. It was a most satisfactory victory.

"You dance quite well, sir." She acted as if nothing important and intimate had passed between them. He clearly needed a minute to collect himself. She enjoyed studying the grim line of his mouth. "Though you do need some instruction in proper hand placement."

He blinked and shook his head. Then he cocked a brow. The confident American was back. "Trust me, love. I am very well versed as to where my hands are supposed to be, as you will soon find out. Unfortunately, you have on far too many clothes."

Noelle pretended to yawn. She wouldn't let him see how deeply the thought of fulfilling the wager had affected her. The chance he'd actually satisfy her needs was slim. She had no intention of bedding him; therefore, no wager. Besides, sex was for procreation, not pleasure. Enjoying his kisses did not make her a vixen in bed.

"Have we returned to that again?"

"Back to what, exactly?" He offered a mock puzzled frown as if deeply confused by her implication. "Tell me details, and leave nothing out."

"I think I shall hire a pinch-faced matron to give you instruction on proper topics of conversation, like the weather. Clearly you have spent much of your formative years with doxies and whores, as you seem to want to turn my every word into some sort of opening for seduction."

He wasn't the least bit taken aback. In fact, despite his sober demeanor, there was mischief in his expression.

"Indeed? Then you must forgive my forwardness, My Lady. Making a wager against my fortune, and your acceptance, has left me reeling. However, I'll not regret the offer. I've been suffering from a serious case of frustration for several days now, and you are the key to my fulfillment."

"See?" She slid her hand from his shoulder and jabbed a fingertip into his chest. "You cannot help yourself."

He sighed and frowned. "I can speak quite eloquently about the weather. 'Twas a fine day today, was it not? There were just enough clouds in the sky to keep the day from becoming overly warm." He looked up. "The night is cool and clear with a few stars to draw the eye. Tomorrow should be much of the same, unless a storm is brewing that we didn't expect. Hence the reason it is considered unexpected." He drew her to a stop when the music died again. "I think it would be wise to ask Lady Penny for her thoughts, as her left foot seems to swell when bad weather is brewing."

Noelle was laughing by the time he ended his haughty speech. His humor was infectious. Not a hint of the American accent could be found in his perfectly proper words. But the stiff manner behind his pontification caused a stitch in her side.

"Well done, Mister Blackwell." She clapped several times. "Stuffy old Baron Wegan could not have done better."

Gavin snorted. "I would much rather talk about your skin. Discussing thunderclouds is quite dreary."

Her laughter faded to puzzlement. "My skin? What about my skin?"

The music began again, and he swept her into his arms. "Your skin is like a sweet siren song that calls me to explore its silkiness. When I press my mouth to it, I have never tasted the like. When I inhale the light scent of lemon and cinnamon, I find I cannot think of anything but how I'd like to nibble every inch until I can assure myself I have fully tasted heaven."

"Oh, my." The words tumbled from her mouth. She expected jests and instead received verse. Not excellent verse. Still, anything that issued from his perfect mouth sounded like poetry.

"And your eyes." He bent slightly to peer into her eyes. "They are the softest, beautiful amber, with a ring of pale green around the center. The color reminds me of new spring grass." He paused. "The way you looked at me the night in the coach, I was certain I had experienced something wondrous, something no man has ever experienced, no matter how many women have passed beneath him. It was the purest desire, and it was directed at me. It was a gift I shall always treasure."

Noelle gaped. Many men had spun odes to her beauty over the years in an effort to woo her, but she'd never heard anything so lovely.

But he wasn't finished. "From our first kiss in my bedroom, I've been able to think of nothing but having you in my arms again, tasting the sweetness of your lips." His eyes darkened. He danced her to the entrance of the rotunda and stopped. "I know it is madness. You are a Lady and a maiden. I have no right to you, to your body, lovely Noelle, regardless of the outrageous wager. I think I should take you home."

Gavin took her hand. He dragged her pell-mell down the path, and she had to totter to keep up.

He wanted her. Not what her title could offer him. Not the obscenely generous dowry her father had left for her. Only her.

At a curve on the path, she dragged him to a halt.

"Wait, Gavin . . . the investigation . . ."

"Damn the investigation," he growled.

Damn everything. They hadn't seen or felt one hint of trouble. The night hadn't gone as expected, but it didn't need to be a failure. She'd steal a bone-searing, body-tingling kiss before he dragged her home.

Without hesitation, she pulled him into a darkened corner of the garden. She gave him no time for questions but pushed him back against a tree and pressed her body against his. Lifting to her toes, she tugged the veil free, clasped him tightly around the neck, and pulled his face to hers. She heard his breath catch the moment she melded their lips together. She kissed him with every ounce of passion inside her.

It was but a moment before he opened his mouth to accept her probing tongue and caught the back of her head with one hand. Her legs melted. His other hand cupped her buttock, keeping her close.

Noelle felt the wonder of his kiss and knew she'd always feel so in his arms. In the moment when he'd spoken about her with such sincerity and passion, she'd confirmed she was becoming far too attached to her pretend American lover.

Attached? Noelle startled when the truth slipped into her mind. She was falling hopelessly in love.

It was a dreadful situation to be in.

"No." Noelle pushed Gavin back, her mind racing. She couldn't love him. She never wanted to love anyone. To do so would open up all sorts of vulnerabilities. And because he'd never love her in return, it promised tragedy for her heart.

"I've made a mistake. Please forgive me."

Turning on her heel, she fled in the direction of the coaches while tears burned her eyes.

How had she allowed this to happen? Emotion was the enemy when it came to men. Somehow this American had breached her defenses without her knowing and dug himself a large spot right in her heart.

Through her tears, she couldn't find Gavin's coach, so she settled into the shadows of the one closest, without a coachman seated above, to review her heartbreak. Leaning against the frame, she let the tears flow down her cheeks, uncaring if rivulets of wetness ruined the powder.

In the distance, she heard him call for her, and she stepped deeper into the shadows, and into something she knew instantly was not part of the coach. It was a movable object of flesh and bone that was much larger than her, and a pair of hands caught her in a viselike grip.

She let out a muffled yelp when an arm snaked around her waist and a hand clamped over her mouth!

Chapter Eighteen

The dampness from his sweaty palm made Noelle gag as bile rose in the back of her throat. Her second scream sounded no more frantic than a kitten mewing. It was nearly impossible to breathe, and harder still to comprehend what was happening. All she knew was that she was in danger.

Her body shook with cold, biting fear. She felt herself being lifted against a burly chest. Then her captor spun and sped off with her.

In a blink, the shock wore off and she realized that in the seconds when she'd fled from the startling realization that she loved Gavin, she'd forgotten about the thieves, the danger, everything.

A mistake that might well prove fatal!

Gavin's calls got farther away as the night swallowed Noelle and her captor in inky darkness. The man pressed against her back smelled of fish and soiled clothing and sour flesh. He was large enough to keep her feet from touching the ground as he raced through the night with lumbering speed.

He had her, and he wasn't about to let her feeble struggles cause him to lose his prize. And struggle she did.

His hold was so tight that she couldn't breathe well, and she felt woozy. The kidnapper moved with surprising agility for one so large, darting in and out around coaches and doing his best to keep out of sight.

If only a coachman or footman would see her plight and come to her aid, or at least call out for her release. All she could hear over her panic were his footsteps and the loud and rapid beats of her heart.

She did her best to make noise behind the hand, managing a weak, muffled squeal or two. A vicious cuff to the side of her head ended her struggle as the world around her went black.

Gavin thought he heard a soft cry, and his stomach tightened painfully. In the seconds it had taken for her to escape from his arms, he knew, just knew, she'd gotten into trouble. He had to find her quickly.

Whatever happened was his fault. If she was injured, or worse, he would forever live with the guilt of allowing her to attend this ball.

Of letting her leave his sight.

He cursed as he searched frantically in the darkness for any sign of Noelle. He'd known there could be danger, and he'd let her unexpected kiss distract him and muddle up his brain. This was the consequence. If the thieves had her, the cost would be devastating.

Terrified for Noelle, he rushed past the coaches, pausing every few steps to listen for signs of which way she was headed. The distant crunch of gravel turned him south at a steady lope, and he hoped he wasn't on the trail of a footman searching for a bush in which to relieve himself.

Fearful that that was exactly what might happen, he said a silent prayer for help and tried to distinguish fleeing footsteps from impatient horses jingling their harnesses and pawing at the hard earth.

"That way." A voice from above startled him, and he looked up to see a shadowy coachman pointing east.

"My thanks." Gavin ran. He was now pretty certain she'd been snatched by one of his attackers. If she'd merely run off, he'd have found her by now. Noelle would know wandering London at night wasn't smart. She wasn't upset enough to forget the dangers of the city. No, wherever she was, it wasn't her choice. Gavin quelled rising panic. Any one of the three men wouldn't think twice about despoiling her, given an opportunity.

A distant moving shadow caught his eye, and he headed in that direction. A large form was moving stealthily past a coach near the end of the row. In the slip of moonlight escaping the clouds, Gavin could see a bit of red skirt and knew he'd found Noelle. There was one coach left, and the bloke seemed to be heading for its safety.

It was a rattletrap conveyance, but for a getaway the kidnapper wouldn't need anything more than wheels and horses. Gavin muffled his footsteps as best he could, hoping he wouldn't be spotted. He moved with care toward the coach, trying to hurry without allowing the man to catch wind of his presence. The man had to know Gavin would be searching for her.

Gavin got close enough to see the kidnapper glance over his shoulder and seem satisfied he wasn't followed. Gavin could barely make out another man high in the seat as the kidnapper reached up, yanked open the door, and stuffed a limp Noelle inside the coach.

"Go! Go!" The burly man clambered inside behind Noelle, and the coach lurched to life. The horses strained against their trappings and bunched up for a run. Gavin darted from behind a gray carriage horse with the kidnappers' coach boot in his sight.

He jumped, catching a handhold just as the team took flight down the darkened street. The speed and pits in the road almost launched him off the boot, but sheer determination kept him on the coach.

He could not let them get away with Noelle!

Rage drove all other thoughts from his mind except saving Noelle. He adjusted his body to the sway of the coach, shucked off his coat, and began a precarious climb to the roof and the driver.

The task was difficult enough when a coach wasn't moving. Fortunately, he knew a thing or two about coaches. He and his friends had often hitched rides on passing conveyances as they traveled around Boston on their boyhood adventures. In addition, years spent climbing ship riggings had made him fairly nimble.

Though he was pushing the grand age of thirty, he felt confident he could make the climb.

Failure could mean Noelle's death.

It turned out that executing the act was easier in his head than in reality. Handholds and footholds were difficult to find in the dim light and made the climb precarious as the old coach pitched and swayed. The driver clearly understood the nature of his crime and planned to get away with Noelle as quickly as the ancient coach could manage and still remain upright.

Gavin ground his teeth each time his foot slipped or his hand was unable to tightly grasp a hold. Though the distance to the top of the coach wasn't great, it took a supreme effort to finally pull his body onto the roof.

The driver called to the team for added speed, and the scraggly-looking horses did their best to comply. The man was so focused on his race that he failed to see Gavin coming.

Gavin saw just enough of the man to recognize him as one of his attackers. The smaller one. The confirmation brought him no satisfaction. It wasn't enough to ambush him on the dock. When they kidnapped Noelle, they'd made an enemy.

The driver didn't see Gavin's fist until it was too late. The attacker grunted and toppled off the seat onto the street. Gavin dived for the reins.

The horses slowed not a bit with the change of driver. Gavin kept the steady pace but changed their destination. He eased the team toward Cheapside and hoped he could remember the address he'd been given. The distance wasn't great, but with Noelle helpless inside the coach with her kidnapper, it seemed like an eternity until he finally turned the coach onto the correct street.

With only a sputtering streetlamp to guide him, he found the town house he sought and stopped the team.

"Blast, Farley!" came an angry voice from within. "Why are we stopping?"

Gavin quickly climbed off the coach as the town house door opened. Mister Crawford, his investigator, limped down the steps, his rumpled shirt halfway untucked from his trousers, his hair askew.

The look on Gavin's face and a quick tip of his head clued the investigator that something was amiss, and he silently took up a position on the other side of the coach's door.

"Farley!" Grumbling followed, and the coach swayed. The door was flung open with a thud. The kidnapper was about halfway out the door, muttering curses the entire time, when two pairs of hands jerked him from the coach. He let out a cry and landed face-first on the street. A few sharp blows to the head and he didn't move again.

"Get him tied up before he rouses from his stupor." Gavin removed his cravat to bind the kidnapper's hands and left him to Crawford. He climbed into the coach and dropped to his knees beside the seat where Noelle lay. She was breathing but unconscious. The bodice of her gown was askew and the hem of her skirt was slightly raised. He cursed, and vowed the stranger would pay for touching her.

A quick examination showed she had not been violated, and he eased her into his arms. She felt so small, so helpless, as her head lolled against his chest. With care, he climbed from the coach and joined Crawford, who was pulling the addled giant to his feet. The investigator shot a quick glance at Noelle, then winced. Gavin had no time for questions.

"She's alive," he said, and headed for the open door.

Between the two of them, they got their prisoner and Noelle into the house. Gavin took brief note of the sparse furnishings as Crawford pushed the man forward and led Gavin upstairs to a small parlor. He quickly stretched Noelle out on a worn settee.

Crawford pushed the kidnapper into a chair and pulled a tie from a drape to bind his legs. The large man glared but said nothing as his heated gaze fell on Noelle. He licked his chops in an exaggerated and disgusting manner.

Gavin straightened, enraged. He walked over to the stranger. His fist caught the kidnapper on the side of the jaw, and his face jerked sideways.

"That is for kidnapping an innocent woman." The second blow split the man's lip and sent spittle flying. "And that is for touching her." He flexed his fingers and knew his knuckles would be aching tomorrow. His voice was low and menacing as he bent and bunched the man's lapels in his hands. "Had you raped her, I would have cut you apart one piece at a time."

The thug's tongue swept over the bloody cut. "Given a few more minutes, I'd 'ave shown the leidy what it means to be with a real man."

The third blow silenced him.

Crawford grinned as the kidnapper's head lolled against the back of the chair. "Well done." He walked to a sideboard and poured two drinks. He handed one to Gavin, who tossed it back. Crawford lifted his own glass and followed suit. "Now, would you like to explain, Blackwell, why you have brought this to my door?"

Gavin cast a glance at Noelle. She let out a small groan. He hurried to her side. Red, knuckle-sized bruises marred her temple and cheekbone. It sickened him to think of what she might have suffered had he not managed to find her in time.

"This was the only place I knew I could come to without stumbling across anyone I know." Gavin brushed back her hair. Tenderness washed through him. "I thought we would be safe here."

"And Lady Seymour?" Crawford asked. "Would you care to explain why you have her and why she's dressed for a costume party? If I'm to risk my neck to shelter her, I'd like to know what I'm facing."

Gavin stared. "I'd forgotten you know her."

Crawford shrugged. He poured himself another drink. "I've done some work for her brother-in-law, His Grace."

This wasn't surprising. Crawford was the man to call on when someone needed investigative work done and didn't want the Bow Street Runners involved. He was known for his skill and discretion. That was why Gavin had hired him to find Bliss's maid. So Gavin gave him the shortened version of events since they'd last spoken about the stolen necklace.

This time he informed Crawford of Noelle's part in the case. There was no reason to keep that from him now.

Gavin cocked his head toward the footpad. "I need your help getting information from this bastard." He broke off further speech as Noelle twitched. Gavin watched her eyes flutter open and confusion fill her face. He dropped to one knee and took her hand. He smiled reassuringly. "Shh. You are safe, love."

Noelle blinked several times and looked around the room. When her gaze caught the unconscious man in the chair, she was visibly startled. "Who is he?" she whispered.

Gavin followed her gaze. "He's one of the men who ambushed me and kidnapped you." He struggled not to walk over to the chair and beat the kidnapper to a bloody pulp. Unconscious and tied or not. Gavin then watched her gaze flick to Crawford. The investigator nodded.

"And him?" Her voice was small and weak. She frowned as if trying to clear her head. "I think I know him."

"It's Mister Crawford, love. I believe we discussed this. I hope the two of us can force some information from our friend."

"Mister Crawford," she breathed, "of course." Appearing satisfied with the answers, Noelle lay back on the pillow. Her face was still marked with worry.

"What is it, love?" He gripped her hand tighter. Her fingers were cold in his palm.

Her amber eyes darted to Crawford. "Can I speak to you

privately?" she said softly to Gavin. The investigator nodded and left the room. It was a moment before Noelle spoke, and she stared at the kidnapper. "Did he, ah, touch me in any way?"

Tears sprang to her eyes. Never in his life had he hated anyone so desperately as he did her attacker at this moment. All the fire and feistiness that drew him to Noelle had been extinguished with the shame of thinking she'd been brutalized. She was like a beaten child, helpless. He never wanted to see her like this again; he needed to assuage her fears.

All he wanted to do was protect her, care for her, take away her hurts, and make her smile again.

"He did not." Gavin hoped it would be enough. He didn't need to tell her about her rumpled clothing or that he suspected the man had touched her in some fashion. All she needed to know was that her innocence had not been breached and she was safe. "I got to you in time."

A grateful smile crept over her mouth. "My hero."

He brought her knuckles to his lips. "I am no hero. I'm responsible for this mess. Everything that happened tonight was my fault. I should never have forgotten the danger and left you unguarded."

Noelle rested her hand on his arm. "No. I got myself into trouble. I forced you to take me to the ball. You asked me to allow you and your investigator to handle the matter, but I wanted to have an adventure. The fault was mine."

Their eyes met. "There is plenty of blame to share." He leaned to press his mouth to her forehead. The sweetness of her skin was marred by the scent of fish. As soon as she was well, he would see that she was scrubbed free of the smell of her ordeal. "I don't know what I would have done had I lost you."

Noelle's heart fluttered. There were several ways to interpret the comment, but she hoped it meant he cared for her. In her muddled mind, she couldn't think of anything more. Her head hurt desperately. She felt like she'd been kicked in the temple by a horse. It was difficult to remain alert and not succumb to the pull of darkness.

It was Gavin's warm hand keeping her from the abyss. Her unrequited love for him aside, if they could not be lovers, then perhaps friends. Outside of the kidnapping, he was the most fun she'd ever had. He made her laugh, and cry, and want to put her trust in him and see where he would take her.

"Be careful what you say, sir." She pressed a hand to the side of her head where she'd been cuffed. Pain pulsed in her temple. The room shifted, and she felt her stomach roll. "I have been known to get into mischief when left to my own devices. Spending time in my company has been documented to be hazardous to one's well-being."

Gavin's teeth flashed. "I shall take my chances."

The room pitched, and she slumped back on the settee. She heard Gavin call out and then felt herself lifted into his strong arms. The room turned to shades of gray as Gavin's face swam before her face in a whirl of color.

"Noelle?" His voice came from a far-off place. It was the last she could remember as the world faded away.

Chapter Nineteen

S he suffered a vicious blow," Gavin said. He kept his face averted from the duchess's accusing eyes. Her Grace sat next to her sister on the bed, her face awash with worry, but her eyes promised his untimely death. "The footpad downstairs cuffed her when he took her. She was awake for several minutes once we arrived here. The physician said it was a good sign her brain isn't injured."

He looked at Noelle. It was impossible to see how deeply she'd suffered when the only outward sign was four knuckle bruises lined up in a row on her skin. "I sent word, as I knew you'd want to see her for yourself."

Noelle was pale as death. His chest tightened. Despite the physician's assurances, and his positive assurances to the duchess, he was terribly worried. It had been hours since Noelle first came around, and with every passing minute, he feared she would never awaken from her deathly sleep.

Her Grace clasped Noelle's hand to her chest, but her gaze was locked onto him. "I should horsewhip you for getting her into this fix, but I know much of this situation happened because she is intensely stubborn. I told her this was a terrible idea, but she cannot see reason when her mind is set." She looked down at Noelle and bit her lower lip to stop its trembling. "However, should she fail to recover, I *will* hold you responsible."

It didn't take Her Grace's admonition to make him feel guilty. The weight of his part in this debacle was like an anvil. "I should've made good my threat and locked her in a wardrobe." He cursed under his breath. "She trusted me to watch over her, and I failed."

Noelle had been lying there still as death for over fourteen hours while Gavin anxiously focused on her every shallow breath as proof she lived. If there was a pause between breaths, he shot to his feet and pressed his fingertips to her neck. He never left her bedside for more than a few minutes, certain his vigil was what kept her alive.

No amount of pummeling the man whom Crawford watched downstairs could assuage his guilt or rage. Eventually the responsibility came back to him. If he hadn't kissed her, or rather, allowed her to kiss him, she wouldn't have been frightened off by his desire and fallen into the arms of the footpad.

"I want her brought to my home," Her Grace said sharply. "I can better care for her there."

"No." Gavin slumped into a chair. His temples pulsed and pain shot through his brain. "The physician said she shouldn't be moved. To do so could cause greater harm."

The duchess frowned. "I cannot leave her unattended and under the care of two unmarried men. I'd attend to her myself, but having me living under this roof would draw attention to this house, and there would be an irreparable scandal if the gossips took notice of our presence here. There would be no reasonable explanation." She sighed. "Though I know and trust Mister Crawford to a small degree, and don't think either of you will harm her while she is ill, it is unseemly. And you have her attacker a floor below!"

What a muddle he'd dropped into. Perhaps sending for the duchess hadn't been a grand idea. She hadn't been happy with him before, because of his indecent attentions to her sister. Now she was fully enraged, and he was wearing a target on his back.

"Crawford will take up temporary residence at an inn and will see to the footpad. He refuses to speak, but Crawford knows a man who can get him to talk." Gavin rubbed his temple and felt the headache pulse beneath his fingertips. There were men who knew techniques of torture from the Far East that could break a man's spirit and leave him a body without a mind. Gavin found such measures abominable. Still, if it meant saving Noelle from further harm, he'd leave Crawford to do whatever was needed. "I have faith this matter will be resolved quickly."

"Excellent. Now not only is my sister's situation dire, but we can add torture to the list of crimes." The duchess turned away and touched her knuckles to Noelle's florid cheek. Deep worry etched tight lines around her mouth. "When you discover the person behind this thievery, I would like to have a hand in the confrontation. My driver has a fine new horsewhip I'd like to try out on his back."

"If there is anything left to use it on." The headache was nothing compared to the ache in his stomach. He'd give all he had to rewind the last several hours. All he could do now was flush out the thief-master and care for Noelle.

He refused to believe her state was permanent. His world would be a dismal place without this beautiful and stubborn chit around to keep him engaged.

Gavin's heart tugged. He was startled by the realization he'd grown to deeply care for her. He wanted her to awaken and give him one of her exasperated glares, then smile unbidden under his teasing; as though to do so was a crime against everything she stood for. He wanted to see her scowl at him for his improper behavior, then sigh the instant his lips covered hers.

Deep down, he had the feeling she didn't find him as distasteful as she'd led him to believe. There were times when he'd spoken or behaved outrageously and was certain he caught a glimpse of humor in her eyes. He knew she saw him as little better than a savage. However, it didn't keep her from melting in his arms and kissing him whenever he pressed his attentions.

"The fewer people who know where Noelle is, the safer her reputation will be," he agreed. His tone brooked no argument. To move her could mean her death. Since he was responsible for this attack, it was up to him to see that she was saved from any further difficulties. "I can care for her myself."

"Absolutely not," the duchess snapped, then immediately lowered her voice. "It is like giving the weasel the key to the chicken coop. Why would I trust you not to take advantage of her weakness?"

Now he was shocked and truly offended. Did he look like the kind of man who would paw at her body while she slept? "You cannot believe me such a lowly wretch as to molest her while she cannot defend herself." He seethed. "I assure you, Your Grace, I prefer my lovers willing and conscious."

She glared. "Who undressed her?"

Gavin dropped his hands to his sides. The woman was impossible. "She needed less clothing to breathe comfortably. And as I'm certain you noted, she is still covered by her chemise."

"And what are your qualifications for tending the infirm, Mister Blackwell?" the duchess pressed. "There will be certain delicate needs that will come up. You have no staff here except a housekeeper. Are your prepared for that eventuality?"

More than prepared. "Though my mother had maids to tend to her as she lay dying, I often assisted with her care. I assure you, Your Grace, I can manage quite well."

Her eyes softened perceptibly when he mentioned his deceased mother. It was a human side of the starchy duchess he hadn't seen until today. And she had every right to be concerned. The conditions here were less than ideal. But he would save Noelle. He owed her that much.

"I'm sorry about your mother." She leaned to caress the side of her sister's face. "Please make her well," she said softly. "I would hate to see you hanged."

Gavin snorted. The sisters were as close to a set of twins as two women born a year or so apart, to different mothers, could be. Both were willful, stubborn, and ill-humored at times. And very lovely, too. There were hints of each other in their eyes and features, but enough of a difference that they could hide their sisterly connection. He hadn't been frightened when he'd been attacked by the trio of footpads. But the thought of meeting the two women in a darkened alley, while they were in a rage, could strike fear in the most toughened heart.

He bit back a grim smile. Noelle would be proud of her sister. She'd enjoy seeing him taken down a peg.

It took another few minutes to convince the duchess to leave Noelle in his care, and a few more to agree to send for her immediately if Noelle's condition changed in any way.

"I will be visiting, and often." With a parting glare, she left him alone with his patient.

Gavin shook his head. Under other circumstances, he knew Her Grace wouldn't allow this state of affairs. But they couldn't move Noelle, and to bring in a chaperone or servants would risk gossips' getting word of her injury. Once that happened, it wouldn't take long for the stories about Noelle to race throughout the Ton.

Crawford assured him his housekeeper was discreet and lived elsewhere. For much of the time, they'd be alone.

With one last check to see that Noelle was comfortable, he left the room and set off to make final arrangements with Crawford to remove from the town house the filthy piece of cow dung who'd attacked Noelle.

It wasn't more than an hour or so before a sharp rap sounded on the town house door. A middle-aged woman with a stern face and a sterner demeanor rudely announced herself as Noelle's maid, Martha something-or-other, brushed past him, and took over the majority of Noelle's care with quiet efficiency.

Despite her seeming acceptance of his promise to take great care of Noelle, the duchess had sent a bulldog to nurse her. He'd managed to learn Martha had been with Noelle forever and wasn't about to allow Gavin to hurt "her girl."

The only time he was allowed near Noelle was when he forced the issue and sent the maid off for food and rest. The next two days were long, and the nights were worse. Noelle was as still as death. He spent most of his time with her, watching her chest rise and fall, and hearing the soft ticks of a clock breaking the silence. He prayed and held her hand and made God and Noelle all sorts of promises if only she'd open her beautiful eyes.

The duchess, dark circles framing her eyes, came twice. After the first morning, Gavin stopped offering assurances of Noelle's recovery. He was losing hope.

Even the physician had little to say. With a head injury, patients either recovered or they didn't. And even when patients came out of the sleep, many were no longer able to care for themselves and seldom lived long.

Gavin appreciated his candor even as he wanted to shake some hope out of the man.

"You should take some rest, Mister Blackwell," Martha said as she set a tray with a bowl of broth beside the bed, in case Noelle awakened and needed nourishment. "I had the housekeeper make you a tray of bread and cheese, and she took it to your room."

Gavin looked at the maid through weary eyes and sensed a crack developing in her dislike for him. He suspected that once she realized he wasn't about to impregnate Noelle in her sleep, and that his intention was only to see her well, she'd allow him time alone with their patient, without hovering outside the open door.

They both had the same purpose, and it drew them together, albeit reluctantly.

He scratched a hand over his head and arched to release the crick in his spine. He needed a bath more than food. He was still wearing the clothes he'd worn the night of the ball and was starting to find himself offensive.

"I think I shall." He squeezed Noelle's hand, then stood up. "If anything changes, please fetch me immediately."

He felt the weight of Martha's curious perusal as he left the room to heat some water.

It was nearing morning on the third day when he woke to a slight stir beside him. He'd lain down beside Noelle last evening as he had the night before, when Martha was sleeping, taking comfort in the soft sound of her breathing. As long as she breathed, he could continue to pray for heavenly intervention.

He listened for some sign of awakening, but there was no other movement in the darkness. He slumped and slid an arm around her. Gently, he pressed his face into her hair. The scent of lemon and cinnamon was no longer present.

Anguish threatened to undo his composure. But throwing chairs about and smashing china wouldn't help her recover. He had to stay positive.

Cursing fate was better left for when he was alone.

"I am sorry, love," he whispered, then curved his body against hers and gently snuggled her into his warmth. He held her tight in the circle of his arm. "If you come back to us, I promise to make amends for the way I mauled and mistreated you."

"Including removing your hand from my left breast?" came a weak reply.

Gavin was startled. "Noelle?" He pulled back and rolled from the bed to light the lamp. When he rushed back and knelt by the bed, her eyes were open. He'd never seen anything as lovely as the small half smile on her perfect lips. "You scared ten years off my life," he scolded, then clasped her hands together in his and pressed two firm kisses on her knuckles.

She looked into his eyes and then moved her attention to his temples. "I see a gray hair," she croaked, her voice thin. "Please explain what happened to me."

Taking the glass from the table next to the bed, Gavin poured some tepid tea and lifted the glass to her lips. Noelle sipped gratefully, then settled back on the pillow. She was pale, and dark circles curved under her eyes. She had never looked more beautiful.

The tight band around his heart eased. "You were kidnapped, and the thug cuffed your temple."

She grimaced. It was a long moment before she spoke again. "I do remember that part. But why was I taken? The men were after you."

Gavin returned the glass to the table and took her hand. "You were a tool. The kidnappers planned to use you to force me to hand over the necklace."

Noelle grimaced. "I never planned for that eventuality. And how long have I been sleeping?"

"You've been unconscious for more than two days." Gavin wanted to whoop from the rooftops. She was frail and weak, but he knew she'd live to scold him another day. Gathering her hand, he pressed it to his mouth. "If you ever worry me like that again, I will turn you over my knee and paddle your buttocks red."

Her eyes twinkled, and she managed a weak scolding. "I thought you had other plans for my buttocks." She narrowed her eyes. "I seem to recall you handling them several times without my permission."

He offered a sheepish grin. "I promise never to take any more liberties. I have treated you badly. You will never have to suffer my ill attentions again."

The frown deepened into a crease between her brows.

"Never?" The corners of her mouth drifted downward. "Then I shall live the rest of my life under crushing disappointment. I have discovered your manhandling and kisses are the most exciting part of my days."

Noelle wanted to giggle when his brows shot up, but she was too weak to do so. She wasn't sure how long she'd lain in the dark in this tiny white room, perhaps as long as an hour or two, listening to him sleep while taking comfort in his warm body beside her in bed.

The shock of discovering she wasn't alone under the sheets had quickly turned to pleasure when she caught his scent and realized it wasn't a stranger beside her. Well, as much pleasure as one could take when one's head hurt and every small movement creaked painfully along stiff muscles and bones.

It had also allowed her time to think about her situation. Having been close to losing her life at the hands of the kidnapper, she realized how tenuous life was. She could fret about her virginity, or rules, or possible heartbreak until her head spun, but none of it mattered. Happiness, even a few stolen moments, was more important than anything else.

All jesting and verbal sparring aside, she wanted Gavin, and she wouldn't be satisfied until she learned if his seductive wager had been bluster or truth. She'd love him for as long as she could and cherish the memories of those stolen moments for the rest of her life.

"You have certainly come to some conclusions since we spoke last. How long were you awake?" he asked.

Gavin looked haggard and in real need of giving attention to his appearance. Obviously her infirmity had taken a toll on him. She wanted to lift her hand to his face but didn't have the strength. In time she'd run her fingers through his glossy hair and down his face and give thanks she'd survived her ordeal to kiss him again.

"I was awake long enough to know I enjoyed the feel of your hand on my left breast. Unfortunately, the right one wasn't so blessed." She locked onto his stare. From the fresh smell of her nightdress over unwashed skin, she knew she'd been cared for. Still, she couldn't remember the details of anything more than a hazy recollection of three men in a room, one of whom was Gavin, and a brief conversation. After that, the last days were blank.

Whatever else had happened since the courtesan ball, it was obvious that Gavin had spent time at her bedside, his rumpled clothing showing that he'd not been attended to by a proper valet.

"I was holding you," he countered. He darted his eyes away from her face. "I didn't realize the placement of my hand over the coverlet was also on your breast."

"So you didn't enjoy cupping my breast?" she teased grimly. "I think I have suffered the greatest injury I can suffer. I have lost the ability to entice a man."

Chapter Twenty

Noelle watched his face and bit her lip to keep from laughing out loud. There were all sorts of emotions playing on his handsome countenance, none of which was disgust. He wanted her, she knew, but in her weakened condition he had to feel like a cad for thinking lecherous thoughts. And he was thinking them, she had no doubt, when his eyes dipped of their own volition to her breasts before they snapped back to her face just as quickly.

She loved him. When she'd been lying there after awakening, she'd realized she wanted to share his bed, not for happily-ever-after but for one night, a string of nights. Maybe they could keep their relationship secret, all theirs, like a pair of star-crossed lovers hiding from the world, unable to give each other up. It would be her grandest adventure of all.

"Your injury has certainly rattled your brain, My Lady," Gavin said, his voice serious. He kept his attention on the wall behind the bed, as if the plaster was infinitely fascinating. "You don't know what you are saying. It is not lady-like to tease a man in such a manner unless you are prepared to accept the consequences."

"Consequences? You mean what happens when a man

and woman come together in bed?" She opened her eyes wide. If she was to break through his newly misguided sense of honor, she had to force him into action. The only way to do that, she mused, was to keep him focusing not on what his mind wanted him to do but on what his body wanted. "I must admit I do lack that knowledge, other than a few general points of the act itself. However, I have decided you should be the man to teach me."

"Noelle," he warned through gritted teeth.

She plucked at her nightdress while completely ignoring his warning. She should hold back her awkward attempts to seduce him until after she was clean and well. She had to be a frightful sight.

"First, though, you must bathe me," she insisted. "I fear lying abed has made me offensive to the senses."

His jaw pulsed. "I shall call for Martha."

"Martha is here?" Disappointment welled. If her maid was in residence, Eva had to know her whereabouts. Martha was the one person Eva trusted to keep Noelle's secrets. And with Martha hovering, seduction would be nearly impossible.

Gavin left her. A few minutes later, he was back. He appeared oddly disconcerted as he slumped into a chair.

"Apparently, the maid has gone on an errand," he grumbled. "Mrs. Hill informed me she won't be back for several hours."

Noelle hid a smile. Much could be accomplished in a few hours. "Then I guess you must bathe me without her help." She looked at him wide-eyed. "Please, Gavin? I'm starting to itch." She scratched her arm to emphasize her point.

"It is improper for me to bathe you, Noelle."

From beneath her lashes she cast him a laughing glance. "Who said anything about proper, Gavin? And when did you become such a starchy prude?" She paused and crinkled her nose. "I know little about courtesans and their lovers, true, but I suspect some do share a tub together from time to time. I know my sister enjoys a bath with the duke. I understand it can be very sensuous."

Noelle wasn't sure where this audaciousness came from, only that she was tired of keeping her purity under lock and key. She wanted Gavin. She wanted him naked. She wanted to kiss his perfect chest and stomach. And, of course, everywhere else she wanted to kiss.

After suffering through a near-fatal ordeal, she'd decided life was not to be watched from within a protective cocoon. Life was meant to be lived to the fullest. Stolen moments of passion with a man whom she cared for deeply should not be fought, but celebrated. And she planned to celebrate, bare-bottomed naked, with Gavin.

She could think about her kidnapping, the necklace, and footpads later. For now, they were alone. She'd not ponder grim thoughts while she had this opportunity to forget.

The flickering lamplight gave his face a dangerous appeal. His tight jaw sharpened his features. He was obviously struggling between his concern for her and the lingering effects of the blow to her head, and wanting to take her up on her offer to bed her with all the passion he could muster.

"The physician assured me a head injury can alter the personality of the victim." He stood and paced. When he neared the door, he paused. "I shall fetch Mrs. Hill and arrange for your bath. Once you're made comfortable, you will see things clearer."

Now Noelle was getting angry. She didn't want whoever this Mrs. Hill was to attend her. She understood that she was in no condition to fully seduce Gavin or completely enjoy the delights she hoped she would find in his arms. However, seduction didn't start with the act of copulation itself. Temptation, even in the form of bare skin, would certainly intrigue her reluctant lover enough to drive him to want to sample the delights she offered, soon, when she was well.

Unless he no longer desired her. She touched her hand to her face and wondered about the depth of the damage. She hadn't considered that her injury might have forever ruined her face. Nowhere in the room was there a mirror to check.

Certainly one blow hadn't destroyed her features. So she put that worry aside and scowled.

"If that woman sets one foot in this room, I shall throw myself from the window." She struggled onto her elbows, and the room swayed. She blinked and waited for the space to settle. "I understand my condition is fragile and my appearance questionable. Have I suddenly become unappealing?"

Gavin's head snapped around. "Is that what you think?"

"How can I think anything else?" She felt the press of tears. "My first real effort to tempt a man is failing miserably. I offer to share intimacies with the only man who has ever engaged both my mind and my body, and all he can think of is to put a housekeeper or maid between us." She bit her lip to stop the tremors. "I promise I will recover from this and return to robust good health. Certainly you can wait a few days before deciding you no longer want me."

His shoulders slumping, Gavin stared at the floor for several seconds before lifting his eyes to her and sighing resolutely.

"From the moment I pulled you down on my bed and kissed you, I have ached to make you mine." He rubbed the back of his neck and down over his jaw with both hands. Whiskers shadowed his cheeks and chin. Clearly, his grooming had been neglected while he played nursemaid. "However, as your sister so aptly reminded me, I have no right to do so, in spite of our wager."

Eva. Noelle should have known her sister would meddle. Noelle had once meddled in Eva's affair with the duke. Certainly she should've expected her sister would repay her in kind.

"What I do is none of my sister's affair," she snapped.

"You are meant to make a well-connected marriage. If I bed you, there will be little chance you will ever make a match." He looked into her eyes. "I will not wed you, Noelle."

She let out a low frustrated sound. Was he worried she would hunt him down and force him to marry her? Did he think sharing a bed would change her mind about her convictions? The man's arrogance clearly had no bounds.

"Why can't I make anyone understand?" she said, exasperated. "I do not want to wed you, or anyone else."

* * *

Each word hit Gavin like a blow. He felt like a cad for arguing with her when she looked so fragile. Her skin had a deathly pallor, and the dark smudges under her eyes seemed to deepen with her distress. At any moment, he expected her to crumple back on the bed and expire. Fortunately, his feisty Noelle was made of sterner stuff.

She was recovering and would continue to do so, if only to spend her days tormenting him with her lush and beautiful body.

"All women wish to wed."

"Is that so?" she countered. "The same could be said for men. They enjoy the comfort of a wife to whelp their heirs and mend their stockings while they spread their favors to any willing partner who'll lift her skirts for a toss behind the potted plants. Why wouldn't they want a wife?"

The bitterness in her voice took him aback. He knew Noelle had an aversion to marriage. However, most women got over their reluctance when the right man made an offer. His faithless Anne had sent many men on a merry chase, until his heavy purse had brought her around. He would have cherished her forever if she hadn't betrayed him. "Not all men are lecherous cads, Noelle. Some men truly love their wives."

"Name one." She crossed her arms, her eyes flashing with challenge. He paused a bit too long before answering, and she nodded with grim satisfaction. "See, you know of none. Eventually all men will be unfaithful. It is in their nature."

Ire stiffened Gavin. She was so certain she was right, he felt utterly insulted. Damn! He'd not be thrown on the same shit pile with all other men.

"You may find this impossible to believe, but I was once engaged to the most beautiful woman in Boston. I was building a house for her that would have been the finest anyone had ever seen. I cherished her and worked long hours to be able to afford to give her anything she desired." He frowned as the unpleasant memories unfolded. "One afternoon, her father and I caught her frolicking in the straw beneath a groom. The engagement was over."

"Oh, Gavin." Noelle reached over and placed her hand on his arm. Sympathy and sadness filled her face. "I didn't know."

He snorted, and his gaze met her red-rimmed eyes. "I would have been faithful to the deceitful witch."

Their glances locked. "We make quite a pair," Noelle said, her smile cynical. "Neither of us sees marriage as the wondrous institution sung about in ballads."

Gavin didn't know her full history but suspected she'd also seen the dark side of relationships. Perhaps one day she would share her tale with him. "Then you can see why I have no intention of marrying."

"I can," she said. "But have I ever asked you to marry me?"

"Do you understand the ramifications of making love with me? There could be a child."

Her narrow shoulders lifted. "I understand there are ways to prevent conception. I shall leave that to you." She ran her hand through the tangles in her hair. "We can discuss the particulars later, as well as the wager and how you intend to win it. First, I desperately need that bath."

Gavin had much to ponder. He wanted to believe her injury had left her addled. Looking back at their previous encounters, and her responses to his kisses, he knew she wasn't addled when she asked him to love her. Her body was frail at the moment, but her mind was sharp. The offer to become his lover wasn't made without careful consideration. He knew enough about Noelle to understand that much.

"Yes, My Lady." He bowed formally, and she smiled. "I also need to advise your sister that you've awakened. She's been terribly worried."

Noelle shook her head. "Please give me a few minutes to bathe first," she pleaded. "I'd like to be clean and clear-headed when Eva arrives to fuss."

"I'll tell the coachman to drive slowly."

Noelle smiled softly. "Thank you."

He fell into her beautiful eyes. How she could ever believe he didn't want her was a puzzle. Even in her current state, she drove him to madness. He knew that during the next hour or two, he'd have to make a decision about the course of their relationship. Hell, in a few minutes she'd be naked, and he would be unable to think clearly.

Damnation! When had his life taken such a mystifying turn?

Gavin went to order some hot water from Mrs. Hill, and Noelle rose slowly from the bed. She felt as helpless as a babe as she walked across the room to a narrow table pushed against the wall and sat down on a three-legged stool. The red and cream carpet beneath her feet was threadbare and stained, and the room was the size of a moderate pantry. If not for the bright quilt on the bed and the faded rug, the space would be devoid of color.

Someone had left a silver brush and comb on the table for her use. Though she wanted to believe Gavin had made the gesture, he wouldn't understand how a simple brush could be so important to her pride. She suspected Eva had been the gift giver. It had a woman's touch.

Each stroke of the brush pulled painfully at her scalp, but she wasn't satisfied until her hair was free of the tangles and knots. At the moment, she was grateful there wasn't a mirror. It would be impossible to be courageous in her attempt to entice Gavin if she looked a fright. Better to think of herself the way she was before her injury.

She cleaned her teeth and sipped some tepid tea and felt some confidence return.

Gavin arrived sometime later with a hip bath. He settled it by the fire before leaving to retrieve buckets of water. Noelle enjoyed watching him work, his muscles flexing beneath his shirt and the strength of years of hard physical labor showing in every movement.

Noelle sucked her bottom lip between her teeth as he leaned over and poured a bucket of steaming water into the small bath. His bottom tightened with the movement, and she took advantage of his inattention to caress his buttocks with her gaze. He was a virile man from his glossy hair to what she suspected were nicely formed toes.

Though she'd offered to share with him, the tub was too small to accommodate them both without them sitting face-to-face with their knees jammed up under their chins. She'd just have to wait until the accommodations were better suited for the first steps of seduction.

"Your bath is ready, My Lady."

"I thank you, sir, for your efforts on my behalf." She stood and walked gingerly toward him. While lying abed, she'd thought she could manage a romp. After gaining her feet, the full impact of the footpad's cuff became clear. Tonight there would be no seduction. She did not have the strength.

Gavin must have seen her struggle. He hurried to her side and swept her into his arms. He grinned into her eyes. "Though I appreciate your desire to divest yourself of your virginity on my manly staff, you'll just have to wait a day or two until you've recovered. Then we will speak of it again."

Noelle nuzzled her face to his neck, inhaling his warm male scent and reveling in the feel of being in his arms. She let out a little groan of protest that the distance was not longer when, a few strides later, he slowly settled her onto her feet and reached to steady her with his hands on her shoulders.

"Can you remove your nightdress, or will you require assistance?" he asked, drawing back her attention.

There was hesitation in his voice. She suspected it was more for her fragile state than for his lack of desire to see her standing before him naked. She bent for the chemise's hem, and the room whirled. She stumbled a half step sideways. Gavin caught her arm and shook his head.

"Allow me." With infinite care, he bunched the fabric in

his hands and carefully slid it up her body and over her head. Noelle heard his breath catch as he freed her of her rumpled nightdress and bared her body to his gaze. She watched his face and saw his struggle not to look down at her breasts and, lower, at the thatch of curls between her legs.

He might well be an untamed American, but he was also a nobleman-gentleman to his core. Noelle noted his discomfort with satisfaction. Eventually, he'd break and make passionate love to her. She looked forward to the day.

Though she knew he'd tended her while she lay in her befuddled state, she suspected Martha had been pressed into service for the more personal matters. By his reaction, this was the first time he'd seen her in her glory.

Her skin flushed. She'd spoken of intimacies they'd share, yet when it came down to actually removing the protective layer of clothing, she found acute embarrassment in the intimacy of this moment. When he met her gaze, she lowered her eyes. A long stretch of silence passed before he spoke. "I have never seen anyone so beautiful."

Noelle tipped up her face. Soft humor and desire lit his eyes. She crossed her arms tightly over her breasts. She knew she was a frightful mess. His well-chosen words were meant to ease her shame.

"Then your choices have been limited, sir." She resisted the urge to dart for the bed and sweep a sheet around her. "A mangy mutt has more appeal at the moment."

Gavin lifted a hand to cup her chin. "Though it is in bad taste to bring up previous lovers with a future lover, I have seen my share of female bodies." He looked downward to encompass every inch of her. "Using my considerable experience to guide me, madam, yours is beyond compare."

Noelle looked down and dropped her arms. Her breasts, though not large, were nicely shaped and tipped with rosy nipples. Her legs were long and shapely. Her stomach was not hard and rippled, as his was, but she supposed it wasn't unattractive. And she did have nice feet. Overall, she figured she was appealing enough, though not incomparable.

"You have a way with words, sir, but it isn't necessary to flatter me. I know my limitations." Bracing her hand on his forearm, she lifted her leg to step into the bath.

Gavin grumbled, "Even sick, she's difficult."

Noelle smiled wickedly and sank into the tub.

The water was decently warm, and she groaned at the delicious feel of it on her aching limbs. Without footmen to help carry the buckets, and pressed into service to tend her without years of servant training, Gavin, her temporary footman-physician, had done well with both.

She wondered who was watching his shipyard. She hoped her infirmity hadn't cost him his navy contract.

Guilt tugged at her. If his business fell to ruin, it would be her fault for running off when she knew danger could be lurking in the shadows. Now he felt obligated to help her. As soon as Martha or Eva arrived, she'd insist he return immediately to his shipyard.

For the next few minutes, she'd enjoy her bath. Once she was settled and comfortable, she glanced around in vain for soap and a washing cloth.

"Lean forward."

She looked behind her and found her face very nearly eye level with the front of his breeches. Gavin sat on the spindly stool, legs spread wide open to better reach her. Proof of the effect of her bare body still showed beneath the perfectly cut cloth of his breeches. His desire for her hadn't waned. The outline of a lingering erection was visible beneath fine stitching.

Forcing her eyes up, she saw he was holding soap and a cloth in his hands. One eyebrow hiked up as her cheeks burned. She realized he'd been fully aware of where her gaze had rested. Inwardly, she winced. For a woman who just minutes ago had offered her body to him without compunction, she certainly was racked with a sudden bout of shyness.

This wouldn't do. She had to remember she was a courtesan-adventuress, and keep her flushes and fumbles to herself. Otherwise, Gavin would never seduce her and satisfy both her curiosity and the terms of their wager.

"I thought I would start with your hair, My Lady," he said, his voice husky. A slow grin tipped up his mouth. "Unless you'd prefer I start with your breasts?"

Chapter Twenty-One

Luckily for Noelle, Gavin was behind her and couldn't see what she suspected was a burning red face. Try as she might, she couldn't pull up the adventuress inside her and make some sort of tart reply. The idea of his hands on her wet breasts left her flustered. It was easy to speak boldly about desires. It was another thing to put those same desires into practical use.

Especially when one was an innocent.

"My back would be fine." She jumped when the cloth touched the back of her neck. Never in her life had anyone unnerved her as Gavin did. Nothing in her entire existence up until this moment could compare to the contradictions she felt in his presence: a tangle of good and bad Noelle, with the bad Noelle struggling to win out.

"I can call for Mrs. Hill." Gavin swiped the cloth over one of her shoulders and then the other. "It isn't too late."

She closed her eyes. He was being a perfect gentleman. It was the light brush of his fingertips as his fingers traveled across her skin with the soapy cloth that made it impossible to remain unaffected. It felt so good. She wanted to return to his earlier offer and ask him to start with her breasts instead. But her mouth wouldn't wrap around the words.

"The window isn't locked," she said, reminding him of her earlier threat to jump from it if he called for the house-keeper. To get over her hesitation to give herself to him, she had to overcome her anxiety. "Continue as you were."

She didn't have to see his face to suspect he was smiling at her discomfiture. She leaned forward in the shallow water, and he slid the cloth down her spine to the cleft of her buttocks and back up again. With precision, he covered the entire surface without touching anything he should not be touching.

Still, the act did have some effect on her. A little tingle here, a little shiver there. She was naked, after all, and he was the perfect male specimen with whom she wanted to eventually share a bed. And his hands were anything but soft. Each time a callused fingertip gently scraped across her skin, she nearly moaned aloud.

With her ingrained belief that bedding a man was entirely for procreation, and his pleasure, why did she want to bed him at all? It was as if her rapidly warming body knew something her mind did not. Was it possible Gavin could actually satisfy her carnal urges? That she might truly find some pleasure frolicking with him among tangled sheets?

He had pleasured her in the coach.

Though Eva seemed to find satisfaction in her marital relations, not all women felt that way. Noelle had always considered herself somewhat frigid. Was it reasonable to believe, now, after the seductive coach encounter, that she was capable of making love with Gavin and actually enjoying his skills?

Suddenly, she wanted more than anything to find out what it felt like to have his hands on her private parts. The brief time in the coach had been only enough to tease her to curiosity, and she'd been fully dressed.

Unfortunately, he wasn't making any effort to comply. He seemed very content to wash a groove in her spine and keep well away from her bum, her breasts, and the juncture between her legs. Any normal man would take advantage of the situation by at least "accidentally" touching something inappropriate.

Not Gavin. He was entirely proper.

"I think my back is satisfactorily clean," she grumbled. "Move on, please, before you wear a hole in my skin."

"Yes, My Lady."

Noelle felt a tremor of frustration build when he lifted her right arm. He swept the cloth down the underside, then over her rib cage, careful not to touch any part of her breast. He moved to the left arm and repeated the action until her underarms had to be sparkling clean.

She gnashed her teeth. Her breast was uplifted with her arm over her head, yet he didn't once move in for a fondle, a nipple tweak, nothing. And she was intently hopeful he would. She jerked her arm out of his grip and petulantly stuck out her bottom lip. The place between her legs pulsed, and she was burning up.

The man was certainly not acting like a lover. Any maid could serve just as well.

A sound came from him, and she wasn't sure if it was frustration or humor she heard. Was he purposely tormenting her, or was he as uninterested as he appeared?

"Close your eyes," he commanded.

He squeezed the cloth above her head, and soapy water trickled over her face. She blew water off her lips and scowled. Frustration made her grumpy. He washed her hair and rinsed it from the bucket. Not once did he comment on the gentle curve of her neck or the satin texture of her skin. He was treating her with clinical care, and she hated it with everything inside her. She had to bring an end to this torture.

"Wash the front, please." Noelle flopped back in the small tub and water splashed about. She hoped she'd gotten his boots wet. It would serve him right. "My breasts are highly soiled."

It didn't matter if her breasts were covered in lard or as

pristine as well-polished silver. She wanted him to touch her intimately, even if she had to pull his hand to her nipples or shove it between her legs.

Her entire body burned.

Pressing her legs together didn't help squelch her need. In her discomfort, she was shifting in the water. She couldn't help herself. Never had she felt such a driving ache.

How could he not sense her struggle?

The warmth of his low chuckle teased her senses. "Yes, My Lady." Gavin stood up and dragged the stool around to the side. His sleeves were rolled up to the elbows, but the water had gotten on them anyway. The fine hairs that she remembered on his broad chest showed beneath the open collar of his shirt. Where dampness from bathing her had wetted the front of the linen, it clung to him in patches.

She wanted to draw her tongue across the damp spots and feel the warmth of his body beneath his shirt. She wanted to climb into his lap and rub her core against him as she had done in the coach, to fulfill her driving need.

Staring at the man through besotted eyes made him appear even more desirable to her than he had during their first meeting. However, even if they were both old and wrinkled, she knew she'd always find him the handsomest man in all of England.

"Left or right?" His voice cut into her seductive musing.

"Left or what?" she asked absently. She pulled her attention from his chest to his face. He had a blank expression.

"Left or right breast?" he asked again. His face was a stoic mask, but there was devilishness in his eyes he couldn't hide. "Where would you like me to start?"

It took her no more than a second or two to realize he was tormenting her on purpose. He knew she was heated up, and he'd do his best to keep the fire lit. She shot a glance to his open legs and his erection pressing the limits of the seams. Gavin wanted her as badly as she wanted him. He was keeping his emotions in check to torture her.

And doing a right fine job of it, too.

Wickedness raced through her mind. If he could play games, so could she. By the end of the bath his suffering would be the likes of which he'd never suffered before. He'd beg her to ease the pain between his legs, regardless of her weakened condition. The courtesans had mentioned the aches men felt when they couldn't satisfy their urges. Her reluctant lover would suffer a similar fate.

"Left, please." She hid a smile. "And be sure to put extra effort in. I have been wallowing in filth long enough."

Noelle stretched out as much as possible in the limited space and dropped her knees open against the sides of the tub. The soapy water was just deep enough to hide the patch of curls between her legs from view. She put her arms on the edges of the tub and leaned back with her eyes closed, knowing her nipples were pointing upward for his perusal.

His breathing took on a ragged quality, and she wanted to grin like an idiot. Finally!

Squish. The cloth slopped over her breast, and her eyes opened. Gavin's stare was innocent. He jerked the cloth left and right like he was buffing a tea service. "Like this?" He swirled the cloth around her nipple, and the peak hardened. "I am not well schooled in the art of breast washing. You might have to give me detailed instructions."

Oh! The man was intensely exasperating! Then why were her nipples already forming tight, rosy peaks?

"Do what you will," she snapped. Just as quickly as she had wanted to play this game, the desire to best him fled. She'd not beg him to help end her suffering. "Just be quick about it."

Leaning her head back, she waited for his awkward fumbles to finish. For all his handsomeness and, she suspected, his great knowledge of bedding women, he was clearly as clumsy as a schoolboy in the art of pleasing a woman in her bath. She wondered how she would spend her winnings from the wager; how far she'd travel on one of her beautiful new ships.

With all her mental grumbling, she wasn't immediately

aware of the gentle caress of the cloth over and beneath her breast until the sweep of his rough fingertips brushed the hardened peak.

Noelle looked down and found that his scrubbing back and forth, like a washerwoman on a marble floor, had been replaced by a more seductive stroke. Slowly he moved to the right, to begin a sensuous assault on her other breast. He swept and swirled the cloth over the sensitive nipple, sending a shocking wave of heat down her body.

Her woman's core pulsed harder in response.

Gavin leaned to place his mouth to her ear. His breath caressed her like a feathered kiss. "Better?"

Noelle nodded dumbly. Rivulets of soapy water ran down her chest as Gavin soaped and caressed her breasts as only an experienced lover could. He'd decided to stop his torture and give her what she needed. She arched back and lifted her buttocks off the bottom of the tub. The thatch of curls danced on the surface of the moving water. She couldn't turn her eyes away from his hand as he lowered the cloth to circle her navel.

She moaned helplessly.

"Yes. More." She didn't realize she'd spoken aloud until the cloth dipped beneath the water and over her inner thigh. He drew it up between her legs, and it skimmed across the sensitive bud he found there. She let out a small cry.

Somehow the cloth disappeared in the water and was replaced by his searching fingers. Noelle gasped in shock when his fingertip brushed her most intimate place. He teased and played with the bud until her body responded by bucking recklessly against him. Gavin dipped his head and pulled a nipple in his mouth, sucking the peak until she was mad with heat. With a gasp-cry, her body exploded into a mass of sensation as he brought her to a shuddering release.

Noelle's breaths came in small gasps before he caught her mouth with his and kissed her deeply. She played her tongue with his and lifted her hand to run through his soft hair. When he broke the kiss and peered deep into her eyes from beneath his tumbling hair, she knew that even if she lived to a very old age, she'd never love another man as she loved this man.

"My thanks," she whispered as her lids drooped. Sated and fatigued, she hardly felt him quickly finish her bath and step away. Beneath halfway lowered lids, she saw him spread a clean sheet across the bed and make an awkward attempt to smooth the edges. The result was a lumpy mess across the surface.

"Your skills lie elsewhere, Mister Blackwell," she teased softly. She couldn't bring herself to leave the bath and help. "However, we are not abed. The wager still stands."

Gavin gave up on the sheet and returned to her. He pulled her to her feet, dried her with a well-used towel, and carried her to the bed. Easing her down, he tucked a warm blanket around her. She nestled in, knowing he'd sacrificed his own pleasure to satisfy her need. Once she was well, she vowed, she would return the gesture tenfold. He'd be her lover even if she had to get him thoroughly drunk and take advantage.

"Sleep," he whispered softly, and his hand slid over the top of her damp head. "The wager can wait."

It was the last Noelle heard and felt before she drifted into deep slumber.

Gavin waited until she was breathing softly in sleep before leaving her to rest. He went downstairs to ask Mrs. Hill to fix a bowl of broth for Noelle, then found Crawford sprawled in a chair in the small library. The man had his bad leg stretched out on a footstool and held a tumbler of something Gavin assumed was cheap whiskey.

"Is the Lady recovering from her ordeal?" the investigator asked, taking a sip from his glass. Oddly, the sparsely furnished house and inexpensive spirits didn't quite fit what Gavin knew of the investigator. Crawford had to be a man of some wealth. He was well paid for his services, and

Gavin wondered if he had another place he called home when he wasn't working in London, a hideout away from the dangerous men he crossed during his cases.

That was likely the case. This town house was almost unlivable, as spartan as it was. Not the sort of place one would consider a home. Crawford had given up this town house for Noelle's use without hesitation. Clearly he wasn't overly attached to the place.

Gavin nodded. "She has awakened and is speaking coherently. I am confident she's suffered no lasting ill effects from the injury." He went to the sideboard and poured a glass of the spirit for himself, and discovered it was watered-down wine. He grimaced.

"Remind me to send you a case of the good stuff." He swallowed the rest of his drink and poured another. "This swill isn't fit to wash the windows with."

Crawford grinned. "The ladies don't seem to mind."

Dropping into the other chair, Gavin grinned. He liked the man. He wondered what sort of trouble they could get into, given the proper time and setting. "Then you aren't spending time with the right sort of ladies."

Crawford peered over the rim of his glass. "With what you're paying me, I'll soon be able to consort with the right sort." He looked around the sparse room. "And be able to purchase some furnishings, too."

Gavin snorted. "I think your tastes run much higher than this drab den." He scanned the room. "But you can keep your secrets. Every man is entitled to keep some part of his life tucked away from prying eyes." As long as he found the information Gavin needed, Crawford was free to do what he wished with his time and money.

"Has our friend broken his silence and given you what we seek?" Gavin asked, sobering. He turned the glass on the arm of the chair and braced himself for the report.

Slowly, Crawford nodded, his smile turning into an evil grin. "He did give new information, though he does not know the name of the woman who hired him. The extent of their contact was a brief glimpse of her face when the maid climbed from a coach to pay him a deposit for his services. She clearly works for the second woman and was placed in Bliss's household. He, too, knows the maid only as Freda. I assume that isn't her true name."

"There's a second woman?" Gavin sat upright in the chair, his eyes hard on Crawford. Had he heard this news incorrectly? "The person behind this case is a woman?"

Never during the last week had he suspected the mastermind behind the theft of the necklace was female. He expected, wrongly, that the master thief would be male. This clearly turned the case on end and sent it in a new direction. He pinched the bridge of his nose. The culprit list was expanding. It was quite possible that the necklace had been only part of a grander operation. But how did Bliss figure into all this?

"I suspected the maid wasn't capable of setting the plot into motion alone but thought a man was certainly handling the puppet strings," Gavin said. "This is an interesting development. Could Bliss's maid be traveling from house to house, under the guise of a servant, to steal valuables? Mistresses often get expensive gifts."

Crawford stood and walked to the bookshelf. "It is possible. A woman wouldn't arouse suspicion in thefts as much as a man would." He picked up a sheet of parchment and examined it closely for a few seconds. "The footpad believes the woman he glimpsed is a Lady of means, and he managed to give a fairly apt description."

"A Lady?"

Crawford moved over to Gavin and held out the sheet. "Just because she has wealth does not mean she is an aristocrat. Stolen jewels can buy nice clothes and a fancy coach."

To Gavin's surprise, a face was sketched on the parchment in ink, a very nice likeness of a woman with pretty features. There was something familiar about her, but there wasn't enough detail in the rendering to bring the owner of the face to the front of his mind. Still, it was well done by an artist of talent.

"Where did you get this?" he asked, and lifted the page

into better light. He ran his gaze over her nose, her cheekbones, the cut of her brow; memorizing every curve. If she was a woman of society, he intended to watch out for her.

"A Lady with whom I am acquainted uses the artist to sketch suitors for her matchmaking services." Crawford leaned to look at the page. "I know she is pleased with his work, so I asked for his help. The footpad described the face as he remembered it, and the artist made the sketch. You will find his payment on your bill."

Gavin smiled slowly, stood, and felt confident for the first time since he had stumbled into this pit of mire that they might actually solve this case.

"Well done, my good man." Gavin stood and clapped Crawford on the shoulder. He wanted to get back to Noelle. She was recovering well, but he still had to be vigilant lest she take a downward turn. Besides, he'd developed a habit of watching her sleep. "Get this concluded by the end of the week and I'll triple your fee."

The older man grinned. "I shall do my best."

After Crawford left, Gavin jerked open the drapes and took a few minutes to carefully study the sketch. He realized rather quickly that there *was* indeed something familiar about her, but he couldn't quite put his mind around how he knew her.

She looked very much like Lady Crowley, a former lover of Charles. Could she be behind the necklace caper? Their arrangement had ended unhappily.

If the likeness was even close to correct, she didn't have the bluntness to her features of the lower classes. The footpad was correct; she was a Lady, or could pass as one with the right trappings. And in order to pay someone to coerce Bliss to steal the necklace, and a trio of thugs to steal it back, she had to have some wealth.

The question, then, was why?

What could have caused this woman to set into motion a theft, an attack on him, and Noelle's kidnapping? He knew women could easily be as devious as men, but their reasons usually came down to money or jealousy.

If she was wealthy in her own right, he could set aside that reason. If she was indeed a woman scorned, certainly that would explain much. It would be easier to accept that the necklace had been stolen by a woman out to punish Charles rather than by a random band of thieves. He peered into the face. The woman also somewhat resembled a mistress Charles had had before Bliss. *Maria*, he thought. He'd seen several of Charles's former lovers during his brief time in London. His cousin liked to boast about women with whom he'd once shared a bed. And Charles certainly had a look he favored. That relationship with Maria had ended on a sour note with breakable objects being thrown at Charles's head.

And what of the wealthy widow his cousin had dallied with before Maria? She'd nearly been killed after throwing herself in front of his moving coach after he'd explained to her that their association had come to an end. Although Gavin had never seen her, she could be added to the list of suspects.

Since the necklace belonged to Charles, the seeds of the plot had to return to him. He'd had a string of lovers over the years, many not at all pleased to be set aside for a younger or lovelier new mistress. Any one of them could be behind the theft.

Gavin frowned. His cousin certainly had a talent for picking the wrong mistresses.

The leader of the thieves had to be someone who knew by now that they were cousins, or at least friends, and that Gavin was staying in Charles's town house. Certainly the initial mix-up couldn't last forever? But why come after him? Had the woman known there was a possibility he might have ended up with the necklace? If so, then someone was probably watching the town house the night Noelle climbed the trellis. She had stumbled across danger that evening, and neither of them had known it was lurking there in the dark.

She was lucky she wasn't taken then. No one but a silly courtesan would have known she was missing. Bliss would never have called for help. To do so might have caused her arrest, and Gavin couldn't imagine the chit sacrificing her hide for Noelle.

He carefully scanned the sketch one last time, as all the questions worked to come together in his mind, to match with answers. Nothing up to this point made sense, but one thing was certain: The sketch gave him confidence.

He had to give Crawford a list of rejected mistresses, as many as he could recall from Charles's indiscreet tales, so they could be eliminated one at a time.

Gavin grinned. The clues were quickly adding up.

Chapter Twenty-Two

Gavin returned to the bedroom with the sketch at almost the same time Martha returned to the house, Eva on her heels, to the excitement of learning Noelle had awakened from her stupor and was recovering. He allowed a few minutes for a happy reunion, then ushered the maid into the hallway. Low-voiced conversation followed after Martha left the three of them alone. Eva had no interest in the mysterious woman, only in Noelle, and the sketch was temporarily set aside.

Reprimand came quickly when the duchess discovered Noelle was clean and that Gavin had bathed her. Then Her Grace had shooed him out and made him wait in the parlor, cooling his heels, while she helped Noelle dress.

"Mister Blackwell has certainly become an intimate friend," Eva said, annoyed. "I don't suppose he managed to wash you with his eyes closed?"

Noelle flushed. "He was a proper gentleman."

Eva made a disbelieving snort. "Improper, perhaps."

"Don't lecture," Noelle said quickly, before Eva could work up an argument about her behavior with Gavin. She was beyond behaving herself. "I know what I'm doing."

Her sister looked ready to argue but held her tongue. "We can discuss this later, when you have fully recovered."

Noelle sighed resolutely, still too weak to argue. "If we must."

They joined Gavin an hour later.

Well, actually they brushed past him, pulled on capes, and Eva dragged Noelle out the door with a scowl on her pretty duchess face. She wasn't about to leave Noelle alone in the town house with Gavin one minute longer. Or so she said. There was no telling what kinds of mischief he'd get Noelle into.

Gavin didn't put up a fuss as he joined the three women in the coach for the ride to Collingwood House.

O nce Noelle was settled in Eva's expansive cream and green drawing room, the women finally got to the business of examining the sketch.

"Who is she?" Noelle asked from her place on the settee, the sketched face staring at her. For a woman capable of evil, this stranger was without fangs or a warty nose below hairy black brows. Her pretty face could be any face Noelle passed on the street. "I don't recognize her."

"That's what I'm hoping to find out," Gavin replied. "So far we have come up with nothing," he added grimly, and peered at Nicholas. "If the four of us do not know her, it's possible she isn't a noblewoman, as we thought, but perhaps a courtesan who felt wronged by my cousin."

"This is becoming a muddle," Noelle said. "There are so many ways to look at this puzzle. Is there a band of thieves, one errant maid, a scorned lover, or an unhappy courtesan behind this crime? Which path do we choose?"

"A courtesan knows the rules of arrangements," Nicholas said. "I find it difficult to believe one would turn on the earl because he ended their association. If she is skilled and beautiful, she would have no problem procuring . . ." He paused and glanced briefly at Eva and Noelle. This wasn't a topic one discussed in front of a wife and sister-in-law. "Another lover."

Noelle nodded. "However, we cannot rule that out. Men see such arrangements as business. Still, one shares oneself in an intimate manner, so there is the chance emotions can be engaged. It's possible one of the women fancied herself in love."

The two men looked at her like she was an oddity. Clearly the opinion was hers alone.

"I shall keep watch for her," Eva said, distracted, giving only a cursory glance at the sketch. She fluttered around Noelle like a bird with her chick. "If she turns up at the school, I shall send for you immediately."

Eva smoothed the blanket so high around Noelle that it almost completely covered her sister's green gown. Noelle glowered and slid the blanket back down to her waist. It was too warm in the room, and her sister had somehow decided burying her was an excellent idea—as if doing so would help shake off Noelle's last lingering headache.

"You are smothering me," Noelle told her. They were so close together that only the different colors of their gowns showed where one ended and the other began. "Perhaps you can throw open a window, Sister?"

Eva remained tucked to her side. Instead, Gavin moved to do her bidding and cracked open the sash, letting in a late-day breeze. Noelle sent him a grateful nod. He winked back. She warmed under his regard.

They hadn't been left alone for a moment since Eva and Martha had gotten their hooks in her that morning. She was deeply disappointed. There wouldn't be a repeat of the bath under this roof. So she had to satisfy her lust by drinking in his presence with her eyes.

He was dressed entirely in black, except for his white shirt and charcoal waistcoat. His hair was carefully combed back, though it looked on the verge of falling over his forehead, as was its wont. When he was mussed up, he looked very dashing, like a pirate on the sea. Today he was formally handsome. He'd taken the time while Eva was dressing Noelle at Crawford's town house to change and shave. Afterward, Eva had bustled them so quickly to Collingwood House that Noelle hadn't had a chance to thoroughly examine the cut of his manly figure. Clearly he didn't need help getting dressed. Even his cravat was in perfect order around his neck.

Eva dropped a sugar lump into Noelle's teacup and stirred the tea vigorously. Noelle shot her a frown. "I can stir my own tea."

Eva smiled patiently. "You have endured a trauma. You must be careful not to suffer a relapse."

With the blanket tucked around her and Eva hovering, Noelle felt like an invalid. She'd been on her feet no more than an hour after her bath and nap when her sister kidnapped her. She'd endured the coach ride, an elaborate meal, endless questions about her head, and general fussing. She hadn't had a chance to speak to Gavin privately or to advance her seduction. Now she was trapped with Eva, and there was nothing she could do but suffer her sister's ministering.

Noelle turned her eyes to Gavin and silently begged him for help. He shrugged. Nicholas followed suit with a similar gesture, and Noelle encompassed both handsome men with a scowl. Obviously, neither of them would come to her rescue and face the wrath of the duchess. They chose to remove themselves to the fireplace, where it was safe.

"It isn't as if the footpad thumped me so hard he cracked my skull and my brain matter is leaking out." Noelle reached for a plum cake and took a vicious bite out of it. She chewed the flaky pastry and scowled at Eva. Her sister's patient smile never wavered. "I am fine. I just need a day or two to rest."

Eva leaned back against the cushions. "I will be the judge of your fitness."

Noelle simmered. Not only was Eva treating her as if any slight movement would shatter her into tiny shards of glass, but by stealing her from Gavin, she'd destroyed any chance of Noelle becoming his courtesan. Gavin wouldn't dare sneak into Collingwood House and abscond with her or risk an unwanted marriage.

It was difficult enough to have been left virtually un-chaperoned for several days with Gavin. Martha and Mrs. Hill hardly qualified as proper watchdogs as far as Eva was concerned. Noelle wasn't completely certain Eva wasn't planning a wedding anyway. Her sister had an unreadable expression in her eyes whenever she looked from Gavin to Noelle. If that was what Eva was plotting, Noelle had to keep vigilant.

No wedding. Not today, not ever.

After what he'd done to her in the bath, she very much looked forward to the next lesson. She didn't need wedding vows to share in such delights. Spinsters lived by a relaxed set of rules, and as long as Noelle kept her relationship with Gavin private, she was free to indulge her passion. Eva had come in and ruined her ruination. And she wasn't happy in the least.

Noelle looked over to the men and discovered they were no longer concerning themselves with the women and were focused on other matters. They were speaking about ships and trade routes while drinking brandy and casually loiter-ing in a pair of high-backed chairs.

She'd always thought Nicholas the most handsome man of her acquaintance, with his dark hair and nicely filled-out frame. His brooding nature had been difficult to warm to at first, but since finding love with Eva, he'd become an excel-lent brother-in-law. Caring, amusing, charming, devoted.

However, now she found she much preferred lighter hair with a touch of sun, easy teasing laughter, and the lean, muscled frame of her future lover. Though Nicholas was a cut above dandies and puffed-up society princes, she had eyes only for Gavin. She cared not if he was in trade or found working for a living an honorable pursuit. It was his rough edges that kept her enticed and hungry for his kisses.

Gavin chuckled at something Nicholas said, and Noelle watched his blue eyes light up. The tension he'd been suf-fering over the last few days eased in the safety and comfort of Collingwood House's drawing room. No band of thieves would dare harm Noelle here.

He turned his eyes to her, and suddenly she understood why he hadn't insisted she stay under his care. Gavin could have fought Eva, and won, if he'd wanted to keep her. But he knew very well she would be safer with the duke and duchess. In more ways than just worrying about the thieves, he was protecting her from himself. He wouldn't be tempted to take her innocence if she wasn't always underfoot. And from previous experience, he was *very* tempted.

"I made the right decision," Eva broke in. Noelle turned to find her sister looking keenly at Gavin. "With the blow to your head, I knew you wouldn't be able to make a clear and rational decision where that man is concerned. You look at him as if he is covered in cream and strawberries and you haven't eaten in weeks. It was only a matter of time before you gave in to your desires and ruined yourself."

Ruined herself? Of course she wanted to ruin herself. That was entirely the point. A point best kept to herself.

"I am not a child. I'm older than you." Noelle's voice was louder than intended and drew the attention of the men. She turned pointedly away and lowered her voice. It didn't take shouting to show her displeasure. "If I choose to take a lover, it is my choice."

Eva sipped her tea, then lowered her cup to the table. "I agree. I am not one to judge. Nicholas and I were lovers before we wed." Eva's eyes softened as she looked at her husband. "However, I'm a courtesan's daughter, and you are gently bred. You have to live by a different set of rules."

The love in Eva's eyes made Noelle's heart ache. When Gavin couldn't come up with a single happily married couple who were devoted and loyal to each other, Noelle could. Nicholas would give up a limb rather than ever look with lust at another woman. If all matches were so happy, Noelle wouldn't have such qualms about marriage. Unfortunately, they weren't. Eva and Nicholas were the exception.

Her sister continued, "Your connection to Mister Blackwell is built on the excitement of this game. Now, I am not saying you wouldn't find Mister Blackwell attractive in a dull setting, too, so do stop scowling. However, you need to look at the situation rationally. A few days ago you were determined to dry up like autumn leaves in your spinsterhood, and now you want to take a lover?" Eva shook her head. "If Mister Blackwell can get you to give up that notion and take you to be his wife, not only will I accept your choice, I'll push you into his bed and lock the door on my way out."

Noelle stared, surprised. Not too long ago her sister and she had shared the desire not to wed. Now Eva was happily matched, Margaret was happily matched, and both had turned on her, determined to find her a husband she could love.

It didn't matter what she wanted.

"I want what's best for you," Eva added. "And I want you to make the choice with a clear mind." She reached out to close her hand over Noelle's. "And I want you to be safe. I need you."

"I need you, too." Noelle patted her hand.

"Then it is settled." Eva nodded. "You will do as I say and keep away from that man. He is troublesome."

Noelle frowned. When, exactly, had she consented? "I never agreed to do any such thing." She blew her breath upward and fluttered her hair. "When did you become so disagreeable, Sister dear?"

Lately Eva had become a grumbling bear. Even the maids fled when they saw her coming. It was an odd change. The staff of Collingwood House adored their new duchess. They usually ran to her, not away. Something was amiss, and it didn't entirely encompass Eva's concern for her. She'd been unsettled for several weeks, since before the necklace caper. "Where is the sweet sister I have grown to love?"

"Sweet" would not be the best word to describe Eva, and they both knew it. Contrary, stubborn, loyal, opinionated, fearless, beautiful. Sweet was Margaret. She was the opposite of Noelle and Eva in temperament. Well, truthfully, opposite in every way.

Eva's eyes welled as she peered at Nicholas. Noelle was

taken aback by the sudden rush of emotion. Was the marriage not as happy as she'd thought? Was he mistreating Eva? If he'd harmed her sister in any way, there would be serious consequences.

She shot her brother-in-law a dark glower. He grinned.

"If you continue to dice up my husband with daggers in your glare," Eva said, "our child will come into this world fatherless."

Noelle gaped as the comment took a heartbeat or two to sink in. "A child? You're having a baby?"

She let out a squeal and jumped to her feet. In seconds the sisters were clutching each other tightly and crying. Noelle pulled back, smiling. "I cannot believe you're to be a mother." She sniffed and hugged Eva again. "What a difference a year can make."

Nicholas joined them, and Noelle hugged him, too. There was none of the stiffness usually associated with a ducal title between him and his new family. Too much had happened in their recent past to stand on formality.

When the initial fuss settled, the duke put an arm around his wife. They beamed at each other as if the child was the greatest gift ever accomplished between two people. And it was. The child would be adored by its unusual little family.

"I will be an aunt. Again," Noelle remarked softly. Margaret was days away from giving birth. Soon there would be two babies to love.

Noelle was stunned that, along with her joy, there came a sudden rush of sadness. She'd never know what it felt like to hold and love a child of her own. It wasn't something a spinster could do without the baby being born a bastard. Until this moment, she had never truly considered what she was giving up when choosing not to wed. A baby. Gavin's baby?

Involuntarily, her eyes went to Gavin, who stood just outside their small family group. He was looking at her with an odd expression.

Could he see the aching need in her eyes? He'd never bed her if he knew that deep inside, she was wishing his seed would find a fertile home in her womb. Just as quickly, she felt somewhat ill at even considering the notion of purposely wishing him into fatherhood. And Noelle would never want a bastard's life for a child of hers.

Her womb would remain barren.

She coughed, hoping to hide the tears rising behind her lids. "Excuse me. All this excitement is overwhelming. I need some air."

Noelle felt three pairs of eyes on her as she fled the room, down the hallway and out the front door.

Dusk was settling, giving the sun a respite behind the horizon. The brisk, damp air of a brief earlier shower hit her flushed face with a slap, and she inhaled deeply. The scent of wet leaves and damp grass was pulled into her lungs as she gasped past the overwhelming desire to cry for a child she couldn't and wouldn't ever have.

What was wrong with her? Not once had she ever longed to be a mother. Not until a few minutes ago. Watching her mother live with her unhappiness in marriage and, truthfully, in motherhood had long quelled any desire to make her own family. Why had this changed the instant she'd discovered Eva was with child?

She was thrilled for her sisters! She was! Then why was there a crushing burn of envy in the pit of her stomach?

Noelle rubbed her arms and bowed her head in shame.

Behind her the door opened with a muted creak. The booted footfalls crossing the narrow porch toward her were not Eva's. She didn't need to turn around to know it was Gavin. How easily she'd grown capable of feeling his presence, even when she couldn't see him.

His coat brushed against her back as he stepped close and his hands came down on her shoulders. She closed her eyes and lowered the side of her face onto his knuckles.

"Your sister is worried you've taken a turn." He eased her back against him and slid his arms around her. "I had to convince her it was the heat of the fire you were suffering from, lest she call for the physician."

There was understanding in his voice. He, too, had

learned to read her emotions. At the moment she needed him, he'd come to her again. Her rescuer, the man she loved.

"I am excited for them, I truly am." She felt the need to explain herself. She didn't want to be selfish. "The last year has been overwhelming."

Noelle felt adrift. "It was always Margaret and me together. My mother never wanted much to do with us. Our nanny was the woman who raised us. Mother saw us only as extensions of our father, and rarely spent a moment concerning herself about our welfare." Noelle leaned her head back, and he put his chin on her head. "I knew about Eva for years and wanted to meet her. It was bumpy at first, but I grew to love her. We are three sisters now."

She eased from his embrace and faced him. "She was already involved with Nicholas when we met, and they married shortly after. It was only a few weeks after Margaret married Harold." She hated herself for feeling selfish but had to go on. "Now they are both carrying babies, and I feel—" Her throat closed. She was a horrible person. Just horrible!

"Left behind?" Gavin finished for her. He reached out to take her hands. She bit her lip. "You lived with a cold, heartless mother who spilled her bitterness onto her innocent children. In spite of that, you chose to love a sister whom most people would scorn for her illegitimacy. Now both of your sisters are carrying babies. It is understandable that you are envious of their good fortune."

Her eyes widened. "You don't think I am terribly selfish to want more time with Eva, just us two?"

Gavin smiled softly and bent to kiss her head. "It is a bit late for that, love. But don't fret. You and she will have many days together, before and after the babe comes." He looked into her eyes. "I saw the joy in your face for the duke and duchess. You reveled in their happiness." He lifted her hands to his mouth and pressed kisses on each set of knuckles in turn. "As you said, this is all overwhelming. You must give yourself time to get accustomed to all the changes in your life, before you decide to drown yourself in the Thames."

Noelle let out an unladylike snort, and her mouth quirked. "I would never take such a measure. Leaping from the Tower of London is swifter." She sighed, her smile turning pensive. "I will be the best spinster aunt two children could ever want." The idea of spinsterhood had never looked so bleak. She forced herself to move past her gloomy thoughts. "My sisters will resent all the spoiling."

Gavin grinned in the lamplight. "I cannot see you tucked behind high, stiff lace, your corset so snug that you have a permanent pinched expression, and a tight bun pulling your eyes back to a cat-slant. Such circumstances are better left to young ladies without beauty or prospects. Not for you."

The last several days had changed her somehow. It had become more and more difficult to imagine, after how much she'd enjoyed the sensuous liberties Gavin had taught her, spending the rest of her life without kisses and seductive touches.

She looked into his eyes. "I shall get used to it. Women through history have lived with much worse. I have family and wealth. I do not have to worry about living in poverty. My father made sure my mother, sisters, and I would be cared for in the event of his death. For his consideration and the freedom it brings, I will always be grateful. I can be a spinster if I choose."

"If I were you, I wouldn't settle for such a grim and lonely path, dearest Noelle. You never know what your future will bring."

Noelle didn't look up but stared at his lips as his head lowered. Silently she begged him to kiss her, and when he did, she melted into him.

Watching from the window above, Eva tensed. Blackwell kissed her sister and slipped his arms around her. Noelle hugged him around the neck and knitted her fingers in his hair. Even from a distance, Eva could see the passion flare between them. If they weren't careful, she thought angrily, they'd set fire to the house.

"Mister Blackwell has no shame," Eva said through clenched teeth. The forward American needed a hearty slap. Unfortunately, that didn't look like her sister's intention. Noelle was too busy pressing her breasts against the man to consider any sort of propriety. "Anyone traveling past the house can see him take advantage of my sister."

Nicholas walked over and looked out. He slid an arm around Eva's waist and snuggled her against his side. "The trees give them a measure of privacy from the street. You needn't worry, darling. Noelle can take care of herself." He leaned to nuzzle her temple. "If you recall, she took me to task several times when I misbehaved with you before we wed. She is a strong-willed woman and not one to rush into fire. She will make a right decision when it comes to Blackwell."

Eva rested her head against his shoulder. The happiness and then sadness in Noelle's face, when she heard about the baby, had wrenched at her heart. Noelle's desire to remain unmarried was clearly warring with her intense capacity to love a family of her own. And Eva had seen the way Noelle looked at that blasted American. Though she might not realize it yet, Eva's older sister was very much in love.

"How can I not worry? She has never met anyone like him. He was raised among savages. He could be a dangerous felon."

A soft chuckle sounded. "There are no savages in Boston, sweet, and Blackwell is no criminal but a man of means. Need I remind you he comes from good stock? No matter how much he wants to ravish her, he will do right by your sister."

Eva narrowed her eyes. "Can you make me a guarantee?"

"I cannot." Nicholas ran a hand up from her waist to her rib cage and teased the side of her breast with his thumb. "I can assure you, your worry or wishes will not change her feelings. If her nature is as passionate as yours, sweetheart, there will be nothing you can say or do that will stop her from plunging into an affair." He glanced out the window and grinned. "A steel bar couldn't break them apart."

"Her ravishment is what I worry about." Eva grimaced, even as she warmed under her husband's casual fondling. Nicholas did know how to distract her. But at the moment, she was having none of it. She caught his hand to cease further exploration. "You tease, but when she begins to swell with child, it will be you, as head of our family, who has to deal with the consequences."

Her dark and handsome husband spun her around and tucked her tightly against him. Nicholas bent and nuzzled her neck. She sighed. "Then I will drag him before a priest myself," he said as he nibbled her earlobe. "Men cannot seduce and impregnate a Harrington woman and escape shackles. Even if I have to chase him all the way back to Boston myself."

Nicholas eased her away from the open draperies and pressed her against the wall. Eva knew he couldn't be too free with his hands; the hallway door was open, and her sister and guest were kissing below. Still, a few stolen caresses would be delightful.

This time it was Eva who grinned as she slipped a hand around to cup one of his sculpted buttocks. Months of marriage hadn't dimmed her desire for Nicholas in the least. He was a passionate man, and she was a very lucky woman. "I shall hold you to your word, Your Grace. For I intend to see my sister wed, and from the looks of the improper behavior below, I suppose Blackwell will have to do."

Nicholas lifted his face. There was a look of pity in his eyes. "Lord help poor Mister Blackwell."

Chapter Twenty-Three

"Though this outing isn't meant for my rescue, I thank you for saving me from my sister," Noelle said early the next afternoon when Gavin arrived to take her on an excursion to Hyde Park. He wanted to ride through the park to see if he could spot the mysterious woman in the sketch, and Noelle insisted on tagging along. The day was cool and threatened rain, but when he offered to cancel and return on a better day, she literally dragged him from the house by the hand. "I think Eva has decided to practice her mothering skills on me. If she chooses to continue the practice of smothering with the baby, the poor little dear is in for quite a time of it."

Gavin chuckled and maneuvered the gig around a stopped carriage with well-executed skill. "If she reaches for a nappy, run. Fast."

Noelle smiled and scanned the area as the horse trotted down the tree-lined path. The air was thick and the sky overcast, yet the park was ever so lovely in vibrant green. After her recent days spent cloistered inside, this park and fresh air were a welcome respite.

Gavin and Eva had protested profusely over her choice

of outing wear when she'd come down the stairs to greet him. Tucked under her cloak, Noelle had donned a courtesan disguise, complete with a wig and veil, and refused to change.

She'd suffered enough at the hands of the footpads and wasn't about to be seen in public with Gavin, for fear of alerting possible spies to her real identity, until the criminals were rounded up and jailed.

By now they had to have figured out Gavin and his cousin were two different men. Too much time had passed not to come to that realization. The attack on Gavin at the shipyard had been perpetrated by three men without a clear set of facts. Though the earl had invested in the shipyard, he certainly wouldn't toil there. Obviously, they'd seen only Gavin come and go from the house the day after Noelle's break-in, and it had confused the thugs.

Noelle nervously glanced around. "Do you think you, we, are still in danger?"

"It's hard to determine," Gavin said. "The necklace is very valuable. It would be difficult for the thieves to give it up after all they've done to steal it."

"But the earl has it now."

"True. Do the thieves know that? It's hard to say." He flicked the reins. "We suspect they figured out the necklace had been returned to Charles's town house. Bliss admitted she'd expressed fear of arrest to the maid after she'd taken the piece."

"And she ran off immediately afterward," Noelle said, "before the maid could get her sticky fingers on it."

"So the maid probably assumed Bliss had gone to Charles and confessed her crime. They'd have no idea she'd fled to the courtesan school."

"And turned the necklace over to me," Noelle said grimly. She very much wanted to put the entire caper behind her.

"Charles left early that next morning, so I was the only person, aside from the staff, to be seen at the town house in the days following Bliss's disappearance. The thieves are probably so confused right now, as they have no idea where the necklace is. All we can do is hope they end their obsession over the piece."

"I agree." If not, and the culprits were still lurking, she wasn't about to let the remainder of the trio, and their leader, remain free to harm another soul while she sat in her sister's stuffy parlor under a heavy pile of blankets and Eva treated her like a blasted invalid. Though she dearly loved Eva, living with her was proving to be a challenge.

Hence the disguise. Gavin could still be in danger. Everyone around him could still be in danger. Her attendance at the ball was proof of that. She hated the idea of putting herself in danger again, and had struggled over what to do. But until she was absolutely certain the trouble was over, she had to fight her fears. She couldn't bear the idea that he could be injured or killed over the necklace. She had to help, and the disguise was the only way to stay close to him while looking for the mysterious woman.

The quicker Crawford and Gavin made sure the danger was over, the sooner Gavin would no longer have to look over his shoulder. Then Noelle could be seen with him publicly, as herself, without the thugs regarding her as a possible tool to get him to turn over the necklace.

"What of Charles? He might be targeted."

Gavin nodded. "I sent word. He assures me he is taking precautions to keep his family safe."

When she decided to throw off caution and become an adventuress, she hadn't thought that just over a week later, she'd be aching for her normal life. She desperately wanted to return home and sleep in her own bed. With Gavin, if she had her druthers. Tossing and turning at night in a heated state had become unbearable. She needed him without delay. And to accomplish her wish, she had to get well enough for Eva to give her blessing for Noelle's escape from Collingwood House.

Then her life would again be her own.

"I don't see Mister Crawford or the men he hired to watch over you," Noelle remarked as she looked about.

"If you see them, then they aren't doing their job properly.

Now stop craning your neck before you fall out of the carriage and ruin your disguise."

Self-consciously, she reached up to assure herself that her lower face was still covered. Without the added blessing of darkness, she felt exposed. "Are you certain no one will know me?"

Gavin gave her a brief look. "Love, even I don't know you," he assured her for the tenth time.

Beneath her dove gray pelisse, she was dressed in a very low-cut gown of rose silk with cap sleeves and tiny roses framing the bodice. Her wig was pinned securely on her head, and with the powder covering her face in a thick layer of white, she portrayed a cherished courtesan, a role she intended to continue once she got Gavin alone.

She touched the beauty patch. "Truly?"

"You are unrecognizable, love." Unlike married men, Gavin had no qualms about being seen gallivanting about London with a mistress seated beside him. As an unmarried man, he could publicly consort with whomever he chose. In fact, doing so with a lovely courtesan would probably elevate him in the eyes of his male friends.

Noelle chewed on her bottom lip. "Are you certain you weren't followed to Collingwood House?"

"Crawford assured me he would follow whenever I go out. Since he didn't sound an alarm, all is well."

Still, Noelle wished she could at least know where Crawford was, in case one of the thieves decided to show himself. She was aware Gavin had a pistol tucked in his waistband, as it had bumped up against her several times during their drive. She took comfort in knowing her kidnapping would not be repeated. Gavin would kill anyone who tried.

So she settled back to scan faces in coaches and carriages for women who resembled their target. Though the weather kept most of society inside, there was a decent crowd filling the paths. She hoped to see their mystery lady in the mass.

After about five minutes, she was fidgeting in her seat again and emitting more than a few impatient sighs. Not a single face even slightly matched the sketch. "We'll never find her. She'll remain a mystery, and you shall have to live your life looking over your shoulder."

Gavin pulled over to the side and reined to a stop. Eva's fat little gray pony-horse, Muffin, dropped her head to rip up some grass. Relatively new to London, and temporarily living under his cousin's roof, Gavin hadn't yet purchased a carriage horse or rig. He had no need for anything but his horse or a hackney to get around, so Eva had offered hers for the outing. What the little mare lacked in the refinement of the grander horses favored by the gentry, she made up for with a sweet disposition.

And since Muffin was mostly retired from service and wouldn't be recognized as belonging to the new duchess, she was the perfect choice to squire them about the park.

"We've spent an entire"—Gavin paused and looked down at his pocket watch—"seven minutes driving about. Surely you can summon up the patience to manage seven more before deciding this outing is a waste of time and energy."

Noelle stared at his cocked brow and eyes alight with humor, and notched up her nose. "Must you fault me for wanting to see this caper end with a quick and satisfying conclusion?" She skimmed her fingers over the tender spot at her temple.

"Everyone is working quickly and diligently to see this end," he reminded her. "You will have your justice, Noelle."

A carriage slowly rumbled past, carrying the Baroness Brightman and her pretty but dreadfully dull daughter Minerva. Noelle resisted the instinct to wave. Courtesans did not wave at baronesses. She lowered her hand and waited until the carriage rounded the corner before turning back to Gavin.

"I plan to find the mystery woman and see her covered with honey and staked over a nest of ground wasps," she said sharply. "And that is only the beginning."

Gavin shook his head, smiling. "Remind me never to anger you, My Lady courtesan. You have a very evil mind."

"Perhaps wasps are a bit harsh. A week in the stockade, then off to Australia for an existence of hard labor should be satisfactory. Anything less than life in a penal colony would be a travesty for what this woman has done to me."

Still, no matter how the woman's actions had caused her suffering, Noelle couldn't see her locked in Newgate. No woman deserved that vile place. She still lived under the lingering worry that the earl would yet decide to have her and Bliss arrested. There was only Gavin's assurance that she was safe.

"Once she has been sent into exile and this case has been settled, what are your plans?" Gavin eased Muffin farther off the path as a large coach bearing an unfamiliar crest hurried past. "Will you go back to planning your spinsterhood? Or will you cast word about that you have decided to forgo such a charming institution and are seeking a husband after all? I'm certain there are several men who would eagerly line up for a chance to wed you."

She stared blankly into his face. Her chest tightened.

The causal way he mentioned a husband took her aback. Would he be happy to see her wed some humorless, whey-faced nobleman with sweaty palms and a permanent pinched expression? Would it be so easy to fob her off on another man and forget her?

She'd almost died to help him. She'd risked her heart. Now he casually mentioned marrying her off as if he had no feelings for her in the least.

Once the danger was over, he'd simply walk away.

Take me home." Noelle clenched her jaw to keep from crying. Thankfully, the veil hid the telltale tremble of her bottom lip.

"Noelle, what is it?" He reached for her arm, but she pulled free.

"Take me home," she repeated. "If you cannot follow a simple instruction, then I will find someone who will." She glanced down the path and saw the Earl of Blakemore heading toward them at a clip on the back of a large white horse. "The earl will make an excellent escort."

She made to rise, and Gavin caught her firmly by the arm. "Have you lost your senses?" he snapped. He jerked her back down in the seat, and his jaw twitched as he watched Blakemore ride past. "You cannot wave him down dressed like a courtesan. What would he think to discover you are Lady Seymour?"

In her haste to rid herself of Gavin, she'd forgotten her disguise. She slumped back on the seat.

"Taking you home is an excellent idea. Clearly your head injury is worse than I feared. You have gone insane." He grumbled something about her, the earl, and the footpads under his breath. And it wasn't flattering.

Noelle took satisfaction in knowing she'd angered him and he had no clue why. It mattered not what he thought about her. She averted her head to keep him from seeing her tears.

Gavin Blackwell: American, Englishman, shipbuilder, cad. Why did he have to be the one she'd given her heart, just to have him stomp all over it with his polished boots?

She never should have fallen in love with him! It changed her perspective on her life, marriage, and children. She never planned to have either. And they were still barely on the fringe of consideration. But the fact that she was considering them at all, with a man who clearly didn't think of anything beyond sharing a bed, was painful.

Perhaps she *should* find herself a husband just to spite him. Then again, he'd have to care to feel the spite. And since she had no father to see her wed, he'd probably walk her up the aisle of the church and gladly hand her over to her new husband. Maybe even toast the newly married couple at their wedding supper.

He'd likely be happy to rid himself of her troublesome presence. She'd been nothing but a bother since they met. His face still held proof of her crimes in faded smudges of yellow beneath his sun-dark skin.

"Do you plan to tell me the reason for this sudden change of temperament, or do you plan to ride the rest of the way back in silence?" The question came out in a growl. She stubbornly refused to answer. "As you wish."

Gavin clucked his tongue. Muffin sped up from slow to not as slow. The horse had only one speed.

It was several long minutes of misery before Gavin finally pulled up to the stable behind Collingwood House. By then, Noelle was covered in her cloak to hide her disguise, and she didn't wait for him to alight and help her down. She scrambled from the gig as the groom took control of Muffin.

She brushed past Gavin, pushed open the garden gate, and hurried up the path. If she'd hoped her curt dismissal would keep him from harassing her further, his footsteps behind her divested her of that notion.

Just outside the kitchen door, she quickly pulled off her veil and wig and shoved them into her valise. She dug for her handkerchief and quickly scrubbed off the beauty mark and makeup as best she could without a mirror. He stopped a few steps from her, but she refused to acknowledge him and jerked open the door.

The kitchen staff openly gawked as she stomped through the warm, yeasty-smelling space and into the hallway.

Continuing through the house at a rapid clip, Noelle managed to get to the stairs before he caught up with her.

"Noelle."

Before he could continue, a door opened above, and Eva and Nicholas walked into view. Eva must have seen something on Noelle's face that caused her to ask, "Is there something the matter, Sister?"

Noelle expelled a harsh breath. "Men are so daft."

Without a look back at Gavin, she turned and walked stiffly up the stairs.

Gavin rubbed his hands over his face and sighed. Women were so difficult to understand and so emotionally unstable. Quick to smile, quick to tears. One minute he and Noelle were having a perfectly innocent conversation, and the next she was behaving like he'd committed a crime against her. And she called him daft?

"If I have learned anything from living with a Harrington woman, Blackwell, it is that you cannot understand them, no matter how hard you try." The duke came down the stairs and joined him in the huge foyer. "I think you need a drink."

Gavin followed the duke to the library and accepted a splash of brandy. "When dealing with your sister-in-law, one needs a suit of chain mail to fend off the arrows she shoots from her sharp tongue." Gavin downed the brandy and held out his glass. His Grace chuckled and filled it to the top. "May I live to a right ancient age, I will not understand her."

"The duchess led me on quite a chase from our very first meeting." His Grace grinned widely. "Before I realized what was happening, she'd stolen my heart." He gave Gavin a pitying glance. "I think, sir, you have been hooked by a Harrington."

"Nonsense." Gavin scowled. "I have no intention to wed."

His Grace laughed with open merriment and clapped him on the shoulder. "Eva stole my courtesan. I despised Eva. She was a drab spinster with not a single interesting quality. You wouldn't know it by looking at her now."

Gavin stared. "Her Grace, a drab spinster?"

The duke nodded. "I planned to live my life a bachelor. My father was an angry bastard, and I was following the same path. I couldn't wish my temperament on any woman. My wife tied me into knots until I knew I couldn't live my life without her." He winked and threw back his brandy. "I wouldn't have it any other way."

A grunt was Gavin's answer. He moved to the fireplace and gulped down half of his second drink. It slid smoothly down his throat. If only his dealings with his courtesan-thief went so well. Noelle twisted him around until he couldn't breathe without thinking of her.

"Noelle is the most contrary woman I have ever met. When I'm with her, she leads me on a merry chase," Gavin grumbled. "When I'm away from her, I cannot push her from my mind. I am an hour or two away from Bedlam, and know not what to do to rectify this situation."

A knowing nod followed the pronouncement. "You *have* been hooked, Blackwell, and there is no solution to your predicament. I know." His Grace clunked his glass on the table and stretched his legs out. Knitting his hands over his stomach, the duke settled down to grin. "You might as well send for the parson, you poor bastard."

Noelle knew Gavin had left after an hour locked up with Nicholas in the library. Eva's maid, who'd been sent down to spy, had informed them when he'd exited the premises. Only then did she stop listening for sounds of him coming up the stairs to confront her again, and she took a deep, calming breath.

After she'd gone up to her room and Eva called for a bath, Noelle had ranted about men and all their foibles for a good half hour. She'd finally admitted most of her bad behavior with Gavin to her sister, in hopes of finding an ally. Instead, she'd been left with Eva threatening to see them wed. Noelle spent another quarter hour convincing her sister not to stomp down to the library and demand that Nicholas write up a marriage agreement.

"He should marry you," Eva said several times during Noelle's rant, and she wasn't about to be put off. Whatever the baby was doing to her body, the little mite had left Eva irritable and fiercely protective. "The man knew the potential consequences of his shameful acts. He shouldn't get away with this unscathed."

Noelle swirled her hand around in the soapy water. No matter how angry she was with Gavin, nor how hurt, she couldn't help wishing it was he, and not Eva, who was tending her bath. "You can force us to marry and turn Gavin and me into my mother and our father." She looked pleadingly into Eva's eyes. "Would you want that life for me?"

Eva sat on the bed, her face awash with concern. "You love him." It wasn't a question but a statement.

Biting her bottom lip, Noelle nodded. "Sadly, I do." She ran a finger over the rim of the copper tub. "He doesn't love me. I will be forgotten once the thieves have been rounded up. He will move on to the next woman, and I will be just a memory."

"I don't believe that." Eva placed a hand over her still-flat belly beneath her simple green muslin gown. "I've seen the way he looks at you. He cares."

Noelle smiled wryly. "I care for lemon tarts. It doesn't mean I wouldn't give them up if my waistline expanded."

"I would hardly put you in the same pile as lemon tarts. Lemon tarts are sweeter," Eva teased soberly. "I think we need to think about Mister Blackwell, and this situation, in an entirely different manner."

"How so?" Noelle braced herself for another press for marriage. Once her sister got a notion in her head, she seldom changed her mind. In that, they were similarly stubborn. Eva was likely already thinking of the cut and fabric best suited for Noelle's bridal gown.

"Do you want to marry him?" Eva asked.

Noelle thought for a moment and answered truthfully. "I'm not certain what I want."

"Still, you want him to love you?"

"I'd be happier if he did." Noelle hated to admit that she wanted Gavin as desperately in love with her as she was with him.

Eva nodded and started to pace. "I have discovered that it isn't the greatest beauties that men desire most, though their first attraction is usually a pretty face. No, what men want is a woman who intrigues them, who has a certain quality about her that is unforgettable." Eva pushed to her feet and walked to the tub. "You intrigued your Mister Blackwell when you broke into his bedroom. Now you need to find a way to make absolutely certain he will never be able to forget you."

"Such as riding through Hyde Park wearing nothing but my hair draped over my breasts?" Noelle's saucy comment was rewarded with an impatient look from her sister.

"That wasn't what I had in mind," Eva replied. "You know him better than I do. I'm certain you can come up with something grand."

She patted Noelle's hand and left her to finish her bath. Eva did have a point. If Noelle wanted Gavin to want her desperately, she had to do something outside the usual. She'd have to come up with an intriguing plot to spin his head around until he could think of nothing but her.

But what if she did hook him and he fell desperately in love with her? What if he flung all caution aside and wanted to marry her? Would she give up all the reasons she never wanted to wed and take him as her husband? Could he vow to remain faithful to her for the rest of his days? Could she trust him at his word even if he made that vow?

She leaned her head back and looked at the ceiling. Was it in her best interest to use her parents' miserable marriage as the measure for every relationship? Her two sisters were gloriously happy in spite of their parents' misery. But would their bliss last for the next forty years?

Somehow, deep inside she knew the love matches would hold. Harold loved Margaret deeply, and Eva and Nicholas had a love so rare that people often remarked how envious they were of the profound happiness of the duke and duchess.

Suddenly, Noelle wanted more from Gavin than a tryst. She wanted what Eva and Nicholas had.

She wanted to marry the exasperating American!

With lightness in her heart, she stood abruptly, spilling water all over the floor. An idea took root that would so shock and delight Gavin that it had to work.

She reached for the towel and vigorously scrubbed her skin. Lemon and cinnamon swirled around her from the bath oil. The scent was a step toward the downfall of Gavin Blackwell. But only the first step. She needed to push him off the cliff.

Padding across the floor with damp bare feet, she went to the wardrobe and dug around in the bottom. Once she discovered the items she was looking for, she caught them against her bosom, giggled with delight, and spun round and round until her head whirled.

Before the evening gave way to dawn tomorrow, Gavin would be fully and completely hers.

Chapter Twenty-Four

Confidence and an overriding desire to show Gavin she was unforgettable made the climb up the trellis easier the second time around. She'd sent a footman to inquire, discreetly of course, as to the whereabouts of the earl, and learned he was still in Bath with his family. This left the town house, and Gavin, to her.

She'd borrowed Thomas from the courtesan school, knowing he would keep her secrets, and asked him to help her get to the earl's town house undetected. To her surprise, he was quite good at sneak thievery. They passed through several gardens and over a fence without raising an alarm. If there were spies watching the town house, they'd certainly not seen anything unusual.

Eva had a way of finding men who were fiercely loyal, and had shadowy histories, to protect her courtesans. Noelle was pleased to discover Thomas was a perfect, if a bit stoic, partner in mischief.

And he'd promised to continue to watch over her until she was safely inside the house. She was grateful for his help and for his not judging her behavior.

Now, if she could manage to put her feet on level footholds, and not drop to the ground in a bloody heap, she might actually prove to Gavin she was worth his attention.

And love.

If she ever wanted to take up burglary, she might very well have a successful career, she thought, as she managed to get the window open with ease and step into the darkened bedroom. One would think they'd have learned a lesson from her previous break-in and would have locked the window. Obviously, it wasn't a matter of great concern.

Thank goodness.

In a matter of minutes, she was through the green bedroom and into the hallway. A thin trail of light flickered beneath Gavin's door as she paused to steady her heart and to summon up courage. She was about to take a huge plunge into the unknown, and she wanted to be bold. Knocking knees and quivering hands did not an adventuress make.

The door was unlocked and gave naught but a small squeak as she pushed it open and stepped inside. Though the light was low and the room dim, she could see Gavin stretched out on the bed, a sheet partially covering his lower body.

Pity. Still, his finely sculpted chest was flushed with golden firelight and bared for her perusal. She touched her tongue to her bottom lip, her hands aching to caress him, wanting desperately to draw her mouth over his beautiful body.

Unhurried, yet eager to begin the seduction, Noelle took a few steps forward. As she closed the distance, she discovered he was not sleeping, but intently watching her approach.

"Good evening," she said, stopping in her tracks. She offered him a small, and what she hoped was a confident, smile. "I was passing by with my first mate, Thomas, and saw your light on. With his help, I managed to cleverly avoid the patrol and slip into the garden unseen. I thought I'd pop in for tea and cakes."

One corner of his mouth cocked up into a crooked grin. "You look like a pirate, Milady."

Noelle looked down to her uncle's black breeches, which she'd taken and hastily hemmed, and the borrowed white shirt whose sleeves she'd rolled up to the elbows and covered with a dark coat. He was in India and would never miss them. A square of red scarf tied casually around her waist held the trousers up, and another tied her hair back at the neck. Her slippers were out of place for the costume, but her uncle's boots were too big for her to wear when making the climb up the trellis.

"That is why I was traveling through the neighborhood." She shucked off the coat and shifted her hips to a jaunty angle. "I was on my way to steal a ship to sail the seven seas. And since we are friends, and you saved my life, I couldn't leave these shores behind without saying good-bye or making a heartfelt apology for my earlier behavior."

His mouth twitched. "I accept your apology." He locked his hands behind his head and nodded. "Well, good-bye, then. Be sure to write."

The casual farewell didn't match the heat and intensity in his eyes as he lowered his attention in a sweeping path over the oversized shirt to where her nipples pressed the fabric in tight buds. He knew her game and was as open to playing as she was. The night was theirs to explore.

"Certainly, a life saved calls for a more enthusiastic farewell, my dear Mister Blackwell." She reached up to untie the scarf from her hair. The effort caused the shirt to stretch over her unbound breasts. She knew rosy flesh showed through the thin cloth. His breathing stopped.

She'd breached his reserve.

A shake of her head tumbled her hair over her shoulders and down her back. She had his full attention. He'd never allow her to leave the room now, game or not. They both knew how the evening would end and eagerly welcomed the hours ahead.

"You have beautiful hair, My Lady pirate," he said softly. Gavin shifted, and Noelle saw proof of his arousal beneath the sheet. He was steely hard. "You should never wear it bound."

Several strands fell over her eye. She peered at him from beneath the silky mass. "I do think my hair has merit." She reached for the scarf tenuously holding up the large breeches. "I have always wondered about my legs. I used to think them skinny. Perhaps you can offer an opinion." With a tug, the trousers were around her ankles. She casually kicked them aside.

Gavin jerked his eyes wide. The move had been unexpected, and had the hoped-for effect on him. Noelle smiled seductively and slowly peeled off her garters and stockings. She let them flutter to the floor. Only a little wedge of shirttail kept him from viewing the patch of pale curls at the vee of her thighs.

She turned this way and that, assuring herself he could see her legs from all angles. She had been a skinny child. No more. She thought her legs one of her best features. From the look on his face, he wasn't disappointed.

"They're passable." His voice was tight. He shifted, and Noelle suspected his erection was growing painful. She understood from the courtesans how men sometimes found full arousal uncomfortable. She intended to raise the stakes until he was mad for her body.

"Passable?" She frowned. She knew he teased. He couldn't keep his eyes off her thighs. "Then I shall cover them so as not to offend." She turned sideways and bent to retrieve the trousers. The shirt slid up to expose the curve of one hip and buttock.

A groan broke from him. "Don't you dare touch those trousers."

Slowly, Noelle straightened, leaving the trousers where they lay. She opened her eyes wide. "Hmm. There must be something about me you find interesting besides my hair?" She tapped a fingertip on her chin. "I think I know." With deliberate slowness, she slid her hands down her body to catch up the hem of the shirt with her fingers. She turned around on her toes.

She lifted the hem just enough to expose a tiny bit of the lower cleft of her bottom.

"Dear God, woman." His voice was hoarse and tight.

Noelle squelched a laugh. She dropped the hem and spun back. "Clearly my rump is not to your liking either. You seem pained to look upon it." His face was flushed, and she was certain there was a dotting of sweat on his brow. His body was tense, coiled, and hard. And so very wonderful.

He was nearing the point of breaking. It wouldn't take much to throw him off the cliff. So she reclaimed the hem with both hands and grinned wickedly.

"Perhaps this is more to your liking, sir." With one swoop, she drew the shirt up over her body and cast it aside. Her hair fell in waves about her. She was fully bared to his eyes.

"You are a wicked wench, Lady Seymour."

Noelle hadn't had time to savor her victory when he launched himself from the bed and padded barefoot to her, his fully aroused male member saluting like a steel staff as he walked. Clearly the man was unashamed of his body. From what she could see, he had no reason to be anything but confident.

She let out a small yelp as he bent to lift her and carried her to the bed. Gavin dropped her in the center with a bounce. She had just enough time to gasp before he was over her and claiming her mouth in a bruising kiss.

Ripples of pleasure flashed over her skin. He lowered himself enough to tease her with parts of his muscled frame as he brushed against her bare body with his equally naked hips and chest. The friction of their skin aroused her further.

He kissed her breathless, plunging his tongue into her mouth, mating their tongues together. When he finally lifted his head, she fell deep into his intense eyes.

"You drive me to madness, love." He dragged his mouth over hers, briefly, and then trailed kisses across her jaw and down the side of her neck.

"I want you so desperately," she breathed, and ran her hands through the thick softness of his hair. He rained kisses over her shoulder blades, down between her breasts, then up to pull a nipple into his mouth.

Noelle let out a cry-gasp. The pleasure of his sucking mouth left her weightless. He laved the peak with his mouth and tweaked the other nipple with his fingertips. She felt like she was floating outside of her body, but oddly, she wasn't afraid. She watched him tease and delight her with his mouth, until he lifted his face to grin into her eyes.

"If you like that, you will love this." He pushed backward down her body, kissing and caressing the entire length in slow, measured strokes. Her sighs encouraged him, and he occasionally grinned against her skin. Before she could collect clues to his ultimate intentions, he had her legs spread and all but the top of his head had disappeared between her thighs.

A thrill of alarm broke through her the second she felt warm breath on the tight nub, the core of her femininity. She tried to close her legs. His seeking mouth wouldn't allow her to succumb to embarrassment. His tongue brushed across the pulsing spot, and she cried out as a thrill of pleasure arched her backward. He had delighted her body with his mouth for a time when she felt him slip a fingertip inside her damp sheath.

She gasped out his name when her body became no longer her own. She was burning, moaning, begging him with sobbing breaths to ease the torture and give her the release she sought.

He moved his finger gently inside and out, tugging at the nub with his lips, while she bucked against his hand and mouth. Frenzied, with a final cry, Noelle plunged up and over into a whirling abyss.

Gavin chuckled as she went slack. He moved up and over her to press a few more kisses on her breasts, her neck, and her lips. Noelle smiled sleepily as he positioned himself between her legs and pressed the tip of his erection against her body.

"Make me yours, Gavin," she begged softly.

With one hand, he placed himself at the opening of her sheath. She writhed against him, encouraged him, wanted him, with quiet desperation, to end her innocence and finally let her know what it meant to be a woman. Gently, he eased inside her and she encompassed his hard length.

"Careful, sweet." He leaned to kiss her. "I understand a woman's first time can be painful."

Noelle locked onto his gaze. The tenderness in his eyes closed her throat. He would never intentionally hurt her; she knew it in her heart. "I trust you, Gavin. Completely."

Suddenly, his expression changed, softened. Noelle ran her fingertips down his rib cage, and the muscles flexed under her searching hand. His body was strong and powerful, yet tender, too. He didn't release her gaze as he eased himself further inside her. When he reached the barrier of her innocence, he thrust deep.

She whimpered. The breach caused some pain, but not extreme discomfort. Gavin rocked gently, giving her time to adjust to his presence. Within minutes, pleasure built again.

Instinct took over, and she rocked with him as his thrusts deepened and became more intense. She moaned softly, reveling in the feel of him inside her, and his soft skin beneath her hands, as she drew them over his muscled back and down to cup his firm, thrusting, and perfect buttocks.

He reached between them and again touched the tiny bud.

For the second time, Gavin brought her to the release she sought. Brief moments later, he groaned and buried himself to the hilt, shuddered, and spilled himself inside her.

Sated, Noelle closed her eyes and pulled in a deep breath. Never in her life had she felt so complete, so loved. And to think she'd once planned to cling to her innocence and spinsterhood with both hands. It would have been shameful never to experience the delights of lovemaking with this handsome and giving man.

As she lay beneath Gavin and slid her hands over him, she didn't regret the loss of her virginity.

"Are you hurt?" he asked. He eased off of her and settled beside her, a bent hand tucked beneath the side of his head. He examined her body carefully, touching a small red mark on her rib cage where he'd nipped her.

Shaking her head against the pillow, she slipped a hand around his neck. His expression was slack, sated, his hair falling across his eye. There was a boyish happiness in his expression, as if he'd been given a fantastic new toy to play with.

But it was she who'd been given a perfect gift. She brushed a fingertip over his smiling mouth that had pleasured her so fully. "Just the opposite. I feel wonderful. Though I fear I have lost the wager. I thought sexual encounters were only an unwelcome means for procreation. I'm pleased to find I was mistaken."

Gavin grinned and nipped her finger. "You are a minx, My Lady pirate." He bent and pressed a light kiss on the tip of her nose. "I will treasure this night always."

"As will I."

G avin kissed her lush mouth and inhaled the fragrance of lemon and cinnamon and lovemaking. He'd suspected fire in Noelle from their first kiss. However, these moments with her had changed everything he thought about her, about virgins, about women in general. There was nothing about her, in her, that was deceptive or false, as Anne had been. Noelle had come willingly to his bedroom with nothing more than the desire to share herself, with him to guide her. She'd wanted him as he wanted her, and her passion had stolen his breath away.

His Lady courtesan-thief was bewitching, beguiling, and beautiful. His heart tugged as he looked into her face, into her soft and gentle eyes.

There'd been so much to learn about Noelle, about Lady Seymour, when he'd explored beneath her sometimes prickly surface to see what she kept hidden. She'd used her often unhappy childhood to protect herself from harm, and he suspected this was the first time she'd ever fully let her walls come down.

Why she'd chosen to do so with him was a puzzle. She'd

trusted him with her innocence, though he'd made her no promises of a future together.

"Had I known you were such a magnificent lover, I'd have come sooner to your bed," she said wistfully. "I have wasted several days when I could have been enjoying your services."

Gavin gave her a funny look. Her gentle touches skimmed over him, exploring. She seemed to want to run her hands over every inch of his flesh, as if she was marking him with her lemony scent, claiming him as hers. And he discovered he was thoroughly smitten with his pirate-courtesan.

"As I recall, you did enjoy my services, twice," he reminded her. "In the coach and in the bath."

She smiled softly. "Yes, but neither compared to this. It was worth my losing your fortune." She let out a dramatic sigh and drew a fingertip across his chest. "You have done some very scandalous things to me tonight that I am sure in some countries could get us both beheaded."

"Indeed?" He dipped his head to circle his tongue around a nipple. The delightful taste of her skin left him light-headed. "You should point out all the things I did that could cause fatal consequences, My Lady. Then I can refrain from doing them in the future."

Her fingertips dug into his flesh. He looked into her eyes. She was frowning; scowling, actually.

"You will not change a thing." She flattened her hand, removing her nails from the flesh of his rump. He suspected it was quickly becoming one of her favorite parts of his anatomy. "I will risk life and head if you do everything you have done to me tonight over, and over, again."

When she'd dropped the breeches, he'd nearly come off the bed. When she'd stripped off her shirt, he'd almost spilled himself on the sheet. Now, as he lay beside her, happily basking in the aftermath of their lovemaking, he was eternally grateful for overgrown ivy on the town house walls and for her trellis-climbing skills.

Gavin raised his brows and stared into her eyes. She

wasn't the slightest bit shy when asking for her needs to be met. He had never known anyone like her, and suspected he never would again. "Everything?"

"Everything," she replied.

He reached to take her into his arms and pulled her sweet body beneath him. "As My Lady wishes."

Chapter Twenty-Five

※◎◎※

Gavin met with Crawford late the next afternoon in Gavin's study. The investigator had turned the battered footpad over to the Bow Street Runners with only a vague explanation of the attack upon Gavin at the wharf, leaving out the rest of the story to protect Noelle's identity and the identity of the woman in the sketch.

Neither Gavin nor Noelle thought revealing the plot would solve their problem, since they hadn't a clue to who the woman was. Getting the Runners involved might drive her into hiding. Then ever finding her could prove an impossible feat. They couldn't take that risk.

"They will hold him until you make a formal complaint, Mister Blackwell." Crawford rocked back on his heels after making his report. "I'm certain you were not the first victim. There may be further charges."

If not for the need to hide Noelle's title and position, they'd have added kidnapping to the list of crimes. That would have seen the thugs locked up for a very long time.

Noelle. Gavin's mouth twitched. Racing the sunrise, he'd regretfully sneaked her out of the town house and insisted on seeing her home. They retraced Thomas's path through the garden and over the neighbor's fence, caught a hackney a few streets over, and managed to get her back to Collingwood House just as the first ray of light broke the horizon. The lengthy and delightful kiss she'd left him with, before she'd slipped into the manor, had capped off an enchanting and memorable night together.

He'd made sure to keep a wary eye open as the coach plodded to Collingwood House, with Noelle tucked against his chest, and then as he returned to the town house. He saw no one lurking in the shadows beyond the streetlamps, and took some comfort in knowing there was little chance the thieves had discovered Noelle's true identity.

"I shall file a complaint in the morning." Gavin looked around the study and couldn't help feeling the loss of Noelle's presence in the house. In a matter of hours, he'd been changed by her. Even now, his body stirred with the memories.

"What of the other two men?" Gavin added, relieved his seat behind the desk hid his rising erection. "Have you discovered any information on them?"

Crawford nodded. "I have learned the identity of a man who suffered serious injuries the night of the kidnapping." He eyes twinkled. "Apparently he broke both an arm and a leg falling from a great height. Though I haven't been able to confirm it was a tumble off a coach, I am off to the hospital to see for myself. I hope to have that mystery cleared up this evening."

"Excellent." Another puzzle piece was moving into place. Two thugs had been eliminated. Gavin was pleased. The sooner the danger to himself and Noelle eased, the quicker he could begin courting her publicly as Lady Seymour.

It didn't matter if their relationship ended in marriage. She was his for as long as they both wanted it to remain so, and he planned to make good use of the time they had together.

A throat cleared and brought his attention around. Crawford was staring at him. He pointed to the housekeeper standing patiently in the open doorway.

Mrs. Mayhew nodded. "The young lady has arrived."

Gavin's heart leapt, and for a moment he thought Noelle had foolishly ignored the danger and showed up at his door. He quickly realized she was not the visitor and settled back in his chair. Crawford rose, went over to welcome the woman, and helped her out of her cloak.

Bliss was indeed stunning. Her dark hair was upswept in a crown around her head, and the deep russet muslin gown she wore accentuated her delicate beauty. It was easy to see why Charles had been besotted with the chit and why Crawford fawned over her as he led her into the room. Had Gavin seen her first, he might well have fought his cousin for a place in her bed.

However, Gavin found he much preferred his pirate to the courtesan. Though most would find the lush beauty of the courtesan more to their liking than the less flashy beauty of Noelle, it was the adventurous spirit and charming wit of the latter that he coveted.

"Please sit down." Gavin skipped pleasantries and indicated a chair. Though Noelle considered Bliss nothing more than a pawn in a game, Gavin couldn't dismiss her completely as a suspect until they questioned her more deeply.

Hence the decision to remove her from the protection of the courtesan school and bring her here for a last interrogation. Thankfully, Crawford had known the address from his previous dealings with Eva, and sent off Charles's steward with a coach to collect her. They didn't have to go through Noelle and the charade of the coach and blindfold. And the duchess had reluctantly given Crawford permission to have the courtesan picked up, as she trusted the investigator.

Even if the young woman was innocent of the bigger charges, she had taken the necklace and set the whole caper into motion. At the very least, she was a thief. But it was up to Charles to determine if there would be charges in that matter.

"We want to hear the story behind the necklace one

more time," Gavin said once she was settled opposite the desk. Without Noelle and the courtesan rescuer, Sophie, lingering at the school to come to her aid, Bliss was unsettled. It would help to keep her honest. "Mister Crawford hopes to find some information in your story."

Bliss's face tightened. She perched uneasily on the edge of the chair, as if she expected to be arrested at any moment. Gavin felt confident. She should be fearful.

"I . . . ah"—her composure started to slip—"please, it was a mistake. I didn't mean to take the necklace!"

Gavin frowned. "We did not bring you here to have you arrested for theft. The matter has moved beyond that. We need to know everything you can recall about your maid. Down to the last detail. She seems to have fled London, and we hope to discover her trail. Did she mention family or where she was from?"

Bliss shook her head and twisted her fingers together. "I don't remember any family. I think she was an orphan." The courtesan's shoulders slumped. "I'm certain she mentioned that once." Her brown eyes narrowed. "She fixed the beds and dusted the furniture. Why did I need to know anything beyond how well she cleaned?"

Gavin felt a rise of annoyance. The courtesan cared nothing for the maid yet allowed the woman to convince her to steal a very expensive necklace. Bliss wasn't intelligent enough to plan and execute the theft without encouragement, and she certainly was no mastermind behind a theft ring.

"And you have not seen the woman since that day?" Crawford asked, frowning.

"I have not." Bliss clasped her hands tightly in her lap. "It was a horrible, horrible mistake," she cried. "I tried to put it back, I did. But Charles distracted me, and by the time I remembered the necklace, he was gone."

"And the maid?" the investigator pressed.

The courtesan slumped. "I didn't see her after I went for help. I'd heard of the courtesan school and knew if anyone could help me, it was Miss Eva. I dressed and quickly set out. Freda was nowhere in sight when I left."

The two men exchanged glances.

"The woman was probably meeting with her cohorts and didn't expect Bliss to take off with the necklace," Crawford said. He rubbed the old injury to his leg. "She must have been livid to find both Bliss and the necklace gone."

Gavin lifted the sketch off the desk, rose, and walked over to Bliss. "We have placed a face to the woman we suspect is behind this." He held it out to her, and she took the sketch.

She crinkled her nose. "It isn't her."

Gavin shared a second glance with Crawford and nodded. "As we suspected, this wasn't the maid." He turned back to Bliss and leveled a hard stare on her. "Do you recognize her?"

Bliss shook her head. "No. Though there is something familiar about her face. It is as if I've seen her before."

Gavin felt hope rise. He'd thought the same thing. "Do you know where?"

Another shake of her head. "I don't believe I've seen her in person. Perhaps from a painting?" Bliss said. She pressed her lips together for a moment. "No, I am certain we haven't met." She squinted and looked closer. "Drat! I cannot place her face."

Disappointment welled in Gavin. Every clue failed to connect and seemed to lead nowhere. Still, they were getting closer, in spite of the labyrinth of unconnected paths. He felt it in his bones. "If you remember anything useful, please pass the information on to Miss Eva immediately."

Bliss nodded and sighed. "Yes, sir."

There was nothing left for her to offer. Gavin dismissed Bliss and settled back behind his desk. Crawford placed the young women back into the care of the steward and returned moments later.

"Someone knows her." Crawford lifted the sketch off the desk. He tapped a closed fist against his mouth, then a fingertip to the sketch. "We are very close. We will find you, mistress thief."

"I agree." Gavin leaned back in his chair and tapped his fingertips on the arms. The excitement of the chase welled.

It was only a matter of time before they'd have their answers. "My cousin is the key. I think it's time to force Charles to get involved. He cannot continue to avoid the matter for fear of causing scandal to his family. Bliss was his mistress. He must have seen the maid during his visits, and he may have information. I shall write to him at once and demand his return."

The letter never materialized. As Gavin collected the parchment and pen, Charles arrived, flushed from the long ride from Bath. He looked first at Crawford and then at Gavin, frowned, and said, "What in hades is happening here?"

Noelle visited the courtesan school as the charitable widow and helped Eva teach the young ladies how to host a dinner party. Well, helping wasn't what she was doing, exactly, considering her mind was on her handsome and extremely skilled lover. His hands, his mouth, his perfect male form all captured her interest more than china place settings and silver.

After several failed attempts to hold her attention, Eva finally took Noelle's hand and pulled her from the small dining room. She led her down the hallway and into the parlor.

"Would you like to tell me why you're walking around in the clouds today?" Eva closed the parlor door behind them and stared. "And with a dreamy smile pasted on your face?"

Noelle knew spending the night with Gavin, and gifting him her virginity, was probably better kept secret. But she was so happy; she couldn't keep it to herself. If anyone understood how wonderful it was to share one's body with a man you loved, it was Eva. She spent all her nights with the handsome duke. Certainly Eva could see how happy loving Gavin made her.

"I spent the evening with Gavin." She smiled slyly. "I no

longer worry he will forget me. After last night, there is little chance of that happening."

Eva gaped. "You sneaked out in the middle of the night?"

Noelle nodded and grinned. "Perhaps you should have posted a guard at the door." Eva was clearly mortified, less about the seduction and more about Noelle's wandering the streets at night without an escort. "Not to worry, Sister dear. I took Thomas with me. He is very skilled at creeping around undetected. Someday you must tell me his history."

"You involved Thomas?"

Nodding, Noelle said, "He was reluctant at first but realized I was determined. He knew you'd be unhappy if I came to harm. So he agreed."

Eva groaned and dropped into a chair. "Not only was my sister parading around town in the middle of the night—"

"Dressed like a pirate—"

"Good lord!" Eva pressed a hand to her forehead. "Dressed like a pirate, and she seduced a man who has no desire to wed her." She sighed deeply and pushed the spinster spectacles farther up the bridge of her nose. "And if the virile beast has planted his seed in fertile ground, my husband will have to beat him to a bloody pulp."

"Fertile ground?" Noelle giggled. "I hardly think such a consequence is possible. We were together only one night."

One glorious night.

"Old Lord Chatsman impregnated Lady Chatsman on their wedding night, then proceeded to drop dead the next morning," Eva scolded. "So it can happen."

Noelle waved a dismissive hand. The tale had frenzied the gossips for weeks with speculation on how vigorous a lover the young Lady Chatsman was, to kill off her husband in bed. Since then, she'd become a very popular widow with the cads and rakes. "That is her story. I myself find it odd that her son looks very much like her handsome, dark-haired footman."

"Either way," Eva retorted, "the deed was done that evening or shortly thereafter. It doesn't matter who the lady spent those first few days with after her wedding, and Lord Chatsman's funeral. The boy was born almost nine months to the day after and is the old letch's heir."

Watching her sister run a hand over her belly made Noelle wonder what it would be like to be carrying Gavin's child. She let her own hand drift to her flat stomach and knew if he had gotten her with child, she would love the little mite with all her heart.

"You cannot be considering bearing his bastard?"

Noelle's eyes snapped up, and she realized Eva was staring aghast at the path of her hand. She jerked it off her belly and flushed deeply. "Of course not."

"I will not have a niece or nephew suffering the shame of my situation. I am a bastard. We do not need another in our family." Eva's eyes clouded. "Even now, we hide the truth of our connection. I want nothing more than to claim you as my sister to society, but I cannot. The Harrington family does not need a courtesan's bastard, or Blackwell's illegitimate issue, hanging from their family tree."

Noelle dropped to her knees and took Eva's hand. "I wish the same, but I see this differently. I am not the least ashamed of you." She brushed a tear off her sister's face. Eva wasn't the overly emotional sort. But since finding herself with child, she'd been both cranky and weepy. "It is you who chooses to hide our sisterhood."

Nicholas wasn't ashamed of Eva's paternity either. He loved her. And in spite of the shaky start to her entrance into society as the Duchess Stanfield, Eva was a popular duchess. Some members of the Ton might have initially scorned her because of her mysterious past, but eventually they'd come around with Nicholas standing firm and protective beside her.

"I'm not ready." Eva brushed the remaining tears from her face and sat upright. "Perhaps after the babe is born, we can revisit the topic again? People will begin to notice when he or she calls you 'aunt.'"

Noelle pressed Eva's hand to her cheek. "I cannot wait to publicly claim both a new sister and the precious babe as kin."

After Eva had excused herself to return to her class, Noelle decided to head back to Collingwood House for a much-needed nap.

She'd had only snippets of sleep in Gavin's arms. The man had decided sleep was wasted time when he could be loving her. She'd not complained a single word about his enthusiasm, as she'd felt the same. Now, however, the lack of rest was creeping in and fogging her brain. A nap was just what she needed.

Luckily, a hackney pulled up to the curb as she stepped outside the courtesan school. She wasn't surprised to see Bliss alight. Gavin had casually mentioned his plan to speak to her with Crawford. He just hadn't mentioned when.

A small bit of jealousy formed as she watched the beautiful courtesan smile at the driver, who grinned. Had Gavin felt lust with Bliss? He'd have to be blind to not notice her seductive draw while questioning her.

Noelle brushed aside her annoyance. He'd met Bliss once previously. Surely, if he desired the courtesan, he wouldn't have been so eager to bed her last evening.

Bliss looked as if the world was pressing down on her shoulders as she stepped away from the hackney. Her face was pale, and she looked on the verge of tears.

"Miss Noelle." Bliss had taken two steps toward her when a man darted around the hackney and slammed into her. Bliss let out a pained cry. A second man appeared from nowhere and caught Noelle tightly around the waist. An enclosed coach with bars on the windows raced around the corner and down the street, rapidly drawing to a halt beside the hackney. The two men dragged Noelle and Bliss toward the coach.

Both women screamed.

Chapter Twenty-Six

The prison guards waited until they were well away from the town house before stopping briefly to shackle Bliss and Noelle together. The women struggled fiercely, but to no avail. The largest man was quick with his hands, touching places he should not, and grinning evilly as he did so. Noelle managed to keep the worst of his fondling at bay with her nails. Still, the horrid man left her feeling unclean when he finally settled against the back of the coach, leaving them huddled together in a near-hysterical lump near his feet.

They'd been arrested, likely illegally, and without a magistrate to oversee the matter. The guards had probably been bribed to take them. Somehow Bliss's whereabouts had finally been discovered. Where Noelle fit into this, she didn't know. All she could think of now was fighting off the guards.

The two women clung to each other on the dirty floor as a toothless guard stared at them with hard black eyes.

Bliss sobbed quietly on Noelle's shoulder while Noelle glared at the man to warn him off. She was fully prepared to fight for their lives if he dared touch either of them in a lascivious way. She and Bliss might well be smaller and weaker, but the men would not find abusing them easy.

Her nightmare had come true. They'd been arrested. But who had made the charge? Gavin? Deep in her heart, she didn't think so. He'd been so tender, so loving. He wouldn't turn on her without feeling anything after what they'd shared.

If it wasn't Gavin, then who? The mysterious woman? She certainly was up to something. Her goal was the necklace, wasn't it? Since Bliss and Noelle no longer had it, why would this despicable stranger go to this trouble? Or had the earl finally figured out the real reason for the sudden reappearance of the bauble and decided Bliss should be punished?

She'd left his bed. Perhaps he *was* the vengeful sort? Had Noelle just been at the wrong place at the wrong time?

A shudder of dread filled her as she tried not to imagine the fate that was heading toward her like panicked horse. It took all her strength not to join Bliss in tears.

Any sign of weakness would give the guard a reason to maul them again. She steeled herself. Bliss needed her to remain focused on finding a way to extricate them from this nightmare.

Once they reached their destination a short time later, Noelle had only a moment to glimpse the outer prison walls before they were dragged inside by the chains that bit into their fragile wrists.

The door slammed closed behind them. This was an entirely new world composed of danger and terror. It was dark, vile, and without rules.

Newgate. Bile raced up the back of her throat. At least Bliss was shackled to her, and Noelle had something real and comforting to hold on to. The dim, dank passageways were filthy and rat-infested. The two women stumbled along, their skirts tangled together, desperate not to be separated. Bliss was no longer crying. Her tears had turned into whimpers as they faded into the bowels of the prison.

Sounds of despair came from barred cells, as if the occupants had long ago given up their sanity. Shrieks and moans and mumbled voices filled the passageway, and clawed hands reached through the barred doors toward her, until Noelle was certain she'd go mad with fright.

She felt sick and struggled not to empty the contents of her stomach on the unswept stone floor. Bliss needed her, and she would be strong.

The guards finally shoved them into a cell, the floor covered with straw and, likely, vermin. The toothless guard unshackled them, taking his time with Bliss. The girl tried to twist away when his hand groped her breast.

"Ye are a beauty." Spittle droplets sprang from his mouth, no teeth to block the spray.

Noelle pushed his hand away and shoved herself between them. "Don't touch her." She stood to full height. The top of her head barely came to his chin. "I have friends who will see you hanged if we are harmed."

Whether it was her tone or her aristocratic speech that caused him to back away, Noelle couldn't know. But he finally left them and slammed the heavy door closed behind him.

"What is happening?" Bliss asked, her voice high. "Mister Blackwell swore he wouldn't see us imprisoned."

Noelle scooped her into her arms. "I am positive he isn't responsible for this." But not as positive as she'd like. She petted Bliss's hair and made soft, soothing sounds. "We have to hope that someone saw us taken and will come to our rescue."

Noelle watched a pair of mangy rats move over the straw, searching for edibles, their black beady eyes intense. She led Bliss to the soiled cot, eased her down onto it, and joined her on the tattered surface. Both women tucked their legs up beneath them in hopes the rats wouldn't come in for a closer look.

Rat bites were suspected to cause disease.

"We have to remain strong." Noelle clutched Bliss's cold hands and tried to manage a smile. When that failed, she managed to force out, "Someone will come for us. I know they will."

As the hours passed and their situation became more desperate, Noelle began to worry they'd never escape. The guards took turns looking through the small barred window of the cell, their evil eyes burning through their clothing, silently promising it was only a matter of time before they violated the two women. Eventually the bravest of the group would overlook Noelle's obvious aristocracy and threats and would pounce.

She tried twice to gain the attention of a guard, hoping if she told him her name and title, she could gain release. However, the men seemed content to ignore her pleas.

It took some time before the occupants of the adjoining cells settled to sleep, and Noelle suspected it was nighttime. Without exterior windows to confirm her suspicions, it was but a guess. Bliss had fallen into a restless, exhausted slumber with her head on Noelle's lap, her soft breathing uneven.

Noelle kept watch, glaring at the guards as they passed. The smells of disease, urine, and filth helped to keep her vigilant. Two sleeping women were easy prey. And though Noelle knew that eventually they would be victims, she'd fend off the inevitable as long as possible.

Time passed without notice, and Noelle didn't realize she'd dozed until a sound snapped her awake. The toothless guard and another man had slipped silently into the cell and loomed over the cot. Bliss came awake at Noelle's cry and screamed. The two men grabbed for them, one jerking Bliss to the floor.

Noelle clawed at her attacker, barely noticing Bliss being pushed down into the straw. The toothless guard tore at the courtesan's clothing while the second guard shoved Noelle down on the cot and climbed atop her. His weight was so great, she couldn't push him off. He tore at the opening of his trousers, at the same time shoving up her skirts. Noelle pummeled his face with her fists, hoping to break his nose.

"Get off!"

Bliss fought as well, kicking the toothless guard with her slippered feet. He slapped her hard, and she went still.

Noelle whimpered, gouging her attacker's eyes with

her nails. It was a replay of the night of the courtesan ball. The man grinned sickeningly. "Ye might well lay back and enjoy it."

"Never." She spat in his face. The man glowered and closed a fist. She braced herself for the blow. Instead, he reared up, his face filled with shock and surprise. He tumbled off the cot onto his face and went still; a knife was buried deep in his back.

Her eyes wide, she saw Gavin standing behind the fallen guard. "Gavin!" she screamed. Noelle scrambled from the cot, only then noticing the toothless guard similarly prone on the floor, a knife in his neck. The Earl of Seabrook reached down to gather the stunned Bliss into his arms.

Gavin took Noelle by the hand and pulled her against him. "Are you hurt?" She shook her head. "Come, then, we must go."

Gavin took the lead, dragging Noelle behind him. The earl, carrying Bliss, brought up the rear. They made their way quickly through the darkened passageway. Noelle had no sense of direction in the maze of passages and had to rely on Gavin to lead them to safety.

Shock kept her from questioning his appearance or doing more than notice that Crawford had joined them at the back door of the prison. They were quickly hustled into a waiting coach. The investigator rapped his fist on the roof. The coach jerked forward, and the prison was soon well behind them.

Gavin snuggled her close to his side and looked into her eyes. The blue depths of his eyes showed how deeply concerned he was for her. Both relief and worry were there. "Are you hurt?" he whispered. "Did he—?"

She touched a fingertip to his lips. She couldn't speak about her near-violation now, while it was still fresh. "We are both unharmed. You came in time." She watched his eyes fill with relief. "How did you find us?"

"Your sister saw you taken, and sent for me." He leaned to press a firm kiss on her brow, then another. She felt his body shudder against her, and she realized how truly fearful he'd been for her. She clung to his coat and held on. "Crawford bribed a guard to look the other way."

Noelle pressed her head to his mouth and resisted tears. He was warm and stable in a day gone mad. Had the rescuers' arrival been delayed by minutes, there would be nothing left of her to save. She would have killed herself rather than live with the aftermath of her violation.

"Thank you for coming," she whispered, and nuzzled her face to his shoulder. His scent washed some of the lingering stench of the prison from her mind. It still clung to her clothing, and she longed to rip off her soiled dress and toss it out the window. She'd see everything burned.

"You're welcome." He caught her hand and pressed it to his lips. "When I discover who did this, I'll see her hanged."

Noelle tucked her hand under his arm, fearful she'd awaken from this dream and find herself back in the prison. If she held on tightly enough to him, she could stay safe forever.

"How many kidnappings does one have to endure in one's lifetime?" she asked, resigned.

"If I have my druthers, this was the last," Gavin replied. "I plan to see that your life from now on is normal on every front."

Normal sounded wonderful. She clasped his hand. "I will hold you to that promise." She turned to smile gratefully at Crawford. He grinned and nodded. She'd thank him properly once they were well away from Newgate.

"How is Bliss?" Noelle asked softly. She watched the earl smooth the courtesan's dark hair back from her face. Her head was in his lap, her lids open slightly as Bliss roused and looked up at His Lordship. He gave her a smile and cupped the side of her face.

Bliss smiled weakly. "Your Lordship."

"You stole Hortense's necklace." He shot her a teasing glare. It was as if Noelle, Gavin, and Crawford were not in the coach. "I'd paddle you if I didn't think you'd suffered enough for your crime."

"I didn't mean to take it," she said. Tears sprang to her

eyes. Bliss was filthy and mussed up, her gown torn and her hair in disarray. Her condition didn't seem to bother the earl in the least. He held her close. "I would never steal from you."

"I know." The earl shook his head. "Rest now, dearest. There will be time later for a discussion on how not to be led astray by the whims of your maid."

The pair slipped into a quiet conversation. Noelle finally submitted to exhausted slumber, her head on Gavin's shoulder and his arm tucked snugly around her.

Gavin felt Noelle go slack, and he sighed. When he'd seen his beloved courtesan-thief beneath the guard, fighting for her life, he'd felt a burning rage like no other. He hadn't hesitated when he'd buried his blade so deep into thick flesh; he'd known the man would not live to attack another defenseless woman.

When Eva had sent him the frantic note, he'd gone icy cold with fear. Crawford was the first person he'd thought of who could help. The investigator had connections all over London. Gavin suspected what had happened from Eva's note. He knew Crawford could confirm that the women had been taken to Newgate and could help plot their rescue. And he was right. For that, Gavin would be forever grateful.

He'd heard of the vile things women prisoners suffered and knew they had to mount a quick rescue. Gavin and Charles collected Crawford on the way to Newgate.

The distance to the prison was not great, though it seemed like an eternity as they raced through the streets. All he could think about was Noelle suffering, and the terror of not knowing how he'd find her. His heart felt torn asunder.

It was in the moment he saw the guard tearing at her clothing that he knew, somehow over this last week, he'd fallen deeply and completely in love with her. He'd kill a thousand men, if it meant keeping her safe and at his side forever.

No matter how this caper ended, or how Noelle felt about the matter, he'd find a way to break past her fear of marriage and wed her as quickly as a special license could be arranged. Then he'd spend the rest of his life making sure she never regretted her decision to accept him as her husband.

A few minutes later, the coach rolled to a stop outside Charles's town house. Once the women were carried inside, Gavin sent a note to Eva, via a footman, to assure her both women were safe. He knew Her Grace would be angered he hadn't brought Noelle to Collingwood House, but she'd just have to live with her disappointment. Never again would Noelle spend a night anywhere but under his roof.

Well, for the moment, Charles's roof. It was far past time to find his own house.

Perhaps he'd leave the matter of picking out the perfect house to Noelle, since she'd be mistress of the household. The idea of having her in his life and bed, and children, too, filled him with happiness and contentment.

An odd sentiment for a man with his own fears about the institution of marriage.

"You are smiling," she said, and slid her hand down the side of his neck. "Would you like to tell me why?"

"Later," he said. There was time for courtship once she was bathed and had recovered from her horrid ordeal. For now, he was content to hold her.

"You can put me down," Noelle said as he headed for the stairs with her clutched high in his arms. "I can walk."

He snuggled her tighter. "I think I shall keep you like this always. I like having you in my arms."

Noelle smiled into his eyes, and his heart lurched. She had such beautiful eyes. "I smell of Newgate. Surely you can gather me back into your embrace once I've bathed and you've changed." Her fingers plucked at his dirt-smudged coat. "Then I shall thank you properly for coming to my rescue."

Gavin carried her up the staircase to one of the bedrooms along the hallway. Once they were over the threshold, he kicked the door closed behind them and lowered her feet to the floor.

"I think you should thank me now." He pulled her to him and kissed her. Noelle melted against him. He pushed aside thoughts of Newgate, brutal guards, rats, and anything else Noelle might have suffered, hoping his kiss would help erase the horrors of this nightmare. He wanted to tell her he loved her, but the moment wasn't right. She needed time to collect herself. So he kissed her instead.

When she pulled back, she was smiling. "You are an expert kisser, Mister Blackwell. Now please send for some hot water. I am offending myself."

He lifted her dirty knuckles to his mouth. "I think it is time you finally stop calling me Mister Blackwell, don't you? I much prefer that you call me Gavin."

She said nothing as she reached for the door handle. She opened the door and, pushing gently against his chest, eased him backward into the hallway. "Perhaps," she said, and closed the door in his face.

Gavin chuckled and went to do her bidding.

Once the women were settled in rooms upstairs and baths had been arranged with the staff, the men gathered in the study. Gavin and Crawford seated themselves in over-stuffed chairs before the fireplace while Charles spoke to the housekeeper.

The chill of Newgate had left Gavin cold to his bones in a way that no expensive brandy could wash away. Once business was concluded, he intended to soak in a very hot bath.

"I cannot thank you enough, Crawford, for what you did for the women, for me." Gavin lifted his glass. "If I can ever return the favor, you need only ask."

Crawford nodded. "The duchess has always been kind to me. I couldn't see her sister harmed." He shot a quick glance toward Charles and leaned forward in his chair to take Gavin into his confidence. "And Bliss is too lovely and sweet-natured to suffer at the hands of those animals. I am pleased they're dead."

Clearly, Crawford was smitten with the courtesan. Though he was nearly fifteen years her senior and walked with a limp, Gavin suspected some women would find him easy to look at. Still, putting Crawford and Bliss together as a pair of lovers was absurd. It was like linking a parrot with a sparrow.

Gavin let the comment lie and turned his attention to business. They had to catch the rest of the thugs, and the mysterious woman, before they caused further harm.

The leader of the thieves was clearly without a conscience. Today had proved his theory. Gavin opened his mouth to begin the discussion when he noticed Charles peering down at the desk, his body tense.

"What is it, Cousin?" he asked, and watched Charles lift the sketch and stare at the mysterious woman. His face was tight, and his jaw clenched and released beneath his skin.

Charles turned the sketch toward Gavin, his eyes dark and puzzled. "Why do you have a sketch of my wife?"

In the chair, Gavin went still. Crawford made a funny sound. Only the clock on the mantel broke the silence with soft *ticktocks*.

"Hortense?" Gavin stared at the sketch in disbelief. Though he'd never met the woman, he'd heard tales of both her exceptional beauty and her spiteful nature. Never once had he considered she might be behind the plot. Yet somehow, it all made sense now, in a very strange way. If anyone wanted to hurt Charles, she topped the list. "Are you certain?"

"Down to the small mole beneath her right eye."

The cousins locked stares. How did he break the news that Charles was married to a woman who set in motion events that almost killed Noelle?

There was nothing he could do but be direct.

"She is the woman behind the plot," Gavin said regretfully. He hated to break such awful news, but it had to be done. His own thoughts would have to wait until later.

Charles sat on the edge of the desk and rubbed his free hand over his face. The strain had etched lines on his face. In that moment, he aged ten years.

"I always knew she was troublesome. Her father paid me well to marry her, and she has often tried my patience.

Still, she is a loving mother." He looked at Gavin, and there was pain in his eyes. "How could she do this? How could she cause so much hurt? Hell, Lady Noelle was almost killed by the footpad. And Newgate? The women were about to be brutalized." His voice trailed off as if he couldn't finish his painful thought.

Rage burned through Gavin. Hortense needed her neck wrung. She was a Lady. How had she sunk to such low depths to do . . . what? Ruin Charles to get revenge for his unfaithfulness?

"I certainly would like to know her reasons," Gavin said. If there was neck wringing to be done, he planned to do it himself.

He leaned to speak a few whispered words to Crawford. The investigator nodded and left. The matter was now to be left to family. Any action taken from this moment forward was between himself, Charles, and the despicable Lady Hortense.

"I need to get to Bath." Charles pushed off the desk. He folded the sketch and put it in his coat pocket. There was dark determination in his clipped movements and tight face. "I shall change and leave immediately. My wife must be confronted before she hurts anyone else."

"I shall go with you." Gavin knew the woman couldn't fill his cousin's head with lies with him there to keep Charles focused on her crimes. What Charles would decide to be her punishment was another question. She was a Lady and the mother of his children. No matter the depths of his villainy, those facts would be considered when passing judgment.

"Be ready in an hour." Charles walked to the door, his narrow shoulders bowed. He shifted his eyes to Gavin. "My dear wife is about to face the full measure of my wrath."

Chapter Twenty-Seven

I'm going with you." Noelle pulled on her gloves and reached for her velvet cape. "I have the right."

Gavin's scowl didn't deter her. If he wanted her to stay at the town house, he never should have mentioned Lady Hortense. To know the wife of a peer was behind the plot to destroy Bliss and, by a twist of fate, Noelle herself left a bitter taste in her mouth.

And she'd not be swayed from her determination to confront the dreadful woman. The countess should face the depth of her anger. So she stared down Gavin, her jaw stubbornly clenched.

"I suppose arguing will accomplish nothing?" Gavin eyed her carefully, as if checking one last time for any lingering effects of Newgate, her head injury, anything he could use to keep her from the trip. He'd hovered for the last hour as the maid finished giving Noelle a bath and quickly dressed her. If the maid found it scandalous for an unmarried gentleman to be in the presence of a Lady during Noelle's bath, and after, her face revealed nothing. She accomplished her work with quiet efficiency and then left the two of them alone.

Noelle's scowl melted into a smile. "You know me well. And if you intend to spend time with me in the future, you have to accept that I am stubborn to a fault."

Crossing the room, she slipped into his arms. Though he frowned, his eyes lit up as he slid his hands around her body. He desired her. Risking his life, and possible arrest, to save her from Newgate had proved to Noelle she wasn't just a casual bed partner to him. He hadn't dropped to one knee and begged for her hand, but knowing of his affection was enough.

She'd give him her love, and hope that eventually he'd love her in return. But not now. They had business to finish.

"So I've discovered, My Lady-pirate-courtesan." He leaned to press a kiss on the side of her neck. It tickled, and she twitched. "Mixed with beautiful and seductive and all of those headache-inducing traits you have, which I've grown to recognize and tolerate. Perhaps we should leave Lady Hortense to her husband and test the sturdiness of yonder mattress."

"If you hope to distract me from my mission by insults, or by loving me until I'm too weak to stand, you're wasting your time." She pressed forward. "Though it will give me great pleasure to spend another night with you, I will have my justice." She brushed a tiny piece of lint off his coat and smoothed his lapels. "I'll follow you all the way to Bath on the back of a horse if I must."

Gavin shrugged and kissed her deeply. He teased her tongue with his and groaned when he broke the kiss. He locked on to her gaze and cupped her chin. "We need to have a lengthy talk when we return. There is much I have to say to you."

Her heart fluttered and her face tightened. "Can you give me a hint of the topic?" Her worst fear was that Gavin would see this caper concluded, then tell her he no longer desired her company. No more shared intimacies, no more laughter. No chance at all for any sort of future. He was as against marriage as she was. Or had been. She was no longer sure what she wanted.

After twenty-five years of vowing never to love a man, Noelle had allowed her heart to be compromised, breached by this imposing and dangerous American. She might soon suffer from a shattered heart.

"Why so grim, love?" Gavin smiled. He tucked a curl behind her ear. "You have no reason to worry. Certain topics require privacy, and we have no time to waste. Charles is waiting downstairs with the coach. We must be off before he leaves both of us behind."

The trip to Bath was the longest of her life. Charles and Gavin had little to say to each other, or to her, and a borrowed middle-aged maid slept through most of the journey, awakening only when they stopped for food or rest, or when her particularly loud snores snapped her from slumber.

The earl faced a grim reality and was too troubled to converse on mundane topics like the weather. His wife was responsible for several dangerous misdeeds that could have cost lives. He had to feel the weight of this bearing down on him. He'd married this woman, had children with her, and vowed to care for her for the rest of her days. Now he had to decide her fate. A monumental task.

Throughout his heartfelt apology, Noelle felt his pain and held him largely blameless, though she suspected his misbehavior had led his wife to desperate measures. Still, he seemed to be a decent sort. Perhaps once they cleared up this matter, she could consider him a friend.

The trip seemed to take an eternity with horse changes and stops, and Noelle was fatigued to her bones when they finally arrived at Kirkwood Manor, just outside Bath. The house was immense and reminded Noelle of a medieval monastery, complete with perfectly manicured flower beds and a lawn that seemed to stretch forever. She almost expected to be greeted by monks as she stepped down from the coach and was ushered across the gravel drive toward the house.

From somewhere in the expanse, Noelle heard children laughing. She knew the earl had four children, knowledge that left her with a heavy heart. She hoped their mother's sins would not affect them too greatly.

"Where is my wife?" His Lordship brushed past the butler standing in the open doorway while shucking off his overcoat and tossing it in the general direction of the man. The butler caught the coat and hung it on a peg by the door without blinking an eye.

"She is visiting Mrs. Shaw, My Lord." The butler collected Noelle's cape and Gavin's coat. He asked a passing maid to bring tea, and she hurried off toward what Noelle assumed to be the kitchen. "She is expected back shortly."

Charles grimaced, clearly put off by the delay. "Tell her she has visitors in the yellow parlor, but do not tell her I'm here. I'd like to surprise my darling wife."

The man bowed his gray head. "Yes, My Lord."

Charles led them through the entryway to a narrow hallway that passed under a wide stone staircase. Noelle saw hints in the unusual stonework of her earlier assumption that at least parts of the manor could have originated as a monastery or a medieval keep. They walked by several rooms until they arrived at what was obviously the yellow parlor.

With the exception of the colorful carpet, the room was decorated entirely in various shades of sunshine. From its dark yellow drapes to the pale yellow stripes on the settee and matching chairs, it was a bit overwhelming.

"I would have kept my hat had I known we would be in the sunshine," Gavin whispered. Noelle appreciated his attempt at levity but nudged him with her elbow.

"Behave," she whispered, and Gavin refrained from further comment.

The earl walked to the window, and Noelle and Gavin settled side by side on the settee. Tension twisted her belly sour, and every sound outside the parlor seemed magnified as Noelle waited to confront the horrid woman.

She supposed tearing out Lady Hortense's hair and gouging out her eyes wasn't proper behavior. Still, it should be acceptable to tear and gouge if a situation warranted such actions. And at the moment, Noelle wasn't beyond rolling up her sleeves and giving the woman the pummeling she much deserved.

Click-clicks from rapid footsteps in the hallway brought Noelle's attention to the door. It didn't take introductions to know the woman who stepped into the parlor. The sketch had been surprisingly accurate. Though diminutive in size, she carried herself with a queenly bearing, as if all of England was meant to bow at her tiny feet.

Noelle knew she was not yet thirty, yet lines of disapproval and scorn had etched grooves around her mouth and between her brows. Had she lived her life with happiness and laughter, she could have been a rare beauty. Instead, she'd been spoiled and pampered and never made to suffer for her misbehavior, to the point of becoming a shrew.

"Surprise, Wife," Charles said and turned away from the window. His posture gave the appearance of casual indifference, but his face showed he was anything but calm. A visible undercurrent of anger simmered in him. "Did you miss me?"

Lady Hortense's dark eyes darted from one face to another, and all the color fled her cheeks. Clearly she possessed the intelligence to know that finding Gavin and a strange woman in her parlor did not bode well for her. Obviously, her evil henchmen had kept her abreast of the goings-on in London. Whether she knew Noelle's true identity, and how her plot had entangled the highly placed Lady Seymour, remained to be seen.

The countess forced a grim smile. "Charles, darling. Back so soon?" She must have decided to steer away from her husband, and instead crossed toward Gavin. "You must be the American cousin my husband has spoken so much about. His description was apt. I feel like I know you—"

"Stop." Charles's voice boomed through the room before she could reach Gavin. She jolted to a wavering halt.

Lady Hortense winced with each slow step as he trod toward her, his eyes pinning her in place. "How could you do what you did and not hide your face in shame?"

She swallowed and her face paled. "How could I do what, My Lord?" She tried to smile but grimaced instead.

"Gavin and Lady Seymour were almost killed because of this sickening game you played to punish me for my indiscretions. How can you stand there and act as if you did nothing wrong?"

Her gaze snapped to Noelle. "Lady Seymour?" she croaked. "You were involved with the necklace?" Evidently, her henchmen had not put Bliss together with Noelle. It was one thing to harass a courtesan; it was quite another to attack a noblewoman.

The countess seemed to shrink inside her well-cut rose gown. Clearly she now realized the seriousness of her situation.

"I want to know, why Bliss?" Charles demanded, and the countess jerked her head around to her husband. "I have had scores of lovers since our marriage. Why this one?"

Noelle watched her expression flash to intense anger. Lady Seabrook might have been surprised by their arrival, and by Noelle's part in the drama, but she wasn't done fighting just yet. It didn't take much to see the feral cat in the countess.

"You want to know why I had Fanny—Freda, as your whore knew her—convince your pretty plaything to steal my necklace?" She rose to her full height and closed her fists. She barely came midchest on her husband. "You called out her name in your sleep—'Bliss, Bliss'—in our bed. You mooned over her like a calf-eyed puppy." She paused. "I overheard you speaking to Lord Bennington in the library about your beautiful courtesan. It was clear you were besotted." Her voice grew shriller with each spewed word. "I know you've never loved me, but could you have had the decency not to speak of her to Bennington in our home, and not mutter her name in our bed?"

Her cheeks turned flame red in her rage. Suddenly, Noelle realized that in spite of her husband's obvious affection for Bliss, and his cavalier attitude about their marriage, the shrew loved him. Everything she'd done, all the deception and dangerous plotting, had been to remove Bliss from his affections.

"I sent Fanny to watch over her, looking for an opportunity to do some harm. That is when the necklace became useful. Fanny saw how enamored the whore was by the piece and encouraged the theft. Fanny knew that once the chit stole the necklace, I could have her arrested and tossed into Newgate. Then you would see her as nothing more than a lowly thief." Her voice caught in a sob. "You would have had to come home to me."

Angry tears burned a path down her face. Noelle looked at Gavin, and he was just as enthralled with the drama as she was.

However, it was Charles who appeared most stunned by the confession. Obviously, he'd not been aware of the love, twisted though it was, that his wife felt for him. He'd wedded and bedded her for many years yet was blind to her feelings.

Pity. That was what Noelle felt in that moment. Though Lady Hortense deserved to be whipped for what she'd done to Noelle and Bliss. Noelle's own mother had suffered the shame of marriage to an openly unfaithful husband. Though theirs had not been a love match either, the humiliation of knowing her husband had loved Eva's mother must have been a dreadful weight to bear.

Love match or not, realizing one's husband found passion and joy in another woman had to be a blow to one's pride. If Noelle was wed to Gavin, and he left her bed to enjoy the pleasures of a mistress, she'd be devastated.

That was why she'd never wanted to wed. The price was too painfully high. Could it still be?

"Why, after the necklace was returned, did your thugs continue to demand the necklace?" Gavin pressed. "And how did they find Bliss?"

The woman averted her eyes. "I promised them a large reward once Bliss was arrested. When that failed, I refused to pay them any more than the initial payment. I cut off contact." She paused. "Obviously, they saw my necklace as their reward. They couldn't know Charles had already returned it to me."

Noelle could see Gavin's outrage in his trembling body. The duchess had started a dangerous game that she quickly lost control of, leaving her thugs to carry on unfettered. Havoc, pain, and near-fatal consequences followed that fateful decision.

"How did they find Bliss?" Charles asked.

"I don't know," the countess said, her voice thin. "After several threats to harm me, I didn't hear from them again."

Gavin looked at Charles. "The thugs must have paid the guards to take Bliss in order to force payment from the countess. Noelle was caught in the ambush."

Lady Hortense stood stock-still in the center of the room. Her crimes clearly weighed on her. "What is to be done with me?" she whimpered.

Charles seemed to struggle inwardly over the right thing to do. He had a wife who didn't think twice about harming others, yet to have his wife arrested and hanged, leaving his children motherless, would be a dreadful burden.

Gavin stood and walked to his cousin. He clapped a hand on his shoulder and Charles started, as if he'd forgotten others were in the room. Gavin pulled him out of earshot. The two men spoke quietly for a few minutes until Charles nodded, his face bleak. Gavin returned to sit next to Noelle. Though his expression was grave, he winked.

Puzzled, Noelle watched the earl face his wife. "I cannot leave you to your devices, Wife, out of fear you will further endanger others with your spite. If only your father had seen fit to paddle you as a child, we might not be in this dilemma." He dragged his hands over his head. "Gavin and I have come up with a punishment, if Lady Seymour agrees." He flicked his glance at Noelle. "Kearney Castle in Scotland is a long-neglected property belonging to our family. It is cold, drafty, and isolated, with only enough staff to keep it from falling into the sea. I think it will be a fitting prison for you, for the period of one year."

"No!" Lady Hortense wobbled and her face crumpled. "You cannot do this to me."

Charles glared. "Consider yourself lucky. Newgate was my second choice." He walked over to pour himself a brandy. "You'll have plenty of time to ponder your sins. Perhaps when you return, you will have a change of temperament."

"But what of the children?" Lady Hortense begged. "They cannot live in such conditions."

"The children will stay with me in London."

"No, please." She covered her face with her hands.

Charles turned to Noelle. She knew the ultimate decision was hers. To be isolated and removed from her children was a greater punishment than anything, save Newgate, she could come up with. Lady Hortense deserved to suffer for her crimes. She admired Charles for standing up to his wicked wife.

Noelle pulled in a deep breath and faced the countess. She felt powerful for the first time since this ordeal had begun. "You endangered and almost killed me, and set into motion the events that landed me in Newgate. Bliss and I would have been violated by the guards, if not for the intervention of Gavin and your husband. Had that happened, I would have seen you hang." Noelle paused. The countess's fate was in her hands. It was the children she considered most, not the countess. A year was a long time without their mother. Unfortunately, there was no other reasonable choice. "I would like nothing more than for you to spend one day, one hour, in Newgate, but I cannot inflict such a punishment."

"Thank you, My Lady," Lady Seabrook whispered, but Noelle raised her hand.

"Do not speak," she snapped. "I do not accept this punishment as fitting for all you have done. However, for your children's sake, I will not ship you off to a penal colony. I cannot in good conscience allow innocent children to live their lives with the shame and heartbreak of knowing their mother is gone forever, and that I was the one who had sent her away."

The countess crumpled into a chair and sobbed. Whether she came back from her exile changed or not remained to be seen. But the threat of imprisonment would certainly keep her from ever repeating her crimes. And it was enough for Noelle.

"Exile it is," Noelle agreed.

"It is settled, then." Charles downed his drink and nodded. He did not look at his wife but leveled a grateful glance at Noelle. "I will make the arrangements."

Gavin rose and took Noelle by the hand. He led her from the room. Once they were safely away from the doorway, he stopped.

"You made the right choice." He took both of her hands and bent to hold her gaze. "She loves her children deeply. The separation will be excruciating."

She squeezed his fingers. "I almost pity her." She smiled grimly. She felt the earl was also culpable in this affair. It was unfair that he'd get off without punishment. Still, his wife was ultimately responsible for her actions. "Almost. After what she did to Bliss and me, I still cannot help but wonder if the separation and exile will be sufficient for my own desire for vengeance."

Gavin chuckled. "I visited the castle once with my father when I was a boy. It is a horrible place. And there are no noble neighbors within a decent day's drive. For a woman who loves to socialize as Hortense does, that alone will be torture."

Smiling, Noelle leaned against him and slid her hand into his coat. "Then perhaps we should suggest that she pack books."

Charles offered to put them up for the evening before they headed back to London. But the piteous weeping from somewhere deep in the upper floors of the house, and the unhappy prospect of spending even one night under the same roof as the countess, fed their desire to be off immediately. Gavin gathered up Noelle and the maid and escorted them toward the coach.

Charles took Noelle's hand and kissed her gloved knuckles. "I thank you for your understanding in this matter, Lady Seymour. I know the punishment doesn't cover all her crimes, but I had to consider my children."

Perhaps he should have considered them when making the choice to humiliate his wife in her own home, Noelle thought, but she knew men of his ilk were seldom faithful. It wasn't in their breeding, and she couldn't fight the institution of courtesans and noblemen.

The earl had a spark of fire in his eyes. Noelle had a feeling he was hoping for a changed wife upon her return from exile. Miracles could happen. Maybe he'd even grow to love his shrewish countess.

"Perhaps, then, you should give consideration to allowing her to become a loving and dutiful wife." Noelle knew she should keep her advice to herself, but she had to speak her feelings. "She loves you, you know. Her happiness rests on a husband who is both loving and faithful."

His brows went up, and Noelle smiled. A knowing look filled his brown eyes, and he nodded almost imperceptibly. She suspected he'd accepted that his behavior had cost them all so much. Whether he'd take her advice and change, too, was difficult to gauge.

Noelle turned and took Gavin's hand. He helped her into the coach. The two men spoke briefly before Gavin joined her. He seemed very happy as he settled close and took her hand. Something had happened in the last minute or so to lift his spirits.

"What has brought that grin to your face?" she asked curiously as the coach rolled away from the manor. "You are awfully smug after such a sober occasion."

Gavin leaned in to keep the maid from overhearing and whispered, "My cousin has decided that if I do not keep you, I should be drawn and quartered for my stupidity."

Noelle grinned wickedly. "Your cousin is a wise man."

Chapter Twenty-Eight

Noelle relaxed back on the cushions. Now, with the thief-master exiled, and Crawford on the trail of the remaining culprits, there wasn't a reason for Gavin not to return to his life, and she to hers. He had ships to build, and she, well, she had spinsterhood to settle into and her uncle's household to run in his absence.

The idea left a cold place low in her belly. She'd been ready to risk all and marry Gavin. The last hour had scrambled up that notion. Each time she changed her mind about marriage, something happened to change it back.

"I'm the one who is wise," Gavin muttered under his breath. "It is I who share your bed."

"Hush," Noelle urged. She darted a glance at the maid, Dory, who had resumed her usual position, her head against the window frame and her eyes closed. Noelle wondered if perhaps she wasn't sleeping at all, but listening for interesting bits of gossip.

If that were the case, she'd learn little during this particular journey. The trip from London had been without interest to a potential gossip. The trip back would be similar. Noelle had no intention of doing anything scandalous with the maid sitting across the way.

Gavin had other ideas. She felt his hand slide from hers and move stealthily to her thigh. Noelle shot the maid a second glance while closing her fingers tightly over his hand to stop him from mischief. Gavin grinned wickedly.

"You must keep your hands to yourself," Noelle whispered, and felt a bubble of laughter rise up. He was completely shameless. "We have an audience."

"Not for long." He didn't have to explain as the coach turned off the road and stopped before an inn set against a small copse of trees. The building was an unimpressive two-story structure with a thatched roof and had the look of general neglect. Still, it appeared to be sturdy.

They hadn't traveled more than a mile or two. The maid popped upright when the coach stopped, her face puzzled.

Gavin said, "We have traveled many miles in a short span, and I am tired. If we sleep here tonight, we can resume our journey tomorrow, refreshed."

Noelle knew fatigue wasn't the true reason for the stop. Gavin wasn't looking at her with sleep in his eyes. Truthfully, she didn't care what his intentions were. She was exhausted. The trip had been very draining. A meal and a bed would both be welcome.

"Will you excuse us?" Gavin asked the maid, and she quickly exited the coach. Once the door was closed, he grinned again. "I have instructed the coachman to ask for the rooms: one for the maid, one for the coachman, and one for us to share. There will be a fourth, for appearances, of course. If you have a problem with the arrangement, speak up, for I intend to spend the hours between now and dawn taking full and complete advantage of that lovely body of yours."

A flash of desire tingled through Noelle. She knew very well that she should protest, loudly. Or share a space with Dory, as it was her reputation he risked. Yet, she couldn't. The idea of spending a full night with Gavin, without the fear of discovery by sister or servant, was deliriously appealing. And Dory could think what she wanted. Noelle no longer cared.

So she slid her hand down to cup his arousal and leaned close to press her breasts against him. Her nipples tightened in anticipation of his heated mouth.

"The coachman had better hurry." She pressed a kiss on the side of his jaw. "For if you do not have me naked in the next ten minutes, I shall be terribly put out."

It took seven, and Noelle was quite pleased.

Noelle awoke to a rooster's predawn crow and cursed the bird for his lack of a decent clock. Gavin had loved her, and taken her, and shown her a full collection of skills, including several positions one could twist into for optimal pleasure. Noelle didn't think she could find enjoyment in lovemaking with her ankles near her ears, or on her hands and knees. She was wrong.

"What time is it?" Gavin said sleepily, and reached to pull her close. Noelle snuggled to his side.

"There is no clock." She looked out the window and saw the slightest hint of daylight breaking the blackened sky. She pressed kisses on his bare chest. "We have an hour or two before we should consider getting out of bed."

She licked his nipple and rose to straddle his hips. His erection pressed her core. He reached to twist his hands in her tangled hair and attempted to pull her down for a kiss, but Noelle had other ideas. She smiled seductively, guided the tip of his cock inside her, and then swiftly impaled herself with a blissful moan.

Gavin groaned and lifted his hips. Noelle leaned to tease him with her mouth, flicking his tongue with hers. She slid up and down him, letting her pleasure build, assured by the hunger in his face that he was equally engaged. They rocked together, hurrying toward their pleasure, until they gasped and plummeted headlong into release.

Exhausted and satisfied, Noelle collapsed on his chest.

Gavin ran a hand down her hair and pressed a kiss on

the top of her head. Noelle nuzzled his throat. She loved him so much, it frightened her. The protective barrier around her heart had no longer completely shut out the idea of marriage. Then she'd seen the earl and his countess as another example of why marriage wasn't a grand idea, and she'd pulled back again.

It would be simpler to be Gavin's lover without having to worry that someday he'd betray their marriage vows and disappoint her. And she enjoyed being his lover very much. Maybe too much.

Gavin played with her hair. "Marry me," he murmured.

Startled, Noelle lifted her head. "What?"

"Marry me." Gavin smiled and brushed the strands of hair out of her eyes. "I want you to marry me and bear my children. I want you to spend the rest of your life both engaging and exasperating me." He looked deep into her eyes. "I love you, Noelle. I don't want to spend another day without you."

Shocked, all she could do was stare dumbly. It took a moment to fully grasp what he was saying. He loved her? When had that happened? She hadn't suspected or expected he'd fall in love with her. Panic welled. "I thought we both agreed marriage wasn't what we wanted? Now you want to change the rules?"

Inside herself she knew this wasn't what Gavin wanted to hear from her. Unfortunately, the words just tumbled out.

Gavin pushed her gently off him. He came to his knees. Noelle rose and settled onto her bum. She wanted to reach for him, to tell him she wanted very much to marry him, but the proposal had come as such a surprise, she couldn't think clearly. The unhappy confrontation between the earl and his betrayed countess was still fresh and raw.

"Rules can be changed, Noelle," he said tightly, his body visibly tense. "Do you love me?"

She wanted to tell him how deeply she loved him, how fully he'd captured her mind and heart, but all she could do was nod. At the moment, it was impossible to explain the contradictory thoughts running through her head.

"Then we will marry as soon as the arrangements are made." He grinned and reached for her.

With a quick maneuver she moved out of reach. She slid back on the bed and held up her hands. "Please don't. You must give me time to consider your proposal, Gavin."

Noelle knew she was on the edge of ruining what they had and forcing him out of her life forever. However, she couldn't instantly change everything she'd ever believed and wanted for herself and her future just because she enjoyed his company and had grown to love him. Love alone did not a successful marriage make. He could break her heart. In all likelihood, he *would* break her heart.

What did she really know about him? She'd known him only a couple of weeks. Would they be compatible in marriage? Could he forgo mistresses and only love her? On which side of the bed did he prefer to sleep? How did he like his tea? She felt a rising flush of panic.

Tension crackled in the room. "I never planned to wed," she said softly. "You felt the same. This is an unexpected change. We must take time to think with clear minds."

Disconcerted to be having this discussion naked, she stepped off the bed and reached for her chemise. Oddly, she was unable to meet his eyes.

"I see." There was an underlying current in his voice that left her feeling he didn't understand at all. Then, "This is about Bliss and Charles, and all men who take mistresses and hurt their wives. You think I could turn into your father all over again."

Noelle's stomach tightened. "No." Yes.

"That's exactly what this is about." Gavin rolled from the bed and rummaged in a heap of clothing on the floor for his shirt. He shoved his arms into the sleeves, then reached for his breeches. "I cannot take away your unhappy childhood, nor can I do anything more than promise to love you and be faithful to you for the rest of my days. Beyond that, you have to trust me."

There was such bitterness in his voice that Noelle winced. She knew how he'd been hurt in the past by his

unfaithful fiancée, but Gavin had chosen to give Noelle his
heart anyway. And she'd rebuffed him quite cruelly by
actions, if not words.

Desperate to make amends, she walked over to where he
stood, his back to her, and placed her hands on his shoulders.
"Gavin, please." She pressed her cheek against his
spine. "I do love you. I have for some time now. But this
has nothing to do with love. I'm afraid."

He turned and took her arms. "That is something I cannot help you with, Noelle. You've had years to formulate
the notion that all men are cads in expensive clothing, waiting to ruin their marriages." He briefly closed his eyes,
then looked down at her. "You will have your time to
decide. Just know I will not wait forever, nor will I marry a
woman who spends our marriage anticipating the day
when I'll be unfaithful, just to prove she was right. I'll not
live that way, and neither should you."

Gavin released her arms and finished dressing. Once his
cravat was knotted to his satisfaction, he silently helped her
into her gown. There was nothing further to say.

By the time the sun rose and he called for the coach, the
strain between them was intense. Noelle had to blink to
keep from tears. The remainder of the journey to London
was without the affection they'd shared before the proposal. He didn't speak unless the situation warranted it,
and she had no words he wanted to hear.

Once he dropped her at Collingwood House and into
her sister's hands, he left her with nothing more than a curt
nod to sustain her. No last affectionate glance, no kiss on
the hand. As the coach rolled away with the finality of
clopping hooves, Noelle burst into tears and raced up the
stairs to her room.

She won't eat, she won't bathe, and I haven't seen a smile
since before she left for Bath." Eva met Nicholas's eyes
and worked her bottom lip between her teeth. "All I know
is that the case is closed and the countess banished to some

obscure Scottish castle. Otherwise, she will not offer me a single clue to why she is so unhappy."

"You must not worry so, dearest. It isn't good for you or the baby." Nicholas moved to take her hands. "I have learned that your sister received a proposal of marriage that she promptly rejected. I believe that is the reason she's moping about, and not some unnamed mistreatment."

Eva stilled. She probed his stare. "And where did you discover this news, husband?"

He lifted her hands to his mouth. "You cannot be privy to all my secrets, my dear wife. Let's just say I made a visit to a certain gentleman and discovered your sister was not in any way abused. Her unhappiness is all her doing."

This explained much. Every time Eva cursed the misbehaving American, Noelle was quick to leap to his defense, an odd turn when the man was the cause of her distress.

"Have I ever told you what a darling you are?" Eva glanced out the open parlor door and a slow smile crossed her face. She turned back and pressed a kiss on Nicholas's mouth. "My stubborn sister has been shut up in her room for far too long. Now, with your help, I have what I need to shake her from her melancholia."

Noelle jerked upright on the bed when her bedroom door banged open against the wall, shaking the panel on its hinges. Her formidable sister came over to the bed and glared down at her. Noelle winced.

"Get up." Eva jerked the coverlet to the bottom of the bed, and a flush of cool air skimmed over Noelle's skin. "It is well past two, and far past the time for coddling." She walked to the window and pushed open the drapes. Light flooded into the room. "I have never heard of a woman taking to her bed over a proposal of marriage by a man she loves. Of all things!"

Noelle grimaced. Her secret was out. Somehow Eva had discovered the truth and wasn't pleased. Her tight face and impatient manner showed that Eva was on Gavin's side.

"You don't understand."

"Oh, I do quite well." Eva moved a few steps closer. "I was you a year ago. I worried how every choice I made in my life would affect, and possibly hurt, my mother. But you know that. I wasn't about to let Nicholas, and my love for him, open up our lives to scrutiny and further destroy her fragile mind." Eva walked to the wardrobe, flung open the doors, and rifled through the gowns. She found a green frock and threw it on the bed. Stockings followed, with an array of other items, until there was a pile on the mattress near Noelle's feet.

"You have nothing to hold you back from love but your mother's misery." Eva returned to Noelle. "Do you ever wonder why your mother is so unhappy? Do you ever remember a time, well before my mother met Father, when she was a happy, loving wife?" Noelle shook her head. "Did she ever exchange loving glances with Father? Did she ever laugh at his jests or caress his hand when she thought no one was looking?"

Not ever. Noelle shook her head again and slid up to position herself against the pillows.

"Now that she is free of him, does she laugh or dance or flirt with men, just for the enjoyment of doing so?" Eva didn't wait for another head shake. She wagged her finger. "Your mother lives to be miserable and to provoke misery in others. Had she made any sort of effort in her marriage, she could have been happy. I know Father loved her when they wed."

Taken off guard by the revelation, Noelle gaped. "Who told you he loved my mother?"

"I overheard a conversation once between him and Mother." Eva sat down on the bed and fluffed out her skirts. "Your mother was a great beauty, and he was smitten, so much so that he didn't see the unhappiness inside her until after their vows were spoken. It was during an argument on their honeymoon trip when he learned she'd loved a man her father disapproved of, and his suit was rebuffed. She did not want to marry Father, but Grandfather arranged the match against her wishes. In spite of this confession, Papa tried everything to please her, to earn her affection. And as you know, it came to naught."

The shock of the tale overwhelmed Noelle. Her mother had loved someone once and had been forced to wed Father instead?

"I didn't know." All these years her mother had a secret of her own. Thwarted love. No wonder she was so bitter. "Why didn't you tell me this before now?"

"I thought with Father gone, it didn't matter anymore. I thought you'd see how happy Margaret and I are and open yourself to finding love." Eva paused and closed her hand over Noelle's. "When I heard you'd stubbornly refused Mister Blackwell, I knew I had to do something. It is high time you forget the past and look forward to a happy future."

Noelle put her hands over her face. All her notions about marriage and men were clouded by misinformation. It wasn't her father who hadn't tried in her parents' marriage. Her mother had pushed him away.

"How stupid I've been," Noelle said miserably. She'd chased Gavin off. Three days had passed without a word. He was probably pleased to be rid of her and her antics.

"Not stupid. Misinformed," Eva said, as if reading her mind. "You saw only what was placed before you. Your mother and our father never stood a chance in their marriage when your mother loved someone else. That was why he fell in love with my mother." Eva placed a hand to her head and smiled. "It is a wonder we three sisters are not inmates of Bedlam, with the upbringing we've had."

"Truly," Noelle agreed. She leaned back and looked at the ceiling. "What a muddle. Gavin will never have me now. He declared his love and I stomped all over it. How he must hate me." He should hate her. He'd taken a second chance at love and she'd scorned him. What else could he think?

"Nonsense." Eva stood and pulled her roughly from the bed. Noelle stumbled to gain her footing. "In fact, I am so confident Mister Blackwell will wed you, I have sent Nicholas off to make the arrangements."

"You've done what?" Noelle asked, but her sister had

already walked to the wardrobe and stuck her head inside. So Noelle stood, twisting her fingers over the news, unsure of the next step. Eva had taken her future in her hands, and Noelle was left either to accept that a wedding was imminent or to run screaming for some far corner of the world like a coward.

It an instant, she chose the former.

Eva found a pair of gloves and then dug through the pile of undergarments with fervor until she found the two stockings. The items fluttered when she dangled them from one hand. "Don't just stand there like a stone. We must get you dressed. You have a proposal to accept."

"Yes, Your Grace."

Eva's happy enthusiasm was infectious as she bathed and dressed Noelle, then called for the maid to fix Noelle's hair in a loose twist at the base of her neck. There was no time for anything grander. Every minute that ticked by pushed Gavin farther away. Noelle had to get to him, and quickly.

Maudlin no more, Noelle felt her heart lighten for the first time in the three days since Gavin had unceremoniously dumped her on the stoop and left her to wallow in her misery. Though she wasn't certain he'd have her back, or still wish to marry her, she had to try. It was high time she closed her eyes, leapt from the cliff, and trusted Gavin would catch her in his strong arms.

When Noelle was dressed and coiffed to her sister's satisfaction, she gave Eva a big hug and grinned widely. "Wish me good luck," she said, and hurried from the room.

Fish smells, salty air, and gulls greeted her when Noelle pulled up in front of Blackwell Shipworks in an open and grand ducal carriage. There was no need to hide from prying eyes anymore. She didn't care if all of society knew she was visiting an unmarried man with the intention of begging him to wed her. She wasn't about to leave this shipyard without Gavin knowing that she loved and trusted him wholeheartedly.

She'd be the intended bride of an American-Englishman, Gavin Blackwell, before the day's end, or expire trying.

The sun was high overhead as she looked at the lovely blue sky and inhaled deeply. If she was to become the wife of a wealthy shipbuilder, she needed to become used to the smells of the sea.

Several men stared as she alighted and scanned the row of ships for Gavin. There was no sign of him, but the beautiful ships took her breath away. The idea of traveling the seas for adventure filled her with excitement. She would have to insist that Gavin take her on a sea journey once they married. She very much wanted to feel the salty air dance across her face.

She looked for a few moments more. No Gavin. As she worried he was elsewhere, a worker in faded clothing pointed toward the office. She nodded her thanks and headed in that direction with a confidence she didn't quite feel.

There was a very good chance he'd toss her out on her bum and lock the door behind her. He had the right. But if that was his intention, she'd fight him with all her stubborn nature.

The office was cluttered with drawings and stacks of papers on every surface when Noelle opened the door without knocking. Gavin sat at a high table, his back to her, sketching something that looked like ship parts. Only the sound of pen on paper broke the silence.

"I think we should adjust the lines along here just a bit for added speed," he said, and she instantly realized he thought she was someone else. "If we lengthen the sails as we planned, the ships will be unbeatable in a chase."

She ran her gaze over his sun-kissed hair, to his broad shoulders, to his narrow waist, and down to his perfect buttocks clad in black trousers. Her throat caught. Lord, how she'd missed him! If only he'd missed her, too!

Collecting herself, she straightened her spine one vertebra at a time until she found real confidence.

"Are you planning to outrace pirates?" Noelle asked,

and watched his head jerk up. He spun on the stool, his face stern. "Or have you taken to piracy yourself? If so, you will definitely require added speed to outrun our British navy."

It took a half second for annoyance to rim his eyes and tighten his jaw. "What are you doing here, Noelle?"

His shirt was open. Dust marked his skin, and there were bits of wood shavings in his hair. Her heart fluttered wildly. He had never looked more desirable.

She wanted to run into his arms and press kisses over his face. But his anger stilled her feet. So she took her cues from her steely determination and stepped into the room.

There was no time to be cowardly. She'd say her piece and let him decide her fate. "I came to ask you to marry me."

There. Simple and right to the point.

If he found the gesture romantic, it certainly didn't show. "It took you three days to decide that I was worthy of your hand?" He put the pen in the inkwell and crossed his arms. In doing so, smudges from his ink-stained fingertips soiled his white shirt. He'd send his laundress into fits. "That doesn't inspire confidence, Noelle."

There was a touch of hurt in the angry tenor of his voice.

"No. It took me three days to realize that I never wanted to stop loving you. And if I desired any chance to be happy, for both of us to be happy, I needed to rush down here before another second passed and our moment was lost forever." Noelle felt tears well with the rush of words. "I love you, Gavin."

He said nothing but just stared at her for what seemed like an eternity before he spoke again. "Do you trust me?"

She nodded vigorously. "I do. Completely."

"And every time I speak to another woman, or take a turn around a dance floor with someone other than you, you won't be wondering how long it will take for me to bed her?"

"Not once." She took another step forward. "I will be confident in your love and know that you would never hurt me or be unfaithful." Tears streamed down her face. She sniffed and dabbed her face with her sleeve. "Please marry me, Gavin."

Without hesitation, he stood and opened his arms. With a glad cry, Noelle threw herself against him and buried her face in his shirt. "I love you so very much. I truly do."

He kissed the top of her head, then leaned back to cup her face. "I love you, too, Noelle. I always will."

Bending, Gavin captured her mouth in a tender kiss that left her legs wobbling and her heart swelling with happiness. All his love was exposed in that simple show of affection, and she knew he would indeed love her forever.

The next few days were a whirl. A wedding to plan, invitations to send out, and in the midst of it all, Gavin arranged for Noelle to visit several available properties in the area to choose a home.

She quickly settled on a house, a mansion, one street over from Collingwood House, chosen so Eva would be close. It was four stories high, built of sandstone brick, and had enough room for a large family. Gavin also promised to purchase an estate somewhere between her two sisters' country homes, to make frequent visits among the trio manageable.

"You are spoiling me, my love," Noelle said during a quiet moment, properly chaperoned, in Eva's parlor. Her sister insisted they stay apart until the wedding, lest any offspring of their union fall short of the nine months required between wedding and childbirth. Noelle didn't mind, for it gave Gavin a chance to court her properly. Something they'd skipped. "My head is spinning."

Gavin drew her into a corner, away from the open door and the pair of footmen lingering outside. "Then this may only add to your distress," he teased. He reached into his pocket and drew out a long box. He placed it in her hands.

Noelle smiled. She'd never fully admit to herself that she was beginning to love surprises. Gavin was proving to have the ability to choose just the right gifts for her. From trinkets to gowns, he had very good taste. So, eagerly, she pulled off the blue ribbon and opened the box, then almost dropped the gift on the floor.

Looking up, she stared, confused. Nestled in black velvet was Lady Seabrook's beautiful sapphire and diamond necklace, complete with spider clasp. "I don't understand."

Gavin took the necklace and walked behind her. He settled the item around her neck, and it felt warm against her skin. Noelle touched the smooth stones.

"Charles and I decided you'd earned the necklace, as he and I know what it has cost you." Gavin closed the clasp and returned to face her. "Not only will it disturb his wife to lose it, but you more than deserve a reward for what you did for his children. Though they will be without their mother for a time, having her arrested and hanged would be worse."

Noelle felt a tickle in her throat and peered lovingly into his eyes. She'd been quite prone to tears lately. Love had unleashed her emotions.

"Although the necklace has been instrumental in several dark moments for me, it brought me you, and for that, I will cherish it always." She walked to the window and stared at her reflection. The jewels sparkled in the sunlight. "It is beautiful. Thank you."

Gavin slid his arms around her waist and dropped his chin on her shoulder. "Whenever you wear it, I will fondly remember the night we met."

Their gazes met in the reflection. "As will I."

After a moment, he turned her around. "I have another gift. Well, two gifts."

She pulled free and raised both palms outward. If she didn't put an end to his generosity, and quickly, she'd need two new houses to hold all his gifts. "Please, I cannot take any more presents. This house is already stuffed with my things."

He chuckled. "You will be pleased with this. Lady Seabrook's maid and the last footpad have been arrested. They made a dash for Scotland, but Crawford had alerted the Runners and they were caught just outside the border. They will be charged for my attack and various other crimes. Turns out, even had they been paid, they'd planned to keep and sell the necklace. Hortense wouldn't have gotten it back."

Noelle smiled as she caressed the heavy piece. For all her plotting and deception, the countess would have lost her necklace anyway. She was pleased it had found a home with her instead.

"And the second gift?" she asked.

"Though her husband, the baron, loudly protested his wife's decision to travel with the birth of the babe mere hours away, your sister Margaret is currently upstairs resting under Eva's care and awaiting our wedding." Gavin brushed a kiss on her temple. "So I will leave you to ready yourself for the ceremony tomorrow, and drink myself silly with my two future brothers-in-law. I've heard marriage to a Harrington sister requires copious amounts of whiskey."

Noelle's mouth dropped open with an exasperated sound as he sidestepped out of reach and strode briskly from the room, his laughter following his exit. She giggled at his impudence and vowed to spend the rest of the next three months, while they were honeymooning on her first journey aboard a ship, making him very sorry for that outlandish and impertinent comment.

And she did.

Read on for a special preview of
Cheryl Ann Smith's seductive romance

The School for Brides

Available now from Berkley Sensation!

From this moment forward, you will not wear any gown that shows even a trace of areola, a length of thigh, or any other part of your bodies normally covered by an undergarment."

Miss Eva Black paused impatiently while muslin, crinoline, and satin rustled as several pairs of hands reached to jerk up unacceptably low necklines. A shadowy hint of the curved crests of at least one pair of rosy peaks disappeared from view behind stiff lace.

"Proper clothing is the first outward sign of a lady and the first rule that cannot, and will not, be broken." She sighed, resisting the urge to tug at the high, scratchy neck of her gray wool gown. In the heat of the parlor, she felt trapped beneath the heavy layers of her spinster's garments.

It took determination not to shuck off the dress and kick it into the overstoked fire with her slippered foot. With the rain whipping against the window, throwing open a sash wasn't a viable option. She really had to give the maid simpler instructions on whether a fire was appropriate when the morning was warm, lest fainting become the order of the day.

The next several hours loomed ahead like a dismal and

itchy fog, yet Eva forged on. Her suffering was unimportant. An example had to be set for her young courtesans at all times as they looked to her for guidance and the chance to free themselves from their desperate situations.

She continued, "With one's breasts exposed, one can expect every reprobate for fifty miles around to come running for a peek. This is an unacceptable situation I intend to change over the course of the next few weeks. You must behave like ladies, if I am to have any chance of finding each of you a husband."

More giggles and a flurry of whispers followed her pronouncement. The young ladies took a moment to settle before five pairs of curious eyes turned back to Eva. She pulled her fingernails away from her neckline and settled her hands in her lap. A lady did not fidget nor show discomfort in public. Eva was always the picture of ladylike serenity, even if she was no Lady by birth or marriage.

Lady Watersham's book, *Rules for Young Women of Quality*, spelled out every societal rule in precise detail, and Eva had eagerly read and memorized every page. Now she passed those teachings on to others desperately in need of guidance and a chance at a life outside a courtesan's lot.

So she wouldn't fidget, even if pushed to the brink of insanity by the confounding prickles.

Out of sorts today for some unknown reason, Eva felt her mask of stiff propriety settle in the shape of an invisible noose jerked tight around her neck. Just once she wanted to giggle like a ninny with other girls, slouch against the back of the settee with her bare feet outstretched, or scratch her neck like a dog overrun with fleas.

Though only twenty-three, at times she felt eighty-three. She'd skipped the frivolity of youth for the weight of responsibility. At times it was almost too much for her narrow shoulders to carry.

"But how will a fellow know what he's buying if he can't see the merchandise?" Rose asked, pulling Eva from her thoughts of self-pity. The tiny redhead was a confection in pink satin and enough lace to cover several gowns from hem to neck.

"Merchandise?" Eva asked.

The perfect heart-shaped face turned sober as Rose seemed to reach for the correct way to express her ideas. She finally nodded her head. "Miss Eva, a fellow always wants a taste of what he's purchasing before he proposes a contract."

Rose's bright blue eyes were remarkably innocent for a girl who'd spent the last four years of her life servicing an elderly duke. A loose curl settled over her right eye, making her look much younger than twenty-one. However, it was her frankness when speaking of her sexual experiences that gave her a decidedly less-than-innocent air.

Pauline, a buxom twenty-six-year-old blonde in yellow, nodded, nibbling on a knuckle. "A man will pay a higher price if he likes what he sees beneath a corset and drawers. Plump breasts and a nicely rounded bottom are most favored among the gentry."

The comment was so matter-of-fact it took Eva a blink for her spine to catch up with her ears and draw her back from her moments of inattentiveness. She straightened one vertebra at a time, exasperated that a woman had to care what any man, or men, thought about her figure. If a lady wanted to eat so many pastries that her bottom grew as wide as the Thames, she should be able to do so without the judgment of the male species.

"Except for Lord Fitz," Rose interjected with a knowing glance at Pauline before Eva could respond. The two friends nodded their heads in unison, setting their curls to bobbing. Rose put an open hand to the side of her mouth and lowered her tone to a loud whisper. "I hear he likes his mistresses to look and dress like footmen—"

"Let's move along, ladies," Eva interjected sternly. From deep within, and past the beginning of a headache, she hung on to a tiny thread of patience. All she wanted to do was pull the nearest pillow over her head to shut out the light and the world.

Running this school, as she called it, was never easy. Nor was it simple to turn her courtesans into proper ladies and match them with husbands.

However, the importance of saving young women from lives of servitude on their backs, with pompous lords riding them like grunting, sweaty jockeys, was the foremost reason for her to get out of bed every day and make the journey across town to Cheapside.

Each well-made match produced a rush of relief that there would be one woman less to end up broken-spirited and left to live in poverty and quiet desperation, once the line of rich and lecherous patrons dried up.

Any bedding these five courtesans would indulge in from this moment forward would follow a wedding in front of a vicar and with papers signed to legalize the union. That she'd make sure of.

Though her temples pulsed, she would get through this introduction to the rules, send the women off to contemplate the lesson, then rush home to put a cool compress on her head and take a long nap between soft sheets.

"A man should choose you as his partner based on your intelligence, your disposition, and the joy you bring to his life. Not, Pauline, what you have beneath your corset. So, that said, you shall never again, for any reason, wear fabrics thin enough to see through outside your marital bed." Eva scanned the room and was satisfied all the women were now decently covered. "Advertising one's wares to the masses is no longer permitted if you intend to change your circumstances and find a respectable mate."

Audible groans and hushed whispers again sounded from around the modest yet tasteful blue room. Change did not come easily for her courtesans. However, Eva was confident that by the end of the month all her charges would step forward to meet the challenge she set forth: to make her, and themselves, proud.

"Trust me, ladies. You will have no difficulty finding a husband once I am finished with your instruction," Eva said. "And he will care more about the strength of your character than the circumference of your breasts."

Pauline knitted her hands in her lap and screwed up her face. Several emotions played across her delicate features.

Eva watched as a measure of understanding dawned in the young woman and the start of a new way of thinking passed through Pauline's pretty hazel eyes. Satisfaction filled Eva's heart; one enlightened courtesan and four to go.

The five women were of different ages, were from varied backgrounds, and had varied educations. They were all brightly wrapped from head to slippered toes in a selection of red, pink, blue, orange, and yellow feathers and bows, like exotic hens preening as they sought a cock with whom to mate.

Eva squelched a frown as she contemplated each in turn, perched together on the pair of rose-patterned settees. There was no dull mouse in the lot.

The women had been instructed to wear simple, unadorned clothing this morning. Perhaps next time she should be more specific about the cut and color of the gown. If this was the best each could come up with, a day of shopping was clearly in order.

Truthfully, catching the attention of a breathing, wealthy male had been their life's work up to this moment. And the second requirement was likely more important than the first.

"But His Grace says a woman is judged by her beauty and figure," Rose said innocently as she smoothed out her skirts. "And education is wasted on a woman. As long as she knows how to please a man and walk upright, she needs no further instruction."

Eva scowled. "His Grace needs to be horsewhipped. Walk upright and service men, indeed! Next time the old buzzard visits, Rose, jerk his cane away from him and beat him senseless with it."

Rose's eyes widened, then the corners of her mouth twitched in response to the peals of laughter of the other

girls. A spark of mischief lit her face. Clearly this courtesan did not share the view of her ancient patron. "I think I
shall do just that. It would do the wretch a wealth of good,
and his wife and daughters would certainly be grateful."

While Eva sat shamefaced over her outburst about the
arrogance of noblemen, the other women voiced various
treacherous ways to make the old duke suffer for the crime
of ignorance.

"Let us turn that stallion into a gelding," said Abigail
softly as her cheeks pinkened beneath wisps of brown hair
that framed her round face. She was twenty-four and had
been a year into her career as a courtesan, since her father,
a tenant farmer, died in a fight over ownership of a flock of
sheep. Only her beauty and some education had kept her
from selling her wares on the docks.

"Stallion?" Rose said with a laugh and pressed her fingertips to her mouth. Her eyes flashed. "A suckling colt has
more vigor with a mare."

The jesting continued until all but the stern-faced Sophie
were happily satisfied the duke had been verbally battered
to a pulp. Though Eva suspected this particular gaggle of
young women could try the patience of even the most stoic
magistrate seated on a high court, she found she enjoyed
their company. With all the darkness that marked her days,
laughter and silliness were a welcome diversion. She even
managed a smile at the image of the old duke slathered in
pudding and covered with duck feathers.

Still, she had lessons to complete, and now was not the
time to socialize if she were to keep on schedule. "As
enjoyable as it would be to geld the duke, we are fresh out
of rusty medical instruments to do the deed." She waited a
moment until she had their full attention. "Now, let us continue. I have matched former courtesans with husbands for
three years, and I understand how difficult it is to give up
your seductive ways. Yet, none of you were chained up and
dragged here to sit through my teachings, and each of you
is permitted to leave any time you choose. Harold informed
you before he brought you here that the school is entirely

voluntary. As you saw when you entered through the front door of this town house, the solid oak panel does not have metal bars."

A secret network operated by word of mouth had brought each woman willingly to Eva's door. Since most of the courtesans had worked from the time they were young, this made her efforts challenging. They'd been taught early that earls, dukes, and barons cared less about what lay above the neckline than what treasures could be found below. It was her job to change their perception of life and themselves. They had value beyond their bodies, and by the end of the month all five would know just how high their worth was.

"Henceforth, the only time any of you will show any private parts to a man is on your wedding night and beyond. Your pasts are almost behind you now, and a new life dawns. If you follow a few simple rules, you'll be ready to wed before the month is out."

Unfortunately, the task was never quite so easy. Especially for those like Sophie, who'd worked as a courtesan for twelve years, since the tender age of seventeen, when her parents died and left her penniless.

Older women like Sophie and Yvette had played the coquette for so long they used seduction and their beauty to keep a roof over their heads and food in their bellies. It was difficult to break free of such a past and accept the idea that life held other possibilities. But Eva enjoyed a good challenge and her rate of successful matches was high.

"A gentleman does not need to see your parts exposed in order to make a proposal. A marriage proposal." She leveled a glare on each woman in turn and pursed her lips. "If any one of you does not see your future as a proper wife and mother, Harold will bring the coach around. I will not waste my time and your monies on a futile endeavor."

The courtesans peered at each other and then back to her. All shook their heads in unison. Two blondes, two brunettes, and Rose the redhead. All highly paid in their previous profession. Some wanted children, some wanted a home of their own, and some just wanted one man in her bed to love. Whatever their reasons, Eva would find them their perfect mate.

"Excellent. Let us get started." Eva walked over to the bookcase and pulled a thick volume off the shelf. The women watched, openly curious, as she returned and settled into a high-backed chair.

"From this moment onward, you will not use vulgar terms for genitalia, breasts, or sexual positions as topics of conversation in polite company. You will stick to topics such as the weather, or Parliament, or current fashion. I care not which, as long as it isn't immediately followed by a man shoving his hand down your corset."

Several snickers followed, then faded quickly when Eva failed to join in. "You will learn deportment and manners and clever ways to begin a conversation, and all of you will learn to carry yourselves with the grace of a duchess."

Eva turned the book to show its gilded black cover. The women stared as if the words were written in Latin. Though only shy Abigail couldn't read well, five puzzled faces gazed at the large gold-inlaid word at the top of the cover.

Husbands.

Eva's eyes softened and she nodded. "I promise a husband is now within reach for each of you."

"I do so want a husband," Abigail said, sighing.

Eva smiled at the beautiful girl. "Then a husband you shall have, Abigail."

If not for the limited number of positions for which women could seek employment in this society, and the beauty of her charges limiting the chances of finding work in any household where a husband resided, she wouldn't have needed to use her matchmaking talents to this end.

Eva herself had no interest in marriage and considered the institution dreadfully archaic. But her ladies really had no other choices. So marriage it was for her courtesans.

"Inside this book are information and sketches of men seeking wives; they have no compunction about your lack of virginity." Eva opened to a page and turned the book so the girls could see the first face. "I asked each man to answer some questions. I wrote down the questions, and their responses, here." She pointed to the page opposite the sketch. "I've verified the information myself, so each of you will know exactly what kind of man you are choosing and what he expects of his wife. When a man is matched, we remove him from the book so there will not be any confusion."

She flipped to a page where the sketched face was blacked out. She'd kept his page in the book for an example to show the sort of man she would not tolerate. "Men who abuse women are immediately refused, as are men with drinking or gambling problems. These are respectable men who want a respectable wife."

"But why would they want to wed one of us?" Yvette, a twenty-six-year-old brunette with tired brown eyes, crossed her arms over a sizable bosom and frowned. She'd had eight lovers during her six years as a courtesan, and her unhappiness with her lot showed in the hard lines on her face. She would be the most difficult to place without substantial effort on Eva's part. "What is wrong with them? Hideous scars? Rotten teeth? A missing limb?"

"Yes." Pauline nodded, and the yellow feather in her upswept hair fluttered along the side of her round face. "Men do not marry women like us unless there is something awful they are hiding. I want a husband, but could not abide a twisted troll with claw hands pawing at my soft parts."

Eva's shoulder blades tightened. Odd, women who willingly bedded the highest bidder had lofty standards when it came time to choose a mate.

She grimaced. The itchy gown was making her irritable. Of course she should have a pleasing mate.

"I assure you there isn't a single troll in this book, but neither are there dukes or earls or kings." Blunt honesty sometimes was exactly what these women required. If they expected to someday be addressed as "Lady" anything, they'd be sorely disappointed. "Men of stature require a virginal wife of impeccable birth to wed."

At least until they whelped an heir or two to continue their perfect bloodline into the next generation. After that, they set up young women like these in apartments or town houses, away from their wives, and played their lascivious games.

The concept of unfaithful marriages was one Eva found distasteful. Once a man and woman wed, they should forsake all others. Perhaps if the matches were born of love and not for financial gain, it might be the case.

It was rare when a couple found true love. Even then, it did not guarantee a happy ending. She knew the dark side of love well.

Shaking off the press of bleak thoughts, Eva added, "Every one of these men is apprised of the general circumstances of your lives, and they have chosen to be included in this book." She turned a few more pages and revealed several more faces. Some of the men were quite handsome, and none had claw hands. "They include barristers and shopkeepers and even a baron's younger son. I do not hide what I do from my clients, and select them carefully for stellar character and financial security."

"Yet they look for whores as wives," Abigail said quietly, and shared a sidelong glance with Yvette. She plucked at the sleeve of her blue gown and sighed. "Perhaps you should explain to us their reasoning."

Eva did not judge her charges for the lives they had led, for many had sad tales of desperate circumstances that led them to a courtesan's path. But neither could she understand how resistant they became once under her tutelage.

They came to her.

By the time a courtesan reached Sophie's age, she was well past the first blush of youth and no longer able to command a high price for her services. Suddenly, with age came the realization that her charm, sensuality, and pretty face were waning, and younger courtesans were ready to take her place. It was usually then that the woman became desperate.

If a courtesan had the sense to put aside coin for her future, she could close up shop and disappear into genteel retirement, or flee to the Continent for new adventures.

For others like these five, who had spent most of what

they earned on fripperies and were without means enough to retire into obscurity, finding a decent husband was their chance for security.

Eva closed the book. "The reasons vary with the men." She leaned back into her chair, the book settled on her knees beneath her flat palms. "Some have businesses to build and do not have the time to find a potential wife and court her. Some travel extensively and seek a woman of adventurous spirit to follow him to exotic locations."

"Oh!" Rose bounced up and down on her seat and raised her hand. "I love adventure!"

Nodding, Eva smiled. The saucy little redhead would be a wonderful companion and wife for several of her clients. She still had the enthusiasm and blush of youth that men craved. "Excellent. I'll keep that in mind, Rose."

She turned her attention to each woman in turn. Their beauty should be only one part of what men saw when choosing them. Not the main or only reason.

"Truthfully, there are some men who seek to marry only women of rare beauty, far above the type of young lady they could normally attract. They want a peacock on their arm, not a sparrow. For that privilege, they will overlook a questionable past. Over the course of the month, you will be able to study the book and choose several men you feel will best match you. Then we will have a party where the introductions will be made."

The courtesans fell silent. Each knew the men paid generous fees for Eva's services, and the arrangements were business-based. Even so, several of them she had tutored and their suitors went on to make love matches. It was an end to which many aspired.

"What differs from your old life is that you all have choices here in this house. You pick the man, you decide what kind of life you want, and I put you and your suitors together. It is up to you how the relationship evolves. If you reject one match, we shall find you another until you, and he, are satisfied and we finalize the arrangement with marriage vows."

Soft sighs filled the room.

"It sounds wonderful," said Yvette wistfully. Apparently, even the most hardened of courtesans longed for love.

Eva ran her hand over the book and thought of how lucky these women were not to have fallen in love with their bene-factors. It had happened with several previous clients and ended with broken hearts. She let out a pensive sigh of her own and blinked back the press of tears. If only Charlotte Rose had had a place like this to turn to before she fell into the love trap, her circumstances could have ended differently.

She mentally shook herself. It was not the time to drift into gloomy thoughts. Today was a day of new possibilities. "Though your suitors have no qualms about your pasts, they do require the public air of respectability. That is where my lessons become invaluable." Eva peered over the top of her spectacles. "They have mothers, sisters, and families who might not be pleased with a former courtesan as the wife of their son or brother. From this moment on, you will forget everything you've done, every man who once warmed your beds, and live a modest life. And if you cannot do this, you are free to go. I do not force anyone to follow my directives. From now on, your future is your own responsibility."

A sniff drew her attention, then Rose burst into tears. Pauline slid across the settee and squeezed her hand. "What is wrong, dearest?" She pulled a handkerchief out of her bodice and handed it to the distraught girl.

Rose dabbed her eyes and hiccupped. "Ever since my mother tossed me out on my bum when I was seventeen and her second husband took an interest in me"—she blew her nose loudly into the handkerchief—"I have relied on men for everything." The last word had a high pitch to it. "I've done things I cannot even confess to my priest, for fear God will hear and strike me down." She let out a low wail. "I don't know if I can take care of myself." She fell into a round of soft sobs. Abigail moved over and took a position on her other side. She rested an arm around Rose's shoulder and clucked her tongue.

"Miss Eva will help us," Sophie said firmly from the other

settee. "And you will no longer have to suffer His Grace's cold hands and limp—" She looked sheepishly at Eva and cleared her throat. "She'll find you a man of adventure who knows how to love you as you deserve to be loved."

Rose dabbed her tears and peered at Eva with measuring eyes, then slowly nodded her head. "Then I shall put my trust in her hands."

"We all will," said Abigail, and the others nodded.

Eva set the book aside and stood, hope for a successful outcome to this class springing once again into her breast. Sophie's unexpected show of tenderness to Rose clearly had an effect on all the women. They were no longer facing this as five separate women, but as a collective and supportive group.

With one show of tears, Rose had done what usually took days or weeks to achieve. Togetherness.

Eva walked to Rose and pulled her to her feet. She tipped up the girl's chin and looked into her shimmering eyes. "You need not worry, my dear Rose. By the time I've finished with you, you will be well able to care for yourself."

With a wavering smile, Rose nodded and pulled her into a tight hug. Eva flinched but allowed the embrace. The other women stood and circled around, their excited chatter infectious. Eva had opened her mouth to offer further reassurance when her butler, Harold, came through the open door with a troubled expression on his face. Eva gently extricated herself from Rose's embrace and stepped away from the group.

A sudden chill seeped into her bones, and she shivered. She looked to the windows, certain one had blown open to invite the cool morning into the stuffy room. But the panes were securely closed and locked and the heavy blue drapes showed not a flutter.

Strange. This was the second time in a week she'd felt that same dank chill slide through her body. If she wasn't a woman of solid mind and not one to dabble in fits of fancy, she would worry that this chill was a sign of impending doom.

Rubbish. She shook her head to clear it and faced Harold.

She was a bit ruffled by his intrusion, as her orders were clear: He was not to interrupt the lessons unless it was an emergency. She stepped close, out of earshot of the women. "What is it, Harold? Has something happened to Mother?"

He shook his head firmly. "No, Miss."

Harold led her to the open doorway by her elbow. Her butler was tall, nearing thirty, and built like a pugilist; a perfect guard for the door of both this house and her home. He kept the girls safe and the riffraff off her front steps.

And Eva trusted him with her secrets. All her secrets.

He leaned toward her and whispered, "A man, a gentleman, is at the front door. He insists he has business with you that cannot wait." He glanced down the hallway and scowled. "When I informed him you were not taking callers today, he said to explain to you that if I send him away, he will return with a Bow Street Runner in tow and have you arrested."